JUNK MAGIC AND GUITAR DREAMS

OTHER BOOKS BY T. JAMES LOGAN

THE LYCANTHROPE TRILOGY

JUNK MAGIC AND GUITAR DREAMS

BY

T. JAMES LOGAN

BEAR PAW PUBLISHING
DENVER

IV

PAPERBACK EDITION

ISBN 978-1-62225-433-0

Bear Paw Publishing
Denver, Colorado, USA

www.bearpawpublishing.com

DEDICATION

For the Dreamers.

Hang on to your dreams with all the
strength you have.

The world needs yours.

ACKNOWLEDGMENTS AND THANKS

I would like to express my profound thanks for all the readers who helped shepherd this book into readable form.

Hannah Beresford, James Beresford, Kaea Beresford, Jim Breyfogle, Jeanne Cavelos, Ido Doron, Richard James Errington, Chanel Heermann, Kaylen Helgason, Mike Howard, Chris Mandeville, Veronica Roland, Virginia Vernon, and Katie Yelinek. You are all awesome, and this book couldn't have happened without your thoughts on the early drafts. Thanks as well go to the astute eyes of Joshua Essoe and Colleen Kuehne for the final polish.

PART I

DISINTEGRATION

CHAPTER ONE
KEEP ME IN YOUR HEART

Otter flung open the door and stepped into the trailer, letting his backpack slip off his shoulder and thump to the floor. "Mom?"

The front door slamming behind him brought her half up out of the sofa, across the living room. "Over here, kiddo." She lay back into it, half-swallowed, shrunken, her ears cupped by headphones, a coil of cord bobbing between her head and the stereo.

The air in the trailer smelled sour today, as if her sickness now permeated the house itself. With another pained effort, she swung her legs out so she could sit up to greet him.

"That's all right, Mom. Don't get up. Just rest," he said.

As she righted herself and removed her headphones, he saw her cheeks were wet, her eyes bloodshot.

"Mom, are you okay?" His arms began to tremble, and the words felt thick, his breath coming in gulps. Was this going to be it? Was today the day?

She gave him a wan smile. "How was the last day of being a freshman?"

"A waste of time, like every other day at school." He lofted his Mudskippers ball cap like a frisbee toward his backpack beside the front door, where it landed perfectly on top, then ran his fingers through his hair to stop the tremors from spreading.

"School is never, ever a waste of time," she said sternly. "I know you're bored there. You're so smart, and you have an old soul in so many ways, but you don't know a damn thing about how the world works. And I'm not going to be here to teach you."

His heart clenched and his voice caught. "Stop saying that."

She sighed. "Sorry. It's been a rough day. How's Angelika?"

He shrugged. "She's Lika, emphasis on the 'leak.'" It was an old joke that went back to a time when Lika had laughed so hard she almost wet herself. His response sounded more indifferent than he intended but the truth was, Lika Walker was the only person who ever gave a damn enough to listen to his stupid poems and lyrics and read comics with him. Everyone else just looked at him like he was too weird to live.

"Sometimes friends are the only family we have."

Lika had a regular, normal summer ahead of her. Otter did not.

On the floor around the sofa lay wadded-up tissues. Had Mom been crying all day? "Is it the pain?" he asked. "You need me to go to the pharmacy?"

"Just having a bad day, that's all."

There was no money to go to the pharmacy anyway. The money from selling the car was all but gone.

The last strains of Johnny Cash whispered from the headphones, the last verse of "The Highwayman," a bittersweet song about the endless reincarnations of a highwayman through the centuries. It was mournful, as the man died over and over again; with each verse a new life and a new death, culminating as a starship captain contemplating his place in the vast universe. Immediately after it ended, he recognized the opening chords to Warren Zevon's "Keep Me in Your Heart," a song she'd been listening to a lot lately—a song that was Zevon's last goodbye to his friends as he was dying of cancer.

She was listening to her darkest playlist. He had to do something to pull her out of it.

"It is now officially summer, and I'm now officially a sophomore," he said, "so let the good times roll." He headed for his bedroom and returned to the living room with two guitar cases, hers and his.

"Otter, honey, we need to talk about some things."

No, they didn't. He didn't want to hear it. So he unsnapped her case and lifted out her battered, old acoustic-electric.

She said, "I haven't played that thing in months."

"I know. It's past time. It's jam time."

"Please, honey—"

"Mom! Take it!" His voice shrilled like a seventh-grader's again for a just second. He cleared his throat.

She sighed and clasped the guitar by the neck. While he brought out his bass and warmed up their little two-channel amp, she tuned hers by ear.

He couldn't look at her sunken, gray cheeks or her skeletal fingers on the fretboard. She looked a hundred and fifty years old, not thirty-two. If he held still, he would cry. As he puttered, he felt her eyes on him.

She strummed a chord, but it buzzed and rang with off-notes. "Oh god, I can't even play a G-chord anymore."

"Sure you can."

"Honey, I'm too weak."

"You just need to get warmed up. Come *on*."

She sighed and strummed a few more. They got a little better. "What are we going to play?"

"Queen." He thumped the first bass riff of "Another One Bites the Dust."

She gave him an indulgent smile that brought some light back into her eyes. "I have raised you well, my child." A quick nod, then, to tell him to keep going, so he did.

She didn't sing. Her voice was so raspy and broken these days that she only picked the melody on the strings, but she managed it. She used to have the voice of an angel. He would have given anything to hear her sing again like she used to. Her hair used to be a lustrous red, now the brown of fallen leaves.

They grinned at each other, and some color returned to her cheeks.

And then, at the second chorus, her fingers stumbled over the strings and she sagged back against the couch, the guitar falling flat into her lap. "I can't anymore."

"But—!"

"Michael! I *can't*!" She was gasping with exertion, and she only called him Michael when things were serious.

"I'm sorry, I'm sorry."

She set the guitar aside and heaved herself forward, taking his face in both hands. "It's okay. Shh. It's okay."

Her breath carried an acrid, chemical odor. Dammit, he *was* crying now.

"Honey, we have to talk about some things," she said again. "Some very serious things."

"I don't want to."

"You knew this was coming. You've known a long time."

He nodded. "I still don't want to." If they talked about it, it became more real, like a blurry picture sliding inexorably into focus.

"We have to. Sit." She patted the couch cushion beside her.

He set his guitar down and joined her.

"There's a pile of paperwork in there on the kitchen table."

A manila file folder rested on the table.

"I'm going to tell you what it is. We're going to fill it out."

He wiped his cheeks dry. "What do you need?"

"This is about what you need. I probably won't see you start school in the fall, so we need to take care of what happens to you. You're not old enough to live on your own. And I don't want you to end up in foster care—or worse, in an orphanage."

"What about Aunt Misty?"

Her face tightened. "That is not an option." Her tone was like all the other times he asked about Aunt Misty. She wouldn't answer any more questions. He had three cousins, triplet girls, living across town. He remembered playing with them when he was a little kid, but they had fallen away from his life for reasons he never understood.

"What about Grandpa? Couldn't I live with him?"

She wiped a quiet tear of her own. "Grandpa and me, we're in the same boat. River Styx, thataway."

"What? You talked to him? After all this time?"

"He called to tell me. Doctor gave him three months."

"What else did he say?"

"He asked if he could come and see me."

"And you said—"

"No. After seven years, old habits die hard. Sometimes things don't work out like we want them to." She swallowed the hardness in her voice with effort, then continued. "So, foster care, bad. Orphanage, no way. I've written up a will that leaves you this trailer house. You'll have to keep up with the lot rental. This is why I put you on my bank account. This is why I've been teaching you to be independent, how to be a grown-up. I wish you could stay a kid a little while longer, but that's not in the cards for you. I'm really sorry about that."

He nodded. He'd been the Man of the House for some months now since the diagnosis.

She continued, "So we're going to file in court for you to become an emancipated minor."

"What does that mean?"

"It means we have to convince the court that you're mature enough to handle your own affairs, that you don't need me. You would be legally allowed to live on your own, handle things like legal contracts, that sort of thing, stuff that minors can't do. You won't become a legal adult until you're eighteen, but hopefully this will keep you out of foster care."

"What's so bad about foster care? Not like I *want* to go, but…"

"You remember my friend Kathy? She's a social worker, used to tell me stories. *Bad Things* happen to kids in foster care. Not all the time, mind you—there are some good foster families—but for teenagers the risks are just too high."

"Got it. Grown-up. No foster care." In a strange way, it made him feel good that she thought he was grown-up enough to handle his own affairs. At the same time, the yawning Grand Canyon filled with all the things he knew he didn't know—all the boring things like bank accounts, taxes, school—was terrifying. How was he going to learn how to drive?

"But being an emancipated minor means that someone is going to be watching you from the court. You have to have a job, and you have to support yourself."

"More hours at the car wash."

"Right. And you also have to keep going to school. You have to be working toward graduation. Those are the two basic things. Without that, they'll revoke your emancipated status."

"Straight into the system."

"Smart man."

Even as she said the words, his spine straightened. He seemed to feel his voice fall for good into the adult male range. "I'll do it."

By contrast, her voice was getting weaker, far away. "Thank you, Otter. I know I can count on you." She tucked a few strands of blond hair behind his ear. "This has been so hard on you, and I'm sorry. But you've been my rock." Her voice fractured, sobs peeking out from a deep crevasse of emotion. "This has been so hard on you."

"Hard for *me?*" He wasn't the one who was dying.

"There's something I want you to remember. When you're going through hell, keep going."

"What's that mean?"

She smiled wanly and cupped his cheek. "Would you really want to stop *in* hell?"

"Oh."

"You *will* get through this, you hear me? There hasn't been any normal in your life for a while now."

He didn't even remember what normal was like.

She went on, "But you'll find it again. It'll take some time, but you'll figure it out. Do you believe me?"

He nodded, but couldn't meet her gaze. Nor could he fathom, not even slightly, what life would look like without her.

"Good Otter," she smiled again, a mere flicker. "And stay away from that new guy across the road. What's his name…?"

"Zeke."

"That guy is bad news."

"He's all right." Zeke had a super-cool motorcycle and wore enough leather to look like a supreme badass.

"I get a really bad vibe from him. Listen to your mother."

"Okay, okay. Are we done talking about serious stuff?"

"For now. I need to try to sleep for a while. I can feel it coming on."

He wanted to ask, *Feel* what *coming on?* But he didn't.

She staggered upright and tottered back toward her bedroom, an ashen scarecrow. "Make sure your homework is done."

"Okay," he said, slamming the floodgates down to stop a deluge of tears.

CHAPTER TWO
FADE TO BLACK

She died on July 4th, to the sound of fireworks in the distance.

There was no money for a funeral or memorial service, only a brief cremation ceremony the following day. He was the only one there. She had made all the arrangements herself, including getting him a pair of secondhand dress trousers and a white shirt, the kind of clothes he tended to grow out of before he could wear them a second time.

Someone asked if he had written an obituary for the newspaper, but he didn't know how.

He didn't call his grandfather or Aunt Misty. They were strangers.

The funeral home gave him a box of ashes afterward, and he scattered them at her favorite picnic spot on the riverbank, like she had asked him to do. It was a bright, hot day, the kind that only come in July.

He sat there for a while and watched her ashes float away on the swirling current. He had gone beyond crying to a vast, desolate plain of numbness. His stomach was twisted into a sour fist. Even his lungs felt tired of breathing.

Would he ever feel like living again? He had no desire to follow his mother into death. He had a whole life to live, after all. But that life lay on the other side of an impenetrable black fog. Not only could he not yet try to find his way through the fog, he had no interest in trying.

The guy in the suit at the funeral home had said some things to Otter, things that were supposed to offer comfort, but he couldn't remember what they were.

Otter didn't know if he believed in Heaven, but that's what everyone talked about when someone died. Mom had not been the churchgoing type.

Did it make him feel better that she might still be out there somewhere, watching over him? He thought about the song "The Highwayman" and the nature of souls. Had Mom moved on to her next life? Would she be a starship captain? He could still feel her presence in the world as if she would be there when he got home, just like she had always been. But if the opposite were true, if everything she had ever been, her whole life, was now ashes in a river, sinking once again into the planet that had borne her, didn't that lend more weight to the life she had lived, to what she had left behind? To the fact that he himself was all that remained of her?

It was like he was watching a bright, sunny afternoon in July on television from a pitch-black room.

Across the park, a couple of kids, maybe sixth or seventh graders, were laughing with delight on the swings. The chains creaked as they pumped themselves higher and higher, so high the chains went slack at the apex of their arcs. They were just kids, having fun. A stab of fresh pain went through him.

He thought for a moment how much he used to love the swings. But his days as a kid were over. He would never swing again. He was a man now.

There was someone he had to tell.

He pulled out his cell phone—a cheap, pay-as-you-go model—and called Lika. She used to swing with him.

"Hey!" she answered brightly. "How are you? I haven't seen you since—"

"Mom's gone," he said.

A long pause hung between them.

"Oh, Mike, I'm so sorry. Are you okay?"

He had no inkling of how to answer that question. "I just scattered her ashes."

"Oh, god…" Lika's voice cracked. "I'm so sorry."

He could hear Lika's mother's voice in the background, "Is that Mikey? Let me have the phone, baby." Lika's mother, Loretta, was a sturdy, statuesque woman brimming with fire and kindness. When she was angry, her voice could split a tree stump at a hundred yards, but most of the time she was as sweet as marshmallow fluff. Loretta took the phone and said, "I'ma send Marvin over to pick you up. We want to have you over for dinner."

Something in her voice would brook no refusal, even though he couldn't imagine eating anything. "Okay. I'm at the Smith Park picnic area." There was something else, too, hidden in her voice, a purpose for the invitation.

"You stay put."

"Yes, ma'am."

CHAPTER THREE
BRIDGE OVER TROUBLED WATER

Lika Walker waited on the porch swing for her dad to show up with Mike.

While she waited, she fretted over how Mike had gone through his mother's final days alone. He and his mom lived in a poor trailer park on the outskirts of town, hemmed in by industrial areas, pawn shops, and liquor stores. Lika felt guilty that, all the while, she had been going about her summer like any normal fifteen-year-old, dreaming her own dreams about bands and music, listening to old James Brown songs just to listen to Clyde "Funky Drummer" Stubblefield, and wondering if she'd ever have the guts to play in front of an audience. And while she'd just been bopping along on her own merry way, her best friend was drowning in death and despair.

They had come together in the third grade to team up defending the class nerd, Billy Parks—complete with Coke-bottle glasses—from the infamous sixth-grade bully, Danny Akers. She and Mike had simultaneously stepped up side by side and laid into Danny Akers like Batman and Robin. As they grew older, her other friends teased her about being friends with a white boy. They either said they were sorry or they weren't friends any longer.

Mike's mom had dubbed him Otter for his early swimming ability and lanky playfulness. Lika had loved Mike's mom. Such a beautiful woman Maggie MacIntyre was, with an amazing singing voice. Then another spasm of guilt shot through Lika at how she had stopped going over to Mike's house when Maggie's cancer started to show. It became too painful to watch what was happening to her. Or maybe it was because Mike didn't want Lika to see it happen that he stopped inviting her over. For the last several months, they only saw each other at school and at occasional rehearsals of the band their friend Toby was trying to put together. But those practices had ceased when the school year ended and the three drifted into their separate summer universes.

Dad's headlights rounded the corner, and the shiny, black Caddy slid up into the driveway. In the dashboard glow, Mike's face looked like that of a still, gray corpse. While her father retrieved Mike's bicycle from the trunk, Mike shuffled toward the porch, hands in his pockets. His hair was combed and he was dressed up in slacks and a white, button-up shirt; an unusual attire for him.

Stepping down from the porch, she met him with a hug. He hugged her back, tentatively, but he wouldn't meet her gaze. Such displays of physical affection were not normal operating procedure, which was to throw a high elbow or two, complete with snark barbs and veiled taunts.

He said, "Your hair's getting long."

She ran her hands over the two globules of dark frizz, one on each side of her head like Afro Princess Leia. "Yours, too." She sighed at her lame attempt at conversation, but she couldn't think of anything else to say, so she took him by the hand and tugged him inside so that Momma could fuss over him.

It was a sumptuous meal of cheesy casserole and bacon-steeped collard greens, enough for ten people, but he only nibbled at it, as if from politeness rather than hunger.

Afterward, in the dark, the two of them sat on the porch swing, spatterings of leftover fireworks popping and crackling in the distance, warm breeze ruffling their hair. The weight of things that should be said hung over them like black clouds threatening rain. She could hear her parents inside talking in quiet, solemn tones.

"How's the band?" he asked, as if trying to drive away the silence between them.

"Toby says we're having practice soon."

"Can I still be in it?"

"Of course you can! Why wouldn't you?"

He shrugged. "I don't belong anywhere anymore. I don't have a family."

Lika leaned toward him. "That's not true."

"I don't know if I'll ever play the guitar again."

"Mike!" she gasped, but she couldn't form any more words than that.

"I mean, you, you're an amazing drummer. If you go after it, you'll be famous."

She clamped a hand over her mouth. How, after not seeing him for so long, could he give voice to every worry and hope she'd had all summer long? Lots of people told her she was good, but parents didn't count. There was one real question. Was she good *enough*? Then again, she shouldn't be so surprised. They had long been in tune with each other.

Footsteps approached from inside the screen door. Her parents filled the doorway and came out onto the porch. Her father, massive and broad, loomed over both of them. At 6'6", he weighed in at about three-hundred pounds, nearly all of it muscle. All the other cops on the force looked up to him, and nobody wanted to face him in the boxing ring.

"Mike," he said, "we have something we want to talk to you about."

How many times had Mike heard those words since Maggie got sick? He looked like an old hand at it.

"Okay," he said.

Lika's dad said, "We think you should come and live with us. It's not that we don't think you can handle it. But everybody needs a family, you know? You're practically family already."

Mike listened thoughtfully, clasping his hands on his knees.

Lika had expected this was coming, but she hadn't prepared for it. Having Mike as a kind of foster brother? That would be weird. They had been friends a long time, but family? She decided she could put up with weirdness if it meant that he would stay off the street or avoid getting swallowed up by the system.

The Walkers lived in a decent neighborhood, a mix of races and ethnicities, a suburb of boxy, brick houses showing their age but maintained with pride. Only in the last year or two had Lika become conscious of the circumstances of Mike and his mother, living in a rundown trailer court with no car. Mike went everywhere on his bicycle. Maggie knew all the bus routes backward and forward. No father for Mike or boyfriends for Maggie had ever been in the picture, and Lika had often wondered why. As beautiful as Maggie was, she must have been swarmed with men whenever she went out in public. How did such a beautiful person, inside and out, stay romantically unentangled? All of Lika's friends at school were an endless, tiresome swirl of who's dating whom, and yet this woman had seemed to walk outside of it all.

Lika's dad was still laying out the case, but she stopped listening until his deep voice, like an avalanche of concern, rumbled to a halt.

Mike sighed. "Thank you—really. But Mom set me up pretty well.

I have my own house, my own bed. I got a job. I just need to be there by myself for a while."

Lika's mom said, "Didn't your momma die in that house?"

"In her bed, yeah," Mike said.

Could they not afford hospice?

Lika's mom said, "You need to be out of there, Mikey, be with people who love you. You got to heal."

"I can handle it. She taught me everything I need to know. We did all the paperwork. I'm a man now. I can handle it."

A well of despair opened up in Lika's stomach. He didn't look like a man at all, but a scared boy who was in over his head. The black community Lika had grown up in was full of too many boys who thought they were men.

Dad thrust his hands into his pockets. "Comes the day you can't handle it, you call us, all right? We would love to have you."

Lika's face tightened with frustration. They were just going to let him *go*? What would he *do*?

"I will," Mike said. "I'll be okay, I promise." He gave Lika a wan smile.

Even as he spoke, it was like he was riding away on the caboose of a train bound for nowhere, and she could do nothing except watch him go.

PART II

APPETITE FOR DESTRUCTION

CHAPTER FOUR
SUNDAY MORNIN' COMIN' DOWN

TWO MONTHS LATER...

"What am I supposed to do with all this crap?" Otter whined as he looked down at the ragged cardboard box in his arms. The lawyer folded his hands on the mahogany desk. "Your grandfather's will was very specific. He bequeathed you this box and its contents."

Otter's eyes felt like a dusty gravel road, and last night's wreck-fest with Zeke had left what tasted like a coating of dead mouse on his tongue. Nothing in the box looked remotely valuable. Trinkets. Knickknacks. Cheap plastic toys. He'd be lucky to get five bucks at Big Jimmy's Pawn. He'd spent two hours on a bus, missed work when he desperately needed the money, risked angering his boss over the last-minute no-show, and put his job in jeopardy for a box of useless junk.

"Load of horseshit," he muttered as he retook his seat next to Aunt Misty. Beside her, in this office of hardwood, leather, and entitlement, he felt like a vulture among prize fowl. He pulled the bill of his Mudskippers baseball cap lower over his eyes. The air in the lawyer's office smelled like leather, fresh carpet, and at least three conflicting perfumes.

Aunt Misty flashed him a brittle, stone-gray look of disapproval at his language. Her face was a plastered mask of beauty a decade past its expiration date, framed by a golden-blonde mane more luxuriant than the hair of girls half her age. She belonged on her new anesthesiologist-husband's mantelpiece. Her handbag was worth as much as his ramshackle trailer house. Too bad she hadn't seen fit to share any of that wealth, or else

Otter's mom might still be alive. Otter remembered old Uncle Sal, Misty's first gig, from the days when they had all still been a family. Sal had been a good guy. He'd have helped out in Mom's last days. But living with Misty must have put too much strain on the old ticker.

When Otter had first walked into this room—ten minutes late—and Aunt Misty had turned to look at him, he was immediately angry at how much she looked like his mother.

The lawyer went on, "'…and also to each of my grandchildren—Michael MacIntyre, Mia Kowalski, Mara Kowalski, and Maya Kowalski—the sum of fifty thousand dollars…'"

The utterance punched Otter straight in the heart. A kaleidoscope of possibilities exploded in his brain, everything he could do with fifty thousand dollars. A smoking-hot motorcycle, up to his armpits in smoking-hot girlfriends—starting with Amber, that girl at the music store—the smoking-hot Les Paul hanging behind glass in the guitar store. Of course, Mom would have paid bills, set up a college fund for him, maybe go to college herself, all sorts of boring stuff. But like Zeke always said, school was for losers. Best to just enjoy life as it came. He deserved some fun after what he'd been through, what he was going through. Didn't he deserve to escape his crappy life, just for a little while? So he'd happily toss back a few celebratory beers and weed and pizza and video games and—

"'…to be placed in an interest-bearing trust until such time as the beneficiaries reach the age of twenty-five.'"

His hopes and visions collapsed into heaps of ash. Twenty-five was *old*. Most days he couldn't imagine twenty-one, much less twenty-five. That money was a lifetime away.

About six months older than him, his three cousins, the triplets, looked like M&Ms, little blonde duplicates of their mother sitting just on the other side of her, wearing different colors of candy-coated shell.

The weight of the box on his legs further angered him. Otter hadn't seen his grandfather in seven years. And with all that money, why couldn't Grandpa have given some to Mom? He could have at least paid for hospice. She wouldn't have had to die in agony. Otter wouldn't have had to watch her die by inches, wallowing in squalor, every day for the last few months.

Otter squirmed in his chair as the lawyer droned on like a floor buffer.

He peeked into the box and spotted an old Orange Crush bottle cap. His lips tightened with disgust at being the proud new owner of a box of useless crap.

He reached inside and drew out the bottle cap, turned it over in his fingers. The old, glass pop bottles were still around in specialty shops, but everything else was plastic nowadays, cheapened. The bright, sunny flavor of orange soda crept into his mouth, sweet and blazing citrus. He could almost imagine playing in empty lots with his buddies, darting through wooded hidey-holes not yet swallowed by pavement. The smell of orange, the smell of fresh-cut grass, of hot dogs at the ballpark, of the leather of his baseball glove, of dirt on his pants. The sounds of children playing, the laughter, the taunts, the jeers, the challenges, of the crack of a bat kissing the ball, of leaves rustling in a zephyr. The taste of an Orange Crush float, essence of orange made creamy by a scoop of vanilla ice cream at the Dairy Freeze. The weariness of having run hard, climbed hard, played hard, hard as he could, until the light failed and fireflies emerged from the shadows under the trees, and he collapsed with weariness in his bed with a summer breeze wafting through the window, and yearning for another orange soda pop.

What the heck was a zephyr anyway?

The lawyer snapped shut his binder and yanked Otter back into the present. "Thank you all for coming."

Otter caught himself with a grin on his face, in spite of his annoyance at the proceedings. The intensity of all those memories made him scratch his head, especially because he had never played sandlot baseball with a group of his buddies or visited a Dairy Freeze. And yet, it all felt so familiar.

Then he snorted and chucked the bottle cap back into the box. He didn't have time for such childishness anymore.

Downstairs in the high-rise's first-floor lobby, the Green M&M, Mia, approached him. "Hey, Mike, how are you doing?"

He compared this pretty girl, tall and lanky, her long, honey-gold braid draped over her shoulder, to the skinny little towheaded kid from his memories. A dozen snarky retorts hovered on his tongue, but she hadn't earned any of them personally, so he said, "Surviving."

"Sorry to hear about your mom. That had to have been really, really hard."

He sniffed. "Thanks." Should he accept her concern?

His hesitance must have prompted her to say, "We didn't know what was happening with you guys."

And whose fault was that? He really didn't know. It had to be because Aunt Misty was somehow awful, and probably Grandpa, too. Mom would not have cut ties so thoroughly without good reason. "Adults. What are you gonna do?"

She quirked her mouth into a smile that looked genuine. She had always been the least snooty of his three cousins—that much he remembered. "How's the band going?"

His ears warmed. "Where did you hear about that?"

She pointed to the guitar case slung over his shoulder.

"Oh, well, I haven't seen them much since school got out." Since his mother got really sick. "But we almost have a gig lined up."

"Cool! Where?"

"At the Black Line."

"Never heard of it."

Of course she hadn't. It was a million miles from her sphere of reality. But it was also a million miles away from his. There was no such gig, only hopeful talk of such a thing, and three-months-old talk at that. They hadn't had a rehearsal since school closed in the spring, and he hadn't seen Lika since that night at the Walkers' house. She'd called him a few times. He'd answered once or twice. The weight of grief still felt like a wall between him and the world.

He hadn't even picked up his guitar since that last time trying to play with his mom. It was too painful, but the absence of it was doing things to him he didn't understand, making him cranky. So he had brought his mom's six-string with him today, thinking he might do a little strumming in a park or on the bus. Bitterness had settled into his thoughts, but he didn't know what he could do about it. It did feel good to have it with him, though. He was a bassist, but when you wanted to make music all by yourself, you needed a six-string.

"But it sounds fascinating!" she said.

"It's a big rave club. All industrial Gothic."

The light of interest in her eyes guttered. "Mom would never let us go to that kind of place."

He leaned closer. "You could sneak out. You have a driver's license by now, don't you?"

The Black Line was a pipe dream, so why was he spinning this tall tale? To impress this relative he barely knew anymore?

Mia snickered and glanced at her mom, who was watching them from across the lobby with the Blue and Red M&Ms.

Aunt Misty tucked her four-figure purse under her arm. "Let's go, Mia. I'm sure Michael has a bus to catch."

"We could give him a ride," Mia said.

"There's no room in the car," Misty said.

And by "car" she meant her eight-passenger Lexus SUV.

Otter turned away. "See you, Mia."

Mia pulled a *Hello, Kitty!* notepad and pen out of her purse, scribbled her phone number on it, and handed it over. "Let me know about the show!"

"Sure." He stuffed the paper in his pocket.

"Family should support each other, right?"

He restrained the impulse to scoff.

"It was good to see you. Bye!" She waved and hurried after her sisters, leaving him standing there with this cardboard box of crap.

He considered chucking the box into the first garbage can he found. But then, maybe there was something valuable in there. He needed to do an inventory first.

CHAPTER FIVE

CRAZY LITTLE THING CALLED LOVE

The stench of diesel crept into the rear seats where he sat with the box on his lap, this last remnant of an old man's life. Otter opened a ragged flap to peruse the contents again. He propped his head on one fist and sighed. Stuff like this only mattered to the person who had it.

Big Jimmy's Pawn already had some of Mom's stuff, stuff Otter didn't need. Every time he handed over a curling iron or an alarm clock, though, a pang pierced his chest and his lungs constricted, but he went through with it anyway. Mom's cancer had dragged them both along the jagged edge for months before she succumbed. There was nothing left in the bank account, no savings, no cushion to fall on. His job at the car wash had slowed the tumble, but it was like a car trying to brake on an icy downhill. Something bad was going to happen at the bottom.

The box felt warm against his knees, as if it had something alive in it, like a puppy or a cat.

His head still ached from last night, and the dead mouse had curled up behind his tongue. He couldn't keep doing that, the all-night game-fests. But Zeke was the only person who seemed to understand Otter's situation. Beer and weed and an eight-hour video game marathon were the only combination that let him block it all, the pain, the memories, the confusion. And then there was Amber.

For about a week after Mom died, he had wandered the streets of town aimlessly, determined to be in the sunshine. Being at home was simply too painful. Mom should *be there*. But she wasn't.

In his wandering, he had come upon a used vinyl and CD store called

The Flip Side. Thinking he might be able to bring some CDs to sell, he left his bicycle out front and shambled inside to check it out, only to find behind the counter the most beautiful girl he had ever seen.

She was sitting on a stool, sorting through a stack of CD cases. Raven hair with a long, scarlet forelock draped over one eye, a heart-shaped face, button nose, and lips made for kissing. He didn't even know he'd been dreaming of her his whole life until he saw her right there.

He stood there are stared at her, his mouth going dry, until she noticed him. She said, "Hi."

The best response he could manage was some caveman-like grunt.

She looked roughly fifteen, wearing a colorful T-shirt that read "Siouxsie and the Banshees," cut-off denim shorts, and a skater-girl vibe. She otherwise ignored him, and he was forced to steal glances at her as he meandered the aisles helplessly. Eventually, he weirded himself out and left without saying a word to her.

He went back a few days later, this time with a handful of CDs. They were his mom's, but none of them were by bands he cared about.

"You'll have to bring these back when my uncle is here," she said. "I'm not allowed to buy used stuff."

"Oh."

"Weren't you in here a few days ago?" Her eyes looked into him so deep he would never forget them. Deep blue, rich blue, with pale ring around the iris, holding him fast.

"Yeah, that was my first time." His ears heated, cheeks flushed. She remembered him!

"We don't get a lot of customers. Nobody gets their music from CDs anymore. It's all MP3 files."

"Buggy whips," he said, lamely.

"What?"

"My mom used to tell me about how buggy whips were a huge business a hundred years ago. Before cars." God, he sounded stupid.

She smiled. "Right. I get you. Welcome to the internet generation, old farts!"

Beside her on the counter was an aging stereo system, complete with dancing equalizer lights, a ten-disc CD changer, a vinyl record player, a cassette deck, and even an old reel-to-reel. "Is that what's playing the music?" Over the store speakers came a smooth, laid-back but repetitive song that went, "Sweet, sweet Jane."

eah, that's the coolest part of this job. I get to listen to whatever I she said.

'This is not bad. What kind of stuff are you listening to today?"

A stack of CD cases stood beside the sound system. She scooted them toward him. "This is Cowboy Junkies' 'Sweet Jane.' It's a Lou Reed cover, but I like it better than the original. Then we have Siouxsie and the Banshees, Patti Smith, Joan Jett, The Pretenders, Amy Winehouse, Alanis Morissette, Fiona Apple, ZZ Ward…"

He nodded with appreciation. All of it music with meat on its bones, not bubblegum. Mom had some of this in her collection. This was a girl with thoughtful musical taste. Music *meant* something to her. The music she chose was a conscious expression of who she was.

He had returned a few days later, the longest he could make himself stay away. She had asked him, "So do you go to Elm Creek High School?"

"Theoretically," he said. The truth was, he was so caught up in keeping bills paid that he couldn't fathom the necessity of studying geometry and frog entrails.

She laughed. "So do you or don't you?"

"I haven't decided if I'm going back there next month."

She nodded sagely. "I've had a similar situation."

When she didn't elaborate, he started feeling so awkward that all he could do was blurt, "Hey, what's your name?"

"Amber."

"Call me Otter."

She smiled again, broader this time. One of her incisors was adorably crooked. The strength left his legs. "Okay, Otter."

The bell tinkled above the front door, and a skinny, hairy dude shambled in, hair tied in a loose ponytail. He looked like a rock-n-roll musician thirty years past his prime.

"Hey, Uncle Terry," she said.

The man grunted noncommittally, his gaze scrutinizing Otter. "Did you finish sorting that box of stuff I took yesterday?"

"Not yet."

"You go do that, and I'll watch the counter."

"Okay." She gave Otter a little eyeroll that threw his stomach into a loop.

Otter took that as his cue to depart. The next few times he had gone back to the store, only Terry had been working there.

In her absence, meanwhile, Otter did something he had never done before. He wrote a song. A song for Amber. He carried it next to his brain, carefully folded and tucked inside his baseball cap. Like he would ever have the guts to give it to her. He would probably never see her again.

When the new school year had started, he couldn't bring himself to go. He had more adult concerns than doing history homework, like keeping the lights turned on and food in the refrigerator.

The box in his lap shifted, as if something had moved inside. He flipped open the flaps again and studied the contents. He dug his hand through the stuff, but found nothing that might be moving.

A strange array of scents wafted out of the box. It didn't smell like dust or mouse droppings, but…he couldn't say what it *did* smell like. He stuck his face in and breathed deep. Spices maybe? Someone's perfume? Food? But what kind of food? Bread? Baking? Rice? Fish?

So weird.

When he sat up again, a girl about his age, pretty, olive-skinned, backpack on her lap, was looking at him with amusement. His face flushed with the urge to talk to her—and he had just had his face neck-deep in a cardboard box. She smiled at him, braces gleaming, then pushed the button for the next stop.

Something inside him reached out to this other girl he would probably never see again—she had such pretty eyes—but he didn't know what to say. Then she was gone, leaving him with his box of stupid, weird junk.

CHAPTER SIX
BORN UNDER A BAD SIGN

The sun was hot on Otter's back, even in the approach of evening, as he trudged down the road from the bus stop toward the Starlite Trailer Court. Cicadas sang in the roadside trees, and the wind brushed the ditch grass into undulating waves of green and brown. A massive dually pickup truck blasted him with gravel as it roared past on its way to the interstate.

He rounded the bend into the trailer court's driveway and glanced toward his house, which occupied the end lot of a dead-end street.

Out front was a car he didn't recognize. A newer, ugly beige, four-door. The kind of car government agencies bought.

Without him immediately understanding why, a chill like cold dishwater dashed over his flesh.

He lunged into the trees and ducked behind a plum thicket, heart pounding. A suspicion crawled over him, needing confirmation.

He hid the box in the plum thicket and then stole through the narrow strip of woods between the trailer court and the highway, toward his house. The woods paralleled his street and abutted the rear of their...*his* lot. There was no *their* anymore. He would stay out of sight in the trees.

Sticks and leaves crackled under his feet. A ninja he was not. But he found one of the narrow game trails and crept the rest of the way through coarse branches and leaf litter.

He passed behind the Millers' trailer, a retired couple who were probably old when Mom was born. Their house smelled like Ben Gay and peanut butter cookies. Mr. Miller liked to carve landscapes into wooden planks with a Dremel tool.

After their house came Mr. Simpson, or as Otter called him, Old Man

Cheapson. A couple summers back, Otter had mowed his lawn every week for three months, and every week Mr. Simpson had told him he'd pay him next time. Then when September came and Otter still hadn't been paid, he and his mother had paid Mr. Simpson a visit, asking directly for a whole summer's lawnmowing wages. Simpson had scowled and said, "Boy oughta be grateful for the chance to do some hard work. Builds character." Then he shut the door in their faces.

Next was the Polanskis' trailer, Bob and Delora. Bob was a retired trucker, Delora a school teacher. They had a stunningly beautiful granddaughter, a few years older than Otter, at whom he had goggled since he was eleven, and a grandson about Otter's age who had apparently grown out of his fascination with setting fire to toads. He and Otter had never seen eye to eye.

Next came Mama June, as she liked to be called. Mama June had been one of Mom's stable of babysitters when Otter was small. A wizened up old apple, she stank of cigarettes and had a voice like scuffed leather, but she was kind, and little Mikey had fallen asleep many nights on her living room floor with his fists full of Hot Wheels and old Looney Tunes tapes playing in her VCR. He hadn't seen much of her this summer; she said she was spending more time with her sister in Arizona.

Finally the corner of his house emerged from behind Imelda's trailer next door, then as he crept farther, the propane tank, then his front door, then the front bumper of a car, then the woman sitting inside. On the door of the car was a logo that read "Department of Human Services."

Mom had warned him this would happen.

Otter was an emancipated minor, but he was still under the supervision of the court. Someone would be tasked with making sure that he was able to make a go of life on his own. At the first sign of slippage, *zip!* Straight into foster care.

Through the leaves, he studied the woman in the car. She was an old lady, at least forty, hair pulled tight into a bun, and so short she had to look *through* the steering wheel, like she was sitting in a hole. Her gaze kept flicking to the mirrors, over her shoulder, her fingers drumming the wheel. It had to be getting hot sitting there in the sun with no air-conditioning. As the shadows of the trees swung long and orange tinged the clouds, she drank some water, then got out and crossed the gravel street to Zeke's house.

Gary and Freaky, Zeke's pit bulls, pelted toward the chain-link fence, snarling and barking as if she was on the menu. The scary thing about that fence was that it was only waist high. One good jump and those dogs could clear it. Otter had met other pit bulls that were total sweethearts. Not those two.

The woman called something from the gate but got no answer from the house. She gingerly retreated from the slavering hellhounds. Their assault shook the entire length of the fence. Imelda's house was her next try.

Out of Otter's view around the corner of the house, the woman knocked on Imelda's door. Otter heard the distinctive creak of her screen door.

"*Si?*"

"Good afternoon. My name is Louisa Pritt. I'm from the Department of Human Services. I'm looking for a boy named Michael MacIntyre. Does he live here?"

"*No hablo Ingles.*"

The woman, Louisa Pritt, then launched into a repeat of what she had just said, but in immaculate Spanish.

Otter's Spanish wasn't so good, but he was pretty sure Imelda said she didn't know anything. She said something about Otter's house.

Louisa Pritt's voice grew shrill with frustration, but she remained polite as she thanked Imelda and then got into her car, slammed the door, started the engine.

Otter crept to the edge of Imelda's house, peered around the corner as the car slipped into gear, tires crunching on loose gravel, and backed into the street. The engine revved and the car spewed tails of gravel behind it as it drove away.

He sneaked up to Imelda's door before she even finished closing it. "Boo!"

At the sight of him two feet away, she jumped back and clutched her chest. "What are you doing, *mijo!* You kill me! Heart explode! Drop dead!"

"I just wanted to say thanks for giving that lady the run-around. *Muchos gracias.*"

"*Much-*as *gracias,*" she corrected him but smiled doing it. The scents of cinnamon, roasted chilies, and hamburger wafted through her screen door. Imelda was a short, barrel-bodied woman with an eyebrow like a carefully scribed line of charcoal across her brow, coal-black hair in a wild bun, and an explosive, Day-Glo muumuu. "You know her?"

"Never saw her before."

"She was looking for you. She say she want to help you."

"I don't need her kind of help. Who's got two thumbs and no interest in foster care?" He pointed both of them at his chest. "This guy."

"Oh, *mijo,* you a good boy, but still just a boy."

He restrained the eyeroll.

Imelda said, "You stay away from Zeke. Hang out with kids! Not... guys like him. How you gonna make it, you get high and skip school? You go to school, right?"

He had not, in fact, been to school since the school year started a couple weeks ago. He needed money more than he needed algebra and *Catcher in the Rye*.

"You go to school, *right?*" she asked pointedly.

He nodded, and she relaxed a bit.

"And stop asking me for weed! You too young!"

"That's a little hypocritical isn't it?" he said, teasing.

"Your brain not..." she gesticulated above her head, "...not done cooking. My brain is already refried." She laughed, loud and breathy, but then jabbed a crimson-taloned finger at his nose and gave him a scary, wide-eyed look. "You be good!"

"I will be good, Imelda."

"You want enchiladas?"

His stomach roared like Gary and Freaky. "I would love some."

Back in his own house, Otter sat down at the tiny kitchen table with his steaming plate of enchiladas and dug in. He would have sworn these were the best enchiladas he had ever had. Cooking like this every day, it was no wonder Imelda was built like a barrel, but was he ever grateful. He'd have to do something nice for her.

His trailer was dark and empty and hot, like always, even with the windows open. He switched on the box fan in the corner. At least Mom had managed enough insurance policy to pay off the place, even if the deed would be crawling through probate court for a year, and he still had to pay lot fees. Across the gravel drive, Gary and Freaky were savaging their supper. Next door, Imelda was on her deck reading a Spanish magazine and smoking a strange-smelling, brown cigarette, fuzzy slippers up on the two-by-four railing.

He pulled out his phone and saw the icons indicating three voicemails.

The messages were probably from Jeff, the car wash manager, and he didn't want to hear them, so he just savored every last forkful of enchilada, every kernel of rice and beans, and when that was gone, licked the plate clean.

But the voicemails were still flashing at his brain.

The first message went, "Yeah, Mike, this is Jeff. Where are you? You're supposed to be here today. Javier couldn't reschedule, so now we're a man short. Get here as soon as you can."

Otter had told that butthead he couldn't come in today. What the hell, was he supposed to be at everyone's beck and call?

The second message went, "Mike, this is Jeff again. We got a rush down here today. We really need you, buddy. Call me as soon as you get this."

The car wash was closed by now, so there was no point in trying to call Jeff. Otter wasn't in the mood for a butt-chewing anyway.

The third voice struck him like a Five Finger Death Punch to the heart. It was from Toby's number, but the voice was *not* Toby's.

"Otter! Rehearsal! Where the hell are you?"

It was a girl's voice. Familiar, but it wasn't Lika's. There was amusement in it, relishing the confusion he must be feeling.

Then Toby's voice came on. "Yeah, get your butt over here, dude. I found us a lead singer."

Could it be…? Was it Amber's voice?

He checked; the message had come about half an hour ago.

Otter choked out a stream of words Mom wouldn't approve of and sprang for his bass guitar case, where it leaned against the couch.

Guitar case slung across his back, he charged out the door, dragged his bike from its hiding place in the lilac bushes behind the house—as an afterthought he tossed the box of Grandpa's junk inside to deal with later—and put the sneaker to the pedal.

CHAPTER SEVEN
OTTER B. GOODE

The thrill of hearing what could be Amber's voice on *his phone* went ten rounds with wondering what she was doing there. She must be the new lead singer Toby was so excited about. Having not played since May, how badly was he going to flub everything?

He was pedaling with crazy abandon when he called Toby back.

A pang of disappointment struck him when Toby's voice answered. "Otter. Dude."

"I'm on my way!" he huffed.

A car zipped past him at three times the speed limit, blasting him with fine gravel and exhaust.

He said, "Hanging up now so I don't die!"

The ride from the trailer court was twenty minutes into the proper suburbs. Toby's house was in an older suburb on the verge of decline.

Lika's drums and Toby's guitar echoed from two blocks away. The chattering rattle and rumble-thud of Lika's immaculate, intricate rhythms drove his legs to greater speed, his breathing ragged. Sweat plastered his T-shirt to his back, slicked his neck, but he managed to turn a twenty-minute ride into fifteen.

He rolled up into Toby's driveway and skidded to a halt before the open garage door. Three faces turned toward him.

He raised both hands. "I'm sorry! I'm sorry I took so long to get your message. I had to go all the way downtown on the bus and just got back."

Toby crossed his arms. "What for?" He was shorter than Otter, blockish, more like a wrestler than a musician, wearing an ancient Led Zeppelin tank top.

"The reading of my grandpa's will." He laid his bike on the grass and unsnapped his guitar case on the concrete.

Lika circled out from behind her drum set. "Your grandpa died?"

For some reason, he couldn't meet her gaze. "Yeah, the funeral was last week."

Toby said, "Sorry, buddy."

Lika came out and hugged him. "I'm so sorry. God, it seems like that's all I have to say lately."

The hug took him by such surprise that he barely had time to return the gesture before it was over. "Thanks."

Then she punched him in the chest. "That's for not telling me." Her black eyes pierced him and she crossed her arms. He would never, ever, in a million years, be able to hide himself from her.

He rubbed the spot. "Sorry?"

Amber stepped out of the shadows, and Otter's breath caught for a moment. Her face was as exquisite as a porcelain doll, round cheeks and huge eyes and pillowy lips that bore an enigmatic smile. "Hey."

"Hey," he said.

Toby said, "You two know each other?"

Lika's eyes narrowed, flicking back and forth between them.

Otter's mouth worked, and he felt the presence of the folded piece of paper inside his ball cap. The song he had written for Amber.

Amber said, "Yeah, he came into the store a few weeks ago."

Toby said, "Okay, cool. Otter, Amber can sing. *And* she's a keyboardist." He thumbed over his shoulder to a keyboard on a stand, a new addition to their gang.

"Since lessons in the fourth grade," she said.

"Let's get at it, how about?" Toby said, his patience wearing thin at all this social behavior.

Otter snatched up his bass guitar, the candy apple red, four-string Fender Precision his mom gave him for his thirteenth birthday. That was before she got sick. She had never given him such an expensive gift, and he never asked her where she got the money. Slinging the strap over his shoulder, he plugged in and tuned up, ears burning with self-consciousness as the other three simply watched and waited.

Toby stepped over to a laptop that had a microphone plugged into it. "I'm recording tonight. If it's good, I'm going to use it as a demo to get gigs. So don't screw up!"

"We always screw up," Lika said.

"Don't screw up *completely*," Toby said. "I can edit out a few flubs."

The added pressure became a clenched fist around the base of Otter's neck. Like he needed any more pressure.

As soon as they started to play, however, that pressure went away and he descended into the Zone, the Underlying Bass Riff of All Things. Toby launched into the opening riff of AC/DC's "You Shook Me All Night Long," and Otter strolled into the familiar bass line just before the first chorus.

Toby was the earth's crust, a place of mountains and oceans, beauty and tragedy, his fingers tearing through chords and arpeggios like landscapes and cloud formations.

Lika was the earthquake, the heartbeat, shuddering and rumbling in surprising directions, but always, always, perfectly on time.

Otter's bass was the dark, throbbing blood of the earth, the deep surge of magma, lending tones to Lika's heartthrob, the bedrock that Toby's guitar danced upon.

And then there was Amber. As soon as she unleashed her voice, it swept him away. Her voice was the wind and sky, at once tragic and deep and passionate and playful. Her voice was the galloping clouds and windy valleys and storm-tossed seas. She was sunset and sunrise, a thousand hues of lavender, copper, and gold, and as her body swayed in her skinny jeans and crop top, she was the lithe, undulating serpent that encircled the earth. With her movements, with her voice, with her spirit, Amber encircled Otter's world around and around and she didn't even know it.

In the Zone, Otter became the bass line, the baseline, the humming undercurrent, and the light outside faded, leaving them in dim, garage bulbs, but they played on.

They belted out Led Zeppelin and Metallica, flashed through Johnny Cash and more AC/DC, intoned Fiona Apple and Alanis Morissette, crooned Aretha Franklin and Amy Winehouse. They wrangled over songs and lyrics, but everybody loved what they played. Sometimes, in the depths of a song three times his age, he felt his thrumming fingers twining through the threads of history, touching something deeper than school could show him.

It was easy to forget the flubs, the missed notes, the wrong chords, because he was *alive*. He was *alive* for the first time in months. He could imagine that he hadn't followed his mom halfway down into her death spiral, could imagine that her absence had left him with his own life still fully intact.

At the end of "Ring of Fire"—a number that desperately needed trumpets to really wail—Toby's dad came out of the house, hands in his pockets, bopping his head to the music. He looked like he hated being the bearer of bad news. "All right, kids, as much as I'm enjoying the free concert, it is now ten o'clock on a school night. Time to wrap it up."

"Aw, c'mon, Dad!" Toby said.

"I ain't gonna be that parent. Wrap it up."

Amber winked at him. "Sure thing, Mr. Paulson."

Mr. Paulson went back inside, and they commenced teardown, sharing high fives.

Toby said, "I might be able to put something worthwhile together for a demo now. We're gonna play the Black Line someday!"

"The Black Line! I love that place!" Amber said. And then she slapped Otter on the backside with a laugh.

He stiffened, and a hot spike shot up his spine and sent him upright like a steel girder.

He had never even *heard* of a girl slapping a guy on the butt.

He wanted to ask Toby about the hypothetical Black Line gig, but he'd just lost his ability to speak and stood there dumbly holding a half-coiled amp cord.

Someone poked him in the ribs. "Hey," Lika said. "Walk me to the bus stop?"

He blinked and brought himself back to the moment. He and Lika hadn't had any time together in forever. "Absolutely," Otter said.

CHAPTER EIGHT
BEST FRIEND

Lika Walker crossed her arms and walked in silence, considering her friend. Otter walked alongside her, guitar case on his back, pushing his bicycle. This wasn't a terrible neighborhood to walk alone at night, but there'd been a couple of break-ins in the last few weeks. The air had cooled with the moist tang of September, the whisper that autumn was coming.

He said, "Sorry we haven't talked much this summer. It's good to see you, though."

Gravel on the sidewalk crunched underfoot. Lika said, "How come you haven't been in school, Mike?" Lika was the only person allowed to call him Mike. And he was the only person allowed to call her Angelika, even though he didn't.

"It's not working out for me. Too much on my mind. Too much to do," he said.

"Your mom?"

Two blocks ahead, the lights of the Kwik Trip near Lika's bus stop bathed the pavement in mercury orange. Several of the streetlights had been shot out recently, leaving this stretch in darkness.

"Not just mom. My whole family has a plague of death upon it." He had probably meant it to sound like a joke, but it didn't.

"I thought you hadn't seen your grandpa in a long time."

"Not since I was eight. And mom wouldn't talk about him, so I don't have the slightest idea what he was like."

"What do you remember?"

He walked a few steps. "Well, I remember once when I was maybe seven, me and Mom were at his house for some holiday, maybe Thanksgiving. His house was this big, old mansion. Really old, really cool, like they don't make them anymore, right? All brick and ivy and hardwood. And there was one room I wasn't allowed to go into, so naturally I had to, right?"

"Absolutely," she said, urging him to continue.

"So I snuck into Grandpa's office and saw these cool Japanese pictures of women and samurai and stuff, and I remember not being able to look away from the bright colors and their weird, exaggerated faces." He chuckled a little. "Some of the pictures were *adult in nature*. People holding severed heads or even…doing it."

Lika laughed.

"I swear, fuzzies in full view."

"No way!"

They laughed harder.

"I mean, what does an old guy need with weird, old porn? Anyway, he had all this other stuff, too. Two swords on a rack, some weird, glazed pottery, this ceramic Buddha, must have been this big." He indicated with about three feet between his palms. "Some porcelain dolls, really beautiful ones, like they were alive… But of course I kept looking at the pictures." He grinned at her.

"Duh."

"I remember wanting to go ask Grandpa about that stuff. But then Aunt Misty caught me in there, and she really yelled at me, '*Never* touch Grandpa's things!' I never told Mom what happened, but I wanted to go hide in the basement. I stewed on it until Christmas, then I asked him about Japan. He gave me this weird smile and said he'd been there many times and he'd tell me all about it someday."

"Did he?"

"It must have been right after that Mom quit speaking to him. That Christmas was the last time I saw him."

"Didn't he try to call you, come and see you? What about your aunt?"

"If he did, Mom never told me. Same with Aunt Misty. I don't think they even know where I live."

"That must have been some huge kinda fight."

He nodded and sighed. "All I know is they're awful people. Mom must have kept us apart for a really good reason."

"What about the will then?"

"He left me this box full of utterly useless crap. And fifty grand I'll never be able to touch."

"Fifty grand!"

"Yeah, except I can't touch it until I'm twenty-five. I'll never see that money."

She waited for thirty yards to see if he would say why, but his silence just dragged between them. "Explain."

He shrugged and hunched his shoulders, gaze fixed on the pavement.

"Mike, are you sure you're okay?" Lika gave him a long, piercing look.

"Yeah, why?"

"You're different now."

He stiffened and looked away from her. "What's that mean?"

"It's just…" She couldn't tell him that there was a darkness in him now, a great, gaping wound.

"How're your parents?" he asked.

"They're gonna be miffed I'm out so late. Dad's on duty tonight. Momma will be waiting up. I can hear it already." The sound of her mom's voice echoed out of her imagination the way only a gospel singer's could.

"Say, 'But Momma, the *band!*'" he said, chuckling.

"I'm lucky she let me come at all on a school night."

"Ask her if she'd rather you practice your drums at home."

She laughed. "That one might get her."

They entered the pool of light around the convenience store.

"Okay, so tell me about Amber," Lika said.

He paused, and his back straightened. "What about her?"

She forked two fingers back and forth between them. "You, me. Third grade. Don't bullshit me. I'm older than you."

He grinned, held out his palm.

She rolled her eyes and fished a quarter out of her pocket and slapped it in his palm. It was a game that went all the way back to elementary school and Lika's mom's Swear Jar. But she didn't mind, especially because she knew he was broke. "So tell me."

"I kinda like her."

She crossed her arms. "Ain't no 'kinda' about it."

He sighed long and deep, recognizing the familiar ache. "I need to tell her or I'm going to explode. Like a toad run over by a semi."

"Not a very romantic image."

"It's all I got."

"I get it. Amber's got it *all* going on. I got my own little girl-crush on her."

"Really?"

"Seriously. And I don't even swing that way."

"Don't you be horning in on my would-be girlfriend." He elbowed her.

"It's not me you need to worry about."

"What do you mean?"

"She's the kind of girl with a ton of guy-friends. I've seen her around school. Transferred this year from West."

"You saying she gets around?" A flash of challenge entered Otter's voice, but there was a tremulous expectation there, too, like a cancer patient's family awaiting more bad news. A painful analogy in Mike's case.

"I'm not saying she's a slut or anything. Besides, who she makes out with is her business. I'm saying you won't know the Friend Zone from the Fun Zone. And if you *do* get with her, the competition will be on your butt the whole time."

His shoulders sagged.

"The first week of school, I saw her get hit on six times in one day," she said. "And those are just the times I saw."

His shoulders fell off and hit the pavement. "Do you think you could help me?"

She sighed for the poor fool. There were crushes, and there were *crushes*, and poor Mike was in the claws of the latter. But how could she say no? He could ask anything of her, and she'd give it.

Damn it.

How did she feel about this crush anyway? The truth was that she didn't know. What she was pretty sure of was that Mike was heading straight for more trouble, and she felt bad about that, especially after everything he'd been through.

As they kicked their love lives around on the parking lot asphalt, the lights in the store dimmed. The manager came out, a short, dark-skinned man with a thick, black mustache, wearing a navy-blue turban. He locked the door, pocketed his keys, and walked toward them. When he spotted them, his teeth flashed white. "Oh, hello, young people!"

"Hey, Mr. Mukherjee," Otter said. "Closing up early tonight?"

"Yes, my daughter is ill. I must go home and tend to her. My wife has a work shift tonight." He spoke with the distinct lilt of an Indian accent. "No customers tonight anyway." He headed for the sidewalk.

"Don't you have a car?" Otter asked.

"No, I am most sadly afoot. Saving for my daughter's college, you know," Mr. Mukherjee said. "How is your mother, young man? I have not seen her in quite some time."

"She died," Otter said, his voice more controlled than it had any right to be.

Mr. Mukherjee's eyes bulged, gleaming. He muttered something in Hindi, then said, "I am so sorry. Please accept my profound condolences."

"Thanks. It was cancer."

"I sometimes wondered about her when she stopped coming. She was such a bright and happy person. Please wait here a moment."

Mr. Mukherjee hurried back to his store, unlocked the door, and went in.

Lika and Otter looked at each other and shrugged.

Lika said, "You know him? This isn't even your 'hood."

"My mom used to come here all the time. Said he had the cheapest smokes in town. Plus, he's a musician so they vibed on that. So I got to know him some."

Mr. Mukherjee came back out carrying a plastic bag. He offered it to Otter. "You must remember that your mother is not dead. She has simply shed her mortal clothes and gone to be reborn. She will soon share her music with others. It is the will of God."

Otter took the bag. It was full of food. A few bananas, apples, sandwiches, yogurt. A stricken look fell over Otter's face, and he stammered. "Thank you, Mr. Mukherjee. Thank you."

"You are quite welcome. Now I must go. A good evening to you both." Mr. Mukherjee bowed slightly and departed.

"That was so nice of him," Lika said, watching him go.

Otter kept looking at the food. "Yeah…"

They moved down to the bus stop sign and stood for a while in the glow of the gas pump lights.

Otter said, "So what do I do about Amber?"

"Look, you can't just tell her. That's too scary, makes girls run screaming for their pepper spray."

"So what do I do?" The desperation in his question tweaked her heart.

"You have to ask her out."

He groaned. "I'm doomed."

The light of the oncoming bus swung around a corner two blocks distant.

As the bus pulled up, Otter abruptly threw his arms around her neck and squeezed. His voice was thick. "Thanks."

Something fuzzed her vision with moisture, and she hugged him back, any thoughts of what to say skittering off into the bushes.

She reluctantly released him, stepped through the open door, turned, and waved, but he was already pushing his bike away.

CHAPTER NINE
DU HAST

Otter's tires crunched on the gravel street as he approached his house, sending Gary and Freaky into paroxysms of snarling and barking. A deep voice from Zeke's deck quelled them. Lined by a splash of light through the window behind him, Zeke Halvorsen sat with his feet up on the deck rail.

"What's up, Otter-man!" Zeke called.

Otter let the gravel drag his wheels to halt. "Still recovering from last night. Good grief."

Zeke laughed. "Gotta learn to pace yourself, bro! I got a little left from last night. Want to come on up?"

It was late, but Otter didn't have to get up until noonish to make it to work on time. Since he wasn't going to school anyway. "Sure, why not?"

He leaned his bike against the waist-high fence. The dogs growled.

"Geri! Freki! Shut the hell up!" Zeke yelled, and the dogs slunk back to the shadows under the deck.

Otter went through the gate and closed it behind him. "I thought their names were Gary and Freaky. You pronounce it different, though."

"You gotta roll the *R* a little. Geri and Freki were Odin's wolves."

"Odin. Isn't that Thor's dad from the movies?"

Zeke laughed. "It goes back a little farther than that."

"How much farther, like to the comics?" Otter put enough teasing in his voice to let Zeke know he was kidding. The wooden steps creaked under his feet. He plopped beside Zeke on a frayed, plastic-and-aluminum lounger.

The scent of beer wafted from the open can between Zeke's thighs. He took a long drink, his long, blond ponytail catching the light from inside the trailer. Zeke's chest and shoulders bulged through his scarlet T-shirt. How could Otter get muscles like that? On the front of the shirt was the image of an inverted hammer, the grim face of a long-bearded, one-eyed man in a horned helmet, and the caption *Viking Warrior*. With a thick, golden beard and eyebrows, Zeke looked the part. "Thirsty?"

"Parched."

Zeke tossed him a can of beer from the twelve-pack beside him.

Otter popped it and leaned back with a sigh.

"Rough day, hoss?" Zeke said.

"Busy. Had to take the bus all the way downtown for the reading of Grandpa's will, had to see my tight-ass relatives, had the Man after me to chuck me into foster care, had band rehearsal…"

"That is indeed a busy day."

"You?"

"Had a club meeting tonight. We're getting geared up."

"What kind of club? Geared up for what?"

"Sort of like a Neighborhood Watch. We're gonna start sending out groups to keep an eye on things. We gotta protect our neighborhoods, protect our own. Too many outsiders coming in."

"Yeah, my friend Toby's neighborhood had a few break-ins lately."

"Yeah, bro, we gotta be out there watching for unsavory types. This whole country is in a death spiral. All these people coming from outside, ruining things for real Americans, stealing our jobs. Drug-dealers and rapists."

"Is that where you get your weed?" Otter meant it as a joke, but Zeke didn't laugh.

"I grow my own. But you keep that under your hat, hear me?" Zeke's pale eyes gleamed like ice in the dim street light.

"Who am I gonna tell?" Otter said.

Last night, he and Zeke had played *Terrorist Apocalypse*, stoned out of their minds, until three in the morning. Between the weed and the game, it was the first time the ever-present splinter of pain that used to be his mom's presence had dulled, if only for a little while. Seeing Aunt Misty today brought it back with barbs on it. And what the hell was he supposed to feel about Grandpa's death? It certainly didn't feel like he needed to stay baked for three solid days, like after Mom's final sleep.

Otter took a long drink of his beer. It tasted a little skunky, but he didn't care as long as he could make that splinter go away for a little while again. "Want to go shoot some towel-heads?"

Zeke shrugged. "Sure." A little unsteady, he scooped up the half-empty case of beer and led Otter into the trailer. He dropped the beer next to the couch before the massive flat-screen TV. Then he flipped several switches to fire up the conglomeration of electronics. Like an explosion, a Tool song blasted over them, a building demolition set to music. Together they grinned and bobbed their heads to the thunderous beat. Then he turned it down and cocked an ear. Across the street, Imelda was yelling at them in Spanish.

They snickered and sank into the tattered, vinyl sofa. A huge black flag covered the wall with an image similar to Zeke's T-shirt, the long-bearded, one-eyed man in the horned helmet, and the inverted hammer.

Otter gestured toward it. "So what's the story with that? Wasn't there last night."

"Got it at the meeting tonight. That's the club colors, bro."

"What's the club?"

"Odin's Warriors. We're all about preserving the Viking ways and protecting our own from outsiders."

"Looks pretty badass."

"Odin was the king of the gods. He sired sons on as many women and goddesses as he damn well pleased. Gouged out his own eye as a sacrifice for sacred wisdom. Nailed himself to Yggdrasil, the great ash tree, with his own spear, for nine days and nights to discover the knowledge of the ancient runes. Like you said, badass. Makes Thor look like a whiny teenager."

"Sounds like a wild story."

Zeke knelt beside a pile of books. Otter caught only one title on the top of the stack, *The Protocols of the Elders of Zion,* before it toppled over and Zeke extracted his quarry. He handed it to Otter, *Song of the Vikings: A Celebration of Norse Religion and Mythology.* "Some great stories about my people in there," Zeke said. "What are your people?"

"My great-great-great-grandfather came from Scotland in the 1800s, I think. On my mom's side. My grandma Rebecca's dad was Jewish. So I'm kind of a mutt." He grinned.

Zeke looked at him for a long moment. "So you're…Jewish?"

Otter shrugged, "Hell, I don't know. I don't know what the rules are for who's Jewish and who's not. Mom never talked about it. Never been to church once my whole life."

Zeke seemed to relax, but Otter didn't know what had triggered the sudden scrutiny in the first place. Zeke raised his beer and clinked Otter's can. "*Skaal.* That is acceptable. Dad's side?"

Otter shrugged. "Mom always joked that I was a virgin birth. She even gave me her last name. I doubt he even knows I exist."

Zeke's eyes narrowed at that, too, but then the huge screen snapped to life with the blood-drenched logo of *Terrorist Apocalypse.* Last night, they had played through at least a dozen missions, killed hundreds of Muslim terrorists in their quest to reach the imam's headquarters. The game's graphics were so realistic he could imagine himself a counter-terrorist operative wielding the most advanced firearms and explosives in existence. The game's A.I. was brutally effective. Hesitate for a moment and the bastards would outflank you, put you in a crossfire, and lights out. How many times had he heard the phrase "*Allahu akbar!*" as the terrorists attacked or died screaming in sprays of gore?

"We'll turn you into a warrior yet," Zeke said as the game booted up.

The thought of being a real warrior, a somebody, a man who stood up for what was right, a man who protected his people, swelled Otter's heart. He was a man now, after all. The world was so much clearer for those with a never-ending supply of enemies to kill.

CHAPTER TEN
SUKIYAKI (UE WO MUITE ARUKOU)

The alarm clock blasted Otter out of bed, casting about for the source of the apocalypse.

He found it on the floor under yesterday's T-shirt. After floundering, fumbling, and flopping, he slapped it silent and rolled onto his back on the floor. The noon light stabbed his eyes like toothpicks. A slow drip of expletives formed as he rolled onto his side and levered himself up.

Four a.m. and seventeen missions later, he and Zeke blasted the terrorist imam to smithereens, saved the hostages, and celebrated with more beers.

But now it was time to be a grown-up and go to work.

He put the last scoop of fresh grounds in the coffeemaker and set it to super-strong, pulled his last can of energy drink from the fridge, and pounded it on his way to the shower.

When he was finished, he poured coffee into the World's Greatest Mom travel cup and sat at the kitchen table to peruse yesterday's mail.

Electric bill: OVERDUE

Lot fee: OVERDUE

At least the propane tank was still full from last winter; when the snow came, he wouldn't freeze to death for a while.

He was supposed to get paid today. And he'd ask Jeff for more hours so he could get these bills paid off.

His stomach unraveled itself and roared, but there was nothing to fill it. He'd pick up some groceries on the way home, too. He could wait until then to eat something. Most of the food from Mr. Mukherjee he had gobbled up when he came home from Zeke's place.

Also in the mail was another letter from the school district charging him with truancy. Perhaps they had forgotten they didn't pay him to go to school. He missed seeing Lika every day, but he had more adult concerns. The thought of seeing six guys a day hitting on Amber made his heart feel like a chunk of concrete.

He plopped down on the couch, picked up the remote, and turned on one of the trashy, day-time talk shows. Baby daddies everywhere, parents and kids screaming at each other, siblings throwing punches. God, some people's lives were *really* messed up.

Something drew his attention to the cardboard box. He could still make it to the pawn shop before work. Wait…he had left it in the bushes out back. Had he been so tired last night he didn't remember bringing it inside?

A little weird.

But it was time to do an inventory.

He upended the box on the floor in front of him. Some of the stuff had Japanese writing on it. He started lining things up. A wooden figure of a man in *lederhosen*. A letter opener in the shape of a samurai sword. A medallion or necklace with its chain broken, of Asian design—maybe Japanese—depicting a crane and a dragon. A cast-iron toy fire truck, most of its paint chipped away. A wooden coin with a buffalo on it that said TOMBSTONE, ARIZONA. A snow globe. A cheap, plastic harmonica. A metal hinge with what looked like a bullet hole in it.

"What a bunch of crap."

There was an assortment of smaller things. Soon he would have to do a real inventory.

He sifted through and picked up a thumb-sized porcelain rooster on a string with a little jingle-bell. He tinkled the bell, and the sound rang surprisingly in the fading light, as if amplified somehow. Suddenly he smelled incense, pine needles, lush greenery.

The scent of flowery incense brought Amber into his mind, and the memory of her smile turned his torso into an aching cavern.

The light dimmed further. Her eyes meeting his, flirting, endless lakes, depths he longed to explore, someone who wanted to understand him, too.

He could imagine her warm hand in his, the sound of her feet on the steps, the moist kiss of the mountain air, the way the mist clung to the bases of the trees, and the profusion of knee-high, red-kerchiefed Buddhas nestled in the rocks along the path.

She looked at him with deep, brown eyes, Japanese eyes, smiled at him with lips that he wanted to kiss more than anything. These stone steps led up a mountainside, under a succession of red-orange *torii* arches, to an ancient temple, toward their first kiss.

(Wait, how did he know what a *torii* arch was? An archway that cleansed visitors to sacred places in Japan…)

Emerald moss, impossibly green, covered everything, even the steps and Buddhas. The excitement in him grew with each step, even though his legs ached and his heart pounded with the climb. He spoke to her, but not in English, and she answered, but not in English, and yet he understood. Her voice was sly, teasing, sharp with intelligence. Maybe they would even make out up there somewhere in a secluded garden. Maybe he'd… No, that wasn't right.

Otter was walking in someone else's movie.

And then on a stroll through the manicured garden, he felt her lips for the first time. The wonder of it echoed through his life, ripples from a pebble dropped in a still pond, ripples in a Zen sand garden, emanating from the point of soft contact.

He had never kissed her before, but somehow he knew it would be the last time he would kiss this woman. Because Sarah had refused to divorce him, tried to commit suicide, and the hospital was threatening collection for nonpayment; and she was *his* responsibility, this dismal, angry, splintered woman who had demanded more of his life than she deserved, an anchor around his neck.

Oh, but the woman beside him was alive, vibrant and vivacious, and she, inexplicably, looked at him with undisguised fascination. He dreamed of coming back to her, taking her hand, and leading her into a new life for both of them.

But even as the warmth of her breath lingered on his lips, he knew that he never would, that he would leave for the airport the following day to take care of his awful business that would drag out for months, and there would never be enough job or money for him to get back on a plane.

Yoko's tongue against his was hot and confident. What a kiss!

And he had carried this charm, this porcelain rooster that she bought for him as a good luck charm that day in the temple gift shop, in his pocket until the day he gave up his dream to go back to Japan.

The joy and sadness swelled in his heart like bursts of scarlet and ultramarine that coiled in his guts like yin-yang snakes, and he cried for what he had lost.

Tears streaming down his face, he jumped to his feet and threw the rooster down onto the pile of junk.

What a coward! What a loser! Why the hell hadn't he gone back? What was he *thinking*? God, she'd been so beautiful!

He shook his head and wiped his cheeks.

But then thoughts surfaced through the flow of memories like stones in a river.

What had just happened?

The world swam around him, and he tried to blink away a disorienting wooziness.

Was this from Grandpa's life? With the Japanese connection, it had to be, but…

Who was Sarah? Grandma's name was Rebecca.

He sank back into the couch and rubbed his eyes. It had felt so good and so painful at the same time. Real love, or at least the promise of it, lost.

Is that what it felt like? That brief fluttering moment like two butterflies coming together, that this first tenuous touch could go wrong at any moment?

It could be that way with Amber. It must be.

Setting the box down beside the stuff, he scooped it all carefully back inside. For a moment, he heard a cacophony of voices, as if someone had just cracked open the door of a crowded social hall. Then it was gone.

As he set the box upright again, a tingle crept through his limbs. The hair on his arms stood erect.

Was he having some sort of hallucinogenic flashback from the weed? Imelda was right to stay away from that stuff.

He stood and kicked the box away from him.

Creep factor: maximum.

Maybe if he went to work early, he would have time before his shift to smooth Jeff's feathers.

As he opened the front door, the box called for one last glance from where it sat in the middle of the living room floor as if waiting patiently.

CHAPTER ELEVEN
CAR WASH SONG

Otter rolled up to the office door of Mr. Chrome Car Wash. Above him on the roof stood a ten-foot-high chrome statue of a man giving a smiling salute. Half a block away, he could smell the soap, wax, and car exhaust.

He took a deep breath and girded himself. This was *not* going to be pretty.

Plastering on a big smile, he shoved open the door and surged inside. "Hey, Jeff!"

The man behind the counter stirred only his gaze, turning skeptically askance, scratching his salt-and-pepper beard. "Mike. You got a lot of nerve being so smiley when you're about to get your ass chewed." He was leaning back in his creaky office chair, sneakers on the desk, smartphone resting on his paunch.

"I'm here, ain't I? And early! Just so I could talk to you."

"So spill it. You really screwed us over yesterday."

"Like I told you, I had to take the bus all the way downtown for the reading of my grandpa's will."

Jeff sat up and chewed on this. "So your grandpa died, huh?"

"Last week."

"Did you go to the funeral?"

"Nope."

"But he left you something."

"Yep."

"So you didn't go to his funeral, but you wanted to see what he left you." Jeff raised a disdainful eyebrow.

Otter stiffened at Jeff's tone, and his voice rose. "I didn't even know he died! I hadn't seen him in years! I got a lot of crap on my plate."

"That I do not doubt. So what am I supposed to do with you? You left us in the lurch yesterday."

Otter grinned. "More hours?"

"I was thinking less hours."

Otter's grin faltered. "Come on, Jeff! I know you need the help. How about Thursday?"

Jeff continued as if Otter hadn't spoken, "Besides, I'm not legally allowed to give you any more hours because of your age. And by the way, school's not out yet, so what are you doing here?"

"Uh, early release day."

Jeff gave him a hard, gray stare. He had a wart at the very tip of his nose, slightly off-center. He seemed to come to a decision and handed over an envelope. "Here's your paycheck. I'm going to give you a little advice: get your poop in a group."

"I'm working on that, Jeff."

"Work on it harder. I know you got a lot of problems, your mom being sick and all. That's the only reason you're not fired." Otter had never told Jeff of his mom's death; he didn't want anyone to know he was an orphan. "But you got to go to school, get an education, and get a job. Be a productive member of society."

"I have a job."

Jeff waved his hand. "I mean down the road. Get you a sensible career. Be a business man, something. You got to do something real."

Otter almost retorted that music was real, but he clamped his mouth shut and restrained his eyeroll. Jeff was a boulder rolling downhill.

"I can see you're not listening, but I'm going to tell you anyway. Maybe something will sink in. If you're not doing something real, you're a drain on society. You're a waste-oid. You want to be living under a bridge somewhere? If not, you work. Period. You don't work, you don't deserve a damn thing. Understand me?"

Otter nodded vigorously. Anything to get out of there.

Jeff waved his hand again. "You're hopeless. Go suit up and clock in."

Otter hurried to the back room where freshly washed, gray coveralls embroidered with his name hung from a peg. Before he clocked in, though, he opened the envelope to see how much his paycheck was. His heart stopped and fell like a chunk of brick into his shoes. The amount should be way more. He *needed* way more. He double-checked the math, double-checked his memory, and then sagged onto the dirty bench. The amount would cover one of his overdue bills, but not both. And it left nothing for groceries. But he had to buy groceries. He couldn't go another week without food, and he couldn't mooch off Imelda every day.

After work, he'd deposit the check. Then he'd buy a sack of groceries, and the rest would go to the electric bill. Maybe they would be happy with a partial payment.

He would also need to look for a second job, maybe one that didn't care whether he was in school.

On the bike ride to the grocery store, Otter's mind whirled with two chords of thought that harmonized beautifully. The experience of touching that little porcelain rooster, the emotions that had flooded him, the feelings that thrummed through his blood—for a woman he had never met.

As weird as that was, he couldn't help transposing those sensations to a girl that he *did* know. Would it feel the same when he kissed Amber for the first time? He yearned for her to look into his eyes the way that other woman had looked into eyes that were *not* his. He imagined Amber's lips parting...

Then he realized he was only halfway across a crosswalk with a truck grille the size of a barn bearing down on him. The truck's airhorn blasted him six inches sideways, and he jumped on the pedals, pumping to get out of the way. His front wheel hit the curb and flipped him over the handle bars. He bounced sideways on the sidewalk, and his bicycle smashed onto him with a clatter.

The truck blasted the horn until it was half a block away and kept going.

He groaned and took a deep, slow breath. "Ow."

At the corner of this strip mall—a supermarket and its usual attendant liquor store, hair salon, and Chinese restaurant—there was no foot traffic. As he lay there bleeding, his nerves only beginning to wake up to the pain of road rash and bruises, there was no one to ask if he was okay. There was only the endless flow of cars, oblivious to a kid lying on the sidewalk with a bicycle on top of him.

Painfully, he extricated himself. Gingerly, he rubbed gravel from the bloody gouges on one palm. Delicately, he checked the hole torn through the calf of his jeans by the main sprocket of his bicycle. There was a grease-smeared slash across his flesh, seeping blood, but at least nothing felt broken.

Easing himself up, he righted his bicycle and inspected it for damage. Everything looked all right until he got on and kicked into a roll.

The front wheel wobbled inside the fork. Hitting the curb had bent the rim, and the deformed ring now rubbed on the brakes. For several seconds, he stood and spewed out his frustration and pain with a string of not-so-creative expletives.

But then he took another deep breath and looked at the wheel again to see how badly it was bent. The deformation was visible but perhaps salvageable. He disconnected the front brakes and let them spring to the sides, open, away from the wheel rim. Then he lifted the front of the bike and spun the wheel. It wobbled but spun freely. He might still be able to ride it, but he wouldn't have a front brake. He would just have to be more careful.

Careful enough not to be hit by a freaking truck.

After a few more moments, he saddled up with a sigh and pedaled to the supermarket, in which resided the bank branch he needed to deposit his paycheck. The wobbly wheel felt funny, but he could steer. The rear brake could still stop him, but not as quickly as both.

But the road rash was starting to sear his hand, elbow, and knee like a branding iron. He stepped into the supermarket restroom to wash the gravel out, hissing with the pain.

After depositing his paycheck via the supermarket ATM, he set about his shopping. The bandages and antiseptic cut deep into his food budget, so he had even less for the electric bill. He rubbed his eyes, his forehead, his cheeks, with his uninjured left hand. At least his fingers were fine. He'd still be able to play guitar.

But he had to be smart about food purchases. The next payday was a week away. For two hours he wandered the aisles looking for the cheapest possible foodstuffs. Ten packages of ramen noodles, cans of generic soup, peanut butter, several cans of pork and beans, on-sale hot dogs, expired bread, creme-filled chocolate snack cakes.

As he counted every single penny in his head, resentment simmered at the fifty thousand dollars he needed desperately *right now*. Willing him that kind of money but not letting him touch it was nothing short of cruel. No wonder Mom cut her father loose.

He walked out of the supermarket with two bulging shopping bags and hoped he could steer his wounded bicycle with the heavy bags hanging from both handlebars.

The hobble home took over an hour, so dusk was fading to dark when he wobbled to the entrance of the trailer court.

That was when a car pulled up, cut in front of him, and skidded to a halt. His hands seized the brakes, but the front ones did nothing. With only the back brake, he couldn't stop in time, nor could he swerve with the heavy weights dangling from the handlebars. He glanced off the driver-side door and toppled into the grassy ditch. One of his shopping bags exploded, scattering half his groceries. The other hit the ground with his bike and sprayed soup cans in all directions.

Through the window of her Department of Human Services car, the lady from yesterday glared at him.

He jumped up and roared, "What the hell is wrong with you?"

The look on her faced melted from determined "Gotcha!" to mortified remorse. Flinging open the car door, she bleated, "Oh my god, are you all right?"

Rage blinded him to any pain he might have felt. "What the hell kind of move was that? You think you're a cop? Look at my groceries, you stupid bitch!"

She bristled. "You're in trouble, young man."

"No, *you're* in trouble. You just tried to run over me! My mom is going to call your boss tomorrow. You'll be on the street by dark!" He swore some more. "Could this day get any worse?"

"I'm so sorry about cutting you off like that. That was a terrible mistake. But I've been trying to reach you for a couple of weeks. You're not returning my calls. But don't lie to me about your mother. We know she passed away back in July."

"What of it?" he mumbled.

"I've been assigned to oversee your case."

"My case?"

"You're an emancipated minor. You have to show the court that you're managing to live on your own."

"I'm doing just fine."

"We'll see about that. I just want to help you." She gave him a plastic smile, cracked at the edges. "No child left behind! Rain or shine or dead of night, no matter what! That's my motto. No child falls through the cracks on my watch."

"Were you in the Marines or something?"

"Semper fi. How did you know?"

"'No man left behind,' isn't that a Marines thing?"

"It is indeed."

"What does rain or shine or dead of night have to do with anything?"

"Nothing, it's just something I like to say. Makes things clear, right up front." The way she talked reminded him of an axe chopping.

"So you just tried to run me over and scattered my food over twenty feet of ditch so you could, what, save me?" He knelt and started scooping up cans and packages.

"Yeah, sorry about that." But she didn't sound sorry. "Look, you're either going to talk to me or you're going to talk to the sheriff."

He'd been letting his anger simmer to see if he might see what she was about, but he could hold back no longer. He jumped up and yelled at her, "Like you'll listen to damn thing I have to say!" His roar drove her back a step. "My mom embarrassed herself in court so that I could be free from people like you after she was gone. You gonna stick me in an orphanage now like Little Orphan Annie? Put me in foster care with some abusive witch housing six other kids for the government handouts?"

Approaching thunder cut off her retort. Zeke rolled up on his chugging, rumbling Harley-Davidson. The green lightning bolts painted on the gas tank blazed in the street light. He was dressed in a leather vest Otter hadn't seen before. On the back was stitched the same emblem of Odin as on the flag. Otter concealed a smirk. Zeke looked *really* mean.

"Everything okay, bro?" Zeke said.

"Well, this lady hit me with her car," Otter said.

Zeke's mirrored shades turned toward the woman. "Is that so?"

Her face went pale as curdled milk. "It was an accident, really."

"What business you got with my man Otter here?" Zeke asked.

She opened her mouth to speak, but Zeke revved his thunderous engine and drowned whatever sound she tried to make. Finally she was able to respond. "I'm with the Department of Human—"

"I can read," Zeke said.

"I'm trying to give him the help he needs, Mister…"

"Mister is enough," Zeke said. "So you're trying to help him by hitting him with your car."

Her hand fumbled limply with her door latch. "As I said, that was not my intention. I'm here doing my job, trying to give Michael the help he—"

"You need any help, little bro? He don't look like he needs any help."

"I think you messed up my front wheel," Otter said.

Her eyes flared with conflicting outrage and embarrassment. "I didn't hit you that—" But she cut herself off.

"We'll call it even if you just leave me alone," Otter said.

She faced him, her voice imploring. "I just want to help you."

"I just told you how."

"I don't think the law is going to allow that, Michael. But I think we need to talk about that another time." She jumped back into her car and shut the door as if Zeke's pit bulls were charging. Then she put the car in gear, pulled away, and did a three-point turnaround as Zeke and Otter watched. She paused and rolled down the passenger window. "Sorry about your groceries!" Then with a last, wary look at Zeke, she hit the gas and was gone.

"Thanks, man. You saved my life right there," Otter said.

"No problem, little bro. Say, you should come to one of our meetings. I think you might fit right in. Plus it'll do you good to hang out with some real men. What do you say?"

"When is the next meeting?" A little thrill went through him at Zeke's belief in Otter's manliness. This was a meeting for *grown-ups*.

"Next week."

"Maybe. I'll think about it." Best not to sound too eager. Plus, he couldn't let it interfere with rehearsal.

"Outstanding. You need any help there?"

"I got it, thanks."

Zeke rolled away.

CHAPTER TWELVE
I CAN'T MAKE YOU LOVE ME

Ramen noodles and a peanut butter sandwich had never tasted so good. His heart still simmered with the awfulness of his day. Fortunately, the pawn shop was open late. He might still get down there before it closed and unload that stupid box. *Now* he needed money to fix his bike, too.

As Otter washed his bowl and utensils, the phone rang. He jumped, splattering himself with dish suds.

It rang again.

What if it was Amber?

What if it was Toby with good news about the gig at Black Line?

He picked up the phone. "Hello."

A woman's voice, unfamiliar. "Hello, is this Michael?"

"Aunt Misty." He tried to keep his voice neutral for the sake of politeness, but wasn't sure he had succeeded. What could she want with him?

Her voice stiffened, as if surprised by having to speak. "Yes. How are you?"

"Getting by."

"That's good."

The brittleness and uncertainty in her voice put him on edge. Why was she calling him? He said, "How are the girls?"

"Well, they're worried about you. We all are."

"Hey, don't you worry about me. I'm just fine."

"I don't doubt that, Michael. You are no doubt very resourceful. But after seeing you yesterday, I've been thinking about something." She paused and he waited for her continue, a silence that lasted an awkwardly long time. Finally she said, "Look, Michael. You're family. And I know you haven't seen us much since…well, it's been a really rough year for everybody, and you're out there in the boonies all alone and—"

"I have a house."

"I know that, and I'm sure you're surviving okay on your own, but you're still just a kid. We'd love to have you come and stay with us. We have the room, and…"

His brain fogged over as she spoke. They lived in a ritzy new development in Centennial Heights, so far from here it was practically in another state. That was where the doctors and lawyers lived. You needed a Jaguar or an Audi to get through the front gate. He would be back in school—*their* school. Visions of nice clothes—turtlenecks and blazers perhaps—organic food and gluten-free kale chips, kids who played Mozart instead of Johnny Cash.

"What about my band?" he asked, interrupting her litany of benefits. He could almost hear the derailment. "Uh, what band?"

"I'm in a band. We have a gig coming up."

"Be sensible, Michael. You're too young to 'have a gig.'"

She faltered at that last bit, as if reconsidering even as the words came out, but it escaped anyway and grated across him like a steel rasp. Jeff had used that word, "sensible." Had Johnny Cash's mom told him to "be sensible," or his teachers, or his relatives?

He didn't know much, but how was he going to have Amber as his girlfriend if she lived an hour away? He'd never see her again, and that thought cut him deep.

"It's really nice of you to offer, Aunt Misty," he said. "It really is. But I'm doing okay right here."

Was that a sigh of relief? "Are you sure?"

"'Course I'm sure. I got everything I need. I even got a box of Grandpa's stuff to keep me company."

"Like I said, you're family, Michael. We're worried about you." She sounded earnest, but he didn't believe her.

"No need. I'm all good. Gotta go, Aunt Misty. Rehearsal's in half an hour."

"Well, okay then."

"Bye," he said, and hung up.

Why the hell did everyone want to take him away from the only things that belonged to him?

It only took Aunt Misty two whole months to feel sorry for him.

Mom died on July 4th. Even as she faded away, she saw the irony of it. "I'm free," she had said, barely a whisper. And now, more than two months later, Misty felt sorry for poor little Mikey and wanted to take in the helpless orphan.

He'd be damned if he'd stand at anybody's door with his hat in his hand. Aunt Misty could take her belated pity and shove it.

He looked at the cardboard box full of junk across the room. "So can Grandpa."

The OPEN sign flashed behind the bars of Big Jimmy's Pawn Shop window. It was getting late, but Big Jimmy's was open late. The check-cashing place next door was closed, but the Chinese massage place was still open. His front wheel still wobbled, of course, which made riding a whole lot less fun, but at least he'd made it.

Otter unhooked the bungee cords securing the cardboard box to his luggage rack. The bungee cords' tension had squeezed the cardboard into something of a deformed wad, but that had helped hold the box in place.

When Otter walked in, Big Jimmy grunted with recognition. He was watching some action movie on a twelve-inch TV screen. He thumbed a remote control and stopped the movie.

They called him Big Jimmy for a reason. He was the size and disposition of a hippopotamus, five hundred pounds if he was an ounce. The act of getting out of his chair made him wheeze with effort.

The air in the shop smelled of gun oil and disinfectant. The shelves and cabinets were crammed with electronic equipment, videos, weapons, jewelry, musical instruments, a dizzying profusion of bits discarded from people's lives, things given up for things needed more.

Otter put his box on the glass counter.

Big Jimmy's voice was thick, as if it had to fight its way past the triple chin, and he looked at the box with an air of disdain. "This ain't your personal garage sale, kid."

Otter ignored the jab. "I got some stuff here from my grandpa. It's all antiques. Some cool stuff from overseas. Left it to me in his will. But I got no use for it."

Big Jimmy sighed himself forward a step and glanced in the box. "What a bunch of crap."

"How about fifty bucks?"

Big Jimmy laughed, then stopped. "Oh, you're serious."

"Come on, man, there's tons of great stuff. Antiques!"

"So have a garage sale." Big Jimmy pulled out the hand-sized wooden figurine of a man wearing *lederhosen,* then tossed it back.

"I've brought you some good stuff before!"

"And when you do again, I might be inclined to give you money for it."

"Twenty?"

"I'm not going to give you five."

"So, ten then."

"Beat it, kid."

"But—"

"Fine. Three bucks. Take it or leave it."

Three bucks would barely buy him a loaf of bread. He bristled. "Never mind."

Outside the pawn shop, Otter sat on the curb and hugged his knees. He should chuck the box into the dumpster over there so he didn't have to cart it home again. Big Jimmy could shove his three bucks up his nose.

Before long, however, his thoughts went back to Amber. She had touched his butt.

He knew nothing. He knew less than nothing. He dug through the box and found the porcelain rooster.

It lay there in his palm, and he half-expected another rush of powerful emotions, a flood of juicy experiences, but as he stroked it with his thumb, all that came were the memories of how all that had felt, the first flush of new romance, a mutual crush coming together. The memories were his now, to draw upon whenever he wanted.

He tucked the rooster into his jeans pocket for good luck, then peered into the box.

Could such an experience happen again? Was it a fluke? A one-time paranormal phenomenon?

He pulled out the little wooden man in *lederhosen.* It was slightly smaller than his hand, the painted eyes mostly flaked away, the color of the chipped paint on the body fading.

Where had the old man gotten such a hideous thing? And why keep it?

Amber crept back into his mind, the physical sensations of that aching, that yearning, the way her deep, brown gaze hovered behind his eyelids when he closed them. The way her blonde hair shone, her smile sparkled, and her laugh lit him up inside and burned away the ashes of loneliness and shame, assuaged the pain in his ribs. For Christmas, before he had returned to the States for Christmas leave and she headed back to Edinburgh for the holidays, two fish out of water, strangers in a strange land. All those days she had checked his bandages, smiled at him, and told him how lucky he was, what a hero he was. He'd given her a beautifully illustrated book of poetry, and she had given him a guy in *lederhosen,* a token of Germany. The heartfelt hug in the entryway of Marina's small apartment in West Berlin, the hope that when he returned to his post after holiday leave, they might do more than hug. And her deep, brown eyes had sparkled at that. All he had to do back home was end it with Sarah once and for all, end the fear, swallow the shame of divorce, and finally be able to act upon this ill-timed infatuation.

His was a romantic gift. Hers was a gift of friendship.

And then Sarah tried to die in a pill bottle. When he finally could return to West Berlin, all he got from Marina was shame. She had not appreciated the fact he was still legally married.

When her contract ended, she returned to Scotland. And he never saw or heard from her again.

A sniffle and wetness in his eyes brought Otter back to the present.

He dropped the figurine. Amber was a brunette with a blazing scarlet forelock. Her eyes were blue.

Otter had never been to Germany.

He picked up that *lederhosen* man again and felt the woman's hug; and the loss, the longing, the heartbreak crashed over him like a breaker foaming with regret.

Where was the Japanese woman? After. The *lederhosen* man still believed Sarah would agree to a divorce. The *lederhosen* man still believed that divorce wouldn't destroy his military career, wouldn't cripple his security clearance and relegate him to a useless desk job. A bitter taste appeared on his tongue, a tightness in his neck, a deep, pervasive frustration too long held at bay.

This beautiful, kind woman with the melodious accent, this Marina, sparkling with a life that Sarah had never known she could reach for. This attraction, this aching maybe, this chance that he might feel some happiness, that he might deserve a little happiness. Ripped away.

"Are you all right, young man?"

The voice had come from an old black woman pushing a shopping cart filled with all her worldly possessions.

He wiped the snot from his upper lip, the tears from his cheeks, tried to give her a smile. "Yeah, fine."

"You lose somebody?"

He swallowed hard and nodded.

She sat beside him on the curb, then pulled a slightly bruised apple from her pocket and held it out to him. He looked at it for several seconds. How could he accept food from a homeless woman? "No, thank you," he said finally.

They sat in silence for a while. He sensed her expectation that he might unzip his heart to her, but he kept it tight, and she didn't pressure him.

Instead, his mind kept returning to what had just happened. The images had been crystal clear, vivid. In the vision, he had *smelled* Marina, and her scent of spices and vanilla lingered as if she were sitting right beside him still. And yes, she was gorgeous, even with that weird, bouffant hairdo. And she was real, and he had *felt* something for her, this person he had never met, in a time that he had never lived, with an ache similar to what he felt for Amber, as if he himself had made a terrible mistake that was nevertheless the only thing he could have done at the time.

What was happening to him?

Was he going crazy? How on earth could he get all that from a cheap knickknack in a box of an old codger's junk? How could his mind create such a realistic picture of a place he'd never been, looking out through the eyes of someone taller than him, when the furniture looked strange, old-style but new, and clothes were weirdly out of fashion? It was like he'd stepped into a movie.

And how on earth could he get all that from simply picking up a ridiculous, little figurine?

He noticed the homeless woman had departed. She was half a block away now, trundling her cart ahead of her down the dark sidewalk.

Otter had never been to Germany.

But Grandpa had.

It was some time in murky prehistory, in that nonexistent time before Michael MacIntyre was born, but Grandpa had been to Germany while he was in the Army, lived there near a No Man's Land with Soviet guns pointed at him. The danger of it, the rumble of distant tanks, the pervasive uncertainty that those tanks could throttle up at any moment and blast through the Wall, the growl of the tanks seemed to pulsate out of the little *lederhosen* man. The growling of the tanks and yearning to make things right with Marina, somehow. Sometimes, you screwed up with someone you cared about and never got the chance to make amends.

Otter dropped the figure back into the box.

Three times now he'd picked up something from the box, and three times something weird had happened. Some kind of displaced memories, phantom experiences. Had he known any of this about Grandpa before picking up the *lederhosen* man? His head swam with uncertainty about where his own memories began.

What else might be lurking in his box? An urge to pull out another piece came, but no. He didn't want to end up crying on the street again like some stupid, helpless loser. But then he remembered that Orange Crush bottle cap. He fished it out and stuck it in his pocket for later. Then he wiped his face again and strapped the box back onto his luggage rack.

CHAPTER THIRTEEN
HE WALKED ON WATER

Otter had a few hours before work at the car wash, so he wobbled over to the library to use a computer for some research.

He quickly found his grandfather's profile on the university web site. The old guy sounded so impressive there, with a distinguished looking photo and biography paragraph. PhD in History, founder of the Asian history program, author of ten books on the history of Japan.

The next thing he found was an obituary in the local newspaper. Loving father, grandfather, and husband. Survived by one daughter and four grandchildren. Preceded in death by wife, Rebecca, son, Michael, and daughter, Margaret. Nana Rebecca had died when Otter was really young. He barely remembered her, but that was after Uncle Mike died. Otter didn't remember him at all. He was killed in Iraq by a bomb, Mom had always told Otter.

It was strange seeing all this information through eyes that were not his mother's. All the information he had was filtered through her. That was natural. She was his only source. But had she told him everything? Especially when she was so tight-lipped about what happened between her and Misty, her and her own father.

The next thing that popped up were his various books. The titles sounded impressive. *The Warrior Ethos in Medieval Japan, Sword and Arquebus: Weapons that Shaped a Warrior Dynasty.*

Did the library have his grandfather's books? They did indeed, three of them. He found one on the shelf in the Asian History section and sat down to look at it. On the back flap was a black-and-white photo of a distinguished-looking professor, a thoughtful, contemplative man. The man Otter remembered from his childhood.

Reviews of the dustjacket flap had high praise. "…Donovan MacIntyre is the definitive Western voice on the history of the East…" The author bio had other information. "Veteran, Purple Heart recipient, and martial artist Donovan MacIntyre is a professor of Asian History at the University of…"

Martial artist?

A Purple Heart? What was that? Something from the military. A quick web search on the library computer told him what he needed to know. "Grandpa was wounded in combat?" he said. His voice, louder than he intended, drew the attention of those around him. His ears heated and he hunched his shoulders.

Wasn't Grandpa in Germany during his Army days? There wasn't any fighting in Germany then. It was so difficult, patching together the things he'd heard but didn't understand as a much younger boy, with the facts presented here. Where were the lines demarking what he knew?

These questions led him down a research rabbit hole about the 1960s—Grandpa was in Germany in 1965, during the Cold War—and about the war in Vietnam.

After two hours of searching and reading, he had answered a few questions, gathered a picture of the Donovan MacIntyre that the world knew. But this picture was not the man Otter knew, and that gap opened up a whole book full of new questions.

He slipped his hand in his pocket and pulled out the bottle cap, turned it over and over in his fingers. It was warm from being in his pocket. Bare metal showed through on the ridges.

He caught the scent of fresh popcorn. He was so hungry, it made his mouth water, his heart beat faster. The taste of Orange Crush filled his mouth, and the sense that he had to be on the lookout for someone who was not Louisa Pritt. He looked around but he was still in the library. But the room darkened, and the movie screen lit up and Eddie O'Neill was sitting next to him, eyes wide with anticipation.

"Do you see the usher?" Eddie asked with mischievous caution.

No sign of the usher.

Between him and Eddie, they had only enough money for a bottle of Orange Crush, no popcorn or candy, much less admission. So they had to make it last, trading little sips.

It had taken them almost half an hour of waiting for the chance to slip past the usher when his back was turned. The usher was a fat man who stank of gin at two in the afternoon.

All Donnie knew was that he'd been too young to see *The Thing from Another World* when it was originally released, but when he and Eddie discovered the Roxy Theater showed old science fiction movies on Saturday afternoons, they had spent every Saturday afternoon of their eleventh summer haunting its alley and entrance to sneak in. Sometimes they had money for admission but it was more fun to sneak in.

By the time the scientific expedition to the Antarctic encountered a blood-drinking alien life-form, his imagination was enthralled. He couldn't take his eyes off the screen. When the Thing's severed arm twitched and moved and came back to life, he practically leaped out of his seat.

Eddie yelped in surprise. "Jesus Christ!"

Donnie slouched in his seat. A chill dashed through him like a bucket of ice water. For the rest of the movie, he was enraptured at the delicious fear and excitement of watching the expedition try to fend off and destroy the creature.

When Donnie and Eddie came out of the movie, they both said, "That was the greatest thing I've ever seen!"

"Way better than *The Blob!*"

"*Them!* was pretty good, though."

"What about *Creature from the Black Lagoon?*"

"Oh, man, it wasn't near as scary as this one!"

Then they had gone to Blue Spruce Park and sat on the swings and lost themselves in thoughts of aliens and comic books and whether Hank Aaron was better than Mickey Mantle and how Eddie had accidentally seen his teenage sister naked in the shower.

"It was the weirdest thing I ever saw," Eddie said, eyes wide with trauma.

"Weirder than *The Thing?*"

"Way weirder!"

Donnie had wanted to know all about it, because he couldn't imagine what girls looked like naked, but Eddie said, "No, you dope! She's my sister!" Eddie shuddered.

The truth was, Donnie kinda had a crush on Eddie's sister. She had a nice smile, cute freckles, and wasn't all hoity-toity like most high school girls Donnie knew of.

And the afternoon passed into a river of other half-formed images, the foggy boats of dreams floating on a river of Orange Crush.

Otter found himself smiling, licking his lips, thinking about summer afternoons, baseball games, matinees, and popcorn.

All of which made his little research project feel indescribably dull. Old movies and summer shenanigans were way more fun than boring old history.

With his car wash shift approaching, it was time for Otter to get wobbling.

For hours in the hot sun that afternoon, Otter scrubbed fenders, waxed hoods, and buffed chrome rims that cost more than he made in six months. Sweat soaked through the back of his coveralls and turned his underwear into a wet baby diaper.

For all the ways that Jeff was a raging tool, he had good taste in tunes. The music he streamed over the sound system ranged from early fifties rock to the music Mom had weaned Otter on. Creedence and Clapton, B.B. King and the Byrds, Neil Young and Nirvana, the Rolling Stones and Ritchie Valens. There was so much of it that he didn't have to hear the same song more than one or twice a week.

While his hands wiped, his mind whirled. He felt like his emotions had been run over by an earth packer, those things like steamrollers with spikes. His grandfather's history was a whole universe of mystery. And then there were the thoughts of women. As if Amber wasn't enough, now he had *three* women on his mind, two of whom he had never met. Except that he had. They were as real and alive to him as Lika. He felt real sadness at never seeing them again, as real as if he had lost Lika.

Lika had always been there for him. She had stood with him at Bellwood Elementary, punched him when he teased her too much, ran with him in the woods behind the ballpark when they sneaked up to watch the Mudskippers lose—again—from fifteen feet up a tree. Lika had been there when Mom's diagnosis came, for the day the loss of Mom's health insurance consigned her to death. Her parents had showered them with comfort food as Mom withered to a gray, desiccated husk. And they had asked him to live with them.

His stomach rumbled at the memory of Loretta's cooking.

He had to stop and lean his forehead against the Cadillac SUV's window.

Inside, Carlos was vacuuming the seats, singing to himself in Spanish. He looked up at Otter. "You okay, man?"

Otter cleared his throat. "Peachy."

Was the entire world an endless parade of cruelty and pain, or just this town? Until Mom had gotten sick, that thought had never occurred to him. He missed thirteen-year-old-happy-Mike.

The next thing Otter knew, he heard the wheels of a skateboard zooming closer, two hands seized his shoulders, and a "Boo!" jolted him into low-earth orbit, bouncing off the side of the SUV as he spun.

Amber laughed and kicked her skateboard vertical. "I thought that was you when I was rolling by." Her eyes sparkled, and the brash curve of her hip kicked his heart like a bass drum foot pedal.

His ears burned. Here he stood in a freaking coverall, dripping with sweat, soap, and mud. "Hey." He couldn't help smiling.

"You're working, I see."

"This is just my cover," he said. "More of a hobby really."

"Your hobby is washing cars?"

"The world is full of road grime. And I must slay it, one car at a time."

She laughed. "You're so funny. So are you doing anything tonight?"

The R&B thump of his heart exploded into thrash metal. "Tonight?"

"Yeah, tonight."

"Um, well, let's see. There's my nuclear fusion experiments, and then there's remodeling my underground lair, then firefighter practice, and then I have to transpose Beethoven's Fifth into bass guitar... After that, I'm free." He wasn't quite sure where this explosion of nonsense came from, or even how it managed to come out because his entire being was silently screaming, *oh my god is she asking* me *out?*

She laughed again. "When does firefighter practice end?"

"About half an hour before whatever you're going to say."

Ask her if it's going to be just the two of you! His mouth could not form the necessary interrogatives.

"Nothing big. Just doing some moves in Blue Spruce Park." She wiggled her skateboard. "Want to hang?"

"I think I can fit it in. But I don't skateboard."

Ask her!

"Don't or won't?"

"I might be willing to learn."

Ask her!

"Good." She winked. "About six."

"Uh, I gotta work till seven."

"Then come at seven." She dropped the board flat and stepped up. "Bye!" One good kick and she rolled away.

Otter could not peel his eyes away from her. They would have followed her all the way to the horizon, but then she rounded the corner of the car wash out of sight.

In fit of half-serious melodrama, he collapsed onto his back on the wet-graveled concrete, clutching his chest with one hand. Sheer, jubilant elation exploded in him, swirling together with cold, black dread like a barber pole. Incoherent noises bubbled out. If something good didn't happen tonight, he might not be able to stand it. When Mom died, finally, after so long, the deluge of grief and relief had nearly drowned him. How much more heartbreak could he endure?

Clouds floated past, high in the azure sky. Otter lay there vibrating like an E-string. Carlos's head poked through the SUV window. "You okay, man?"

Otter tried to gather enough spit to talk. "Swell."

"Wow, she's gorgeous! Is she single?"

CHAPTER FOURTEEN
BACK TO BLACK

In her bedroom, Lika leaned back in her chair. Her science textbook was open on the desk to some of the most disgusting parasites the world had to offer. She could hear her mother downstairs humming a tune to herself in the kitchen.

When the unknown number came across Lika's phone, she almost ignored it, but something tingled in the back of her neck, telling her to answer.

"Hello?"

"Hey, Lika, it's me." Otter's voice came through with about five flavors of worry coursing through it.

"Hey!" She smiled. "Where are you calling me from?"

"Work. I'm on break. I got to tell you about something that just happened."

"You decided to come back to school?"

"No."

"Uh, you ate a bug?"

"Not today, no."

"Something happened with Amber."

"Yeah, she came to my work and asked me to come to the park with her. She wants to show me how to skateboard."

Her enthusiasm for talking about Amber was suddenly in the neighborhood of talking about twenty-foot tapeworms. "Well, that sounds fun." She had to be happy for him, even though she could smell the smoke of an imminent dumpster fire.

"You don't sound very excited for me," he said.

"Neither do you."

"Yeah, I suppose not."

"Why not?"

"Because this could go wrong. Really wrong…"

"Right. She might reject you."

"It sounds so awful when you put it that way."

"I suppose it must suck. It's never happened to me before."

"Of course not, you're a girl."

His comment put her back up a little. "What's that supposed to mean?"

"Girls don't get rejected."

"The hell we don't! We have crushes just like you do!"

"You've never had one, have you?"

"Sure, lots of times, but they were all little ones."

"How many guys have asked you out?"

"I don't know." A few, in junior high.

"How many have you turned down?"

"I don't know!" It wasn't any of his business.

"Hey now, no need to get all prickly."

"All right, fine. No prickly."

"You don't sound not prickly."

"I'm a hedgehog, buddy." She sighed. "So spill it."

He reiterated the story about meeting Amber in the record store, how he thought she might like him but he didn't know, and it soon became clear that every single thing Amber did from that moment until now— every innocuous movement, syllable, or giggle, even though it might have no significance at all—was so overinflated with omen and momentousness in Otter's mind that it would all inevitably explode in his face. His fear showed that he felt it, too, even if he couldn't grasp why.

Boys were so stupid.

Her gaze panned the room, over her posters of Angela Davis, Angela Bassett, and Maya Angelou. As these wise women, these namesakes, gazed down upon her, she asked for strength and wisdom.

Her friend was going to need someone to pick up the pieces.

She said, "So how about I meet you there?"

Relief flooded his voice. "Really?"

"If it all goes bust, we'll go play pinball or something."

"And if it all goes well, you'll…"

A flash of an emotion she turned her gaze away from. "I'll disappear."

"Blue Spruce Park! Seven o'clock!" He sounded like he'd just acquired a shopping bag full of fireworks.

After they hung up, she went downstairs. Her mother was baking ham and sweet potatoes. Drool worthy! Momma was a goddess in the kitchen, capable of making a five-course meal in fifteen minutes, *after* she got home from school, from pocket lint and cat litter.

Her mother smiled at her. "Homework done?"

"Yeah. Where's Dad?"

"He's on night shifts for the next week."

Lika swallowed a lump of worry. Night shifts were when the meth-heads, armed robbers, and angry drunks came out, the most dangerous time for a patrolman. Her mother's face was tight, too. But it was time to broach the subject. "So is it okay if I go over to Blue Spruce Park for a while?"

"Who's gonna be there?"

"Mikey."

Her mother raised an eyebrow.

"Momma! We're not dating."

"Methinks the lady doth protest too much."

"Whatever, Momma. We haven't hung out hardly since his mom died."

"That boy got himself some troubles. He keeping on the straight and narrow?"

"Yeah." She didn't like lying to her mom, but it felt like a violation of Mike's privacy to tell the truth.

"I see it at school all the time, baby. Kids get on the skids, make some bad decisions." She left out that the black community was riddled with such stories. Lika knew a few. "Mikey's a good boy. Be a shame, he ended up in juvie."

Or worse. Lika said, "He needs a friend."

"Okay. Be home by nine."

"Nine!" Lika rolled her eyes.

"A minute later, Angelika, and—"

Lika kissed her on the cheek and hurried upstairs to change clothes.

CHAPTER FIFTEEN
SOMETIME AROUND MIDNIGHT

At the last stoplight before he reached Blue Spruce Park, Otter released the handlebars to flex the feeling back into his fingers. Traffic rumbled past him, belching fumes. Across the street lay the park's green lawns, playgrounds, and concrete half-pipes. Skaters rolled, ollied, and flipped—and occasionally dumped themselves into piles of road rash and bruises.

The porcelain rooster—his new good luck charm for love—was a hard knot against his thigh in the pocket of his fraying jeans. That sense of love he had felt when he first touched it vibrated through him, a delicious murmur. If it had the power somehow to convey stored memories, maybe it had other benefits. Maybe Amber would now find him utterly irresistible.

The traffic light changed, and he pedaled across the street, front wheel wobbling. With only one brake, he still had to be careful with stopping distance.

He spotted a skater girl with a scarlet forelock immediately, and his heart tripped over the curb. The atmosphere itself seemed to be pressing down onto him, squeezing him in a grip he couldn't escape. Nevertheless, he drew in a deep breath. "Be cool. Be cool. Be cool," he murmured as he rolled ever so casually in her direction.

She was not as good on a skateboard as she was on a microphone and keyboard, but the fact that she could roll back and forth in a half-pipe without killing herself made her a thing of wonder. She was wearing a short jean jacket, a short, denim skirt, and black leggings peppered with crimson polka dots. A handful of other skaters watched her with appreciation.

Otter found himself smiling at the idea that this stunningly beautiful person, this goddess, this girl he desired above all things, liked him enough to ask him to come to the park. But then the nervousness thundered right back. He stopped and rubbed the porcelain rooster through the denim of his jeans. For several minutes he watched her rolling, rolling back and forth, the way she worked her center of gravity, swaying, much like the way she swayed when she sang. Another lump formed in his throat.

Then someone punched his arm. Lika grinned at him from astride her bicycle. "Once more unto the breach, dear friend?" she said.

"What?" Otter said.

"It's a line from Shakespeare. The teacher has been saying at the beginning of class every day for two weeks."

Otter rolled his eyes.

"You have no idea how dark and badass Shakespeare was. We're reading *Macbeth*. 'Out, out! Damned spot!'" She raised her fist.

"Whatever. It's nice to see you outside of rehearsal."

"Come back to school and you'll see me every day."

"I don't like you that much."

She punched him, way too hard.

He yelped and rubbed his arm.

The noise caught Amber's attention, and the board zipped out from under her, dumping her face-first onto the concrete. Taking a moment to collect herself and her board, she smiled crookedly at Otter. The sight of Lika brought a surprised widening of the smile. Then a moment of calculation as her gaze went back and forth between them. She approached with more smile. "Hey, you guys!" She paused and cocked a hip. "So are you dating now?"

"*No!*" they both said.

"Then which of you is the sidekick?"

They pointed at each other and spoke simultaneously.

"He is."

"She is."

Amber laughed, then wiggled her skateboard. "So who's intrepid enough to try it?"

"I'll go." Otter did a triple somersault dismount from his bike, but only in his mind.

"You ever been on a skateboard before?" Amber asked.

"Nope."

"Surfed?"

"Do you see an ocean?"

She laughed and laid the board down and gestured for him to step up. Step up he did.

He spent the next several minutes trying to break his record for most contusions and bruises per minute. Several times, she was right there beside him, helping him up—how he loved the touch of her hand—offering tips and encouragement, showing him how to move, how to balance, and most importantly, how to stop. He touched her arm. She touched him back, and her fingers set him aflame.

From a distance, Lika was a patient presence.

Then suddenly he was swarmed by skaters. Actually it was only one skater, but the skater passed so close he could feel the wind, startling him off-balance. He landed hard on his back. Stabbing pain burst up his backbone and struck sparks against the base of his skull.

He lay there moaning, vaguely aware that the newcomer had stopped beside Amber. His entire body throbbed. This fall had reawakened his injuries from his fight with the curb.

Amber rushed up to Otter, failing to suppress the kind of laugh elicited by people destroying themselves in failed internet video stunts. "Oh, I'm so sorry! That looked like it really hurt."

"Yeah," he gasped, trying to catch his breath through the pain. "Yeah, it kinda did."

"Sorry, bro," the newcomer said, a guy outsizing Otter with an extra two inches and thirty pounds. He offered a hand to help Otter up.

Otter took it and was yanked to his feet by a powerful grip and bulging biceps. "Thanks." He bent forward at the waist, hands on his knees, hoping to stretch the pain away.

Lika was there. "You okay?"

"Getting there," Otter said.

Amber gave the big skater a hug, a real one, a close one, and Otter's heart fell into the cauldron of his stomach.

"Lika, Otter," Amber said, "this is Colton."

Colton nodded at them. "Hey."

Amber practically beamed at Colton. "They're in my band."

"Nice!" Colton said. "What do you play?"

"Drums," Lika said.

"Fog horn," Otter said.

They all laughed at that, and he hoped they couldn't see through the brittle mask his face had become.

Amber said, "I think we should sit down for a while. There's a picnic table over there."

Sitting down for a while sounded like a mighty fine idea.

Amber led the way, and the four of them gathered at the picnic table. Who was this guy?

As Otter eased his bruised backside onto the bench, two other guys walked up, both of them looking like football jocks. Amber greeted them brightly, calling them by name. Where the hell were all these extra guys coming from?

Lika gave him a knowing glance.

A gob of cold lead congealed in his belly.

These new guys didn't appear to possess the slightest inclination to converse with Otter. Mostly they looked annoyed that he was there at all. However, their eyes played generously over Lika, who seemed oblivious to it. The longer they looked at her, the greater Otter's distaste for them grew. They looked at Amber the same way, like she was a succulent steak they were waiting for their turn to taste.

Otter's stomach flipped into full ready-to-puke mode.

He was in the middle of Amber's entourage.

Lika's eye stayed on Otter, concern brimming from her gaze. Amber took Colton's hand and held it.

Otter's legs became stone. His lungs became stone. His heart turned to cold mercury.

Amber and the three guys chattered on as if the world was not, in fact, crashing down in a tumult of chaos and agony.

One of them produced a bottle of liquor. Sloe gin, the bottle said.

"Oh, I love that stuff!" Amber said. "Where'd you get that?"

"Found it," the guy said, handing it to her.

She spun the cap off and took a drink. Then she handed it to Colton, who also took a drink and passed it on.

Looking increasingly uncomfortable, Lika quickly shook her head and passed it to Otter.

Otter felt the weight of it in his hand and wished it were the strongest rotgut whiskey in the world, the kind that Zeke drank, something that might burn away the pain in his belly. He took a long pull.

Time passed, an unknown succession of eternities. Darkness thickened. Distant streetlights spread random, unapproachable pools of luminescence.

Crickets began to sing in the trees. The jock-oids tried talking to Lika, to minimal response. It felt strangely like the day his mother had died.

Across the table, Amber and the bros laughed and teased. The sloe gin slammed into Otter's brain, and the way the light gleamed in Amber's eyes, it had hit her, too. She laughed louder, all sassy and breathtakingly beautiful, eyes defiant, perhaps angry at something beyond the horizon. Every time she looked into Otter's eyes stopped him dead.

One of the bros produced a Bluetooth speaker and set it on the picnic table. It launched into some hip-hop beats about bitches and hoes. Is that how they saw Amber and Lika, just bitches and hoes?

From the other side of the circle, Amber called out to Otter. "Hey, you're sure quiet tonight." Seated across the table, her fingers lay entwined with Colton's on his thigh.

Trying to muster air, Otter squeezed his clasped fingers to his chin and nodded.

Amber returned her attention to Colton, leaning in with a beaming smile.

Then the shrill twang of Robert Plant leaped forth from the speaker. *Hey, hey, mama, said the way you move…*

Amber's eyes lit like stars, she jumped up onto the picnic table, gathering the attention of every eye as she began to thrash and sway with Led Zeppelin's "Black Dog." She danced and strutted, standing over Otter, hands on hips, in her short, twirling skirt and black polka dot leggings. Her lips took on a hard smirk as she writhed before him.

It was the sexiest thing he had ever seen. He could barely breathe.

And then, when the song was over, the bros gave her a whistling round of applause and she jumped down into the arms of some guy whose name was already forgotten and left Otter there with his bleeding heart in his cupped hands and the assurance that she would *never* jump down into his arms that way. Colton's expression was the certainty that he would soon "tap that."

Otter was going to throw up.

"You okay?" Lika whispered.

"Not even a little," he croaked.

"You want to go?"

"I can't."

"Why?"

"I don't think I can move."

How could Amber not see his agony? How could she not see that it was because of her? She had to know. She *had* to. How could she not *see?*

Lika's eyes flicked between him and Amber, soft and hard, soft and hard. Right now, her presence was the only thing holding him together. So much pain. All this pain. Like drinking months' worth of his mom's death spiral all at once. One big gulp of sludge and broken glass, raking his throat raw, sluicing down into the writhing ropes of his guts, and as soon as he choked it all down, there would be nothing left of him.

Lika squeezed his arm. "Come on. Let's go."

He swallowed hard and nodded.

"Sir Otter here has to escort me home," Lika announced. "My dad's orders. And I gotta go."

Amber gave a face of disappointment. "Aw, sorry you guys have to go."

"Dad's orders," Lika said.

"See you at rehearsal," Amber said. "Otter, I hope you're not hurt too bad."

He shook himself free momentarily of the avalanche of shattered dreams. "Whuh what?"

"From the fall."

"Oh, yeah. Nothing an overdose of morphine won't fix."

Amber laughed. "You're so funny! If you want to try again sometime, let me know."

He couldn't muster any more words. All he wanted was a bus to throw himself under, a woodchipper to swan dive into.

Lika had him by the arm, pulling him away, into the darkness.

PART III

HIGHWAY TO HELL

CHAPTER SIXTEEN
LEAN ON ME

Lika pushed her bike, her eyes on Otter. In the street ahead, traffic had thinned with the darkness.

She clamped her jaw so tightly it ached, and her hands clenched her handlebars. Her face felt flushed and hot. "That was unbelievably crappy, Mike." With every step, her anger grew until she wanted to go back and slug Amber right in the face. Her dad had made her practice some serious hand-to-hand techniques. She knew how to take somebody down. That whole display had been either incredibly cruel or incredibly clueless. Either way, Lika wanted to put Amber flat on her back.

Otter shuffled beside her as if his feet weighed a thousand pounds.

When they finally reached the edge of the park, she said, "You want to ride? I have to get home."

His voice was a croak. "My legs are too wobbly to ride, I think."

Oh, this was bad.

They paused at a crosswalk for the light to change. Two men on Harley-Davidsons waited on the red. They wore black leather vests, and one had bright green lightning bolts painted across the gas tank. That one had a long, blond ponytail hanging from under a meager black helmet, a scruffy beard, and sunglasses after dark. He looked over at them and spotted Otter. He raised a hand briefly, but Otter was too anguished to notice. The light changed, and the men thundered away.

"Look," she said. "Now you know. You can forget her. You can move on."

"Don't know if I can." His voice sounded far away, as if receding down a tunnel. "Just need to walk for a while…"

"How about I take you home?" If she rode with him back to his house, she would be at least an hour late getting home, maybe an hour and a half. She wouldn't be allowed to go out again until she moved away to college. As much as she wanted to help him, she couldn't face that kind of music.

"You'll get in trouble."

"I could call Momma to come and get us, take you home."

"Nah, too much trouble."

She watched him for several sluggish steps. "Tell me what's in your head."

"Roaring black fuzz. Like an amp that was hooked up wrong."

"No, I mean, what are you going to do?" Ten flavors of suicide attempt flashed a horror show through her brain. When his mom was dying, those last horrible days, the look in his eyes had said he was ready to follow her down into the black.

"What am I going to do?" he said. "What am I going to do?" He stopped, let his bike fall over, and dragged something out of his pocket. A small porcelain object—a chicken with a jingle bell? This he placed on the ground. Then he stomped it as hard as he could. It cracked into two pieces. He stomped it again, and more shards splintered away. He stomped and stomped and stomped until he was gasping, sobbing, and nothing was left except glittering white grains.

Then he wiped his face and let out a shuddering breath. "What do I do, Lika?"

"You have to forget her." She knew the impossibility of this even as she said the words.

"I'll never forget this as long as I live."

She could see how deep this wound went. This night would leave a scar he would carry with him forever. Lika would certainly never forget it, and all she had done was helplessly watch it happen. The callousness of it still stunned her. The way those guys had looked at her had made her skin crawl. What could make a girl like Amber gravitate to guys like that? Despite it all, Lika didn't get the sense that Amber was screwing around with any of them. The hand-holding felt more like some sort of charade, but why she thought so, she couldn't pin down.

"Look," he said, "you had better go. Your mom is going to be pissed if you're late."

"You going to be all right?" The thought of leaving him like this made her heart hurt.

He laughed bitterly. "You worried I'm going to kill myself?"

"Yeah, actually I am."

"I'm not going to kill myself." The sound of his voice suggested otherwise.

"Do you promise?" She squared on him, searched his face. His eyes were blank, empty. "Promise me. Mike. Promise me."

"I promise."

"I'm going to call you at ten o'clock. And if you don't pick up the phone, I'm sending the cops to your house."

"Don't do that."

"Promise me."

"I already did!"

"I don't believe you."

His hollowed eyes were dark in the yellow streetlights. They met hers for only an instant. "I promise, okay?"

She studied him for a long moment. "Ten o'clock. If you don't pick up, I *will* come to your house and kill you."

"Ten o'clock."

She dropped her kickstand and circled the bike to hug him, hard. It was like embracing a wooden board, unyielding, covered in splinters. He hugged her back, just a little. She said into his ear. "It's just one shitty night, that's all. Tomorrow will be better. Just one shitty night."

When they stepped apart, he gave her a hollow half-smile and held out his palm.

"Put it on my bill," she said.

"Ten o'clock." He picked up his bike.

"Answer the phone."

"I'm not going to kill myself."

"Okay then." With one last long look, she got on her bike and pedaled away, her insides clenching as if she had just chosen to let him walk to the gallows.

CHAPTER SEVENTEEN
(I AM) SUPERMAN

Walking by a large, construction dumpster, Otter whirled and punched the steel side as hard as he could. Once, twice—the third time, something popped in his knuckles and pain blasted up his forearm. Tears blurred his vision. Were there any bits of him left that did not hurt?

How many hours had he spent imagining them together, from the moment he first saw her? It had felt perfect, fated, inevitable.

He just couldn't take it. It was a gunshot wound. A cold sword through his bowels. A vise squeezing his head, a fist squeezing his heart, as painful as his new contusions and the massive bruise forming on his back.

Near the end, his mom had wept with her yearning to die. The pain was too great, the weakness too crippling.

If Otter was gone from the world, Lika would be the only one who missed him. Aunt Misty and the M&Ms wouldn't miss him, not really. He had never met Misty's new husband. Sure, they were family, but they certainly felt no stronger connection to Otter than he did to them. Whatever had happened between Mom and them had seen to that. Lika's parents were nice, but he wasn't part of their family. He and Toby were buddies, but the difference in their neighborhoods was a gap that neither of them had chosen to cross.

One thing he had learned all the way to the bone was that the world would not miss him if he were gone. The world didn't give a fizzing frog fart if he was alive or dead. He had no one to count on but himself.

Would Amber miss him?

Would she know it was because of her?

Would she feel bad?

Should he leave a note for her?

He wanted her to feel his pain. He wanted her to know what she'd done. He wanted to see her. He just had to see her. He just had to see her.

But he knew that the moment he did, he would crack open and spill his insides at his feet.

Light washed over him from passing cars, gone again. Could the drivers see his pain?

She knew.

She had to know.

This had to have been on purpose.

Lika had told him before that girls *knew* things like this. So who had been paraded before whom? Was she trying to show off her new boyfriend to Otter? Was she showing Otter that she wasn't interested? Was she using Otter to stoke jealousy in Colton? Was she simply basking in the adulation of the guys who were there? Was she just a callous slut? Otter didn't like that word. Girls had as much right to enjoy making out as boys did. The idea of sex both fascinated and terrified him. He had fantasized about her, but the fantasies were always vague and amorphous, lacking the necessary information to make them vividly clear.

Was he being auditioned for Amber's next fling?

"No!" he roared. "Do *not* go there!"

His mind was a fog-bound hurricane, black and turbulent and sweeping through the same cycle of thoughts over and over again until he shuffled up to his front door.

Zeke wasn't home. From behind Imelda's open windows emanated the sounds of some Spanish-speaking TV drama.

Otter let his bike topple over as he unlocked the front door, and the suffocating black womb of his house yawned open.

He stood there for a moment, looking in. Mom was still there. Would he ever know happiness again?

He entered. Flipped on the kitchen light. Shut the door. Threw his key on the counter.

So many rote motions. It all felt so meaningless, these things.

Paper crackled under his sneaker. A note on the floor, stuffed under the door.

He picked it up and read the hand-written paper.

Next club meeting is Tuesday night. 8 o'clock. Come and be a warrior for the good guys!

Zeke

At the bottom of the note was an address.

His heart swelled at visions of a hulking Viking warrior, sword and shield in hand, blue eyes blazing with ferocity. Such a figure would never allow himself to be brought low by a woman's cruel games.

Maybe he could learn how to be that guy.

Women flocked to such men.

At least he thought so.

And there in the middle of the kitchen table, where he had left it, was that *stupid box*, looking more crumpled and stained than ever.

Memory of the way that porcelain rooster had cracked and shattered under his heel brought back the anger. What an idiot he was! To think that would be some sort of good luck charm. What a load of garbage.

And there sat another load of garbage.

He had let some weird, false memory trick him. He wished he had never gone to the park tonight. He wished he had never touched the rooster, or the little *lederhosen* figure for that matter.

With a snort, he picked up the box, intending to throw it outside.

His phone rang like an explosion. The clock on the microwave said ten o'clock sharp.

He had better answer or Lika's dad would be here in his patrol car within ten minutes.

He answered. "Hello, Lika."

"Hello, yourself," she said.

Silence hung between them.

Finally she said, "You promised."

"I promised."

"Call me in the morning?"

"Sure. Don't worry about me."

"Don't tell me what to do."

"Good night, Lika."

"'Night."

He hung up, his belly quavering again. He spotted the box, and fresh anger rose up. That box had to go. He went to pick it up.

The bottom fell out. Things scattered around his feet on the dusty, worn linoleum.

He swore.

There was some duct tape in the kitchen junk drawer, and a marker. He took those out, repaired the box. Rather than throw it out, maybe his cousin Mia might want it. She knew Grandpa. Otter didn't. He scribbled on the top flap: FOR MIA KOWALSKI. He could get her address some other time.

As he knelt to scoop the junk back into the box, the glint of gold caught his eye.

He picked it up and turned it over in his fingers.

It was a tie tack, on the front of which was the Superman symbol, the emblem the Man of Steel wore on his chest, the big red *S*. Along with all those other things, Grandpa was a comic book nerd?

But what little boy didn't love Superman? It didn't look antique enough to be from Grandpa's childhood. Otter's mind went back to all his flying practice when he was six. He had launched himself from chair to sofa to chair. "Up, up, and away!" Trying to get the right angle, the right speed, never quite achieving the proper trajectory for liftoff. And Mom had been only a few feet away in the kitchen, making dinner or washing dishes, and she never once yelled at him or told him to stop.

Trying the same thing—just once—at Aunt Misty's house had been a *bad idea*.

Superman never succumbed to pain, never gave up. He had a kind heart. He didn't just punch super-villains into submission. He did it all because he wanted to help, because humankind was worthy of help, because he believed in people.

A colleague had given that to him, the most extraordinary man he had ever known, a man who understood the depths of grief, who understood just how relentlessly, grindingly awful life could feel. He'd experienced a long series of life-threatening health problems as a child, first crippling food allergies and then leukemia as a teenager.

In the long months in the hospital, this young man—his name was James, now a brilliant creative writing professor—had kept a Superman novel under his pillow. Looking to while away the endless hours of convalescence, James had wandered into the hospital gift shop, spotted this book, and asked his mother to buy it for him. He took it back to his room and read it all in one day.

There came a point in the book where Clark's stepdad, Jonathan Kent, told the orphaned little alien boy, "I believe in you. You have a greater destiny than this. Do you hear me? I believe in you."

James told of how he had cried like a baby when he read that. When his doctors told his parents that he might not survive, James had thereafter assured them, in no uncertain terms, that he was not going to die, that he did, in fact, have a greater destiny than this.

"I believe in *you*, Donovan," James told him. "Fancy some breakfast?"

But Donovan wasn't hungry.

"I could use a spot of eggs Benedict," James said. "I know a good place near campus." On the walk there, James's hand had been warm on Donovan's shoulder. "You are an amazing individual, sir. I see a passion in you. To hell with those duffers on the hiring committee who can't see that this university needs a scholar of your potential."

Donovan desperately needed the job. This was the last in a string of failed interviews. Rebecca was pregnant. With a PhD in history, he was overqualified for anything except academia. He couldn't even get a job waiting tables or schlepping boxes in a warehouse because he was over-educated. He had written a book on Japanese history, for which he'd had to go deeply into debt traveling to Japan for research. The publisher had backed out of the deal because the editor who'd greenlighted the project had been forced into retirement for health reasons. Donovan had no money and no prospect of money. They were a month behind on their rent.

All this spilled out of him into James' lap over two plates of eggs Benedict. The desperation rose to the brim of his cup.

"Donovan," James said. "In that hospital bed, I didn't just swear that I would live. I swore that I would *Live*, with a capital *L*. Trust me when I tell you, you can live an extraordinary life if you make that decision."

"Really?" He wanted to be polite, but wasn't sure he had restrained his skepticism.

"Really. But you have to make that decision all the way to your bones. As soon as you *decide*, things will start to align around that decision."

That sounded a lot like superstition or useless magical thinking.

"If I'm wrong, you can tell me so next time we meet. In the meantime though, take this." He unpinned the Superman pin from his lapel and passed it across the table.

As the red *S* gleamed in the sunlight, the shell around his heart started to crack. A feeling of such gratitude washed through him that his voice faltered when he said *thank you.* Grown men didn't cry in public, especially not in the middle of the day, so he excused himself to the restroom, let himself heave two massive sobs, one of grief for his failures and one of hope for the future, and put the Superman pin on his lapel.

A week later, he received a call from Bainbridge University. A position had opened up unexpectedly, and he came strongly recommended, and would he be interested in applying for the position?

He wore the Superman pin on his lapel at that interview, and every day in the classroom after that.

And he never got the chance to thank James again in person, even though they corresponded often. James died after being stung by a ray while SCUBA diving in the Gulf of Mexico. Donovan and Rebecca took their young son Mikey, Otter's namesake, to the funeral in England, where hundreds of people came to pay their last respects.

Otter jerked awake in the light of dawn, sitting on the floor against the kitchen counter. His palms hurt. He unclasped hands and found the Superman pin, its corners and edges having engraved scarlet lines into his flesh.

I believe in you. It was his grandfather's voice now. *You have a greater destiny than this.*

"Stupid, cheesy crap," Otter said. But tears of release streamed down his face and his shoulders shook. The rage was gone. The desperate blackness remained, but there was something inside it now, fragile, like a candle flame in a windy cave. If it went out, he was done for.

For now, though, it was there.

CHAPTER EIGHTEEN
TRAVELIN' BAND

As Otter chewed on a piece of toast, he pinned the Superman emblem to his Mudskippers baseball cap.

He hadn't heard his grandfather's voice since he was eight—until last night.

I believe in you. You have a greater destiny than this.

He had awakened with those words ringing in his head. They had led from thoughts of a Zen garden, red-kerchiefed Buddhas, and a beautiful Japanese woman to playing baseball with buddies he never had.

It was so hard to believe it. It sounded so corny, like a line from a bad movie. Had he really heard it? Was it just some weird shard of imagination? Or the really scary thought: was he going crazy? And with delusions of grandeur no less? Would touching those things work for anyone else? Did everything in the box have a memory? Should he tell Lika about it? He didn't know.

But at least for today, Amber could go pound sand.

It was Sunday, and he had work. Without a cloud in the sky, the car wash would be swamped all day.

His body ached like he'd been beaten up. A homeless woman had offered him an apple. Had he fallen so far that a *homeless* woman offered him food? Is that what people saw when they looked at him?

While he packed his lunch—two peanut butter sandwiches and a cup of ramen noodles—into a bag, the phone rang. He picked it up, expecting to see Lika's number, but it wasn't. Apprehension juddered through him. What if it was that stupid lady who'd nearly run him over?

He answered the phone. "Hello, Otter's Fortress of Solitude."

"Otter! Buddy!" Toby's voice exploded out of the phone. "Guess what!" The excitement could mean only one thing. "You got the Black Line gig?"

"We got the Black Line gig!"

Otter whooped and jumped up and down. "When?"

"Two weeks from yesterday!"

A fat lady sat on Otter's heart. "What do you mean, 'two weeks'?"

"Friday night, two weeks from yesterday. It's a three band show. We're first on stage."

"We're not ready!"

"That's why we're rehearsing tonight."

"Tonight." The fat lady wiggled, settling down harder. "Holy crap, we need a band name!"

"Needed one of those to get the gig. 'Toby and the Undertones.' Catchy, right?"

Otter grimaced. It wasn't bad, but didn't feel quite right. And he hadn't even asked them. To be fair, Toby was the organizer and leader of the whole thing, but he should have brought it up. Now, however, was not the time to argue. "Uh, we also need a set list."

"That's why we're rehearsing tonight. And if I can swing it with my dad, we'll have two more rehearsals this week."

"What time?"

"Seven."

"I work until 6:30. I'll probably be late."

Otter could hear Toby's eyeroll. "Fine. But no later."

"I'll be there. One more question, though."

"What?"

Otter looked at his empty cupboards, empty refrigerator, the stack of overdue bills on the kitchen table. "How much are we getting for this? There's gotta be some serious payday, right?"

"Uh, right. I'm still working out those details with the manager. Listen, I gotta go. Two more phone calls of joy to make." Toby hung up, leaving Otter with that steaming pile of dread in his belly.

Rehearsal.

With Amber.

Who had touched his butt.

Who had set his heart on fire.

Who had made him feel special.

And then destroyed him.

How would he be able to look at her a few feet away, singing and swaying like a mythic siren, and not have all that pain come flooding back and drown him?

He would have to figure out a way. He had a greater destiny than this.

The car wash was like a rave gone bad. Two SUVs smooched fenders in the parking lot, snarling up the flow for over an hour as the police came and took accident reports. Chamois and vacuum jobs stacked up like dominoes. The annoyance level of people waiting in their cars ticked upward minute by minute. The sun beat down. Jeff even emerged from his office and chipped in with the labor to help speed people on their way.

As they worked, Otter, Carlos, and Javier sang along with the P.A. music, sometimes in harmony. Carlos's voice was a rich, vibrato tenor.

"You should be in a mariachi band," Otter told him.

"My dad is," Carlos said. "He wants me to. But I can't play guitar."

"Percussion or something?"

Carlos shrugged with a little grin. "Maybe."

At lunchtime, Otter traded Javier a peanut butter sandwich for a bean burrito. Javier was a gear head who spent much of the day talking about the tweaks he was making to a rusty-looking Honda Civic. He called it his Screaming Junkito.

Visions of Amber holding hands with Colton boiled out of Otter's psyche like bones and eyeballs from the bottom of a witch's cauldron, but he poked them back out of sight as best he could. He had cars to wash and a set list to consider.

The songs in the band's repertoire flicked through his mind, and he pondered not only the merits of each, but how they would fit together over the course of the set. On a piece of note paper from the office, he sketched out an order of music that would showcase each of the band members *and* build to a climax that would leave the audience clamoring for encores. He hoped.

But then, about midafternoon, he spotted a familiar car easing up the driveway, the beige sedan with Department of Human Services on the door.

He darted into the office, shut the door, and twisted the lock behind him. Behind the counter, Jeff hung up the phone, an alarmed expression emerging on his face.

"Jeff, you have to help me!"

"What are you, on the lam?"

"Kind of."

Jeff's brow furrowed, and one eyelid twitched. Otter had about half a second before Jeff called the cops himself.

It all came out in a rush. "Look, there's this lady wants to talk to me. I don't want to talk to her. She's stalking me. And now she's found out where I work. She's from the Department of Human Services, wants to take me and put in a foster home or St. Sebastian's Boys Home or something."

"Why would she do that? What did you do?" Both of Jeff's eyes narrowed.

"Before I get to that, I need to tell you something."

Jeff crossed his arms.

"My mom died in July. She had cancer for a long time. It got her."

Jeff's face softened but retained skepticism. "Your mom *died* and you didn't tell me?"

"I was afraid you'd fire me. I don't know why. Look, she's mean. She tried to run over me with her car the other day, just so she could catch me. I'm pretty good at ducking her, you see."

"So where are you living now?"

"In my house, the one my mom left me."

"You're too young to live alone."

"I'm emancipated. My mom taught me everything I needed to know before she died. And I need this job."

"So that's why you're so desperate for more hours. Are you going to school?"

Through the window, Otter saw the beige sedan cruise past in search of a parking spot.

"You have to tell her I'm getting plenty of hours to pay my bills. If she thinks I'm not able to support myself, it's straight into foster care. I won't be able to live in my own house. I won't be able to play in my band—and we got a gig! I won't be able to *work here* anymore. She'll take me away, right now, today. And we've got ten cars backed up to do before closing time. Please, Jeff."

Jeff chewed on this, scratching his beard.

Through the window, Otter glimpsed Louisa Pritt coming across the parking lot.

"Please, Jeff. I'll do whatever you want." Otter edged out of sight of the door, ducking behind the vending machine.

"Fine. I'll get rid of her. For today. But then we need to have a talk. Man to man."

"Absolutely. Whatever you say."

"Cut through the locker room."

Louisa Pritt's shadow fell across the window. She tried the door handle and found it locked, then shaded her eyes to peer inside. Otter caught a last glimpse of her as the door to the locker room swung closed.

"Sorry!" Jeff called. "Just a second."

Otter huddled in the corner away from the door and listened to Mrs. Pritt give roughly the same speech to Jeff as she'd given to Imelda. Jeff listened politely and told her that Mike did indeed work here, but he wasn't scheduled today. He embellished it with a threat that he knew Otter could hear. "If he's in any trouble, he won't be working here for long."

They exchanged pleasantries, and then the door opened and closed.

Otter peeked out.

Jeff said, "A government employee that works on a Sunday? That broad is tenacious."

"I told you!"

"Stay out of sight until she drives off."

But she didn't drive off. She returned to her car and sat there in the heat, waiting for him to show himself. Otter watched her through the window for an hour as she waited. Jeff meanwhile went to help Carlos and Javier outside. Otter stayed inside and answered the phone, keeping his eyes on the woman's silhouette in the car.

After an hour and half, Jeff approached her car and spoke to her. She nodded her assent to something. Then she pulled out of the parking place.

Jeff came in annoyed. "I gave her a free car wash 'for her trouble.' That seems to have hurried her along."

"Thanks, Jeff."

"I'll take her car wash out of your pay. As soon as she's gone, get back to work."

With the surveillance cameras, Otter watched her go through the wash, and when it was finished, she pulled out of the parking lot. But a funny feeling urged him to watch where she went. He peeked out the door after her, and saw her pull into a parking place along the street, facing the car wash.

But he couldn't work as long as she was there. He hissed to get Jeff's attention. "She's still there."

Jeff looked, then rolled his eyes. "Good lord, woman, give it a rest. Mike, just clock out and sneak out the back."

"Thanks! I owe you another one."

"And very soon I'm going to start cashing them in."

CHAPTER NINETEEN
LUNATIC FRINGE

Otter's wobbly front wheel was unmanageable in the gravel streets of the trailer court, so he got off and pushed. Rounding the corner, he spotted the police cruiser parked next to his house, and his hair stood on end.

He swore under his breath and muttered, "Leave me alone!" Then he darted into the woods, stashed his bike behind a plum thicket, and crept nearer.

The patrol car had parked between his house and Imelda's. Arms crossed, eyes red and glistening, Imelda was talking to two officers, a man and a woman. A torrent of Spanish roiled out of her. The female cop, a Latina, was scribbling on a notepad as Imelda talked. Imelda kept gesturing toward her trailer.

From his vantage point he could see nothing amiss, but something had to be going on.

Ten minutes he waited while the cops took her statement. Finally, they drove off, and he emerged from the bushes. Then he saw the side of Imelda's trailer, and his mouth fell open.

On the weathered, white-painted tin was a fresh scrawl of scarlet spray paint: GO BACK TO MEXICO! bitch! "Bitch" was in smaller lettering, as if added as an afterthought.

Outrage boiled up in him. Imelda was one of the nicest people he knew.

Broken glass from the shattered window littered the ground, the window on the front door. Imelda's voice echoed from inside, a half-sobbing, one-sided conversation in Spanish.

He hesitated to knock, but she spotted him through the glass-less opening, then hung up her phone abruptly.

She rushed out and flung her arms around him, sobbing. Uncertain how to respond, he patted her on the back gently. She smelled of cloves and smoke.

"Oh, *mijo!* I go to market, I come back, I see this. I am *chapina!* From Guatemala! Those idiots! They break my windows!"

"That's awful!" he said.

She pushed him out to arm's length. "You see something?"

"I've been at work all day. Just came home. I'm sorry!"

She said something, most likely foul language, in Spanish.

Who would do such a thing? The only people who came to the Starlite Trailer Court were people who meant to. Could the vandal have been one of their neighbors? He knew everybody who lived on this side of the trailer court, and none of them seemed so hateful. Zeke carried on about foreigners sometimes, but he wouldn't do anything like this.

Imelda's face, normally so full of kindness and a unique configuration of Latina spunk, now trembled with a mix of fear and anger.

The vandals also broke her kitchen window, through which years of tantalizing aromas had wafted. Now, the glass was shattered, and flaps of torn screen fluttered in the breeze.

"I've got some old boxes in the back room," Otter said. "We could use a couple of those to cover the holes until you get some new glass."

"Oh, *mijo*, thank you!"

He spent the next half an hour cutting cardboard and securing it with duct tape.

When he was finished, she nodded her approval. "Ugly, but no bugs come in. *Muchas gracias, mijo.*"

"*De nada,*" he said. "And now I have to get to rehearsal."

He hurried inside to get his guitar.

Just inside the door, he glimpsed a guitar pick on the floor, near the area where the box had spilled. He must have missed it. It was a black, rounded triangle. He picked it up and turned it over in his palm.

Seeing the name printed in silver on the black surface, he breathed, "No way."

The silver printing was a tiny signature: Johnny Cash.

"No way!"

All those times listening to Johnny Cash with Mom came whirling out of his memory. Across the room, beside Mom's stereo, was a rack of CDs, many of them by Johnny Cash. There was vinyl, too, but the turntable had stopped working years ago. On Mom's old acoustic, he had taught himself to play guitar with "Folsom Prison Blues," mastering first the chords, then the strumming, then the opening riff, then the twelve-bar blues progression. As Mom sank into the void of painkillers and slow starvation, he often caught her listening to Cash's later work, songs like "Hurt" and "The Man Comes Around" on her headphones.

This pick made him want to grab a six-string and play the opening riff from "Folsom Prison Blues" again.

In his hand was the stuff of legends. Johnny Cash had been a man of complications, great faults, great mistakes, divorce, drugs, brushes with the law, a wildness, a life lived to the hilt, with all the regrets that came with hurting the people he loved. But most importantly, a dark, troubled soul and a capacity for love he poured into his music. Most of all, Donovan appreciated the integrity of a man who lived his art. Johnny Cash was not a poseur, or a wannabe, or a pretender. He was simply who he was, all the way down to the bone. And he had done it all by *deciding* to do it. He *decided* to become the greatest man he could be. The road had been rocky, full of potholes, even a crevasse or two, but nothing had diverted him from his path.

From the third row, he could see all that in Johnny's face up there on stage. An old man now he certainly was, but that soul still gleamed in his eyes, and that wisdom acquired from pain and triumph echoed from his voice. Donovan spent most of the concert in tears, oscillating between rapture and heartbreak, with his teenage daughter next to him.

The life gleamed within her like a sunrise, the promise. So smart, so beautiful. At fourteen, she was already leaving a trail of broken hearts behind her, and within her was a solid, unbreakable core. Even at fourteen, she knew exactly who she was, and no one would ever shake that knowledge.

Otter stumbled back as if he'd been punched.

As Johnny's music flowed over her, her face glowed, her gaze rapt, unwavering.

Between songs, Donovan put his arm around his daughter and hugged her close, tickled her ribs, and she punched him in the side. She would be a small woman, wiry like her mother, but no less fierce. The admiration and gratitude in her eyes when she looked up at him was no less fierce. He squeezed her close and kissed her forehead.

At the end of the concert, as the bows and waves were subsiding, Johnny met the teenage girl's eyes and flicked the pick to her. She caught it one-handed like a miracle.

Never one for such displays, she squealed with delight and threw herself against her father.

As they walked back to the car after the show, she took his hand and pressed the pick into his palm and gave him a look that brooked no arguments.

Mom's face, but younger than Otter was now, full of life and hope and possibility, free of the anger and resignation and despair that had made wreckage of the end of her life. But the same glitter of mischief in her eyes, the same grin, the same teeth—but gleaming white, unstained by cigarettes and coffee.

He clutched the pick in both hands. Once again, as happened so many times, missing her rolled over him like a semi.

But rather than hiding from the grief, hiding from the memories of the broken gray shell his mother had become, he had a new memory of her, fresh perceptions, knowledge that she had once been brilliant and vivacious. And she had loved her father fiercely, just as she had loved her son fiercely.

So why, then, had their falling out been so serious? What could crack such a bond?

Before embarking too deeply on that road of questions, he glanced at the clock. He had to book it, or he'd be late for rehearsal. He stuffed the pick into his pocket, imagining the ghost of the Man in Black hovering somewhere nearby, nodding his approval.

CHAPTER TWENTY
JAGGED, LITTLE PILL

"The only reason you're not dead is Toby told me he talked to you." Lika stood before Otter, arms crossed, lips pursed, eyes narrowed.

"I'm not *that* late!" Otter said.

Her eyes flared like the embers of hell.

An anvil settled onto his chest. "Oh, god, I was supposed to call you."

"You were supposed to call me."

He looked around Toby's garage for a place to hide. Perhaps he could lock himself in that old freezer. "Well, um, I'm here now." He gave her a sheepish grin. "I'm okay."

Toby watched their exchange curiously as he plugged in his amp and prepared to tune up. "Are you guys dating or something?"

"No!" they said simultaneously.

"Look," Otter said, "I'm sorry I forgot to call you. Weird stuff is happening."

"What kind of weird stuff?" she asked.

"I'll tell you about it later."

Amber had not yet arrived, and Otter dreaded the moment she did. What would she say? What would *he* say? A vision of his entire leg going straight into his mouth made him shake his head.

Lika looked at him for a long time, then went back to setting up her cymbals.

When he finished tuning up, Otter showed Toby and Lika the piece of paper with his sketched-out set list. "Everybody gets to show off," he said. "For example, Queen has great bass riffs for me, and Amber can sing like Freddie Mercury. 'Back in Black' for you and Lika—"

"'Under Pressure?'" Toby said. "You want to sound like Vanilla Ice? In public?"

"No," Otter said. "I want to sound like Queen and David Bowie, go back to the source."

"I mean, I love the song and everything—" Toby said.

"We'll throw in a big drum solo for Lika," Otter said. He glanced her, feeling the lingering tension.

She nodded silently, arms crossed.

Toby scratched his chin. "We can try it. It's a great song."

They were discussing Lika's favorites, Amy Winehouse and Aretha, when a car pulled up outside, a rattling, rusty clunker with a hubcap missing on this side, and Amber jumped out. She waved goodbye to her mother and came up the drive.

Otter's heart stopped. Would he ever be able to watch her move and not lose his mind?

Fingers tucked in pockets, she avoided his gaze and said to everyone, "Hi."

"We're just kicking around the set list," Toby said.

Otter's mouth was too dry to speak.

Lika's eyes machine-gunned red-hot daggers at Amber.

Amber looked strangely subdued, her spark dimmed somehow. She leaned in, close enough for Otter to smell the strawberries of her shampoo. "Looks good to me. Who put this together?"

He stepped back, away. "I did." His voice was a croak.

She glanced at him, flashed a little smile, then looked away again. "Good job mixing it up."

"Thanks." The fat lady sat on Otter's heart again.

"Plus me and Lika can do a great harmony on—"

"I ain't harmonizing shit," Lika said.

Amber blinked and stepped back. "What's wrong with you?" Something in Amber's eyes told Otter she already suspected. Was there a flicker of remorse there? Or was he wishing for it so hard he was imagining it?

"Like you don't know." Lika's tone evoked icebergs and angry polar bears.

Toby stepped in. "Okay, what am I missing here?"

Amber crossed her arms and backed up. "Somebody's got a problem."

Toby looked flustered. "Look, ladies. I'm obviously missing something, but we got a gig and less than two weeks to rehearse for it. Can we be professional for a little while?"

Lika said, "All right."

Amber said, "Sure."

The tension between them, however, crackled.

Otter felt bad that it was about him, although there was a warm, fuzzy feeling associated with Lika's protectiveness. At the same time, he wanted just to drop it, forget about it for a while.

Toby said, "Great. We'll use Otter's set list as is for now and play through it, see how it feels."

Meanwhile, Otter struggled to hold his composure. He turned away and pretended to tune. His picking fingers were still stiff and swollen from punching a dumpster, and the palm of his left hand was a patch of scabbed road rash from the bicycle wreck.

Toby started playing riffs, adjusting the amplifier settings.

Moments later, a warm hand squeezed his shoulder. Amber's hand. He jumped away like it was a snake. Her voice was quiet, only for him. "You were kind of a sad sack last night."

His mouth worked but nothing came out. No matter how hard he willed it not to happen, emotion must have flooded his face.

"Is everything okay?" she said.

"Everything's cool."

"Really?" She gazed into his face.

He couldn't meet her eyes. "Really. Absolutely."

She gazed longer.

Finally, his mouth managed something like the truth. "That's not right. Want to hang out for a minute after we're done?"

She drew back and swallowed. "Sure. Until my mom gets here, anyway. She's coming at nine."

He dragged his gaze to her face, forcing himself to hold it there. He had never seen a more beautiful girl in his life, and the power she had over him, power he had given her, made him hate himself a little.

Toby slashed the opening riff to "You Shook Me All Night Long," signaling it was time to commence rehearsal.

Otter couldn't remember a worse rehearsal. He kept losing the rhythm, forgetting chord progressions. His fingers were dumb, chubby bratwursts, painful. The twenty-pound butterfly in his stomach wouldn't lie still. Lika's rhythms felt like the wrong time signature. She kept missing transitions. The magic fled Toby's guitar, his fingers stumbling like a drunkard over the fret board, tripping over strings, and sending sour notes and dull buzzes flying. Amber missed verses, repeated lyrics, sang the wrong notes.

Finally Toby unslung his guitar in disgust. "What a train wreck! Who are you people, and what have you done with my band?"

"*Your* band!" Lika said. "I thought it was *our* band! And you're one to talk, Mr. I-Can't-Remember-the-Chords-for-'Respect.' There ain't that many."

Toby's ears turned scarlet.

Amber said, "We're just having an off night. It happens."

"Yeah, well, it can't!" Toby said. "Black Line! Twelve days! We can't go out there like this! We'll be humiliated! I went online and blabbed it to everybody I know!"

"How about we take a break and relax for a bit?" Amber said. "We've got time for a couple of run-throughs. Five minutes?"

"Fine," Toby said. "You guys work out whatever the hell it is." Then he stomped into the house.

The remaining trio stood looking awkwardly at each other. Lika's eyes flashed fire and ice.

Amber blew out a sigh. "So what is it? Lika, you're ready to stab my eyes out with your drumsticks, and Otter, you look like I just shot your dog. What is up with you two?"

Lika turned her gaze upon Otter, and gestured exaggeratedly toward Amber. Otter couldn't speak.

Lika's frustration with him simmered visibly. "Spill it!"

Amber crossed her arms again and cocked her hip, eyes flashing. "You got something to say, say it!"

"FineI'minlovewithyouokay!"

He couldn't help it. It just exploded out of him. At least he hadn't said *love.* Oh, wait. He had.

The force of it drove her back a step. Her eyes bulged, mouth agape, and it was like he could see his words slowly sink in, as if her face were a sponge. Bewilderment flickered with burgeoning realization.

As the moment hung between them, like Wile E. Coyote's anvil paused to hurtle earthward, Otter imagined dozens of things she might say, and as time stretched past, the bad ones overwhelmed the scraps of hope.

"You can't," she said.

He blinked. "Wh-what?"

"You can't."

"You don't get to pick who likes you!" Lika snapped, then her voice grew quieter. "You don't get to pick who you fall for."

Otter raised a hand to hold her back. This was his struggle. "See," he fought to scrape a few words into an intelligible pile, "I'm not lying. I think you're—"

"Stop right there!" Amber snapped. "You don't even know me."

"I know enough to—"

"To what? Follow me around like a puppy?"

Something inside him punctured and bled. He pursed his lips for a moment. "I'm sure you and Colton will be very happy together."

Her eyes flared. "*You* do not get to comment on who I hang out with. My relationships are none of your business."

"Just wishing you happiness is all," he said, with all the earnestness he could muster, which wasn't much at the moment.

"You don't know anything." Then she turned to Lika. "And what are you still doing here?"

"You had to have known," Lika said angrily. "It's not like he didn't wear it on his sleeve. The boy don't know how to lie! So why invite him on a date you made with somebody else? That's just cruel."

"I texted Colton to come because *he* brought *you*!" She pointed at Otter. "I didn't want to be a third wheel."

"Oh, you've *got* to be kidding me," Lika said.

Otter took off his Mudskippers cap. "I wrote you a song."

"You…you what?" Amber asked.

The Superman pin on the cap glinted in the garage's feeble incandescent bulbs. He pulled the folded piece of paper from inside the cap. It was sweat-stained, soiled at the edges, but it was the song he wrote for her. It was stupid, and lame, but there was no point in hiding it. In having nothing left to lose, no dark secrets to maintain, he was free to act. He handed it to her. "I don't need it anymore."

She hesitated, but then eased forward and took it.

"I'm going to go now." Unplugging his guitar, he turned away and grabbed his guitar case.

Paper shuffled behind him, and he hurried to stuff everything away so he could be gone before she looked at it.

Toby came out of the house, munching an apple, took one look at the three of them, and said, "What the hell, did somebody just drop a grenade?"

Otter said, "Sorry, Toby. I have to go." He shouldered past Amber with his guitar case.

"What about the gig?" Toby asked, mouth full of apple.

"I'll call you." Otter got on his bike and pedaled away as fast as he could.

CHAPTER TWENTY-ONE
WHO WANTS TO LIVE FOREVER

Monday was Otter's day off. He spent the morning practicing all the songs on the set list, playing them over and over along with Mom's CDs.

His fingers felt less sausage-like, and after some warm-up, the bass undercurrents began to flow from his crackly, old tube amp.

This all served to distract him from the thought that kept coming around like a scratch across a vinyl record: what did Amber think of the song he wrote for her? Did she like it? Did she tear it up? Did it move her to love him back? Was she going to call him at any moment?

So he played harder. Concentrated harder.

Until a song came up on one of his mom's mixes that stopped his fingers dead.

Another Queen song, "Who Wants to Live Forever." How she must have loved their music. She always told him this song was from a great movie but he was still too young to watch it. The first strains brought his breath up short, and when the chorus rolled over him, he was five months younger and he arrived home one afternoon to hear this song playing at concert volume through the windows of the trailer, and his mom's voice, inside, singing at the top of her lungs, like she was belting it out at Carnegie Hall; and boy, could she sing.

He just stood there in the doorway and listened to her, amazed. He'd always known she could sing, but he'd never heard her sing like this before. She sang a song about love and dying and living forever and loved ones dying and leaving loved ones behind. She sang as if her life depended on it.

And when it was over, she played it again and sang along.

She was halfway through the second go-round when she noticed him there. Her eyes were horribly bloodshot, and her cheeks glistened with tears. She flung herself across the living room, scooped him up, and hugged him with a desperation that surprised him, with her emaciated arms. She sang, "There's no time for us…" She took off his cap and kissed his forehead, his cheeks, crooning, "the world has only one sweet moment, set aside for us…" Her breath smelled like chemicals and rancid meat, and her skin was thin and gray.

But she sang and she sang, and she hugged him and sang as if her whole life had culminated in that moment. When the song was over, she turned off the stereo and went into her bedroom to sleep.

Two months later, she was dead, and Otter was alone.

But now, his vision blurred by tears, he pulled the guitar pick from his pocket, held it in his palm, stroked it with his thumb, feeling the tiny ridges of the silver autograph, and remembered the youthful face of the girl named Maggie. Endless weeks of gray misery, spasms of torture, faded behind this girl's gleaming smile and sparkling eyes. She was so *alive*. For months now, the cadaverous shell had dominated his memories of her, until now. Her tortured eyes, her awful breath.

His heart warmed at her youthful smile, and the smile unlocked another box of his own memories. Her hands guiding his fingers on fretboard and strings. The times she had played Hot Wheels with him, put Band-Aids on his boyhood boo-boos, yelled at him for leaving his backpack in the front door, cooked him hot dogs and mac 'n cheese, snuggled him to sleep when he cried about not having a dad, chewed out his third grade teacher for turning a blind eye to Danny Aker's bullying at recess, sat out on Imelda's deck drinking Mexican beer and smoking until little Otter passed out on Imelda's couch, danced with him in the living room to music that was old when she was born, came home haggard late at night from bartending, always making sure to kiss him even when he pretended to be asleep. They never had much money, but she made sure they didn't have debt either. She hated owing anybody anything.

And only through the early years of all of that were memories of Aunt Misty, his cousins, and his grandfather.

He remembered his grandfather being very tall, a lanky man, and very old, at least fifty, but with eyes that seemed to look too deep, to look *through*. It always made Otter uncomfortable to look into those eyes for too long. But he had a deep, rich voice and tremendous patience for his four squealing grandchildren. They tore through his ancient house, pretending it was Hogwarts School of Witchcraft and Wizardry, with wands made of twigs from the sprawling back orchard. The M&Ms protested mightily, but only Otter, the boy, could play Harry Potter. Therefore, the girls became Hermione Granger, Wonder Woman, and Princess Leia. Mia always played Princess Leia.

Otter picked up the phone and called Mia's number. She was at school, of course, so his call went to voicemail.

"You have reached Mia's mindless, marvelous menagerie of amusements. Mesmerize me."

"Uh, Mia. It's Mike. We have a gig. It's at the Black Line, Friday night next week. It would be cool if you could come."

Telling someone about it made it feel more real, like something that was coming whether he was ready or not. Something he didn't dare screw up. But it felt important that somebody know about it. It might be cool if Mia actually sneaked out and came to the show.

The long trip down the memory freeway led his gaze to the box on the kitchen table.

What else lurked in there? Maybe there were more memories with Mom.

He opened it up and scanned the contents. God help him, it still looked like so much useless junk, but the guitar pick in his pocket told a different story.

Like a grab bag, he reached in and pulled out the first thing he touched.

A tattered brown paper bag, flat, slightly larger than his hand. From it he pulled a folding street map of New York City. When he unfolded it, Manhattan opened up like a flower. The most famous city in America, open to him, waiting for him to discover it. Famous names marched in a grid of lines—Central Park, Wall Street, Broadway, the Empire State Building. But on this map were the World Trade Center Twin Towers, now only a memory.

He was walking down the expansive steps of the Metropolitan Museum of Art toward Fifth Avenue. Being away from Rebecca and his young son left an ache in his heart, but at that moment he was practically giddy, heart aflutter. This sojourn into the museum had been his celebration for sealing the deal on his first book, *The Wolves of Kyushu: Samurai Lords of the West*. The advance would help make a down payment on a modest house. A studio apartment was no longer sufficient with another baby on the way. Little Michael was fully mobile now, a holy terror, and kept Rebecca's hands full.

Thank god he'd never had kids with Sarah. What an endless debacle of drama and dysfunction his life would have been.

As he walked down the steps, his heart pulsed with wonder, filled to the brim by the artistic marvels in the building behind him. One would have to spend a solid week inside that building to do everything justice. A single afternoon with the Asian art had left his brain spinning.

The Superman pin glinted on his lapel, next to the white rose Rebecca had given him yesterday before he left.

"This rose is as brilliant as my husband," she said, hugging him goodbye. "Now go and keep making me proud."

That embrace still vibrated through his bones and fibers. That woman had changed him, made him a better man, galvanized his purpose in this life. Thanks to her patience, he had two more books in the works, and his editor at the publishing house—it felt strange to think that, after all the years he had worked on these research books—looked favorably on seeing them soon.

The sun painted gold onto the green treetops of Central Park, the joggers, the pedestrians, the readers, the children playing. Hands in his pockets, he strolled, savoring the joys of this moment, the satisfaction of years of effort culminating in success. And here he was in this wondrous city, in this iconic location, breathing life itself in and out.

The warmth of the setting sun joined with his own, and he couldn't stop grinning.

Otter folded up the map, and he couldn't stop grinning. What an accomplishment that had been. But *years* of work? *Years?* He was hoping for stardom within six months. To the top on a bullet. Then no one would be able to tell him what to do, where to live. Maybe the right people would be at the Black Line gig. That was how it worked right? Young bands got discovered all the time. Recording contracts, tours. Cover bands didn't get discovered, so they would have to start writing their own original stuff soon. But this was a *start*.

It was weird, feeling that love from Rebecca—his grandmother. He had only vague impressions of her, a great foam of salt-and-pepper hair, a prominent nose, and wise, playful eyes. She had died when he was only four years old. Experiencing these impressions felt like eavesdropping. They weren't meant for him, but they belonged to him now. What an amazing woman she must have been. What fields of life had been cultivated between this moment and the grandmother Otter knew? What had happened to the women Donovan had loved before her?

He wanted to know more.

He dug into the box and produced a spent rifle cartridge. Stamped into the brass at the base, it read *.30-06 M1 BLNK.*

He had never fired a gun, except in video games, and had no idea what the stamping might mean, but he recognized it as a rifle cartridge. Zeke had a couple of guns hanging around in cases and holsters in his trailer. He turned the brass over and over in his fingers, waiting for the impressions to come. Surely there was a great story behind this, too. If he could get love out of a porcelain rooster, there had to be something exciting here. There was still the story behind that Purple Heart to discover.

If he didn't make it as a musician, maybe he would join the military, become a warrior. The world needed warriors. There was always a war these days, some fanatic "towel-head," as Zeke called them, who needed putting down. Otter found himself using those kinds of phrases in Zeke's company, but it always felt a little wrong. Mom always said she was wild for men in uniform. He envisioned himself in a dress uniform like from the Marine Corps commercials, and then Amber swooning over his studly badass-dom.

The familiar spiral of wondering how she had reacted to his song began, but then a torrent of howling grief blasted through him like a banshee wail, a bullet through flesh.

He threw the cartridge away as if it were white hot, but it was too late. The visions exploded in his mind.

Vision obscured by tears, cheeks hot with them, kneeling to pick up the spent cartridge, ejected from a twenty-one-gun salute, the heart-wrenching "Taps" echoing, fading, a dirge ushering his only son into the ranks of the honored dead. His son, who had died at the behest of rapacious, vindictive men, in a foreign land, over oil and vengeance, killed by cowards who planted bombs on roadsides. And now to lie down among green lawns and endless rows of white crosses.

It was a closed-coffin service. They identified him by his dog tags.

Maggie and Misty supported their mother by the arms. His wife wouldn't look at him.

Mike joined the Marine Corps, she said, to make his father proud. He told his father it was to defend his country from terrorists, to take the fight to the enemy. He was a MacIntyre, descended from a proud clan of highland warriors. All that, only to find himself wading through dust and terror and blood, in a war without honor and only rarely a clear enemy. Mike did not regret his decision, but Rebecca did, deeply, and her silent recrimination showered Donovan intermittently from the day Mike put himself in harm's way.

His son was not allowed to write home about his operations, a restriction Donovan knew well, so Michael sent his father poetry about snatches of daily life, even as he withstood the horrors of war, its endless cruelties, a few, brief, glimmering moments of human spirit shining in the blackness.

Beside the casket, Rebecca hobbled between her daughters, barely able to stand, her face pale. The other funeral-goers dispersed back to their lives, thankful that it was not *their* son.

Donovan lost his son, and maybe, now, the wife he adored.

Dammit, Otter was crying again, sobbing like a baby. Men didn't cry this way. And crying seemed like all he'd been doing for as long as he could remember.

Otter got up and paced the house like a caged wolf, trapped with these feelings he couldn't escape, trying to pace some strength back into his knees.

He didn't want this pain. Didn't he have enough of his own? Now he had Grandpa's, too! But it was too late.

He had been three years old when Uncle Mike died, the first year of the war in Iraq. He had vague memories of a period of intense sadness, being left for a while with a kind but clueless relative, quietly playing dolls and Tinkertoys with the triplets while the adults held each other and cried. It was scary when the adults cried.

Mom had often started to speak of Uncle Mike, sometimes as if he was still alive, and then caught herself, abashed, and trailed off to silence.

Otter picked up the bullet casing again and turned it over and over in his fingers.

If he went off to die in war, there would be no family to mourn him. Lika would miss him, but that was all. The band would find a new bass player. Jeff would find a new chamois jockey. Amber would forget him quickly.

New grief washed up around him. His own this time.

Then he kicked those feelings away and stood, rubbing his eyes and face. He had a greater destiny than this.

In the meantime though, he needed to leave that box alone. A strange headache had settled behind his eyes, and a warm wooziness suffused his limbs, tingling out to his fingers and toes.

The phone rang. Hope flashed that it might be Amber's number. But it was Toby's. Otter let out a long, slow, "Uhhhhhhhhhg," and let it ring. The answering machine picked up and Toby's voice came through. "Rehearsal tomorrow night. Six thirty. Be there. We need you, buddy."

Otter sank back into the sofa with a heavy sigh, covering his eyes with his cap and hoping the wooziness might subside.

CHAPTER TWENTY-TWO
SECRET AGENT MAN

Who knew that spray paint was so hard to remove? Now that the wooziness caused by the rifle cartridge had subsided, Otter stood before the graffiti on the side of Imelda's house, a bucket of ineffectual soapy water in hand. Distant clouds threatened rain, painting the sky a deep gray-blue.

The longer he looked at the spray-painted letters, the angrier he became. Imelda was the nicest lady in Starlite Trailer Court. Who would do such a thing? How many times had she had just enough extra food for him, especially since Mom died? How many times on cottonwood-tuft evenings had Imelda and Mom sat outside drinking beer and smoking? Why did it matter to someone that her English wasn't so good?

The harder he scrubbed, the angrier he became. The spray paint had melded somehow with the paint on the side of Imelda's trailer. The trailer's skin was textured metal, and the grime of decades had settled into the cracks, giving the once-white surface a grayish tone.

For forty-five minutes he scrubbed and scrubbed. He tried a cloth, without effect. Then he tried a kitchen scrubber, and before he knew it, he had scrubbed down to bare metal, so he stopped.

If he knew who the culprit was, he would graffiti the hell out of their car. What a mess this was.

He wanted to surprise Imelda and have this vile crap erased, expunged, before she came home from work, but clearly that was not going to happen.

From his time washing so many cars and listening to Jeff, a guy who knew automobile paint inside and out, he knew that just laying a coat of new paint onto the old would be a mistake, even it was just spray paint.

Unless the side of the trailer was sanded and primed, any new paint would not stick. Attempting to cover it up would be a hack-job at best.

He needed more standing and staring at it to accept this, he knew, but it was inevitable. The graffiti had effectively destroyed the paint job on her entire trailer, and she was forced to look at it every day.

He went into his house, dug out the five-year-old phone book, and looked in the yellow pages for painters. A couple of phone calls confirmed his earlier surmise. Fresh spray paint would eat into old paint. Stripping it would remove the old paint, too. He tried to stop from choking when the painters told him how much it would cost. Instead, he thanked them politely and hung up, disheartened at being stymied in his effort to do a good deed. Back outside, he crossed his arms, staring at the graffiti, and pondered. Maybe he'd make enough money from the Black Line gig to pay for a paint job.

Footsteps coming down the street made him peek around the corner. Imelda walking from the bus stop. She smiled at him as she walked up. "What are you doing?"

"I thought I would try to get the spray paint off, but it ain't going to happen."

Her face melted at that, and she hugged him. "You such a sweet boy! Such a sweet boy!"

He accepted her embrace, and when she released him he told her what he had learned, including the price estimates. She listened with deepening resignation.

"Well," she said finally, "I win lottery, I get new paint." She turned and looked at the hateful words. Then she shrugged. "Maybe in the spring I save enough money." She turned back to him. "Say, why you not in school?"

"Why aren't you at work?"

"Answer my question!"

"Uh, early release day."

Her eyes narrowed.

The pressure of it was more than he could stand. "Got to go, Imelda. I have to work soon."

But he didn't really have to work today. And rain was coming.

Before long, the rain pounded against his tin roof, darkening the windows, darkening the interior, darkening his mood. Thunder crackled and boomed, splashing blue-white brilliance against the windows.

He practiced the set list again. The cardboard box, however, kept tugging at his gaze.

Was there something guiding his hand when he pulled things out of the box? Was Grandpa's ghost there, showing him what he needed to know?

Creepy.

The first couple of items certainly hadn't helped him with Amber. And the last one, the bullet infused with grief over Uncle Mike's death, he never wanted to touch again. He was already carrying around enough grief for a whole town.

When he touched the box, he almost felt a subliminal hum, a suggestion of buzzing as if it were full of ghost bees, and again, the warmth.

He reached in and touched something metal, with thin, rough edges. The metal should have been cold, but it felt almost alive. He pulled out a hinge. It was about the size of his hand, and it didn't hinge very well, because the steel had been twisted by the passage of a bullet, a perfect puncture near the hinge mechanism, almost large enough to poke his finger through.

A shudder of trepidation washed through him. He'd already had one encounter with a bullet-related artifact. He started to feel hot, sweaty, like a steamy shower but without the water. His faded, olive-green shirt was soaked from neck to navel, and his Army-issue boxers hung sodden in his crotch. The sun beat down on the corrugated steel Marston Mat that held back the jungle to create this airstrip in the Laotian jungle. The sharp tang of aviation fuel emanated from a fuel depot nestled under the dense jungle canopy. The half-rotten, half-living aroma of lush vegetation baking in the tropical heat was like nothing he'd ever experienced. It was something. The fat-bodied C-130 Hercules' engines still radiated heat as he carried wooden crates toward the stack of crates alongside the airstrip.

These crates of weapons would be used to help interdict the activities of the North Vietnamese and their Laotian allies, the Pathet Lao, along the Ho Chi Minh Trail. Since the American military wasn't officially operating in Laos, these supplies and this airplane did not officially exist. Nevertheless, the crates were pretty heavy for something that didn't exist.

Sergeant Stapleton was barking orders in French to the Laotians and Montagnards about where to put the crates of weapons and ammunition.

Donovan's French was limited to a few words, so he was unable to communicate much with these Montagnards—French for "mountain people," their allies against the communist North Vietnamese. Watching the mountain people fascinated him. They were so tiny and gnarled, but tough like blocks of knotted hardwood, with flinty eyes and grins missing teeth more often than not. The locals were nervous and babbling about a group of Pathet Lao guerrillas that burned a village a couple of days before.

He set his crate down with a lurch and went back for the next load. The CIA pilot, Evans, met him coming down out of the cargo hold, cigarette clenched in his teeth with a grin, mirror shades and scarlet headband trying to contain a sweaty frizz of salt-and-pepper hair. "Nothing like the smell of jungle and av-gas, right, kid?"

"First time in Laos, Corporal?"

It was.

"You Army Intelligence?" Evans asked. "Thought so. Is it everything you thought it would be?"

Donovan certainly hadn't expected to be shuttling weapons to tribesmen. Sergeant Stapleton was his NCO, and the two of them had been tasked with delivering this particular shipment into the heart of the Laotian mountains.

"Feels weird to not exist, doesn't it?" Evans rested one elbow on a stack of crates beside the cargo ramp.

It did.

"Kind of liberating, too. Puts things in perspective."

Donovan replied that he hadn't thought much about that. He was just trying to do his job, follow orders, and fight communism.

Evans laughed at that. "You're just precious, aren't you?"

Donovan was opening his mouth to ask what Evans meant when splinters erupted from the stack of crates and a twenty-pound sledgehammer slammed into his ribs, knocking him flat onto the C-130's ramp. A moment later, the report of a rifle echoed from a hillside about four hundred yards distant.

Donovan's breath wouldn't work.

Evans yelled, "Sniper!"

The Montagnards scattered. Evans dove into the plane's cargo hold. Sergeant Stapleton was yelling, but Donovan couldn't make sense of the words. Someone was shooting at them. He had been hit, but it must not be too bad since he wasn't dead. He had to return fire, but his M-16 was back in the cargo hold. When he tried to move, however, liquid fire exploded in his side, and his shirt felt warm and wet. The ramp was getting slick.

More shots echoed from the distance. Bullets *pang*ed against the fuselage. The Montagnards scrambled for their hunting rifles and shotguns and unleashed a barrage of indiscriminate return fire destined to hit nothing but jungle.

Evans darted out, grabbed him by the collar, and dragged him into the airplane. "Sergeant! We are *leaving!*"

Moments later, Stapleton was inside slapping the cargo ramp door control. "Hit it!"

As Donovan hovered back and forth around the edge of consciousness, something slid down onto his leg from the closing cargo door. He fumbled for it and found a hinge with a bullet hole in it, blasted off of one of the crates. He grabbed on to it. It had saved his life, after all.

The C-130's four engines began to rumble and whine, even as more bullets slammed into the airplane with a sharp sound like metallic hailstones. The plane began to move…

And then he woke up in Bangkok, Thailand, his midriff swathed in bandages. The day after that he woke up in Bamburg, Germany, in the hospital, with a beautiful, blonde, Scottish nurse named Marina looking after him.

He held on to the hinge. A couple of inches higher, the bullet would have missed the crate and passed through his heart. The hinge had diverted the bullet's trajectory and weakened its power enough to save his life. His whole life had hinged on a hinge.

Otter sagged back, breathing heavy, rubbing a sore spot on his rib cage. Then he rubbed his face, his eyes, wiped sweat that wasn't there from his brow. He got up and paced the room, trying to will his heart to slow down with a series of deep breaths.

"Grandpa was a *spy?*"

That pilot was CIA. That mission was top secret. Grandpa had taken a sniper's bullet and lived.

But he was also just a young man in the military doing his job. He didn't consider himself a hero. He was simply doing his part.

But doing clandestine stuff was pretty cool.

Getting shot sucked, however. Ghostly memories of that sensation lingered in his rib cage. The bullet had glanced off a rib and shattered it. He had been really, really lucky.

Then another realization took hold. If not for that hinge, Otter would not exist.

Suddenly he wanted to know more. He wanted to *know* this man. How might Otter's life have been different with Grandpa in it all these years?

Taking a deep breath, he reached into the box again and pulled out a U-shaped piece of hard, black rubber.

It was a mouth guard, like football players and boxers used. Closer examination revealed a set of teeth-marks embedded in both surfaces.

"Gross!" It was like holding someone's dentures.

The rubber had cracked a bit with age. Were those Grandpa's toothmarks? Had he played football? Had he been a boxer? Mysteries twisted before him about the life of this man he had barely known, daring him to look and see.

What would it feel like to have a chunk of rubber in one's mouth? Probably pretty good if you're the target of an uppercut. In sixth grade, some kid whose name he couldn't recall had decided—wrongly—that Lika's body was subject to grabbing in inappropriate places. Before Lika could overcome her shock, Otter stepped in and punched the kid in the stomach. Unfortunately, the kid responded with a solid right uppercut, smashing Mikey's teeth together in an explosion of stars and pain and landing him flat on his back, at which point little Mikey came unglued and went after the bully like a rabid wolverine. That was when Lika's dad, Marvin, had started teaching her basic punching techniques.

Basic punching techniques, kicking techniques, blocks and takedowns—how many hours of practice crammed into six months with a desperate hunger, a way to escape, a way to make order and routine, to find a quiet center in a life driven off the rails by a runaway-locomotive wife? There was no real escape, only the dream of one, the illusion of one, found in the order of every push-up, every sit-up, shouted in cadence in Japanese in a room of other practitioners dressed in white *gi*. All of these exercises were made more difficult by the burning pain in his side from his shattered rib, a pain that wouldn't ever go away completely. He practiced hundreds of break falls on *tatami* mats soft enough to cushion throws that could still be brutal against the uninitiated.

The repetition of moves built frustration when they would not quite work, not unless they were properly executed, but when they were, the effect was like hitting a baseball with the sweet spot of the bat. Hours of practice not only built his body and fitness but also inured him to pain both immediate and chronic. With the rubber mouth guard saving his teeth, he learned he could take punches and come back fighting. Basic training in the Army had been grueling, disheartening, training young men to kill at a distance with only minimal close-in combat training, mainly with bayonets and pugil sticks.

But this martial arts training was like nothing he'd ever experienced. Exhaustion turned his hands to lead and his arms to ramen noodles. Commands barked in Japanese to a mix of Japanese students and Americans from the military base. The watchful eyes of three black belts and two brown-belts, kind but firm, smiling but exacting, guiding, and shaping.

This was not the stylized punching and kicking techniques of *karate*—*dojos* were ubiquitous here on Okinawa, where *karate* originated—but the down-to-earth, practical brutality of mainland Japanese *jujutsu*. This was the art of the ancient battlefield, of throwing, subduing, finishing an opponent as quickly as possible.

The test for his first belt came only weeks before he was scheduled to return to the U.S. He was determined to win that belt before he left Japan. Back home, bills were piling up and Sarah was a spear in his side. This would be his last chance. He had already failed the test once because his strength—or maybe his will—simply gave out over the two-hour session.

Today he would not fail.

The tests came hard and in quick succession, with stand-up sparring, on-the-mat wrestling techniques, take-down techniques, joint locks, all of them requiring the careful infliction of and the endurance of pain. The smell of sweat and breath close in his nostrils, the coarseness of the thick *gi* they wore, the texture of the *tatami* under his bare feet. After an hour, his strength had dwindled to diminishing spurts, but still he had to go on. After ninety minutes, his breath was like gasping through a straw. The last fifteen minutes of the trial, he was blindfolded and attacked simultaneously by eight combatants who tried to grab and take him down. In a breathless haze, his training emerged from his exhaustion and he blocked their attacks, redirected their blows, and sent them crashing to the mat.

His head swam with exhaustion, one eye starting to swell closed. He was a limp, wet dishrag, utterly spent, bruised, with a fat lip and an incipient shiner, and still his teacher yelled at him in Japanese, *Do not stop!*

At two hours, when *sensei* called the trial to a close, his *gi* was long-since soaked through with sweat in the Okinawan summer heat, and lightly spattered with the blood of himself and others. He and his *sensei* knelt before each other, and his teacher awarded the white belt in both hands. After the ceremony, his fellow practitioners of every grade—from fellow white belts all the way up to the black belts—congratulated him heartily, shaking his hand and bowing, clapping him on the shoulder. Donovan was now an official aspirant to higher levels of training. He had joined a brotherhood of warriors, all of them men with whom it would be unwise to mess. He felt an elation, a sense of accomplishment that he had not felt since the day he graduated from Basic Training.

But this was different. Boot camp had broken down his spirit and identity and rebuilt it as a soldier in the Army. *Jujutsu* training cultivated his spirit, strengthened his identity. This was not training to kill, even though that was its core purpose. This was training to live the kind of life where a threat could be met with controlled, superior force, but only as a last resort. The knowledge that carried at its core a yearning for peace, like an aged *samurai* sitting atop a mountain who *could* kill, but had no need of doing so, no desire to do so, the kind of man who won battles without lifting a finger. That was the core of his *jujutsu* training, and it created a confidence like a mighty tree growing from a simple seed. The Way of the Warrior was not only how to fight; it was also having the confidence to fight only when necessary, to protect the weak, to stand against injustice.

A thrill of accomplishment shot through Otter.

With a broad grin, he jumped up, clenched his fists, and shadow boxed, the power of his grandfather's memories seeping through his muscles like liquid fire.

His grandpa had been not only a spy and a scholar, but a quiet warrior.

He would never forget the sense of serenity, of accomplishment, of pride when the teacher had presented that belt. The knowledge of the techniques seemed to seep through his limbs, but his own movements felt comparatively weak and untrained, awkward, unnatural. Someday, he would learn how to do that, to feel fear but act anyway, to be strong enough to avert violence, or to use it in the most controlled manner possible to protect himself and others.

It all sounded so exotic and cool.

Sadness stabbed through him that he had not known this man better, then anger that he had been deprived of that.

He needed to get to the bottom of why.

CHAPTER TWENTY-THREE
BAD MOON RISING

Excitement thrummed through Lika on the bus ride to Toby's house. Drum riffs pattered out of her fingers onto the seat ahead of her, garnering a few strange looks from other passengers. She just smiled at them.

Her band had a *gig* to practice for, a real one, and she wasn't going to let them down, no matter how much she wanted to throw up every time she thought about playing in front of a crowd. Geez, her stomach jumped into knots just thinking about thinking about it. She was even going to *sing*. Her mother and the other ladies in the choir told her she was a fine singer, even compared her to Whitney Houston, but that had to be just nonsense. She could never be Whitney Houston or Aretha Franklin.

When the bus pulled up to the stop near Toby's house, she spotted Otter sitting on a curb in front of the convenience store with his permafrown. How long would he take to bust himself out of that rut?

At least he was alive.

So it was with mixed relief and annoyance that she walked up to him. "Someone shoot your dog again?"

"I don't have a dog."

"That's probably for the best." She had meant it as a good-natured jab, but his lips turned downward.

"I need you to do something for me," he said.

"Now what?"

"I can't do it."

"Can't do what?"

"I can't go to rehearsal tonight."

Her teeth clenched. "Why?"

"Why do you think?"

"Look, you have to go! We need you!"

"Maybe some other night. It's too soon."

She kicked him on the shin, hard.

"Ow!" he yelped.

"Get your ass up!"

He obeyed, rubbing his shin.

She poked him in the chest. "You're going to rehearsal. You're a professional, right?"

He wilted. "I can't. I just can't. It's too soon. Tell them I'm sick."

"You're going!"

"I've been practicing a lot. I'm getting the songs down—"

"That is *not* the same as playing together, and you know it!"

He couldn't meet her eyes. "I'm really sorry."

"Oh, grow up, would you? Everybody gets their heart broken sometimes."

"Have you talked to her?"

"Seen her at school a couple of times. She's a little chilly, and frankly I don't care right now if she lives or dies. But I'm still going to rehearsal."

He let his breath out slow. "Now I *really* can't go. I'm sorry. Just give me a couple more days. Tell Toby I'll make the next one. I'll be fine then."

"You big baby."

He flinched. "That stings."

"It's supposed to."

"I don't need you mad at me, too."

"Then stop acting like a baby." The low blow hung between them. Then with a heavy sigh, she softened her voice. "I know you're hurting."

His face pointed to the pavement, blocked from view by the bill of his cap. "I have something else I need to do tonight anyway."

"What is it?"

"I'm not sure, but my neighbor Zeke tells me it's important. I'll tell you about it tomorrow."

Her hands clenched her elbows tighter. "You're blowing us off for something you're not even sure what it is? You going to blow the gig, too? Leave us standing on the stage because you can't face Amber?"

He stood and brushed off his backside. "You want a soda?" Without waiting for her to respond he went into the convenience store.

Still steaming, arms clenched, she followed him.

Mr. Mukherjee waved to them both from behind the counter, teeth gleaming. "Good evening, young people!"

She could not help but return the smile. His grin was so bright and genuine. The place smelled of tobacco, and Mr. Mukherjee stood before an entire wall crammed with cartons of cigarettes.

Otter put two Orange Crushes—which she loved—on the counter and handed Mr. Mukherjee a handful of wadded up dollar bills, tips from the car wash.

"How is your band coming along?" Mr. Mukherjee straightened out the bills carefully before putting them in the till, then handed Otter a few coins in change.

"It's coming," Otter said, pocketing the change.

"I should be delighted to hear you play," Mr. Mukherjee said.

"Then come to the Black Line. We have a gig the Friday after next."

"Truly?"

"Yup," Otter said.

"Oh, splendid! I am so excited for you! It must be so exciting!"

Otter wouldn't even glance at Lika. "It is. Scary, too. Lot of practicing to do. Later, Mr. Mukherjee."

"You two have a wonderful evening," the proprietor said with another broad grin.

Otter handed her an Orange Crush as he led her outside. She accepted the bribe, grudgingly.

He settled his cap more firmly on his head and picked up his bicycle. "Sorry, Lika." Without another look at her, he pedaled off.

"Hey, wait!" she called. But he just hunched his shoulders and pedaled harder.

Her anger simmered.

Well, damned if she would let him make a liar out of her.#

Otter eased his bicycle to a wobbly stop before the address on Zeke's note. Nervous moths fluttered in his belly. What would it be like to be one of Odin's Warriors?

It was a well-kept house about a mile from Toby's neighborhood, a nice split-level. Christmas lights in the bay window surrounded a flag like the one in Zeke's living room. Unlike the Starlite Trailer Court, the cars in this neighborhood had all their wheels and hubcaps and lacked rust. In the driveway was a massive Chevy pickup truck, painted fiery red, with oversized knobby tires. It looked like a huge animal ready to growl. From the trailer hitch hung the brass effigy of a massive pair of testicles. He had to stand there and consider for a few moments why anyone would do that. The custom front grill had been laser-cut to read *100% Badass*.

Three huge motorcycles were parked at the curb, one of them with green lightning painted on the gas tank.

Red-capped garden gnomes lined the walk to the front door. Taped to the window on the storm door was a BEWARE OF DOG sign.

He pressed the doorbell, and an explosion of barking shrilled from inside. The pitch of the bark suggested the dog in question was about the size of a toaster.

The front door opened and a massive man towered there, cigarette clenched between his teeth, a hulking knot of muscle, beer gut, and blond hair. Tattoos stretched from his knuckles, up his arms, disappeared into his Odin's Warriors T-shirt, and peeked out over the collar. He looked like a Viking born in the wrong century and with an over-healthy attraction to pizza and beer.

Between the man's feet charged a tiny chihuahua, a frenzy of bulging eyes and white needle-teeth, lips peeled back, snarling. He bent to scoop up the dog with one hirsute paw. "Precious! Shut the hell up!"

The chihuahua silenced, vibrating in the man's palm, but fixed its bulbous eyes on Otter and growled.

The man's gray eyes flashed from under hairy brows. "What do you want?" His voice was deep and gravelly.

"Uh, Zeke asked me to come…"

The man's face softened to neutral. "Oh. You must be Otter. Come on in." He opened the door and stood aside for Otter to enter.

Otter stepped inside, wrinkling his nose at the thick stench of cigarette smoke, dog poop, soiled cat litter, and…cookies baking?

The man held out a dog-free hand. "Duke Cochran. Call me 'Duke.'"

Duke's hand engulfed Otter's. "Call me 'Otter.'"

"We're just finishing up tonight's coverage."

"So how do I get to be a warrior for Odin? Sounds pretty cool," Otter said, feeling like an over-eager idiot.

Duke gave him a grin that was missing two teeth. "Oh, we'll show you."

Otter hoped he didn't have to lose any teeth.

Duke led him into the dining room, where three other men, including

Zeke, sat around an old, yellow table, chrome legs speckled with rust from floor to Formica top. They looked like a biker gang, chunks of tattooed leather wired together with gristle. His stomach clenched. They weren't anything like Grandpa's *sensei,* but they looked tough. If anyone could teach him to be a warrior, it was these guys.

A city map lay spread out on the table, with zones outlined in markers of various colors. They were all drinking some liquor out of red plastic cups. Otter could smell the tang of alcohol. Zeke poured from a dark bottle into a fresh cup and handed it to Otter.

Otter took the cup filled with golden liquid. "What is it?"

"Mead," Zeke said. "Welcome, little bro. A real Viking drink."

A red-haired man smirked. "A real pansy drink." When he talked, his jagged, tobacco-stained teeth made him look even meaner. He had a small bottle of vodka in his lap. Tattoos encircled this man's neck, an indecipherable tangle of dark lines up to his earlobes, spreading up his cheeks to his temples. Acne scars pocked his face.

Otter sipped the mead. Cloyingly sweet but strangely not tasty, like drinking syrup with a weird aftertaste.

"We're still getting organized," Duke said, "but you look like you could be a Viking in training."

"Thanks," Otter said, shuffling his feet. A prickle went over his scalp. These four men could eat him for breakfast and pick their teeth with his bones. He felt like a rabbit surrounded by sabertooth tigers.

"Drink up, little bro." Zeke raised his cup.

Otter raised his and took a long drink. The mead pooled in his belly and lit a spark of warmth. He said, "Zeke's been telling me all about Odin and Vikings and stuff, but what do you guys actually do? Go raiding in longboats or something?"

The four of them traded knowing glances.

Duke said, "We're kind of a neighborhood watch. The cops can't be everywhere, right? We're here to protect our communities. Look for anything out of the ordinary, anyone who's not supposed to be there. There's been a couple of break-ins right here in this neighborhood. So you, me, and Zeke here will take Big Red out on patrol tonight in this neighborhood." He stabbed the map with a thick finger. "Jacko and Smiley here will—"

"That's it?" Otter said. "We're just going to drive around?"

Duke's eyes turned to flint arrowheads.

"Call it a learning experience," Zeke said. "You're a Viking in training, right?"

"Yeah, I mean, I thought you were going to show me some fighting techniques or something," Otter said. "Warriors and all that."

With a broad grin missing more teeth than it showed, the fourth man pulled out a serrated knife the length of Otter's forearm. Otter's eyes bulged. "We can show you some of that," Smiley said.

Otter couldn't take his eyes off the blade, which looked like it could gut a triceratops.

Duke rested his palms on the tabletop, leather jacket hanging open. The butt of pistol in a shoulder holster peeked from inside. A thrill went through Otter, like he'd just walked onto a television show. "You ever been in a fight, kid?" Duke asked.

"Sure, lots of times." As he spoke, he heard the lie in his own words. A couple of elementary school bullies hardly counted.

They saw the lie, too, but they looked more amused than contemptuous. The mead in his belly started to churn.

Then another set of footsteps on stairs caught his attention, coming up from the basement into the nearby kitchen. Light footsteps. They emerged into the dining room with a woman in workout shorts, skimpy tank top, and more cleavage than Otter could stare at in an entire afternoon, everything so tight and sheer she might have been wearing cellophane.

Her sharp, deep-set blue eyes flicked around the room, disdainful of the men, until they fastened on him. A hard glitter of curiosity formed. Her face was too angular, too sharp to be beautiful, but it arrested his attention, like catching oneself alone in the jungle with a black panther. Her raven hair was tied into a tight ponytail, veins and muscle rippling under fair, sweat-sheened skin. In that great vale of sweaty cleavage was a tattoo on her breastbone, a stylized, angular eagle with wings spread across the top of her breasts, standing atop something lost in the cleavage

Her eyes were like someone poking him with an icicle.

"Baby," Duke said, "this is Otter. Otter, meet Baby."

Otter licked his lips and swallowed hard. "Hi." Courage to question her name crawled under a rock, trembling. She didn't look like a baby. She looked like an aerobics instructor from hell. And the vague familiarity of the tattoo raised the hair on the back of his neck, but he couldn't pin down why. But everybody got tattoos nowadays. Why was this one so scary? He had to be overreacting.

"Aren't you going to be out kind of late for a school night?" she asked him.

"Yes, ma'am."

"Does your mother know?"

"I don't have a mother. She died."

"Your old man?"

"No dad either."

Her face softened, and she circled to embrace him. "Oh, you poor thing." Moist heat radiated off her, and somehow, with those breasts squished up against him, he didn't mind that she was all sweaty. He returned the hug, awkwardly, carefully placing his hands on her back.

"Lay off the guy, would you?" Duke said. "Take the estrogen upstairs."

She turned to Duke, met his gaze firmly, smiled sweetly, and snap-kicked him in the crotch.

With a choked gasp, Duke bent like a snapped twig and seized the edges of the table, eyes bulging.

Otter suppressed a guffaw of surprise, which would have gone over poorly.

Her icicle eyes swept the assemblage. "Play nice, boys." Then she crossed through the entryway and climbed the stairs up.

With gritted teeth and ragged breath, Duke said, "We best mount up."

CHAPTER TWENTY-FOUR
RADIO GA GA

Duke's pickup truck rumbled down streets and through neighborhoods like a beast on the prowl. The truck's immaculate interior, without a speck of dust, smelled of Armor All, leather, and cigarette smoke. Duke spent much of the evening with a cigarette clenched between his teeth, grinding it, lips peeled back.

Otter sat in the middle with the gearshift lever between his knees. Atop the gearshift sat a grinning, silver skull with glinting ruby eyes, staring at him, admonishing him for skipping rehearsal. What kind of weakling was he that he couldn't even face the girl he was in love with?

He was too afraid that his song had fallen on indifferent ears. Endless scenarios churned through his imagination. In some, she laughed at him. In others, she told him the song was very nice, but she just wanted to be friends. In a scant, tantalizing few, the few that gave him hope for the future, she threw her arms around him, weeping with joy that at long last their love could be fulfilled, and kissed him over and over. The cycle repeated. What was she saying about him? How did she react when he wasn't there for rehearsal? He would have to ask Lika tomorrow.

Meanwhile, the Big Red Beast growled through streetlight pools.

Still unsure about exactly what they were doing, Otter asked Duke and Zeke, "So what are we doing exactly?"

"Call it supplemental patrol," Duke said. "We're looking for anyone out of the ordinary, anyone who shouldn't be here."

"And then what?" he said. "Call the cops?"

Zeke and Duke exchanged glances. Duke said, "Depends on the situation."

The vagueness of the answer unsettled Otter. "Are we like vigilantes or something?"

Zeke said, "That's a good way to look at it. We're out here protecting people, doing stuff the cops can't do. We gotta protect our own from all these foreigners moving in. Bringing a bad element. Spoiling things. We're protecting what's ours."

"That's the warrior part?"

"Right," Zeke said.

"So can you show me some moves sometime?"

"If you got the money for ammo," Duke said, "I could take you down to the range one of these days."

That sounded pretty cool. He had a vision of himself the hero in an action movie, a pistol wizard. "How much is ammo?" Otter had never fired a gun before. Mom didn't like them, so she never had one around.

When Duke told him the price of a box of ammunition, he had to restrain his surprise and disappointment.

"Uh, maybe after I get some bills paid," Otter said.

They passed a gaggle of well-dressed, college-age women waiting at a streetlight. Zeke hooted at them out the window. One of them gave him the finger.

"Bitches," he muttered.

Otter couldn't quite forget the eagle tattooed on Baby's chest. It felt sinister in a way he couldn't name. "So, is Baby your wife?"

Duke chuckled. "Something like that."

All these vagaries were starting to annoy Otter. He wanted to yell, *How about a straight answer just once!*

The longer they drove around aimlessly, the more annoyed he became. All they saw were a few cars, certainly no hordes of wild-eyed criminals.

Zeke mirrored his sentiment with comments like, "It's too quiet tonight. We need some action."

Duke would reply, "Looks like the 'bad element' stayed home eating tacos."

"And fried chicken!" Zeke snickered.

"Burritos!"

"Watermelon!"

"Beans!"

"With a side of crack and food stamps!"

Duke and Zeke laughed.

Otter said, "What are you guys even talking about?"

Duke and Zeke laughed even harder.

Otter's teeth and fists clenched.

Zeke glanced at Otter and his voice grew more serious. "Sorry, little bro. We're not making fun of you. What we're talking about is where most of the bad seeds come from. Some types of people have more bad seeds than others, right?"

"Right," Duke said. "It's just natural."

Their explanation still felt like it was going over his head, but he didn't want to sound stupid, so he clammed up.

Zeke continued, "Duke here's been in the slammer. He knows where the worst seeds come from."

A trickle of fear cooled Otter's previous anger. He was sitting next to an *ex-convict*. His mouth went dry. "Uh, what for, if you don't mind me asking?"

"'Course I don't mind. I did my time," Duke said. "Did two years for aggravated assault. I beat the shit out of a…black guy who was putting moves on my girlfriend."

"Baby looks like she can take care of herself," Otter said. He had never seen such aggressive boobs in his life, and he would never forget the way they felt against him.

"She can," Duke said, chuckling, "but this was before Baby. We only shacked up about a year ago. But yeah, the joint was an education, all right."

The Big Red Beast was rolling down a well-lit street as part of some search pattern Otter could not fathom.

He spotted a glowing white marquee sign that read: BRING YOUR BAND OPEN MIKE NIGHT SAT 8-12.

Before he even realized what he was thinking, he said, "Hey, stop for a second."

Duke hit the brakes, and the two men peered eagerly outside for some sign of wrong-doing that must have caught Otter's attention. "What is it? See something?"

"Nothing bad," Otter said. "That sign." He pointed. "I won't be five minutes."

The sign was on a building that read Ziggy's Bar and Grill. It was a street of boutique shops, bars, a Chinese take-out place, and empty storefronts with cardboard taped over their windows.

"What for?" Duke growled.

"I have a band and we need practice for a gig."

Zeke said, "He does have a band."

Duke's teeth clenched onto his cigarette butt. "Fine." He herded the Big Red Beast into a parking space half a size too small about half a block down, leaving the engine grumbling.

Zeke opened the door and let Otter bail out.

Otter ran to Ziggy's. Inside, his stomach roared at the luscious aroma of burgers and fries. Half the tables were occupied by working-class families or lone men. Occupying one end of the room was a low stage about four steps across and three steps deep. A long, hardwood bar ran along one side of the room, complete with a huge mirror behind it. Scattered around the brick walls, beer signs provided the mood lighting.

He went up to the bar where a skinny, old man with thick, oiled hair and sharp-cut pork-chop sideburns poured beer from a tap. He smiled a tired smile and said, "And what can I do for you?"

"Tell me about the open mic night," Otter said. "I have a band."

The old man couldn't quite suppress a broader smile. "Oh, do you now?"

"How does it work, the open mic thing?"

"You sign up for a slot. You get twenty minutes. I provide the amps and microphones." The man pointed to the stage. Stacked along the wall were several amps that might have been real vacuum-tube amps, old when Grandpa was born.

"So how do I sign up?"

"You write your name on the list."

Rather than letting his annoyance show at the man's patronizing tone, Otter brightened his. "May I have the list please?"

"Kid, today's Tuesday. You're way out ahead of me. There's no list yet."

Something in the man's tone told Otter that there might very well *be* a list, but he wasn't inclined to let Otter on it. "Do you like AC/DC?" he asked the man.

"Sure, who doesn't?"

"Queen?"

"Righteous."

"Zeppelin?"

"Rock on."

"Aretha?"

"Damn straight."

"Then you're going to *love* us. Seriously. Our singer is Freddie Mercury's long lost cousin and our guitar player is Jimmy Page's unknown love child."

The man laughed. "What do you play?"

"Bass."

"How many of you are there?"

"Four of us. We've got a gig at Black Line next week, so you'll be getting a real band for free."

The man walked to the end of the bar, reached under and pulled out a clipboard, flipped a couple of pages, and picked up a pen. "I've got a slots at 8:20, 9:40, and 11:00."

"8:20, please."

"Band name?"

"Toby and the Undertones."

The man chuckled again and wrote it down. "And you are Toby, I take it?"

"Nope, I'm Otter."

"Otter the bass player."

"Yup."

"Of Toby and the Undertones." That name still clanked like a bad chord.

"Yup."

"Okay, Otter the Bass Player. I have you on the list from 8:20 to 8:40. That includes set-up and take-down time. Make sure you bring your parents. No kids are allowed in here after eight p.m. without their parents. City ordinance."

"No problem. How else are we supposed to get here?" Otter said, with a grin, even though the man's innocuous statement of condition sent a stab of pain through Otter's heart. Mom would have loved to see this. Suddenly he had to bite back tears. "Thank you, sir. I guarantee you will not be disappointed."

"You just bring your little rockin' selves," the man said with another chuckle.

Otter grinned at him and went back outside, tingling with excitement. Toby and the girls were going to be ecstatic. This would be their first opportunity to play in front of live people.

In a dim store window, he caught his reflection and the glint of the Superman pin on his cap. He paused and said to the reflection, "You have a greater destiny than this."

Down the street, the Big Red Beast revved its massive engine, its animal growl echoing among the storefronts and cars, calling him. He wished he had his bike so he could take himself home. Brass testicles, tattoos, knives, and the lack of straight answers made him wish he had gone to rehearsal.

CHAPTER TWENTY-FIVE
CANDLE IN THE WIND

Duke and Zeke gave up looking for "action" about one a.m., disgruntled that they could find no "bad element" that required removal.

Despite all the things that annoyed him, the night riding around with Zeke and Duke had made him feel like part of something important, something bigger than himself, a doorway to manhood. Maybe he needed to prove himself to them somehow before they let him in on all the cool stuff.

By the time they got back to Duke's place, they were calling him a Probationary Member of Odin's Warriors, which made him swell with pride. They looked like a biker gang, but Duke had assured him they weren't up to anything illegal. Otter had enough problems without getting into anything illegal.

Duke had said, "Being in the joint taught me a lot, besides wanting to never go back. I know who my people are. There are bad actors all around. We have to protect each other."

"Who needs protecting?" Otter asked.

Zeke answered, "Well, you, me, all the grannies and kids out there who are afraid of the gangbangers and drug dealers on the streets. You know, the normal people."

That sounded like a worthy goal. Like Grandpa had said, the purpose of the warrior was to protect the weak.

On his wobbly bike ride home from Duke's house, Otter reflected on the evening. Pride swelled his chest that he had successfully landed another gig for the band. It felt like things were coming together. Destiny.

He returned home and then noticed two messages in his voicemail.

The first was from Mia. "Hey, Mike. Mom asked me to call you and see how you're doing. So. How are you doing? I was going to call you anyway, but Mom is pretty worried about you. Maybe you could come to one of our volleyball games! Me and Mara and Maya all made the team this year! It's so exciting! Anyway, call me back, all right?"

That was nice of Mia, even if Aunt Misty did put her up to it. And he liked watching volleyball.

But the next message was from Toby, and all thoughts of volleyball games went straight into the dumpster fire of his existence. "Dude, that was a crappy thing to do. You really screwed us all over tonight. I hate to say it, but if it happens again, you're out."

Otter sagged into the couch with a sigh. Had Lika told them the truth?

He called her and she answered immediately.

"Hey, loser," she said.

"You're still up."

"Can't sleep."

"Did you tell everyone?" he asked, mortification setting in like gangrene.

"You damn right."

"You weren't supposed to do that!"

"I ain't gonna lie for you."

Then it hit him. The truth of it punched through his annoyance with her. He sighed. "You're right. It wasn't fair for me to ask you to do that."

"Damn straight. And you did it because…?"

"Because I didn't want to face Amber."

"Because…?"

"Because…my life is screwed up?"

"That's true, but what I wanted you to say was that you're too chicken."

"Oh, that. Yeah. Are you still mad at me?"

"Where were you anyway?"

"I'll tell you about it later. When I see you." He didn't know why he wanted to keep it secret from her. He tried to change the subject. "Is it always going to be this hard? How do grown-ups manage?"

"Booze and therapy, I guess."

He sighed long and hard.

"I gotta go," Lika said.

"Okay. Bye."

"Bye."

They hung up. As soon as he disconnected, his brain screamed at him about the one huge bit of good news he'd forgotten to tell her, the open mic night. Well, that would be first thing tomorrow.

He leaned forward, elbows on his knees, thinking about the Superman pin, the brass casing, the porcelain rooster…

The cardboard box lay on the floor, one flap open and inviting.

"Whatcha got for me tonight, Grandpa?" he asked.

He dragged it closer and reached inside. Fingers brushing over a corner of folded paper, he seized it and pulled out a rumpled theater program, a simple piece of thick paper folded in half.

The front read:

Elm Creek High School Presents
A Comedie by William Shakespeare
Twelfth Night
Or, What You Will

He flipped the program open. He'd never read or seen any of Shakespeare's plays, nor had he heard of *Twelfth Night*. Lika had been going on about Shakespeare lately. To him, the language always sounded like so much gibberish.

There at the top of the cast list was Maggie MacIntyre playing the part of Viola. Her photo was small and grainy, but there was that same beautiful verve he had seen at the Johnny Cash concert, a little older now. This would have been her senior year in high school.

As he settled into the audience with Rebecca amid rows of folding chairs, waiting for the curtain to part, it all was familiar. The same basketball court with the baskets raised to the ceiling. The same retractable bleachers. The same state championship banners. It hadn't changed through any of his children. And now, here he sat, and his baby girl was all grown up, ready to graduate.

The murmur and shuffle of the settling audience. The lights fading to dark. Applause as the curtain parted. Anticipation swelling in him as he waited for his little girl—his mother, his little girl, his mother, his little girl—to come onstage.

The lights rose, and the Duke strode to center stage in Elizabethan costume, his face patched by sorrow, followed by an entourage. "If music be the food of love, play on; Give me excess of it, that surfeiting, the appetite may sicken, and so die."

If Otter could understand anything, it was somebody caught in the throes of unreturned love. Play on. Play on. Bring the music.

With every word tinged by longing for a woman called Olivia, the Duke barely noticed what his men were telling him.

Just like that, Otter was hooked. Surprise flicked behind the strange overplay of memories, surprise that he *understood*. Even if a few words slipped past his understanding, the meaning was *right there*, laid before him by cadence and action.

And then *she* came onstage, his mother, his little girl, as Viola, washed onto shore with a sea captain and some sailors, an orphan separated from her twin brother. Her face shone with life. He could believe that she really had a twin brother. He could see her intelligence at work in how she would find him and protect herself in a strange country, as she took on the guise of a man. A dizzying array of gender confusion followed as Viola secretly fell in love with the Duke, the Duke pined for Olivia, and Olivia set her sights on the young man Viola pretended to be.

In the fall, she would be majoring in theater at the university. They had a good program, and she was planning to take it by storm. All through her teenage years, she talked of an acting career.

The poetry of the language washed over him in waves of beauty and rhythm, like beautiful song lyrics, filtered through the greater understanding of Donovan's maturity and knowledge.

The Duke professed his love of Olivia to the disguised Viola. "I have unclasped to thee the book even of my secret soul."

The beauty of the language astonished him at every turn, in spite of the often wooden deliveries of the inexperienced high school actors, but they were trying hard, all of them. They *loved* this play.

But Viola was…different. His little girl—his mother—*was* Viola. He could believe that she had fallen in love with the Duke. While the rest of the cast struggled with the language, Viola gleamed with life and truth.

The story and language carried him on waves of tears and laughter. Poignant puns and pregnant glances. Ribald humor and wit. "Many a good hanging prevents a bad marriage!" sayeth the Fool.

The lady Olivia coyly spoke of the Duke with the disguised Viola, "How does he love me?"

Viola said, "With adoration, with fertile tears, with groans that thunder love, with sighs of fire."

Sighs of fire and thunderous love brought a lump to Otter's throat.

His entire life for weeks had been so. He knew the touch of that sentiment.

The Fool struck up a song:

> *Come away, come away, death,*
> *And in sad cypress let me be laid;*
> *Fly away, fly away, breath;*
> *I am slain by a fair cruel maid,*
> *My shroud of white stuck all with yew, O! prepare it.*
> *My part of death, no one so true did share it.*
>
> *Not a flower, not a flower sweet,*
> *On my black coffin let there be strewn:*
> *Not a friend, not a friend greet*
> *My poor corpse, where my bones shall be thrown.*
> *A thousand thousand sighs to save, lay me O! where*
> *Sad true lover never find my grave, to weep there.*

The words hammered Otter. Just a few days ago, that had been him, a blackness from which he had only narrowly escaped.

When Olivia declared her love for the disguised Viola, Viola stood away from her and delivered a speech that strangely brimmed with tears and crackled with ferocity. "By innocence I swear, and by my youth I have one heart, one bosom, and one truth, and that no woman has, nor never none shall mistress be of it, save I alone."

Save I alone, reverberated in his memory, driven deep by the truth of it. No one would ever command her heart save her. Yet there was a wistfulness to it, feelings lurking beneath the surface giving foundation to the words, but hidden.

The Duke lamented to Viola his propensity for falling in love with women who do not return his affections. "For women are as roses," the Duke said, "whose fair flower being once displayed, doth fall that very hour."

With poignant double meaning, Viola replied, "And so they are. Alas, that they are so, To die, even when they to perfection grow!"

His mother, cut down. The husk she became as night to the unsullied dawn onstage.

Throughout the play, Viola sparkled with wit and life, and still that undercurrent of something else lurked. Hidden sadness? Fear? In a play of secrets, some of her lines were delivered thick with conviction and hidden meaning.

On his ragged couch in the ragged house his mom had left him, Otter wept for her. *To die, even when they to perfection grow...*

The play swept him along to its romantic conclusion when all masks were removed, and everyone fell in love with who they were supposed to, and Viola was reunited with her twin brother, and everyone got married to great fanfare.

And as the curtain fell, he stood and pounded his hands together, his throat choked with pride at his gleaming angel. The actors took their turns bowing, but when his little girl stepped forward for her bow, the entire school gymnasium *roared* with approbation, so long and so loud that she stepped forward for another bow, and then another. It was evident even to the rest of the cast that they had witnessed something special, something greater than the sum of its parts, and its embodiment was the eighteen-year-old girl who played Viola.

Otter had never seen anything like this side of her. When he was little, she often clowned around the house with him, for him, making him laugh. She often sang with him. She taught him how to play guitar on that weathered old six-string she'd found in a dumpster. But those instances grew farther between as she got older, as the spark fled from her eyes, little by little, year by year, and disappeared altogether when the diagnosis came. This girl was alive and in the full power of youth, and she was giving it all to the stage.

Then the curtain closed and the gymnasium lights came on, and Otter was sitting on his couch, his eyes misted, his throat thick. It was three o'clock in the morning now. He had seen the whole play in his mind.

Every fiber of him vibrated with the wonder of it.

Along with knowledge of the loss, the knowledge that she was no more.

She could have been famous. She had it all—the charm, the beauty, the talent. A natural performer on the cusp of something greater.

His vision blurred as he looked at her grainy photo on the program. Every letter on the paper blazed fire across his mind.

The date, April 17th.

Seven and a half months before his birthday.

This beautiful girl, this shining actress, this astonishing performer who charmed the crowd into a standing ovation, was pregnant.

With him.

And no one had known. Except her.

Sobs exploded out of him, uncontrollable, fresh tears burst down his cheeks.

He caught himself blubbering, "Oh, Mom, oh, Mom," over and over again.

The sadness overwhelmed him in great crashing waves. How long it lasted he could not remember, but when it finally petered out, when the pain stopped flowing, it was…gone.

No doubt it would return in spurts, but his heart now felt as if a great fist around it—one that had been there so long he'd forgotten its presence—had relaxed its grip. A pressure was gone. A festering wound had been lanced.

Which was good, because that was about all the crying he could take. Warriors didn't cry.

He wiped his eyes and nose and collapsed across the sofa, pulling over himself the quilt that Grandma Rebecca had made, snuggling into it.

For the first time ever, he knew who his mother was.

Sleep rushed toward him, a wave of exhaustion, but before succumbing, his thoughts filled the wave with questions of who his father had been.

CHAPTER TWENTY-SIX
A KIND OF MAGIC

When he awoke, it was two in the afternoon. His first thought was that he had to tell Lika about the open mic night. While he waited for her to get home from school, he practiced his bass riffs and fought with the urge to pull something else out of Grandpa's box.

Last night was too much. He had never experienced such overwhelming intensity of emotion—had never let it happen. When Mom finally died, he had buried it all in beer, weed, and video games at Zeke's house.

Today, Mom's absence still hurt, but it was mixed with a kind of relief, like the time she'd pulled a splinter the size of a spear out of his palm. He'd been playing with Lika in the woods, and they found some old boards that became pirate cutlasses, and in the course of fending off the British Navy, his sword had wounded him. The splinter was agony, and the pulling out was agony, and the blood was scary, but when the thing came out, it left a void. Into that void flowed healing and relief. That was how he felt today.

But as the tide of old pain ebbed, it left behind the detritus of guilt.

What had his mom's life turned into when he was born? Back then, she was only three years older than he was now. Could *he* take care of a baby? Good grief, he could barely manage to keep the lights turned on. Had she ever performed in public again? Had her parents disowned her for getting pregnant? Otter knew this much: she hadn't gone to college, something that had always been a bone of contention with Grandpa, the college professor. Uncle Mike had gone into the military, and Aunt Misty was an accountant. The longest job Mom had ever held was as a bartender for three years. The rest were a series of jobs that sucked her life away like vampires. Otter sensed layers of story he might never know, derailments of life plans—how could his very existence not be one of those derailments?—strains on family ties.

How did a family come unraveled?

Where had his father gone? Why had he left her to raise a kid alone? Did the guy even know he had a son?

There was one person he could ask—Aunt Misty. She would know. He thought of calling her, but then they would both have to think about his "situation." She might try to get him to come and live with them again. He would say no. It would just be awkward.

He called Lika.

It rang four times before she answered. "I'm still mad at you, and I'm getting tired of it."

"I know. But I got something exciting to tell you."

"Before we get to that, you need to know something. I been chewing on this all day. You ain't ever gonna lie to me, or ask me to lie for you, you hear me?"

"I hear you. Promise. Plus, I had a message from Toby. He's gonna kick me out of the band if it happens again."

"That was *our* decision."

"So…Amber knows why I wasn't there?"

"'Course she does, she ain't stupid."

"Um, what did she say?"

"She said she wants to make out with you the next time she sees you."

"What, really?"

"No, not really, you idiot. You oughta know by now she keeps her feelings to herself. It's all I can do not to punch her for being so crappy to you."

Otter sighed. "Look, I'm really sorry about it. I'll be fine from here on, I think."

"So what is this momentous exciting stupendous thing?"

"A practice gig!"

"Do tell." Was that interested inquisitiveness in her voice?

He breathlessly told her about the open mic night, and how he thought it would be great to be on a real stage in front of people, try out their songs, *and* rehearse at the same time. When Mom was working as a bartender, he'd seen a few open mic nights. Some of those acts had to have been pretty awful if twelve-year-old Mikey was snickering behind his french fries.

"So, a trial run," she said. He could hear the growing excitement in her voice.

"I figure we have time for four songs. We pick our four best, one from each of us."

"We would have to pick up my drum set from Toby's house…"

"And Amber's keyboard."

"And my parents would have to come…"

"You think Toby and Amber will like the idea?"

"Call them and find out. Then get back to me."

"Me?"

"Yeah, you! It's your idea, *and* you have some making up to do."

Maybe he could get Toby to call Amber. "Okay."

"And hurry up. I need to talk to my parents about it."

"Okay."

"So what did you stand us up for, anyway?"

"Oh, that. Well, it's this group, an organization, they're kind of like a neighborhood watch—"

"Kind of like?"

"They're thinking about letting me join, but I'm a probationary member. We drove around last night, looking for bad stuff going on."

"Oh, you mean like vigilantes?"

"No! Not like that."

"My dad's a cop. They got a word for that. Unless they're officially a neighborhood watch, it's called vigilantes."

"Look, we're just out to protect the community."

"Hmm." She sounded skeptical.

"It feels important."

"This group got a name?"

"Yeah, Odin's Warriors."

"You mean Odin like the Norse god Odin?"

"Yeah, that one."

"Strange name…"

"And there's something else, too. I've been wanting to tell you about it, but it's kinda freaky. It's been going on ever since I got that box of junk from my Grandpa's will. It's so weird. It's full of his memories."

"Well, of course it's his memories. It's his stuff right?"

"No, I mean the *stuff* holds his *memories.*"

A couple of breaths passed. "You trippin'."

"No, I'm—"

"You high again?"

"No, Lika, really—"

"'Cause if you are, I'm coming over there to—"

"Listen! It's this box of junk right? When I touch the stuff in the box, it's like I see the things that happened to him. It's like I'm there. Last night, I picked up an old program from my mom's high school play and…" His voice cracked.

"And?"

"I *saw it*. Just like I was there, and I saw her, and—"

"You always had a good imagination—"

"No, not like that. You remember last night at the convenience store? We walked in. We talked to Mr. Mukherjee."

"Yeah, why?"

"It's just like that. I'm not imagining it. I'm…*remembering* it, just like it was yesterday. I'm *remembering* my grandpa's memories. You'll like this part. It was a Shakespeare play called *Twelfth Night*."

Her voice turned hopeful. "And?"

"And it was freaking awesome."

"See!"

"You were right, you were right."

"And don't you forget it," she said. Then her voice turned serious again. "There could be some really messed up stuff in there, you know."

"Uh, there already has been. It's like these important moments of his life, all thrown in there in a jumble. I just have to hold the things in my hand for a while and I'm there. I got shot yesterday—"

"Shot!"

"But not really. Grandpa was wounded in Laos on a mission with the CIA."

"You *are* trippin'."

"No, seriously." He felt a burst of pride just telling the story. "I can still feel the wound."

"I was watching a show with Momma a few nights ago about psychic phenomena. There's this kinda ESP where you touch something and you get impressions of who had it or things that happened. It's called…what was it called…Damn, I can't remember."

"Are you saying I'm psychic? As much fun as that would be, I don't think so. It's never happened before with any other stuff…Wait. You don't suppose he's haunting this stuff do you?" Shivers blasted up both arms all the way the top his skull. What made him feel better, though, was how she seemed to be believing him.

"How should I know?" she said. "I've never even heard of this before. So what else have you seen?"

"Stuff about Mom, Uncle Mike's funeral. Lots of stuff I didn't know about his life. Grandpa had a first wife, I guess, but she was pretty insane-o. And there were these girlfriends, and martial arts class, and living in Germany, living in Japan, and…" He let his breath out in a long sigh.

"Sounds like he led a pretty full life."

"I didn't know any of this."

"He wasn't in your life."

"And I want to know why. Something happened between him and my mom when I was seven or eight. That's all I know."

"Maybe you'll get some clues in there."

"Maybe." But could he take another dose of intensity like last night? "So when is the next rehearsal?"

"Friday night."

"Good, we get one more shot, then the open mic night. I better call Toby. He's probably home by now."

"Yeah, you better."

They hung up.

Before he dialed Toby, however, he thought about being haunted. He didn't feel haunted. He didn't feel Grandpa's presence, nobody watching over his shoulder. In those moments, he felt like…he *was* Grandpa.

He cast those thoughts aside and called Toby, who answered immediately.

"What's up, jerk?" Toby asked. "Maybe you can tell me why I should stop looking for a new bass player."

"Look, Toby, I'm sorry. I really am."

"You know how many people at school think you're just a trailer park idiot?"

Otter's ears burned. "Probably quite a few. I'm sorry, all right? I promise it won't happen again." How many people at school did see him that way? "But I have good news. Maybe this'll make up for it."

"Okay, what?"

"I got us a slot at an open mic night on Saturday. At 8:20 p.m. We have twenty minutes. I thought it would be a great chance for us to practice our set list in front of a live audience."

Toby's appreciation came through his voice. "It has possibilities. Good thinking. See you for rehearsal Friday night."

"I'll be there right after work."

They hung up.

One to go.

The Big One.

He took a deep breath. Walked in a circle, swinging his arms side to side. Bounced up and down. Did a couple of jumping jacks.

Then he dialed Amber's number.

Ring once.

Twice.

Three times.

Four times.

Voicemail.

"Oh, thank god!" he breathed as he wilted like wet newspaper. After the beep, he said, "Hey, Amber, I just wanted you to know I got us, the band, I mean, kind of a gig, well it's not a real gig, it's an open mic thing, but we get to play around in front of people—no, not play around that way! Anyway, I, uh, thought it would be a good idea for us to get together—the band, I mean!—but it's Saturday night, I guess we can talk more—about that!—at rehearsal on Friday, see you, bye."

He hung up the phone as if it had just writhed like a snake in his hand, then punched himself in the forehead a few times. "Idiot, idiot, idiot!"

CHAPTER TWENTY-SEVEN
FUNKY DRUMMER

The following afternoon, Otter spotted Louisa Pritt's beige sedan in the car wash parking lot from half a block away. He said a few choice words for the Swear Jar, then paused behind a delivery van to consider his retribution options. Slash her tires with a pocket knife? Potato jammed up the tail pipe? Vaseline under the door handle? "Leave me alone" written in wax on her windows? He had none of those things.

There had to be a way to get her off his back.

Her car looked empty, however. Was she inside talking to Jeff?

He went a block out of his way to sneak in the back. As Otter slipped into the locker room, Jeff's voice boomed out of the front office.

"You're going to have to clear out, lady. This is private property, and you're infringing on my business."

"What about hiring minors to work during school hours? What would the Labor Department say?" Was Louisa Pritt *trying* to revoke his emancipation? Was she inventing an excuse to go to the court and plop him into foster care?

There was a pregnant pause. Otter imagined Jeff stiffening, puffing up, his brow darkening like a thundercloud. "Lady, I run an aboveboard ship. You go ahead and bring it. My records are spotless. You're crossing the line into harassment."

"I will not let this child fall through the cracks!"

"Maybe you should ask him what *he* wants."

"Children do not know what's best for them! When I first started this job, there was a boy like Mike who thought he knew everything. I took my eye off him for one second and then he was dead."

"Of what?" Jeff said.

But she didn't answer him. "Do you know the penalty for contributing to the delinquency of a minor?"

"That's it. You do not come to my place of business and threaten me. With all due respect, get off my property."

A haughty sniff. "Fine."

The front door dinged open and closed.

A wad of papers slapped hard against the desk.

Otter swallowed hard.

"Get your ass out here, Mike," Jeff said.

Otter crept into the front office, checking the window for Mrs. Pritt. No sign of her, just cars lined up to wash. "How'd you know I was there?"

"I know all and see all."

"Look, Jeff, she's a real pain in—"

"*You're* the pain the ass. Tell me why I shouldn't fire you right now."

"Because then I won't have any money to pay my bills and I'll end up homeless and living under the river bridge eating pizza crusts out of a dumpster?"

Jeff's flinty eyes fixed on him.

"I'm really sorry," Otter said. "I wish I could make her go away."

"If I have to have another conversation with that hag, you're fired. You hear me?"

Otter's mouth fell open and his belly clenched. "Yes, sir."

"Is she still out there?"

Otter went to the window, and his stomach clenched tighter. "She's parked across the street."

Jeff rolled his eyes. "Clock in. You can work in the wash bay today, out of sight. Check the fluids and brushes. They're due for maintenance anyway. You know the drill."

"Yes, sir. Thank you, sir."

Lika stood before the Tribunal of Parents at the dinner table, arguing her case. Momma's heavenly lasagna waited, making Lika's mouth water, which counteracted somewhat the dryness caused by having to ask them for this.

"No way," Dad said. "It's a bar."

"And *grill*." Lika said. "So it's like a restaurant, too!"

"I know that place. It's more bar than grill," he said.

"Well, how about if you came and watched us? Make sure nothing bad happens. You could be security."

Her parents glanced at each other.

Dad said, "I'm on shift that night at midnight." This meant that he typically slept during the afternoon and into the evening. He looked tired right now.

"Please?" she asked. "This is our first shot at playing in front of people. We need to work out some serious kinks before the Black Line show."

Dad crossed his arms. "I still can't believe I agreed to that." The look he gave Momma practically simmered.

Momma said, "I think we can manage it, baby." Dad shot her a look of shock, but she squelched it with a gentle smile. "I love listening to you play. You gonna be the next Clyde Stubblefield."

Lika threw her arms around Momma's neck. "Thank you!" Then Dad's. "Thank you!"

Dad patted her arm, giving a sigh and a little eyeroll. "Okay, okay."

They said grace and dug into the lasagna.

Dad forked up a wad of pasta and ricotta cheese. "So how's Mikey doing?"

Lika swallowed a lump of mozzarella and sausage. "Um, fine, I guess."

"I was talking to a deputy from the sheriff's department today. Child Services is trying to find him."

"Oh?"

"He's an emancipated minor but they're worried he's not cutting it. They want to put him in foster care."

"They can't!" she said.

Dad leaned forward, clasping his massive hands. "And why not?"

"It'll kill him! Mikey's been fine on his own for months. He took care of his momma all by himself when she was dying." The truth was that Mike was really not fine. After the catastrophe with Amber, he was hanging on by a thread. She worried about him constantly. Throwing him into an unfamiliar, potentially awful new home situation would destroy him.

"I know all that, baby," he said, "But isn't it more important to be thinking about his long-term welfare?"

"I am thinking about his long-term welfare. They want to yank him out of his own house, put him in with a bunch of strangers. If he can't make this show, it'll..." The rest of her sentence froze on her lips.

Moments passed. "It'll what?" Dad asked.

"It'll destroy him. We want to be real musicians, Dad, especially him. This is a huge shot."

"He's not going to school."

She looked at her lasagna.

"But you know that, don't you."

Her lasagna turned heavy, cooling before her.

He said, "You know it's illegal for a kid his age to not be in school, right? It's called truancy."

"Until he's sixteen, yeah. He told me."

"Are you saying he's never planning on going back to school?"

"I don't know. I ask him, he brushes me off."

"School, food, and a roof. He needs those things more than he needs to play guitar."

Lika had nothing to say to that, because he was right. Her mind wheeled and whirled. "Um, if I can get him to come back to school, will you let him go to the show at the Black Line? Nothing bad is going to happen to him in the next eight days."

"First, that's not my call. And second, how can you be sure?"

"But can't you, I don't know, pull some strings or something?"

He *hmphed*. "You seriously overestimate my pull."

"Please, just don't make it worse for him. Give me a little time to work on him."

He breathed deep and scratched his stubble. "Okay, but I'm going to have a word with him on Saturday night."

CHAPTER TWENTY-EIGHT
ENTER SANDMAN

That night, listening to his mom's mix tapes as he munched on a peanut butter sandwich, dipping it in his chicken-flavored ramen noodles, Aerosmith's "Sweet Emotion" came on. Otter hadn't listened to the cassettes in her Mix Tape box for a long time. Every single one of them reminded him of her absence from the world. But today he wanted to hear her echoes in them, remember the way she used to bop around the house when they were playing.

The opening bass riff caught him up and had him drumming his fingers on the table. He could guess about where it lay on the fretboard, somewhere around the twelfth fret. The intricate repeating pattern through the song's first minute or so mesmerized him. He'd have to talk to the band about learning that one soon.

Across the room, Grandpa's cardboard box beckoned, but he resisted. He didn't know if he could take another night like last night. All that raw emotion had left his insides feeling scraped out.

His questions about father and family lingered, but did he really want to know? "Just do it," he muttered.

He crossed into the living room, snatched up the box, and thrust his hand inside. He pulled out a lacquered medallion or necklace, depicting a crane and a dragon chasing each other in a circle, the size of a large coin. The gold chain was broken, but it had been tied in a crude knot.

Daddy, help me!

A terrified squeal echoed from a telephone into his mind. The sudden boil of fear. His little girl's voice.

Otter threw the necklace down. It landed in the middle of the living room floor, gleaming dully in the lamplight, lying there like a half-coiled snake. Just an innocuous thing, but it seemed to throb with life. It had been awakened and now wanted to reveal its painful secrets.

That scream still echoed in his mind. *Daddy, help me!*

Of the voice's owner, there could be no doubt. His mother. Screaming into the phone, terrified.

The chain lay there, taunting him to pick it up. *Can you handle this?* Wasn't this what he wanted? To *know*?

This one needed him to touch it. It needed him to *take* it, to *hold* it, to *look* into its secrets willingly.

Just a little chain, a limp puddle of links and nicely wrought disc.

He went back into the kitchen and sat at the table where he couldn't see the thing.

That flood of terror was like nothing he had experienced before. Raw. Turning his blood cold. The only thing he could compare it to was when he had come home from school to find Mom unconscious on the floor of the bathroom, pants around her ankles, with a huge bump on her forehead. That day was the beginning of her end.

But this terror was tinged with helplessness. His little girl was across town in some ratty apartment. He'd barely caught the address when she told him. The memory faded like a receding siren, leaving Otter there with his heart beating and his palms moist.

He stood over the chain, looking down, gathering his courage. A warrior felt the fear and charged in anyway.

He picked up the chain, and instantly he was back on the phone.

A man's voice in his ear, Uncle Sal's. "What's up, Don?"

"Maggie's in trouble. I need your help."

There was only a brief pause, then, "I'll be there in five."

Strange to hear Uncle Sal's gruff voice after all these years. It was the kind of voice used to dealing out orders to construction crews and arguing with building code bureaucrats. But he'd always had a sparkle in his eye and good-natured teasing for little Mikey at birthdays and Christmas. A sudden heart attack at a job site had killed him on a sunny Tuesday afternoon.

When Sal's company pickup rolled up out front, Donovan ran across the snow-crusted lawn to the curb and climbed in. A biting wind slashed like fangs through his coat.

Sal punched the gas, squealing the tires. "You wanna tell me where we're going?"

"Maggie's apartment."

"What's going on?"

"She's locked in her bathroom."

"Somebody in her place? She call the cops?"

"I could hear a man's voice yelling her name."

"Boyfriend."

"I presume so."

Street lights *whish*ed past. Traffic lights blinked yellow as the truck roared under them.

Leaning against the seat between them was a Louisville Slugger. The very same one that little Mikey and the triplets played baseball with in Sal and Misty's backyard.

"There's something you're not telling me," Sal said.

More streetlights passed.

"Look, Don. You need somebody's head busted, I'm there for you. But you gotta be straight with me."

Daddy, help me!

An anvil on his chest squeezed his breath short. "Okay. Maggie's been acting weird for months. Started in the summer. She's gotten withdrawn, sullen. Won't look anybody in the eye."

"She just started college this fall, right? Bad grades?"

"I wouldn't know. She hasn't been home since August, weeks before the semester started. Always some excuse."

"Drugs?"

"Once, on the phone with her, I heard a man's voice telling her to get off the phone."

"Abusive boyfriend."

"I've asked her about it, but she denies everything. Something is really wrong."

"Why us and not the cops?"

Daddy, help me!

"I don't know. Run this light. There's no one coming." Sal punched the gas to blast through a red light.

The engine roared loud all the way across town until the tires screeched outside a dimly lit duplex on a seedy street, some unincorporated neighborhood on the fringe of the city limits. Dogs barked somewhere. The place looked like it was built in the 1950s. A single-story ranch structure split into two hovels, snow crusted over everything.

"You sure this is the right place?" Sal asked. "Kind of a slumlord shithole."

"She's supposed to be living in the dorm."

Dull brown paint peeled from the front door. A roaring voice on the other side, a powerful thumping.

He hammered the front door with his fist. "Open up! Right now!"

The shouting stopped.

He beat the door again. "Open up!"

From deep inside the house, he heard Maggie's voice. "Daddy?"

A man's voice just inside the door. "Get the hell out of here."

"I'm going to see my daughter. This door is going to open, one way or another."

Behind him, Sal hefted his baseball bat. "I got a twenty-pound sledge in the toolbox, Don."

The deadbolt clattered open. The door swung inward to the length of the chain lock. Half of a scraggly beard appeared in the gap, along with greasy, blond hair and one bloodshot eye. "What do you want?"

The breath of alcohol belched from the man's mouth.

"I want to see my daughter. Right now."

"She don't wanna see you. Now, beat it."

The door started to close, but Donovan jammed his foot into the gap. Then he threw his shoulder against the door. The blow drove the man inside away from the door. Donovan's second blow ripped the chain lock from the wooden doorjamb, flinging the door open. He plowed inside, Sal on his heels. Bitter cold spilled into the room with them.

The man—no, the kid—scrambled to his feet. He was older than Maggie, maybe twenty-one, wiry, with unkempt, shoulder-length hair and red-rimmed eyes. Strangely familiar. Both hands waved. "Now, look, Professor, we don't want any trouble."

A dimly lit living room. A half-empty bottle of rotgut vodka open on a cheap coffee table.

From deeper in the house, down a dark hallway, sobbing. Maggie's plaintive voice called, "Daddy?"

He called back, "You're all right now. You can come out." Something about what the kid had just said niggled at the corner of his mind.

The kid's eyes flicked between Donovan and the front door, like he was preparing to bolt, but Sal and his Slugger filled the exit.

Down the dark hallway, a lit doorway appeared, with her dark silhouette standing in it, hunched, wearing a bulky nightgown.

"Grab your things, honey," he said. "You're coming home."

The kid said, "Maybe you should ask—"

"Shut up. You've done enough talking."

She shuffled into the light, disheveled, her hair grown long, hanging over her face.

Her midriff was as thick as a beach ball.

"Daddy, I…"

Her voice trailed off, crumbling into anguish.

Suddenly, every mystery of the last six months snapped into focus. Hurrying off to college. The evasions. The loose clothing. The vague reports of how school was going.

A storm of emotions crashed through him, too many to dissect, a flood that staggered him in its power.

His voice was a dry rasp. "We can talk about everything at home. Now, come on. Get your coat. It's freezing."

Her hair hung down around her face. She wouldn't look at him.

"Maggie, baby," the kid said, "you don't have to listen to him anymore."

She flinched at his voice, reached like a zombie for a coat lying rumpled on the floor.

Sal stepped forward and pointed the fat end of the bat at the kid. "You keep your mouth shut." Sal's thick forearms rippled all the way up to his jawbone.

Then Maggie stepped more into the light. Shadows parted to reveal a bruised, split lip, a black eye. Her rolled-up nightgown sleeves revealed rings of bruises—finger marks—on both wrists.

Donovan's world turned crimson.

The kid's throat was in his grip. Something popped under his fingers. The kid's bloodshot eyes bulged like ping-pong balls. His fists pummeled ineffectually against Donovan's arms, his shoulders.

"No, Daddy!"

Maggie's body, crashing into his, knocked his grip loose. The kid staggered back, choking, gasping.

Vile words spewed out of the kid as he flung himself at Donovan with fists and fury. Donovan blocked one punch, another, and then counterattacked with a punishing throw—as automatic as the day he'd earned his first *jujutsu* belt—to put the kid flat on his back atop the coffee table, smashing two legs from under it. The vodka bottle went flying. Half the tabletop crashed to the floor at an angle under the kid's weight. Donovan finished the move by dropping a knee onto the kid's ribcage—something cracked inside—sweeping the interposing arm aside and delivering a solid fist to the kid's orbital bone, slamming his skull against the tabletop. The kid's eyes rolled back, his flailing arms sagging limp. Donovan rose and drew back for another blow, but a weight hooked his elbow.

"Daddy, no!"

He pushed her aside. "Take her outside, Sal."

"No!" she wailed.

Sal had her by the arm, pulling her away.

"Leave the bat," Donovan said.

Sal said, "I don't think that's a—"

"Leave the goddamn bat!"

"No," Sal said, "I'm just going to take it with me." Bat in one hand and Maggie's arm in the other, he dragged her out into the cold.

Winter poured through the open door, cold and brittle.

Donovan stood over the kid.

That's when he saw the necklace around the kid's neck. An oblong piece of lacquered gold and mother-of-pearl depicting a crane and a dragon flying around each other. He had bought it for Rebecca on one of his trips to Japan when the children were small. The crane symbolized his wife's wisdom and serenity, the dragon her strength and vivacity. She had given it to Maggie as a graduation gift. He reached down, seized it, and ripped it free.

Then he picked up the bottle of vodka. Still some left inside. He poured the rest of it in the kid's face. If it wasn't a plastic bottle, he might have bludgeoned the kid with it.

The kid woke up screaming, spitting, clawing at his eyes, rolling on his side in a fetal position.

Donovan dropped a sharp knee into the kid's kidney. Oh, he knew where the pain points were, the nerve clusters. The knee strike flipped the kid onto his back again.

The kid was blubbering now, "Don't kill me don't kill me don't kill me…"

He seized the kid by the T-shirt collar, the necklace digging into his palm. His fingers sneaked back around the kid's trachea.

"Now, you listen to me," Donovan said. "If you ever come near her again, if your phone number crosses her phone, if she spots you from two blocks away, I will break every bone in your body before I kill you."

But the kid was blubbering so hard maybe he didn't hear. Donovan punched him in the mouth, driving out a fresh bawl of pain and sobbing.

"Say it!" Donovan barked. "What did I say?"

The kid spat blood. "Nuh-nuh-never see her again… K-kill me."

"I can mess you up *way* worse than this, you little shit." He seized the kid's right index finger and twisted it until a knuckle popped.

The kid wailed through blood and snot. "Stop! Please!"

Donovan paused, gathered his ragged breath, and stood.

Nausea twisted his guts at the sight of the sobbing wreck on the floor, a sight he could no longer stand. He stalked outside.

On the front stoop of the duplex's other half stood a middle-aged black man, wearing an old bathrobe, arms crossed. He caught Donovan's eye, then he nodded.

Donovan looked at the blood on his knuckles. "Sorry to have disturbed you."

"This ain't nothing," the man said. "I had to call the cops last week. But tonight, I didn't see a thing."

"How long has this been going on?"

"Maybe a couple of months."

The python of nausea in Donovan's belly squeezed tighter. "Oh, god."

Sal called from the curb, "We better go!"

The neighbor nodded in agreement.

Donovan hurried to the truck and climbed in.

He tried to put his arm around Maggie, but it was like hugging a fence post. Her shoulders vibrated with contained sobs.

And that great round belly.

"When are you due?" he asked.

"Couple of weeks." She circled her belly with both arms.

"Is he the father?"

She nodded.

He hugged her close, in spite of her resistance, and told her over and over that everything was going to be okay. Before long, she snuggled into his embrace and cried.

Sal kept glancing at him, wide-eyed and grim. After what Donovan had unleashed here tonight, Sal would never look at his father-in-law the same again, and Donovan would have to live with that.

Maggie said, "What did you do?"

"He'll never bother you again."

"Did you kill him?"

"No."

"Then how do you know?"

"I know." Because he had seen in the kid's eyes the moment he broke him. He had broken the kid just as surely as if he'd put a bullet in him. He'd seen kids about that age in the army, similarly broken.

All the way home on empty streets, an abyss seemed to yawn behind them, right on their tail, a relentless black void.

A few blocks from home, a rational question reemerged from the tumult of rage and nausea. The kid had called him "Professor." He realized why the kid had looked so strangely familiar. The kid had *known* him. He had failed Donovan's senior Asian History class a few semesters before.

He had almost killed that kid. He could have. He'd wanted to.

He held his daughter tighter to keep his hands from shaking.

The crashing emotions and memories ebbed, and in the receding currents, other truths washed ashore in Otter's memory.

That void, that abyss, haunted his grandfather for a long time, even in the midst of the joyous arrival of his first grandson. Even in the waiting room of the maternity ward, he worried over the possible consequences of his actions. If the Kid pressed charges, Donovan could go to jail. If the university found out he had assaulted a student, he could lose his job. If he lost his job for that reason, he might never find another. They could lose the house. But the police never came around. After a few months, he stopped worrying, trusting in the fact that the Kid would cling to his cowardice and slink back into the shadows to fade into the world's oblivion.

The sensation of a finger snapping in his grip—his *father's finger*—sent Otter to the bathroom to spew his ramen noodles into the toilet. He coughed and heaved and spat, shuddering, sitting down on the edge of the bathtub because his legs didn't want to hold him up anymore.

Maggie had met the Kid the day when she had gone to the university campus to tell her father the news about getting the part of Viola in the school play, and she was ecstatic. No doubt she'd been thrilled by the attentions of an older college boy. How quickly he must have romanced her—or forced her—for her to be pregnant by March.

Nowhere in these memories was there mention or knowledge of the Kid's name. That seemed to be the only association in Grandpa's memories. He was forever the Kid Who Got His Little Girl Pregnant and Abused Her.

After that night, Donovan and his daughter never spoke of the Kid again.

That same cold snake writhed in Otter's belly, creature of rage and violence. This guy was where Otter came from? This piece of shit who beat up a pregnant teenager to make himself feel strong?

No wonder Otter's life was an utter train wreck.

Did he have it within himself to abuse a girl he loved?

This knowledge brought into focus some of the conversations he and his mother had had from the time he was little. Conversations about how it was never the victim's fault. They never *ever* brought it on themselves. Usually the spur for such a conversation was a movie in which a woman was abused by a man. These scenes had always made her look sick to her stomach. He had thought it because she was so sensitive and kind. They had watched a lot of movies near the end as she became too sick to work. He had always listened and thought she was right, but only in the abstract sense. These memories, however, now filled her vague expositions with cold, hard concrete.

She had done her best to make sure her son knew how to treat girls. Was it because of who his father was? Was she afraid her son had the same propensity built into his genes? Had she worked harder to drill kindness and respect for women into him because of this?

For years he had dreamed of someday discovering who his father was, but continually slammed against his mother's stone wall when he asked about it. He quietly blamed her for keeping the information from him. Now that he knew, he understood why. Maybe he didn't have to follow in his genetic donor's footsteps. Regardless, he would never call the man his father again.

If he ever somehow encountered his genetic donor, he would…

What, punch him in the face? Kick him in the crotch?

The nausea brought on by that snapping finger gave him pause. Violence carried a cost for the perpetrator, too. Grandpa had known this going into that confrontation and only barely turned aside at the last moment. The knowledge of how far he was capable of going—that he had nearly killed one of his former students—haunted him forever.

The receding emotions left Otter feeling empty and his thoughts muddled. He collapsed once again on the couch under his grandmother's quilt.

CHAPTER TWENTY-NINE
HEAD OVER FEET

The next two days at the car wash passed uneventfully, with no sign of Louisa Pritt. He felt like a ground squirrel peeking out of its burrow, looking for a predator, every time he opened his front door.

He worked hard. He took his paycheck home, paid the rest of the electric bill, started on the phone bill, and bought himself another sack full of bread and ramen noodles. He splurged on a few packages of cheap hot dogs and powdered mac and cheese. He left the cardboard box alone in the middle of the living room floor.

He threw the medallion and its chain into the garbage.

And he worried for two days what he was going to say to Amber at rehearsal.

Lika tried to call him a couple of times and left a couple of voicemails that said, "We need to talk. Call me back. It's about school." He didn't have time to think about school, so he decided to wait until rehearsal.

He rolled up to Toby's garage precisely on time. Toby gave him a neutral "hey." Lika showed up a few minutes later and thumped him on the shoulder. "Your phone quit working?"

"Sorry, I only have a few minutes left on it," he said, "so I figured I would just wait until tonight to talk to you."

She seemed to accept that excuse, and he wasn't entirely lying.

When Amber's mom dropped her off, she walked up the drive, fingers in the pockets of her denim miniskirt. "Hey, everyone."

They gave her a collective "hey."

Otter busied himself with his amplifier cord.

The stiffness in Lika's face made her look sub-zero.

Amber switched on her keyboard, smoothed a piece of paper on top of it, and ran a few bars of a melody Otter didn't recognize.

Toby said, "Nice. What is that?"

"Something I'm working on," Amber said.

They all began to warm up, playing little riffs, limbering up fingers, checking their tuning. Otter's hands had healed somewhat, but they were not yet one hundred percent. He oscillated between trying to catch Amber's eye and trying to avoid it.

Their set list for the open mic would be four songs from their Black Line set. They wanted to open big and end big. They would start out with Queen's "Under Pressure," then jump into AC/DC's "Back in Black," and finish out with 4 Non Blondes' "What's Up" and Aretha Franklin's "Respect." Everybody had the chance to play their favorites and to shine.

They launched into Otter's set list. He grimaced at a series of flubs in the first couple of songs, but by the third go-around the stiffness in his fingers had loosened and he'd caught his groove. Once he had it, he hit the gas. His bass lines picked up little touches and extra riffs.

Toby looked at him with appreciation. "You *have* been practicing."

Otter waggled his eyebrows and hugged the groove.

The third time through their list, they were all trading looks of appreciation, that maybe this "band thing" was not all just a horrible, soon-to-be-humiliating mistake.

By then, Amber's mom was waiting at the curb. Toby's parents were sitting on the front porch sharing a beer and listening with pride.

"You guys are really coming along," Mr. Paulson said.

Amber beamed. "Thank you, sir."

"We're looking forward to your first night on stage tomorrow," Mrs. Paulson said, a pretty lady in yoga attire and baggy sweater.

Amber's mom waved from inside the waiting car.

"Good night, everyone!" Amber waved and started down the driveway.

Unable to withstand the suspense any longer, Otter launched himself after her. "Hey."

She paused and turned, stiffening slightly. "I looked at your song."

"And? Uh, did you like it?" God, what a lame question.

She nodded thoughtfully. "There's a lot of emotion in there."

"Uh…"

"You're much more expressive on paper."

"Uh, really?"

"I gotta go. See you tomorrow."

"Uh, bye?"

She waved at everyone again and turned toward the car.

As she drove away, he clenched his fists and teeth at the sky. How could she be allowed to be so amazing? How could she give him the simplest of compliments and not have him launch himself over the moon?

CHAPTER THIRTY
STRANGE FRUIT

Rehearsal had put Lika in the Zone, and coming down from that left her feeling a little hollow. Some kinks remained to be worked out, but she was hopeful about the open mic "practice," excited to try their work in front of people. And terrified as well. What if their act bombed? What if the audience booed?

Such thoughts had nibbled at her heels ever since Otter had told her about the open mic thing. But at least if they bombed they would have a chance to work things out before the Black Line. They had one week.

As rehearsal wound down, though, and the instruments were safely stowed, the other thing that had been eating at her rose to the surface. She had discovered some things Otter needed to know.

When he chased Amber down the driveway, Lika just sighed and shook her head. When he shuffled back into the garage, his expression was one of pain and bewilderment.

She said, "Walk me to the bus stop."

Otter smiled. "No problem."

Lika sighed. He looked like he was about to explode like a wine glass in a high note.

For a block they chatted about the rehearsal, then she steered the conversation toward school. "So when you coming back?"

He shrugged.

"People ask me about you sometimes."

"What people?" He hadn't had many friends there.

"Some."

"There's nobody asking about me. Nobody cares."

She could say he was wrong, but he wasn't entirely. The society of Elm Creek High School churned on, regardless of who came and went. A blip or two of curiosity about what had happened to Mike MacIntyre, but that was it. "You need to come back."

"I'll think about it." He shuffled onward.

They walked in silence for a few dozen steps while she worked up the courage to tell him what she had discovered.

The lights of the convenience store by the bus stop were in sight when she said, "So the name of that group you were with Tuesday night, Odin's Warriors, right?"

"Yup. Why?"

"I did a little looking on the internet, just out of curiosity." She tried to keep her tone neutral, but the way he looked at her said it had been anything but. She sighed and launched into it. "Odin's Warriors has ties to white supremacist and neo-Nazi movements."

"Huh?" He stopped in his tracks and blinked.

"Did I stutter?"

"I don't get it. You're saying they're—"

"Like the Ku Klux Klan, yeah."

"No way," he said flatly.

"Yes, way."

"They're not like that. Zeke is a good guy. He helped me through a lot. If not for him…"

"That might be true, but Odin's Warriors are bad news. All the way back to World War II. Hitler and a lot of his followers worshiped this idea of a pure white race. The Vikings were the cream of the crap, all blond-haired and blue-eyed warriors. There's some heavy symbolism there, worshiping Odin."

"Okay, but not these guys. You got to be talking about another group. They just like the old stories. They're not Nazis."

She seized his shoulder and spun him to face her. "Look, I read some of the stuff members were saying on the internet. It made me freaking sick! I never saw no old-time lynching photos before, not until this week; people posting those, saying shit like 'The Good Ol' Days!'"

"Lynching photos?" He sounded so confused, as if he hadn't grown up knowing about segregation, the horrors inflicted on black people all across the U.S., but especially in the South, the black people murdered by hanging or burning alive. But why would he know about those things? He was a white boy, and lynchings were simply not discussed in school. Whitewashed history.

Pun intended.

She kept a firm grip on her growing anger and dismay. "Yeah, when the Klan used to hang black people, they took photos and made *postcards.* For *keepsakes.* My dad told me about it, then he had me listen to Billie Holiday's song 'Strange Fruit.' But he'd never let me see…" She tried to swallow the lump in her throat, then wiped a tear. "I ain't slept much this week." Something in her had died at the sight of those images. It wouldn't have been so bad if the people cheering for the lynchings were long dead and gone. But they were right here, right now, walking around. Invisible hate lurked everywhere for her now.

"They say it's about keeping our neighborhoods safe—"

"Yeah, for *white people!*"

Skepticism and confusion mingled on his face, and he wouldn't meet her eye.

"Look," she said, "these guys you're hanging with are probably a new branch of their organization. I couldn't find anything on them. Their websites look like they were typed by four-year-olds. But I found a ton of stuff about the organization. They *claim* they're not a hate group, but there are warnings from the Anti-Defamation League and the Southern Poverty Law Center. Go to the library and look it up yourself, you don't believe me."

As she spoke, he had that expression he got when stuff was just flying over his head. He was one of the smartest people she knew, but this was so far outside his sphere of consciousness, he would need time to process. He was a white kid, but his mom had raised him to be as multicultural as they came. He might not know how awful history really was, and he had certainly never faced bigotry himself.

Three times in her life, she had walked into a store and noticed that clerks started surreptitiously following her around to make sure she didn't shoplift. A couple of years ago, her father had sat her down and talked to her about how black kids needed to deal with police officers when they encountered one.

"Use your Sunday School manners. Don't argue. Don't talk back. Don't wear a hoodie. Don't make any sudden moves. Don't run. Police are not your friends."

"But, Dad, you're a police officer."

"I know, baby, but I still run into a few cops who wish that wasn't true. I grew up having to watch myself. So do you. Dr. King's fight, it ain't over."

Civil rights had come a long way, but there was still a long way to go.

Her life was not Otter's life.

And he still looked very confused, so she did the only thing she could think of. She hugged him. "Just be careful, okay?"

He hugged her back, squeezed her tight for just a moment, and it felt nice. His breath was warm in her ear. "I will."

CHAPTER THIRTY-ONE
PEOPLE ARE STRANGE

Sleep wouldn't come. Plagued by endless ambiguity with Amber and by the things Lika had told him, Otter tossed and turned, switching back and forth from his bed to the couch. Just looking at the cardboard box made him ill. The double dose of painful secrets left him wary. And he couldn't imagine Zeke hanging anybody. They were a rough bunch, Odin's Warriors, but they could teach him how to be a man. He needed someone to show him the ropes, how to fix things, how to defend himself, how to be a stand-up guy. They were certainly more interesting to hang out with than being home alone. But then, Zeke routinely used terms like "towel heads," which Otter was pretty sure Mr. Mukherjee wouldn't appreciate hearing. Otter was a little ashamed that he had used the term himself.

To take his mind off things, he picked up the book on Norse mythology he'd gotten from Zeke and read about the badassery of Odin and Thor, the duplicity of Loki, the nobility of Baldur. He hadn't read a book since school last spring. The next thing he knew, three a.m. was an hour gone.

So once again, it was the crack of noon on Saturday when he pried his eyelids open because the phone was ringing.

How did he become so popular anyway?

He groaned and scratched, still in his socks, and shuffled toward the phone. The screen said MIA KOWALSKI. He raised an eyebrow and picked up.

"Otter's rat race," he said.

"Hey, Mike, it's Mia."

"Hey, Mia."

"Did I get you out of bed?"

"Nah, 'course not."

"Mom asked me to call you to invite you to dinner tonight. Scott can come and get you."

"Gee, thanks, Mia. And thank your mom, too, but I can't. Got a gig."

"Really? Is it the Black Line? I didn't miss it, did I?"

"No, that's next Saturday. Tonight, we're at Ziggy's Bar and Grill. We're playing at 8:20."

"That's sounds pretty cool. Can we come?"

"Yeah, sure, but it's just an open mic thing, you know? I thought we needed some practice before the Big One. So, yeah. Can't come to dinner." Whew, dodged a bullet there.

"Okay, then. I'll tell Mom. How are you doing otherwise?"

"Well, you know, the career is coming together and stuff." He stated this as matter-of-factly as he could manage, as if he had just finished mowing the lawn.

"Was there anything cool in that box of stuff you got from Grandpa?"

He stiffened. What could he possibly say to that? Would she be open to the truth? Finally he said, "Well, you know, I've been so busy, I haven't had a chance to really go through it."

"That's too bad. Grandpa was a cool guy. I really miss him."

A flash of jealousy shot through him. The M&Ms had known Grandpa their whole lives. They hadn't been separated from him at all. And Grandpa *was,* in fact, someone Otter wished he had known better. He'd never gotten to ask him about the Japanese woodcuts, or the samurai swords, or Germany, or Laos, or *anything.*

"Say, Mia, I have a question…"

"Lay it on me."

"What was Grandpa like?" Maybe what he really meant was: what was it like to have a grandfather? "Did you see him a lot?"

"At least once or twice a month. I don't know. He was distinguished, and nice, honorable. I feel like I'm just going to start spewing adjectives. How can I put it all together? He was…Grandpa."

He tried to put the words together the right way, but they weren't having any of it. "So what happened? I mean, somebody had a fight with somebody. Why did Grandpa disown us, me and my mom?"

She paused as if considering. "I'm sorry, Mike, I don't know. Mom doesn't talk about it either." She sounded like she was telling the truth.

"It must have been awful, whatever happened."

"It's too bad. You're still my favorite cousin, though."

"Ain't I your only cousin?" Uncle Sal had been an only child, so there wouldn't be any cousins on that side, and something told Otter there wouldn't be any more kids between Misty and her new husband.

"It's a low bar," Mia said, prompting a chuckle from both of them. She added quickly, "But an exclusive club!"

"Look, I gotta head for work."

"Okay. Good luck with your show tonight."

"Thanks."

"I suppose it's better to say, 'break a leg.' Showbiz and all that, right?"

He smiled. "Absolutely."

Otter was dragging his bicycle out of its hiding place in the woods when Zeke's Harley chugged up the street. As Zeke killed the engine, the motorcycle's falling silence left a void in the air.

Otter walked up to him, pushing his bike. He found himself studying Zeke more closely after what Lika had told him.

"Hey, there, little bro," Zeke said. His voice was jovial, but his face looked haggard and drawn, with dark circles under his eyes and cheeks strangely sunken. Sweat slicked his temples and neck, in spite of today's cool air. He scratched and picked at an unsightly sore on his jaw line. "What's shakin' today?"

"We got a practice gig tonight at Ziggy's Bar and Grill."

"Awesome! I want to hear you guys play."

Zeke's enthusiasm made Otter's ears flush. "Our slot is 8:20." It felt pretty good to have someone that excited about seeing him play.

"Excellent. I'll try and be there."

"Thanks, bro!"

They fist-bumped.

Otter said, "Say, are you feeling all right? You don't look so good."

"Had a rough night. You know how it is." Zeke pulled out a cigarette and lit it. Something flat and cold, like the face of a tombstone, flicked behind his eyes.

Maybe, but Otter had never looked *that* bad after a wreck-fest. There was a sallowness to Zeke's complexion. "Hey, I gotta get to work."

Zeke nodded and turned toward his house.

Otter couldn't believe the things Lika had said about Odin's Warriors last night. Zeke was…Zeke. Zeke's unique brand of independence was something Otter aspired to. Answering to no one. Needing no one. A motorcycle rebel, and yet, a protector. A warrior.

But Lika had been really upset about Otter hanging out with a bunch of guys purported to be white supremacists. But that couldn't be Zeke. If Zeke was there, maybe Lika would see that Zeke was no neo-Nazi, that he was a decent guy who looked out for his "little bro." Otter didn't know if he'd have survived without Zeke for that first couple of months after Mom died. He owed Zeke a lot.

He jumped on his bike and headed for work.

When Otter arrived at the car wash, keeping an eye out for beige sedans, Jeff introduced him to Dashawn, a tall, thin boy about Otter's age. They shook hands and said hi, but there was something in Jeff's tone and demeanor that raised hackles of warning on Otter's neck.

How many times had Jeff said he couldn't afford to hire any more help? If that were true, why had he hired someone new? No one had gotten fired…

Not yet, that is.

Otter's stomach turned sour.

It downright curdled when Jeff told him, "Your job today is to show Dashawn the ropes. Teach him everything you know. Start him on chamois, then vacuum, then dashboards. You know the drill."

Otter couldn't help feeling like a gallows awaited him in the parking lot as he said to Dashawn, "Come on, then."

Dashawn was two parts elbows and two parts Adam's apple, but he tried hard.

The gallows feeling would not go away, though, and it stoked a harsh impatience in Otter when Dashawn asked questions or missed a spot. "Come on, dude! It's not that hard." After six months of working here, Otter could make a fender shine like a mirror.

Dashawn gave him a solid retort of side-eye but kept trying.

Otter couldn't shake the sinking sensation in his belly that he was training his replacement.

That is, until the hour approached six o'clock closing time and his thoughts turned to tonight. Their first night on a stage. He made sure to tell all the guys about his impending triumph. They all nodded and offered encouragement.

When he told Jeff, however, Jeff offered a derisive snort. "Quit before your heart gets broken, kid."

CHAPTER THIRTY-TWO
FOR THOSE ABOUT TO ROCK, WE SALUTE YOU

Otter unslung his guitar case and chained his bike outside Ziggy's Bar and Grill. The street out front lay mostly deserted. He recognized all their parents' cars. He was the last to arrive. He checked his watch: 8:05. On his cap was the Superman pin. In his pocket, the Orange Crush bottle cap and the Johnny Cash guitar pick. His talismans, one of childhood innocence and fearless play, the other of career dedication and hard-fought wisdom. His keys to a greater destiny.

Music filtered through the vestibule, a guy on a stool strumming Neil Young on an acoustic guitar.

Otter recognized the bartender from his previous visit, watching them with combined interest and amusement. What were these four kids going to deliver?

Old dude, you're about to find out.

He walked through the maddening aromas of hamburgers and fries, his stomach roaring, being empty since the peanut butter sandwich he'd wolfed down on his break. He didn't have enough cash to cover a burger and fries.

His bandmates all waved at him as he approached their table. "I'm not late."

"We all just got here," Lika said.

Lika's dad, Marvin, stood like a mountain stretching its legs. His biceps strained the fabric of his T-shirt. His hand engulfed Otter's, and he and gave Otter a long, searching gaze, "Good to see you, Mike. How you doing?"

"Just great, sir," Otter said, withdrawing his hand with all its small bones thankfully intact. It was just getting healed. "You been working out?"

Marvin laughed. He knew that Otter knew that he was a dedicated boxer and weightlifter in his off-duty time. "Getting ready for my shot at Mike Tyson."

"I thought he retired," Otter said.

"The only way I could beat him."

They laughed again. Marvin's paternal gaze warmed him. It would have been nice to have a dad that cool.

Otter caught Lika's gaze. She gave him a huge, teeth-baring smile, then bit her lip and bounced in her seat.

Amber was looking at him, her face guarded, neutral. He took a deep breath and turned toward her table.

Accompanying Amber was a tired-looking woman with friendly eyes, wearing scrubs. She gave Otter a bigger smile than Amber did. "And you must be Otter," she said.

"That's what Mom always called me."

She raised one eyebrow. "Call me Chrissie. Amber has told me a lot about you."

Super-glue seized his feet against the floor. "Really?"

"Sure. She says you're an excellent bassist."

"Really?"

"I used to be in a band myself, back in the day."

"Really?" He clenched his teeth at the way he sounded like a skipping CD.

"A punk cover band. Called ourselves The Raging Misfits. Would you believe this soft, doughy exterior was once a rock-hard screaming harpy on stage? Courtney Love and Joan Jett had nothing on me." Chrissie was a good-looking woman bearing down on forty and losing the Battle of the Thickening Middle, as his mom used to call it. It was easy to see where Amber got her looks and charm, however. There was something warm and endearing about Chrissie.

Amber giggled and rolled her eyes. "Because we should all worship at the altar of punk divas."

Her mother elbowed her. "But we grow out of things, you know?" She turned pointedly to Amber. "We have *kids.*"

Amber flapped her fingers like quacking ducks, good-natured teasing, not derision.

"That's it, little girl," Chrissie said, "You're grounded."

"Mom!" Amber said.

"Until you sacrifice at the altar of the punk goddesses. Now go get me another iced tea."

"Mom!"

"Look, I'm quite happy to keep embarrassing you in front of your friends. The sooner you go, the sooner I stop." Chrissie gave Amber a big, cheesy grin, cocked her head sideways, batted her eyelashes, and handed over a glass full of ice cubes.

Amber snatched it and went to the bar, rolling her eyes.

Chrissie looked at Otter, squarely. "So my little girl tells me you're a songwriter."

If he'd had a drink, he would have sprayed a cloud of mist; but he didn't, so all he could do was choke out, "Yeah."

"Well, good luck." She glanced at her daughter's retreating back, such that Otter wasn't sure she was talking about a song-writing career or Amber.

His brain spun in ever-tightening circles with questions he dared not ask.

At the next table, Toby, his parents, and his two little brothers greeted him with smiles. Toby's brothers, eight and ten years old, picked skeptically at their hamburgers and fries. "They put mustard on it!" said one.

Otter pointed at the stage where a gray-haired man picked and strummed, and, with a cracked, reedy voice, sang a song about an unknown legend. "How's this guy?"

Toby shrugged. "It's an open mic." Behind them sat the mound of their equipment. Lika's drums, Amber's keyboard in its case, Toby's guitar case. "As soon as he gets done, we're on."

The guy onstage finally ended his Neil Young rendition, prompting a spattering of applause from the crowd. Then he opened a new number that had the languid dreaminess of Pink Floyd, but it wasn't a song Otter had heard before.

He swung his arms and tried to contain his agitation.

Loretta said, "Why don't you sit down, Michael? Have you eaten today? You want a burger?"

By all that was holy, he was starving, but he said, "Maybe later? I'm afraid I'd just upchuck it right now." But he did sit down at an unoccupied corner of the table, conscious of Amber's eyes on him from across the room.

The minutes ticked by, his mind descending into the riffs and chord progressions of their upcoming set as he tried to imagine that they were just going to be playing in Toby's garage.

In a heartbeat, the audience was clapping again, and the guy onstage stepped down without ado.

"We're up!" Toby said.

The four of them jumped up like jack-in-the-boxes.

Lika blurted, "Oh, my god I'm gonna throw up." Then she ran outside.

Outside Ziggy's, Lika sat on the curb, hugging her knees. And all she could think about was every flub she'd ever made, how rough rehearsals had been this week, how she did not have the chops to pull off an Aretha Franklin song. She was going to make a fool of herself and embarrass everyone. She had aimed too high. She couldn't pull it off. Her *dad* was here.

Otter was the first to reach her. He sat beside her. "Stage fright?"

She wiped her cheeks. "Sorry. I guess so." Her stomach was a nest of snakes. She hated snakes.

Her parents hung in the doorway, Toby and Amber hovering behind them.

He looked over his shoulder at Toby and Amber. "You guys go set up. We'll be in."

They all disappeared inside.

Otter said, "You can do this."

"No, I can't. I can't even stand up. This doesn't make any sense at all."

"How about if I carry you?"

"What?"

"I'll piggyback you to your stool."

"Shut up." She slugged his arm. "Don't make fun of me."

"I'm dead serious."

She looked at him for a long time.

He continued, "Look, there's nobody here but us anyway. It's just a rehearsal, but in a different place. It was totally empty when I signed us up for this. Dead. The place got condemned weeks ago. No one is going to show up."

She managed to a snort a little chuckle. She considered standing, but her legs were chicken noodle soup.

"I want this back," he said, "but tonight you need it more than I do." He held out a closed fist.

She opened her palm and into it fell a black guitar pick. She gave him a quizzical expression.

"That is a magic guitar pick, from the hand of Johnny Cash himself."

"You trippin.'"

"No, seriously. He played a whole concert with this pick."

"This from the box?"

He nodded. "You feel anything?"

"Not yet." It was just a guitar pick, plastic and rigid in her palm.

"Well, you will. That thing is packed with pure performing power. Put it in your pocket."

"Girl clothes don't have pockets."

"Put it in your shoe, then. It doesn't matter that you're a drummer. It's all about the heart."

She held it in her palm for a long moment. Maggie had been a huge Johnny Cash fan, and so was Mike. The weight of it felt heavier there than any guitar pick had a right to. And he had given it to her. "Thank you," she said, her voice thick.

"Anytime."

Her otherwise useless jeans pocket was just deep enough to fit a guitar pick, so she tucked it in there.

"Feeling stronger yet?" he said.

"I don't know."

He stood and offered her his hand. She took it, and he pulled her to her feet.

The snakes were settling down. She wiped her face again. "I'm such an idiot."

"You got this," he said. "Remember, it's just a rehearsal."

CHAPTER THIRTY-THREE
I LOVE ROCK 'N' ROLL

Moments later, Otter had snatched up his guitar and plugged into an amp, tuning. Toby was checking microphones. Lika's was a little buzzy, but it would have to do. Lika's parents already had the drum set mostly ready. Meanwhile Amber fiddled away at her keyboard with that same melody as last night, a longer snippet of it this time. It was catchy, lilting.

Otter imagined Mom was watching, hoping she was. She'd never once taken him to church, but it was comforting to know she might still be out there somewhere. Of this, she would approve.

Just then, three tall, blonde girls walked in. Otter's mouth fell open.

Mia waved at him as they took a table. He had difficulty distinguishing Maya from Mara, but one of them looked skeptical and the other, curious. Mia wiggled onto her seat, her smile beaming with excitement.

Otter waved back, still questioning his retinas, but kept watching the door to see if Aunt Misty would be following them inside. Nevertheless, his heart swelled. Somebody had come to see *him,* not one of their own kids. Gratitude flushed through him in an abundance that misted his vision.

Their audience had just grown by about a fourth, with twelve people in the room now besides the bartender, including the guy who'd just performed.

Test notes started to flutter through the amps. Dials were tweaked, levels adjusted. Then a chord. Then a few strokes across the high-hat.

Otter studied Lika. She bit her lip and gave him a wide-eyed little nod.

The four of them shared looks. It was time.

Toby stepped up to the microphone. "We're Toby and the Undertones. Hit it."

A high-hat from Lika and Otter jumped into the iconic bass riff from Queen's "Under Pressure."

Bumm-bumm-bumm-buh-duh-duh-dump.
Bumm-bumm-bumm-buh-duh-duh-dump.

A man sitting at the bar said loud enough for them to hear, "Vanilla Ice? Really?"

Amber gave the man a beaming, effervescent smile, and then the finger. "Vanilla Ice doesn't exist!" she sang sweetly. His face darkened and he turned away. Then she jumped into the song's first staccato piano chords.

Smiles spread on the faces of the audience.

Otter grinned and kept playing. Vanilla Ice had sampled the original song by David Bowie and Queen back in the Otter-didn't-know-when days, but it didn't hold a candle.

Bumm-bumm-bumm-buh-duh-duh-dump.
Bumm-bumm-bumm-buh-duh-duh-dump.

And they were *on*. Amber eased into the lyrics like she was Freddie Mercury's little girl, and Toby sang the David Bowie parts. Together they rose into a powerful duet, a hopeful song about life and love in a world falling apart. Toby's lead guitar was crisp, Amber's piano chords sharp, and Lika's rhythms certified fresh. Otter held the bass beat with all the concentration he could muster.

And with the last upbeat piano chord, all twelve people erupted into whistles and applause.

The four of them looked at each other with amazement like they'd just let a genie out of a bottle.

A loud hooting came from a table at the back of the room. Zeke raised his beer bottle in salute. He didn't look well, but at least he was smiling. Otter smiled and waved, a little surprised that Zeke had actually come.

Near the front, the M&Ms' faces formed a spectrum of emotion from amazement to mild disinterest. Mia was whispering something to Mara/Maya and looked at Toby with glowing eyes.

Meanwhile, Toby's dad got up and carried Otter's guitar case to the foot of the stage, where he laid it open on the floor, pulled out a ten-dollar bill, snapped it while pointedly smiling at the audience, and placed the money in the case.

The four of them laughed and shrugged.

"Why didn't we think of that?" Toby said.

The bartender was pouring beer for a couple of new guys sitting at the bar, looking toward the stage with fresh appreciation.

Toby raised his guitar neck, poised, and caught Otter's gaze. Otter struck a flamboyant pose, signaling his readiness to rock.

They launched into "Back in Black" like a locomotive picking up speed. When they hit the first lyrics, Amber abruptly stripped off her denim jacket and flung it aside, revealing a bra-less, skin-tight, black crop-top that hugged her like her own skin. Her mother's eyes bulged. Otter missed an entire bar of the song. He managed to pick it up again, but his ears flushed hot as he hoped no one would notice. Amber didn't need to sing like Brian Johnson's abrasive scream. All she needed was to sing like Amber, bringing a Pat Benatar-like operatic melody to a hard-rocking grind.

As the song built to its final crescendo, then relented like a locomotive fading into the distance before a final slashing chord, the faces of the audience stared in disbelief.

Five men walked in carrying a variety of instrument cases and did a double take when they saw who was playing. One of them slapped his buddy on the shoulder and pointed.

The applause echoed long and louder than before.

Otter's heart swelled like a watermelon. His cheeks started to ache from grinning.

Before the applause had even subsided, Amber punched some switches on her keyboard, changing the sound to emulate an acoustic guitar, started stroking the piano keys with the first chords of 4 Non-Blondes' "What's Up?" After AC/DC, this song was like slamming on the brakes to check out a sunset after a wild ride. Toby slid into the smooth electric guitar riff as if he'd written it himself. It was song of passion for change and yearning for justice and crying for the state of the world and the human race. Amber seemed to feel every word of it.

When the song crashed into the final chorus, she screamed at the top of her lungs, "What's going on!" Chills skittered up Otter's spine and across his shoulder blades. 4 Non-Blondes were only a Nineties one-hit-wonder, but reverberations of the mournful lyrics and Amber's heartfelt delivery turned it into one girl's outcry to the world.

When the final chords faded away, her eyes glistened with tears.

A couple of patrons, a man and woman, had filtered in, sat at the bar, and were now watching in fascination. Surprised hoots and applause filled the dim, brick room in the light of flickering neon beer signs.

Longer still, the applause went on.

Marvin came up and threw a couple of bills into the guitar case, then Amber's mother, then the guy who sang Neil Young before them. He paused before the stage and clapped and nodded with appreciation. Then Mia and each of her sisters. All skepticism had been replaced by looks of wonderment.

Toby thanked them all profusely, his voice cracking with nervousness.

Otter looked at Lika. With a light sheen of sweat now, her grin dwarfed his. She looked like she was vibrating in her seat.

Amber's fingers punched more switches.

Toby stepped up to the mic. "I'm Toby and these are the Undertones, Otter, Amber, and Lika. We got time for one more. Don't stop us if you've heard this one before." Otter winced at the band name. He didn't mind Toby being the band's front man, but there was something about that band name that just clanked.

Amber touched off "Respect" with a chorus of synth-trumpets from the keyboard, Toby jumping in with those first bent guitar notes, and then Lika flying into Aretha's powerful melody. Lika didn't have Aretha's pipes, but she had the attitude, the inflections, the drive, and a few years of singing gospel in church with her mother. Otter, Toby, and Amber sang backup, *just a little bit, just a little bit.*

The audience started clapping along with the beat, swinging their shoulders and arms. Lika's presence seemed to double in size on her stool.

Otter saw something open up in her he'd never seen before. In rehearsal, she'd always sung "Respect" with an underlying timidity, as if she were uncomfortable belting it out like Amber could, never mind Aretha Franklin. Tonight, though, she was singing to the rafters, transformed, transported, mouth wide, aglow with an energy he'd never seen her project. Had it been there all along?

She was gorgeous.

They stumbled over the transition between Toby's solo and Amber's "saxophone" solo, but he hoped no one noticed. *Just keep playing.*

Just a little bit, just a little bit.

The song drew to the crescendo, Toby lifted his guitar neck to signal the final flourish. And *boom.*

It was over.

As the last echoes faded, the applause erupted. Two dozen people could have been two thousand for the size of the lump in Otter's throat.

Their parents stood up and cheered. The M&Ms stood up and cheered. In the back of the room, Zeke clapped his hand against his beer bottle.

The applause ended all too soon, but a few more dollars and change fluttered into the guitar case at the foot of the stage.

The next act, waiting at the back of the restaurant, started shuttling their gear toward the stage.

The M&Ms came to the edge of the platform, and Otter stepped down to greet them.

"We have to go," Mia said. "Mom thinks we went to a movie."

"Thanks for coming," Otter said. "Really. It meant a lot." It seemed strange for him to say that, but it was true. Plus it was nice to bask in the adoration of three beautiful girls, even if they were relatives.

Mia came closer and spoke low, "And Maya wants to meet Toby next time."

The Red M&M bounced with excitement. The Blue M&M, Mara, watched with amusement.

"Why not now?" Otter said. He called Toby over. Maya looked ready to melt across the floor, held together by tension in her ponytail band.

Otter introduced them all. Toby tried to play cool, but his eyes goggled at the sight of them.

"Yeah, dude," Otter said to Toby, "I already have groupies. I bring them to every show."

Mia laughed and punched him on the arm. Then she threw her arms around him. "You guys are really good."

Otter hugged her back.

As she released him, he said, "Are you coming next week?"

"The Lobbying of the Mother has already begun," Mia said, "So we'll see. She's been pretty uptight since Grandpa died."

"Yeah," said Mara, "she needs to get out and have some fun. We'll see what we can do."

"Summon the conveyance, Maya!" Mia declared.

Maya pulled out her phone.

"Until we meet again," Mia said, curtsying, "*adieu!*" The three girls headed for the door, a moving rainbow.

One of the old men—at least fifty—from the next act stepped up to the stage. "You kids expect us to the follow that?"

Another laughed. "We're gonna look like a bunch of old farts playing polkas."

"We *are* a bunch of old farts," said another.

"What's wrong with polkas?" said another.

Marvin came forward to help carry Lika's drums away. "That was phenomenal, baby!" he told her. Her mother was right there, hugging her daughter and showering her with kisses.

She jumped into her dad's arms, half-crying for joy.

Marvin turned to Otter and Toby. "Man, you kids were born in the wrong decade."

The dissatisfaction with the band name that had been niggling at Otter's back thoughts jumped to the fore. "*The Wrong Decades!*"

"What?" everybody said.

"The band name. Toby and the Undertones is okay, but it doesn't say who we are," Otter said.

Toby crossed his arms.

"Yeah, Toby, you put the band together," Otter said, "You're the leader, but a band name needs to *say* something. And we're *not* 'undertones.' Your parents weren't even our age when some of these songs came out. People look at us and think we should be covering the latest bubblegum pop."

Lika stepped down next to him. "The Wrong Decades. I like it. Plus, after tonight, it's not just your band. It's *our* band. Because We. All. Kicked. Ass."

Amber approached. "We did. I like it, too."

Toby stroked his chin, then shrugged. "It wasn't a great name anyway."

Loretta came up to Otter and squeezed him. "That was some mighty fine bass, young man."

Otter's face heated. "Thanks." Then he noticed the next act standing around waiting with decreasing patience for the celebration to end. "How about we finish clearing out for these guys, huh?"

CHAPTER THIRTY-FOUR
KNOCKIN' ON HEAVEN'S DOOR

They all pushed their tables together and sat around laughing and basking in the glory of their triumph. Lika's mom ordered baskets of food. When the crosscut fries and chicken strips and onion rings and fried cauliflower and breaded mushrooms arrived, Otter descended upon them like a starved hyena. He tried to restrain himself from the feast, but couldn't. He didn't know when he'd get to eat like this again.

The elation was still surging through him. This might well be the greatest day of his life. *And* he had seventeen dollars and twenty-five cents in his pocket, his cut of the tips.

The only thing that would make it better would be if he could sit and talk to Amber. Then again, it wasn't talking he had in mind. Tonight, she had been like some otherworldly being. Everyone had seen it. He would never forget the way she moved, the way she sang, the way she *became* the music. Some people had to work up to it, but Amber was a born performer.

It also made her difficult to read, like Lika said. Everything about her true internal life was encased in an impenetrable vault. She and her mother were funny together, and he found himself yearning for the same kind of easy, joking familiarity with Amber, yearning to be part of her inner circle. He couldn't help feeling the gravitational pull. As they sat and chatted, she was friendly, but his constant vigilance for signs of more were fruitless.

Zeke hadn't come up to congratulate Otter on the show afterward. He stayed at his table and nursed another beer and gave Otter a flash of smile and a thumbs-up. A tension in Zeke's shoulders and face suggested some inner discomfort or turmoil. He thought about introducing him to Lika, but Marvin kept casting stink-eye toward Zeke—like he knew him from somewhere—so Zeke kept his distance. The tension made Otter uncomfortable.

Except that he was too busy stuffing his fry-hole anyway. Sitting there, he felt the gulf between Zeke's world—Otter's world, a world of trailer parks and poverty and immense effort spent for little gain—and the nice, suburban, ordered world of his bandmates.

The next group of musicians played their set with an easy familiarity. They had clearly known each other for years, trading banter between songs. Their solos were adequate but uninspired, competent but unimaginative. They weren't on a career path. One of them wore a mechanic's shirt with his name embroidered on it. They weren't looking to break out. Nevertheless their faces lit with the joy of playing music. Their last song was Don MacLean's "American Pie," a number that had everybody in the place singing along with the chorus.

When the gallons of Orange Crush Otter had drunk started knocking in his bladder, he excused himself. The restroom walls were lined with playbills for bands all across town, dozens of them. He felt a moment of terror. Dozens of bands he'd never heard of. How many had recording deals? How many were local teenagers just like him, trying to get a start? How many were established touring acts making big bucks and swimming in groupies? This realization put a tiny puncture in his Balloon of Tonight's Glory.

Tonight was only the beginning.

But it *was* a beginning.

Heading back to the table, he ran into Marvin in the short hallway to the restroom.

"Hey, Mike," Marvin said, "can I have a quick word? Man to man?"

The surprising gravitas of Marvin's voice brought Otter up short. "Sure."

Marvin's voice was deep and powerful, unstoppable. "Lika tells me you're not going to school."

"Uh, not this year, no."

"Why not?"

"I have to pay my bills. Got a job."

"You're too young to work during school hours. The law says you're supposed to be in school."

Otter sighed. "I know."

"Then tell me what's up with you. Maybe I can help."

"I'm my own man now. Mom taught me how, before she died." Anger rose up in his voice.

"Not according to the law, you're not. You're still a kid, emancipated or not."

Otter looked past him for an escape route, his muscles tensing.

"Look, I get it," Marvin said. "You've lost everything. You're trying to keep your head up, just like you did when your mom was dying. But there's people that want to help you."

"Yeah, like that bitch from the government trying to put me in foster care." He clamped down on the gust of anger, glancing sheepishly at Marvin. "She even hit me with her car."

Marvin's eyebrows rose. "She hit you with her car?"

"Bam! Right in the ditch. Groceries everywhere. You think I'm going to let her anywhere near me?"

"I'm sure it was an accident—"

"My ass!" It was disrespectful talking to Marvin that way, but Otter's blood was simmering. "She just didn't want me to get away. Ran me right into the ditch. No way am I going into foster care with her calling the shots. I hear the stories. About brothers and sister torn apart and stuck in separate homes. About people taking in kids just for the welfare money and then abusing them."

"Those are just a few stories, a few bad apples. I've met some foster parents. Most of them really are good people who want to help because they love kids and can't have any of their own."

"A few bad apples spoil the barrel, though, right?" With challenge in his eyes, he met Marvin's gaze.

"Now, just a minute—"

"You think any of those people would give a damn about making sure I got here tonight? About the fact that this is who I am? Can you guarantee they wouldn't try to beat it out of me and jam me into some 'sensible' life, like my boss? Can you?"

"No, I can't, but here's the thing, Mike." He bent over and looked Otter in the eye. "If it's really who you are, and you're one hundred percent committed to it, *nobody* can beat it out of you. They can make your path rocky for a while, but if it's truly who you are, *nobody* can stop you. Now, you want to hear something really counterintuitive?"

"Yeah, what?" Otter sounded like a sullen little kid and chided himself for it.

"It takes a strong man to accept help. Some people think the world is full of people looking for free stuff, that everybody wants a handout. They're wrong. It takes strength to know when you need a leg up, and even more strength to accept it. And here's the thing. You get yourself straightened up, standing up, then you can turn around and help the next person. That's how you pay back the help you got." Marvin paused as if to let this sink in. "You got a lot of strength, kid. But pride is getting in your way. And that lady from Human Services, she'll be back."

"You know her?" Otter narrowed his eyes.

"I know enough."

"What am I supposed to do? Leave my house? Walk away from me and Mom's place?"

"Being a man means sometimes you got to do the hard thing. The first step is getting your butt to school. It's not too late. All other decisions stem from there. They have programs where you can get free school lunch. At least you'll get one square meal a day. Let me guess, you're eating peanut butter sandwiches and pork and beans out of a can."

"Ramen noodles are cheaper." Otter lowered his head sheepishly.

"That's all I got to say. There's people want to help you. You just got to have the strength to ask."

Otter said, "Okay, sir. Thanks."

"Okay then." Then Marvin went into the restroom, allowing Otter to walk back to the table deep in thought, strangely admiring Marvin's well-timed ambush. At least Marvin hadn't chewed Otter out in front of everybody, in front of Lika and Amber.

He resumed his seat, quiet. Lika gave him a long look that said she knew the ambush had been coming and wanted to know if he was okay. He gave her a faint smile.

An hour passed, with more musicians coming and going, more rounds of drinks, patrons coming and going. At some point he noticed Zeke had gone.

At about 10:30, Chrissie looked at Amber and said, "Well, honey, I hate to be the buzzkill, but I have a twelve-hour shift starting in about an hour."

This was the droplet that formed the dispersion. They all went to their stack of instruments along the back wall.

Otter looked around with an awful sense of dread forming in his belly. "Hey, guys?" he said, with alarm growing in his voice and panic tightening a fist around his heart. "Um, where's my guitar?"

They searched the bar for fifteen minutes. They questioned the staff, patrons, and other musicians. They looked outside. As Chrissie had to go to work, Amber gave him a look of fearful, forlorn sympathy.

Otter's guitar was gone.

The bartender had seen nothing. The patrons had seen nothing. The other musicians expressed sympathy at Otter's panic but were busy with their own sets and instruments.

Seeing the growing sense of panic in his bandmates' eyes made his own worse. Without his guitar, they had no bassist for their first gig in just one week.

The certainty that someone had stolen it settled in long before he gave up searching. There was no other way it would have just disappeared. Finally, the moment came when all he could do was stand on the sidewalk alone, weaving, with his chin on his chest and knees trembling and shoulders sagging, his breath a faint wheeze.

From exuberance to annihilation in twenty minutes flat.

His guitar was gone.

And with it, all hope.

He vaguely remembered Lika hugging him, her parents telling him everything would be okay, the Lord would provide. Toby looked horrified, too, perhaps imagining how he would feel if someone stole his guitar.

Lika pressed the guitar pick back into his hand and squeezed. "For luck, right?"

He sighed and tucked it into his pocket.

Mostly everyone seemed to feel as hopeless as Otter. But they didn't feel the violation. A chunk of himself had been wrested away.

Down dark streets and trash-strewn alleys, every wobble of his bicycle wheel became a chorus squeaking *Failure! Loser!*

No way could he afford to buy even a cheap, used bass guitar by Friday. With three, maybe four paychecks he could buy a used one. But he wouldn't be spending any money on food or bills during that time.

And that was the guitar his mother had given him. Another piece of her was gone now, too.

He would have no choice but to let the band down. They would be a no-show at their first-ever gig because their bassist was stupid enough to let his guitar be stolen. He should have had it beside him, welded to his thigh. He should have been paying attention. He shouldn't have had his eyes glued to Amber.

He was too stupid to be allowed to live.

If he ever found the bastard or bastards who did it, he would set Odin's Warriors upon them. He imagined Duke, Smiley, and Jacko going full barbarian on the thief, plus himself battering the thief with fists, tire-iron, two-by-four, baseball bat, and then finishing off with a few solid kicks to the head. Then he remembered the effect violence had had on Grandpa, and all he could do was sigh deeper.

All the way home, the oscillating fury and self-recrimination drove away even thoughts of how stunningly beautiful Amber had been tonight. When he walked in the door of the trailer, everything was simply blackness. He restrained the urge to smash things. He didn't have that much stuff to smash.

Tears of rage and helplessness filled his eyes as he collapsed into the sofa. Those thoughts ultimately gave way to memories of how amazing tonight had felt. Weed and alcohol were nothing compared to this kind of rush, because he was *in* the moment, fully alive, and throbbing with the music. To be able to do that for the rest of his life, he would be the happiest man alive.

The song of crickets rode the breeze through the open screens, fluttering curtains with the moist scent of night.

The cardboard box on the floor beckoned to him.

But the last thing he had touched had brought him the knowledge that his biological father was an abusive wastoid. His mother had been right to excise the guy from their lives. But how far could the apple fall from the tree? How could a good tree grow from a bad seed?

Maybe he deserved all the misfortune that could be heaped upon him. No.

He had a greater destiny than this.

He pulled the box close, braced himself, and reached inside.

PART IV

DARK SIDE OF THE MOON

CHAPTER THIRTY-FIVE
DO RIGHT WOMAN, DO RIGHT MAN

What he held was a palm-sized dial that showed the constellations visible from the northern hemisphere. An interior dial windowed the sky by time of day, and another dial adjusted by month. The other side of the disc looked like a polished chrome medallion, embossed with "Planetary Society" and all the planets orbiting the sun.

He fiddled with the dials but couldn't make much out of the constellations except the Big Dipper and Orion—he could always find those—nevertheless, he marveled at the device's detail and intricacy. It had weight in his palm. He fancied himself a pirate, using such a device for navigation on the high seas of yore.

"Yarrr, me hearties," he said.

But he was not on the deck of a sailing ship, he was under a night sky that was not a night sky. A deep, authoritative voice was talking, a voice he'd never heard before, but someone he knew was famous, one of the most famous voices in all of science.

He looked at the beautiful woman in the seat next to him, stylish wrap over a surprisingly elegant evening gown, with her thick pompadour of gentle curls, eyes bright with intelligence, a smile that had grown warmer as the day progressed. He had never seen her dressed so before. On campus, she was always so staid, so conservative, a dark-socks-and-sensible-shoes kind of woman. Tonight, however, her eyes sparkled with the wonder of their surroundings, the glittering stars projected onto the planetarium dome overhead, moving faster than any real night sky.

From the back of the room, the amplified voice of none other than Carl Sagan. Dr. Sagan was talking about the path of the soon-to-be-launched

Voyager probes, Voyager 1 to visit Jupiter and Saturn, and Voyager 2 to visit Jupiter, Saturn, Uranus, and Neptune. Both spacecraft would ultimately fling themselves, decades hence, into the vast unknown of interstellar space, mankind's first representatives to the stars. Sagan had worked closely on the project with NASA, and also oversaw the compilation of music, other recordings, and images of what humans look like embedded on the Golden Record, a message from the human race to the cosmos, a message that would travel for eons.

It had been such a surprise when Rebecca had invited him to accompany her on this trip to New York, where Carl Sagan had been scheduled to appear at the old Hayden Planetarium.

They had met when they were both PhD candidates. Attraction to her had spurred him to ask her out, but their one date had been somewhat of a disaster, with both of them buried in their work and more than a little distracted. He liked her smile and the sharpness of her intellect, and there was a knowingness in her brown eyes that had the power to arrest him.

She was the first real date he'd had since the final dissolution of his marriage with Sarah, five years before. Sarah had fought him tooth and claw on every smallest thing, offered enough credible threats of suicide that he walked on eggshells for years, terrified that she'd finally snuff herself out and leave a note that would blame it all on him for not loving her enough. He was still paying alimony, deeply in debt, his spirit pinched tight by financial worries.

At the end of the night, he and Rebecca were each more annoyed than charmed with each other. He'd tried to kiss her, but she'd turned away.

They'd remained friends, completed their doctorates, and said goodbye. Until one of those moments when fate seemed to intervene. Two years later—or two weeks ago, time was fluid—they ran into each other at a conference on science and the humanities at Harvard, had a drink, and hit if off in ways that must have been impossible the first time. They spent the last two days of the conference attending presentations in each other's company, even though those presentations were not in their fields.

At the conference, Rebecca acquired tickets for a talk by Carl Sagan at the Hayden Planetarium in Manhattan, sponsored by the Planetary Society, and asked him to go with her. The invitation was a surprise and yet felt completely natural.

As he sat beside her in the planetarium, the wonders of the universe spiraling above, his eyes kept turning to her. He didn't feel the same desperate yearning like he'd felt with Marina, or the bittersweet warmth of Yoko's truncated kiss. For the first time in his life, he was caught by a woman's gravitational attraction and no obstacles stood in the way. She was a blue-green jewel and he was a jagged asteroid flung across the solar system, scarred by meteor impacts, coming to circle her. Perhaps, this time, he wouldn't burn up.

Rebecca's cool intelligence and sanguine temperament made him feel like they were two photons coming into harmony to make a laser beam. The wild, edgy passion that had so long ago attracted him to Sarah felt like anathema now. Now, he wanted a *woman,* not a girl.

And here she was.

When the lights came up again and Sagan took his place at the front lectern, his talk of planets and the universe evoked an expansive sense of majesty.

Donovan bought Rebecca this Planetary Society medallion after the talk. Twenty-nine years later, she died on a Wednesday morning after teaching her first class of the day. He carried the medallion in his jacket pocket for a year afterward.

On the day of Grandma's funeral, once again Otter and the triplets had been left to play and let the adults do the grieving. His sparse memories of her, however, merged with the quietly brilliant woman sitting beside him in the planetarium, this woman who made him feel like a prince among men, this woman who'd pushed him to write the books that would make his name known, at least among aficionados and scholars of Japanese history.

They had been two independent celestial bodies that slowly fell into each other's orbits, rather than flaming meteors crashing into each other, obliterating what they used to be. It took longer, but the bonds of gravity were stronger and less destructive than simple animal attraction.

Knowledge of this, understanding of this, settled into Otter's bones.

Amber was a meteor, a shooting star upon which wishes were born, flaming bright and leaving a streak of shimmering brilliance behind her, inspiring, enthralling, but destructive to anything in her path.

This knowledge, however, did not break the spell. The heart held sway over the brain, and he wondered if that would ever go away, or if he was an asteroid about to fall into the sun.

CHAPTER THIRTY-SIX
UNDER PRESSURE

Otter awoke from a fitful sleep, a night filled with indifferent women and hungry shadows.

His first thought was *I need to get a guitar.*

He didn't often achieve verticalness before noon these days, but he had no time to waste. He knew roughly what bass guitars cost, but maybe he would get lucky and find something that would get him through the Black Line gig, and then he could use the proceeds from that gig to buy a good one.

He rolled up to Big Jimmy's Pawn and walked in.

Big Jimmy said, "Hey, kid. What are you selling today?"

"I might be buying today."

Otter stood under the instruments hanging from the wall. A couple of saxophones, a banjo, a mix of acoustic and electric six-strings. And one bass guitar—a Fender Jazz, two-tone whiskey sunburst. The paint was a little scratched, and the Jazz model offered a different mix of sound than the Precision like his, which predominated with rock guitarists, but it was still a professional axe.

Real professional indeed, said the five-hundred-dollar price tag. With what Otter had in his pocket, he might be able to afford a cigar box with a broom handle and fishing line for strings.

He didn't know how long he stood there before Big Jimmy wheezed, "Got your eye on something?"

"This bass here. Somebody stole mine. I need one for our show on Friday."

Big Jimmy chuckled. "You got a show, do ya?"

Otter bristled. "Yeah, we got a show. We played one last night and brought the house down. Until some lowlife walked away with my bass. In fact, if some scumbag comes in here with a candy apple red Fender Precision, it's stolen."

"I'll keep an eye out," Big Jimmy said, but his tone told Otter he wouldn't.

"So you take payments on this one here?"

"Yeah, I take payments. One."

"Come on, man, can't you work with me? I can give you fifty bucks today and the rest next week after our show."

"Not a chance. What do you think this is, a bank? Besides, I got ten people looking at that very guitar on eBay. It'll be gone by Friday and I'll get full price for it."

Otter wanted to argue more, but Big Jimmy had never shown a hint of altruism. What he showed regularly was a short fuse. Otter wrote his phone number on the back of a business card from the counter. "Remember, if you see a Fender bass, candy apple red…" He handed it over.

Big Jimmy grunted and tucked the card into his sweaty breast pocket.

Otter had time before work to go home and inventory the things he might sell.

His mom's stereo and all her CDs. A waffle iron and a food processor, neither of which he had a clue how to use. The beat up old acoustic six-string. He might get ten bucks for that from someone who was blind and deaf. A TV that was older than his mom. His mom's bedroom furniture probably had some value, but he had no way to transport it. Maybe he could go to the library today and put it all up for sale on the internet. He'd heard of websites for that kind of thing. If he could unload *everything* by this weekend, would all of it, everything he owned, add up to five hundred dollars?

He searched the yellow pages and called all the guitar stores in town, inquiring about their stock and asking them to be on the lookout for a stolen candy apple red Fender Precision.

The time to leave for work came faster than expected. He caught Zeke out front of his house polishing his Harley.

Zeke looked even more tired than last night. "Hey, Otter." His voice was a little hoarse, his eyes red-rimmed and dull.

"You getting sick?" Otter said.

"Probably."

"Stay away from me then. Say, you didn't happen to see a low-down, dirty, shit-stain walk off with my guitar last night, did you?"

Zeke kept rubbing the chrome on his mirror with a dingy rag. "I sure didn't. Somebody stole your guitar?"

"Yeah, and if I catch 'em…"

"Good luck, man. I can't imagine who would do such a thing. You guys really rocked it last night."

"Thanks." Otter had expected more sympathetic outrage from Zeke, but maybe Zeke was just tired. He looked like he hadn't slept since the grunge band era. Lika's information about Odin's Warriors percolated into Otter's consciousness. "Hey, uh, about Tuesday night."

Zeke lit a cigarette and took a long drag. "What about it?"

"I don't know if I can make it."

Zeke's eyes flashed and his voice went hard. "You can't back out now. We need you there."

"But there wasn't much for me to do, and I have to find another guitar."

"You can't let us down now." There was something threatening in his voice, an unwillingness to take "no" for an answer.

"Well—"

"You want to hang with the big dogs, right?"

"I know but, last week was…kinda boring." If Duke and Baby really were leading some kind of white supremacist gang, they might not appreciate being called out on it. Then again, the very idea of it made him queasy.

"We can sure spice it up for you," Zeke said. "You said you wanted to learn some fighting moves, right?"

Otter crossed his arms and frowned. "Yeah, actually I do."

"We can show you how to *really* mess somebody up." Zeke loomed over Otter, his bloodshot gaze drilling into Otter's courage. "We're pretty good at that."

Otter gulped. "I don't doubt it."

Zeke backed off, reassuming his friendly demeanor. "There you go. We'll get you set up. Maybe I can get Duke to come and pick you up."

Otter wasn't sure how he could refuse. Zeke had never steered him wrong before. He owed a lot to Zeke. Without him, Otter might not have gotten through the darkest weeks after Mom's death. And he did want to learn some of Duke's moves. The guy looked like he had a few. Maybe Lika was wrong. Otter could look up Odin's Warriors for himself at the library, maybe tomorrow, but right now, he had to get to the car wash. "Well, okay then."

After a thankfully drama-free shift at the car wash, Otter came home to find Imelda sitting on her deck, smoking one of those thin, funny-smelling, brown cigarettes and reading the Spanish version of a supermarket gossip magazine. She greeting him with a motherly smile, and he waved back. As soon as he rolled to a wobbly stop between their houses, he couldn't help but see the graffiti again. A breath exploded from his nostrils. Outrage on her behalf welled up again.

He stood there gazing at it for a while, racking his brain for ways to erase it. It seemed more important now, somehow.

A couple of minutes passed, then Imelda said, "You see something, *mijo*?"

He kicked the gravel. "Nah, I'm just trying to think of some way to get rid of it without having to paint the whole house. Whoever did this is a real scumbag." He'd been using that word a lot today, scumbag, both internally and externally.

"Don't worry. I'll fix it someday. Today, I see only weakness and feel sorry for them. You had a show last night?"

"Yeah! It was amazing, awesome, and fantastic! Except for the last part." He shook his head in disgust. "Some butt stain stole my guitar."

"No!"

"Yeah, they yanked it right from under everybody's nose."

"Your mama gave you that *guitarra*!"

He nodded sadly.

"So what you gonna do for the show on Friday?"

"Miss it, maybe. I dunno. I'll try to figure something out this week. I have a few days."

"Oh, *mijo*." She sighed and looked at him with thoughtful eyes full of sadness and sympathy. "I tell you a story."

He crossed his arms. He didn't have time for this; he sensed she was picking up momentum.

"When I was a little girl," she said, "in my village in Guatemala, a man had much bad luck. Like you. His wife got sick and died. Jaguar eat his *puerca*. Snake take his chickens. He lose his job because he fall and break his leg. Everybody feel terrible for him, because he was a nice man, a good man. But he was a proud man. He never ask for help. His family all gone. He tell no one he had no money to buy food. He get thin and thinner. People see this, they collect money to buy him some food and a pig. They take it to him, but he was dead." She pantomimed a noose, head cocked sideways, and stuck out her tongue.

"He was kind of stupid, wasn't he," Otter said.

She planted her hands on her hips and raised her eyebrow with a pointed look.

"Okay, okay, I get your point."

"*Mijo,* everybody need help sometimes."

He swallowed hard and released a long breath, shoving his hands in his pockets. "I could use more than help right now." His voice cracked. "Maybe a miracle."

"Miracles come sometimes," she said, her voice soothing, motherly.

Then he remembered what Marvin had told him at Ziggy's about strength and asking for help. He took a deep breath and swallowed something that was bigger than he needed. "Can you help me, Imelda? Please?" He sighed, tried to shrug some tension out of his shoulders, gave her a faint smile. "If you run across a bass guitar by the side of the road, grab it for me, would you please?"

She winked.

CHAPTER THIRTY-SEVEN
MESSAGE IN A BOTTLE

That night he spruced up his ramen noodles with a couple slices of white bread wadded up into little balls like dumplings. He needed a little variety, but his attempt at sprucing up resulted only in soggy lumps in his broth.

"Chalk that one up in the Let's Not Do Again column," he said.

As he ate, he roamed the kitchen and living room, bowl in hand, looking for things to sell. Maybe he could take the old, beat up six-string to a busy street corner and try his hand at busking. But he felt really rusty playing a six-string. Bass was where he'd put all his attention the last couple of years.

The fear of letting his bandmates down gnawed at him. How could he ever face Lika again if he couldn't make this show? Last night, she had gone beyond simply playing drums and singing. She had been *transformed*. Maybe they all had. Something had come together and raised them above what they were. How it had happened he could not fathom, but the second biggest question now was: Could they do it again?

The biggest question was, of course: Could he get another guitar by Friday?

The cardboard box sat on the sofa, open from last night's expedition into Grandpa's life. Otter was still trying to get used to the weird, dissociated feeling of stepping into the movie of someone's life and having those experiences somehow fall into sync or become absorbed with his own memories.

Had he absorbed any of Grandpa's martial arts skills? He assumed a fighting stance and let loose with a couple of punches.

He was starting to feel like he understood his grandfather like no one else had.

A strange thought hit him then. Misty was the last of her family. Both of her parents were dead. Her elder brother was dead. Her younger sister was dead. Even her first husband was dead. What must that be like?

It really was great that the triplets had come to the show. He hoped they could make it to the Black Line. If there was going to be a Black Line.

Tomorrow the search would continue. Maybe a bass guitar would parachute out of a passing airplane. Maybe Grandpa's box held an artifact that would lead him to a trove of buried pirate treasure.

He closed his eyes and reached.

His fingers found a small, glass bottle, slightly dusty, the size of his hand, in which lay a three-masted sailing ship that looked like one of the ships Columbus sailed. The bottle was attached to a faux-wooden base that read *Portuguese Carrack* in English under some writing in Japanese.

The ship was incredibly detailed in its rigging and hull, a replica of the first European trading ships that visited Japan before the shogunate closed the country against foreign trade and influence. He found himself fascinated by how it had gotten into the bottle. He had haggled with the *obasan* over the price, more to practice his Japanese than to get a bargain. Her mouth had tightened when she saw him come in wearing his Army uniform. He was visiting the naval base at Sasebo, Japan, and took a couple of days of leave to visit Nagasaki.

In a meticulously wrapped package, he took his purchase outside into the relentless winter chill, the kind that seeped into one's bones with the wet sea air. Seagulls floated and bobbed above his head on the narrow streets, and the smells of the sea brushed clammy fingers across his face.

Established in the 1600s, an enclave of Dutch traders had existed on the tiny "island" of Dejima, a patch of land large enough for a few modest buildings. Today, it had been swallowed by reclaimed land and surrounded by sea-water canals. Donovan's feet took him past Dejima, an architectural non sequitur of Renaissance era Dutch buildings in the heart of Nagasaki, and into Chinatown where Chinese New Year was in full swing. Thousands of red lanterns bathed the streets and throngs in warm festivity. A raucous cacophony of gongs and firecrackers erupted from a nearby street. Rich aromas of *dim sum* and roasting pork set his stomach roaring. Brilliantly hued banners fluttered in the sea breeze bearing prayers for good fortune, health, prosperity, and early spring.

He could not help but think of Marina. His ribs had healed but his heart had not. What might she be doing now? This was his first trip to Japan, and he loved it. He loved being here, immersed in two thousand years of history that was evident everywhere he went. It was a land of ancient castles, quiet forest shrines, full of kind, industrious people that treated him like an honored guest, even though their relationship with the American military was uneasy and full of friction. Nagasaki and Hiroshima, even though they had been completely rebuilt, were still bleeding wounds in the Japanese psyche.

The succulent aroma of grilled pork from a street vendor soon filled his hands with a paper bag of hot skewers, which he munched as he marveled at the breathtaking beauty of the lanterns, allowing the joy of the atmosphere to seep into him. Some of the lanterns were fashioned into images of animals and Buddhas, but most were brilliant scarlet globes. Chinese music found its way through the tumult of gongs and fireworks.

As much as he wanted to, he could not remain here amid the joy of celebration. He had one more place to visit today. The Japan Rail Line took him a couple of stops north to Matsuyamamachi Station. From there, it was only a couple of blocks to Ground Zero, the site at which the world's second atomic weapon, the plutonium bomb called "Fat Man," detonated about sixteen hundred feet above the city.

On the ground was a series of concentric rings, like a great bull's-eye, with a stone memorial in the center. At the edge of the ring stood a charred brick column, a ragged remnant of the blast left standing as a memorial to destruction.

How many people had been poisoned by radioactivity in the years following the attack? How many genetic mutations and cancers had sickened this now thriving city? But even if the damage had been repaired, the atomic specter still remained, like a human shadow burned into a brick wall, absorbed into the air, water, and land itself. The people here lived with the specter, slept with it, ate it, drank it.

He sat down on one of the concrete rings circling the epicenter of the blast crater.

How many rads of radiation would he have absorbed if he had sat here after the blast, surrounded by rubble? How many was he absorbing now? Would he now develop cancer at some unforeseen, future date? Locals still talked bitterly of cancer and other radiation-related illnesses.

Portuguese traders had brought firearms to Japan in 1543, turning Nagasaki into one of the chief conduits for the flow of European firearms into Japan. Americans had brought atomic bombs in 1945, turning Nagasaki into smoking ruin and killing as many as 75,000 people in a single, civilization-changing flash of heat and destruction. Had the bomb been delivered on target, on the city center, rather than a mile and a half to the northwest, the death toll would have been vastly higher. Such callous numbers in the face of destruction and suffering.

He sat on the concrete circle and wept for the tens of thousands of instantaneous dead, each of whom lived lives as rich and full of joy and sorrow and love and imagination as his, and he wept for the tens of thousands who died of radiation sickness, burns, and later, cancer, in the months and years afterward—men, women, children.

Even in the shadow of catastrophe, however, humans could find celebration. How the city had recovered, seemingly so completely after only twenty years, was a marvel, a testament to their resilience and determination to rebuild, to endure, in the face of the worst destruction the human race had ever wrought.

As he mused on these things, Otter's stomach knotted like a sour rope, and his breath shuddered in and out.

Suddenly his life didn't seem so bad.

He wasn't living in radioactive rubble, drinking poisoned water, eating poisoned food, and suffering from burns that would scar his body until he died of cancer, or exposed to radiation that would liquefy his organs from the inside, with his entire family and everyone he knew wiped from existence by a white-hot mushroom cloud.

Sure, he'd lost his mom. Sure, he'd lost his grandfather. Sure, he'd lost his guitar. But he still had some family left. He still had friends. He had safe food and water and a messy but still-safe house to sleep in.

A missing guitar seemed much less catastrophic now after what he had just experienced, but it made him all the more determined to find another one by Friday.

He lay back on the sofa, the ship-in-the-bottle cradled in his hands, and thought about how to do that until the world went black and he dreamed of pulling Lika out of the radioactive rubble, seeing Amber in the distance and being unable to reach her. He saw his mother with horrendous burns and cried for her, but she smiled and told him everything would be okay. He believed her, because she was Mom. And then he set about picking up hot bricks and stacking them, until morning light crept through the closed blinds and under his eyelids.

Then a heavy fist pounded on the front door. A woman's voice called, "This is the Sheriff's Department. Open up, please."

CHAPTER THIRTY-EIGHT
DESPERADO

Otter sat bolt upright with a gasp.

The woman repeated, "This is the Sheriff's Department. Open up."

His sleep-fogged brain cast about as he stumbled to his blanket-tangled feet. Mrs. Pritt had brought the cops this time. He had to get out of here before they busted through the door.

The curtains and blinds were closed. Stealing across the floor, avoiding the creaky spots, he peeked through a crack between the curtains. In the street were a county sheriff cruiser and the beige sedan of his nemesis, Louisa Pritt.

Voices were outside.

"His bicycle is here," a man said.

"He must be inside," Mrs. Pritt shrilled. "He's not at school, and he's not a work. I'm going to see that the court takes charge of him. You have to go in and get him!"

"Let us handle this, Louisa," said the woman.

Otter's brain whirled. If he could make it to the trees behind the house, he might evade their notice. He tiptoed down the hallway toward the back door. An outside shadow fell upon the curtained window beside him, and through the glass he could hear footsteps moving through the weeds along the side of the trailer house. Another cop less than three feet away.

Otter's heart leaped into his throat, pounding in his ears.

The shadow fell upon the frosted glass of the back door. The doorknob twisted and rattled, locked.

Where could he go?

Beside the washing machine and dryer was a closet. In that closet was a trapdoor to the crawlspace under the trailer house.

The shadow at the door paused, as if listening. Otter froze, holding his breath. His thighs felt like cold spaghetti. The walls on this trailer house were paper thin. The cop could probably punch his way through the door if he wanted to.

Could Otter get the closet door and then the trap door open without the cop outside hearing?

The doorknob rattled again, the walls shaking.

In that moment of noise, Otter seized the closet door and swung it open. He knelt and peeled back the square of carpet covering the trapdoor. The trapdoor was a simple square of thick plywood set in the floor. He pried the door open with his fingernails as quietly as he could.

The shadow remained in place, head cocked.

The trapdoor opening was a solid mass of cobwebs, but there was no time to cringe. He dropped to his belly and lowered himself into spider- and rodent-infested blackness. Then he hooked the bottom of the closet door with his finger, pulling it closed. Oh, so gently, as silently as he could manage. Then he eased the plywood into place above him.

The crawlspace under the house was tall enough for him to crawl on his hands and knees. Daylight seeped through cracks in the plywood skirt that surrounded the base of the trailer. The cool air smelled of earth, cobwebs, and mouse droppings.

The cop on the back step was still only six feet away from him, so he remained still, listening, allowing his eyes to adjust to the darkness. His heartbeat was so loud the cop could not help but hear it.

Finally, after what seemed interminable hours, the cop moved away from the door and continued a circuit of the house. The sound of feet in the grass were easy to follow through the plywood skirt.

By now he could see the cinder-block pillars supporting the house's floor. He wended his way between them, bright lines of daylight peeking through cracks in the skirt.

His hand went into something cold, wet, and squishy, and it stank of something he couldn't identify. His clamped his teeth against a cry of disgust and yanked his hand back, clunking the back of his head against a floor joist. Pain seared through scalp and skull.

"Did you hear that?" someone said.

He put his head down and hurried past the swampy spot. His hand reeked. His head throbbed. He put his head down, squeezing his lips against any peep, and rubbed the spot with his cleaner hand. The other was covered in stinky goop.

He was near the front door now, and voices filtered in from outside.

Mrs. Pritt's voice said, "Can't you just go in and get him? He's not the only child who needs help in this town."

"Look, Louisa, I'm here as a favor to you," the female deputy said. "We don't have a warrant, and we don't have probable cause."

"He's all alone. He'll be homeless by Halloween," Louisa Pritt said.

"I understand you really want to help this kid, but we can't just bash the door down. This isn't a TV show."

"What kind of warrant do you need?"

"Has he committed a crime?"

"Perhaps something can be arranged," Pritt said.

He ground his teeth. Screw that awful bitch! She'd frame him rather than leave him alone.

"I didn't hear that," the deputy said. "Come on, Dalton. Louisa, I've got the photo. We'll keep an eye out for him."

Otter swept a patch of earth free of clods and cobwebs, then rolled onto his back and lay down, resting his head on his arm, rubbing his other hand free of slime on the dirt next to him, allowing his breath to slacken, his heartbeat to dial back from stampede mode.

An engine started, and a car drove away. Just one car.

Here in the shadows and foundations, amid the cobwebs and mouse crap, Otter listened.

Footsteps crunched in the gravel and came up to the house. It had to be Pritt. She stepped up to the wall, paused, moved, paused. Probably trying to peek in the windows. But he had shut all the blinds and curtains a long time ago.

For at least ten minutes she circled and peeked, circled and peeked. Otter didn't move. He just lay there in the cool darkness, enjoying her frustration, and wondering what would have to happen for her to leave him alone.

Would it be so bad going to live with Aunt Misty? Could he withstand a year or two before he got out of there and came back to his own place? This house would still be here. Home wreck home. But it was *his*, and he still didn't trust Aunt Misty. Mom had abandoned the family for a good reason. He just wished he knew what it was.

Maybe the answer was in the box. The latest wooziness that seemed to come with the most intense of the box's memories had faded, perhaps broken by the stark excitement of having the cops on his doorstep. But he couldn't just go touching everything in the box all at once. A flood of memories and emotions like that would drive him insane. The contents of that box were to be sipped, not guzzled.

Lying here in the cool darkness let the tension seep from his shoulders into the ground. He might have dozed.

Until he realized that he had not heard Pritt's car start. She was still here somewhere.

He crawled to the nearest crack in the skirt and peered out toward where her car had been parked, catching a glimpse of a beige fender. He couldn't see if she was inside the car.

Then he heard her voice, right on top him. "I know you're in there, Michael."

Good grief, she was like a snake hunting mice, utterly still until she struck. Then her feet moved away across the gravel toward her car.

The fact that she was so close for so long and he had no clue chilled him.

A cool breeze blew through the cracks in the skirt, bringing with it the smell of rain. That's when he noticed the sky had gone deep gray.

He made his way back to the trapdoor. She could sit out there all day if she wanted to. He was going to have a sandwich.

CHAPTER THIRTY-NINE
BETTE DAVIS EYES

L ika pinned the last of her posters on the school bulletin boards, then stepped back to examine her handiwork.

The Wrong Decades
Starring Toby, Amber, Otter, & Lika
@ The Black Line
Friday at 8:00 p.m.
All Ages Show

With some basic software on her mother's computer, Lika had assembled the poster from a montage of cell phone photos showing each of the members. No one knew their band name, so she wanted their friends and other kids from school to recognize them.

It looked official, professional. It made them real.

She caught herself smiling.

"Wow!" Amber said, coming up behind her. "That's a great poster. Did you do that?"

Lika stiffened and looked over her shoulder. The grudge reared up in her stomach. Even after the success of Saturday night, Lika still had a few choice words about Amber's treatment of Mike. But how to deliver them without fracturing the band? "I did, thanks."

"You're real talented in so many ways."

"Thanks."

"So, um, have lunch with me today?"

Lika faced her. Even before the ongoing romantic mess, she and Amber had never hung out together at school. Amber always seemed to be basking in the attention of five to ten adoring males. The trouble was, her male entourage often included a few other girls' boyfriends. This made her somewhat unpopular with those of the female persuasion. Today, though, her expression was downcast, her hands clasped in front of her, moving with a weighted sluggishness. Lika shrugged. "Okay."

As they walked toward the lunch room, Amber said, "Are you nervous about Friday?"

"Depends on what minute you ask me. A minute ago, I was fine. Now that you made me think about it, though…"

"Yeah, me, too." Amber smiled, and her eyes sparkled.

"I mean, last Saturday night felt so…so…perfect. Like we'd been performing onstage for years."

Amber's voice grew dreamy. "Like we stepped outside of ourselves and into older, more experienced selves."

"That's a little weird, but yeah, kinda like that. It was a huge rush." Lika would never forget the way the energy and confidence had swelled in her with each song.

"Yeah, that's what worries me."

"Worries you? Why?"

"It was *so* good, *so* perfect, that now I'm kinda terrified we won't be able to do it again. Everybody was spot on. Especially you, Lika. You knocked 'Respect' into orbit."

Lika flushed warm. "Thanks."

"But on Friday, we're going to have a lot bigger audience. Thanks to your flaming-good posters, there's going to be kids from school there. So… what if we can't do it again? What if it all falls apart?"

"What if our bass player can't get a guitar?" Lika didn't like casting doubt on Mike, but he was in a difficult situation with no visible means of getting himself out of it.

Amber's shoulders slumped. "That, too. Gee, thanks for the fresh stress."

"Sorry. It's been on my mind."

Amber looked at Lika for a long moment, as if considering carefully what to say next. They entered the cafeteria, where eyes noted this new social development. "So what do we do if we're short a bass player?"

"He'll come through."

"But what if he doesn't."

Lika's voice hardened like quick-set concrete. "He'll come through."

"You're right. He's a stand-up guy."

Despite the missing guitar, Amber had to be thinking about what to do about Otter's feelings for her, at least at some level, but she was a wall, a mask. Would it do any good to ask Amber about what happened in the park, about the song, about her feelings for Otter, or the lack thereof? Or would she just come across as a busybody? Maybe she would just see how this played out.

An unoccupied end of a table beckoned, and Lika steered them toward it. She had told Otter she had a kind of girl crush on Amber, and those feelings were creeping up the back of her neck. Amber was gorgeous, sexy, and incredibly talented. The kind of person who made one think *Am I good enough to hang with her?* Lika was just…herself, a regular girl from the 'burbs, who played drums and sang in church sometimes. Amber even smelled good, like jasmine and vanilla on a spring day.

As they seated themselves and pulled out their sack lunches, Lika noticed some of the girls sniffed with disdain. Amber unzipped her backpack, and Lika spotted something written on it in thick, red marker, then scribbled out. Still barely legible, the red marker scrawled *DIRTY SLUT.*

Lika tried to be discreet about it, but Amber caught her glance. "People are awful sometimes," Amber said. "Somebody got hold of it while I was in P.E. last week."

"That sucks. I'm sorry."

Amber shrugged, but Lika could see that it ate at her. "Have you heard the rumors?"

"What rumors?"

"That I'm the new School S.T.D. Queen." A flash of anger put an edge in Amber's voice.

Lika said, "Like you said, people suck sometimes." But even as she empathized with Amber's pain, she couldn't help wondering if it were true. For all the times they had rehearsed and performed together, Lika barely knew this girl. At fifteen, Amber exuded the sex appeal of a twenty-something woman. She knew only that Amber had been stringing her best friend along for weeks and flaunting her relationships with other guys in front of him. She'd never forget the pain on Mike's face that night in the park, and she hadn't quite forgiven Amber for it.

Amber's face started to crumble, just for an instant, then she sniffed, wiped her nose, collected herself, and pulled out a sandwich. "That douchebag Colton. That one's his."

"That rumor?"

"Yeah. He lusted after me for weeks. We dated a couple of times, then when I wouldn't put out, he started telling everyone I'd given him the clap."

"What an asshole!" Lika said, and she meant it, but a little voice in the back of her head was also saying, *Then maybe you should have better taste in who you hang out with.*

Amber opened her mouth to say something else, but her eyes misted over with memory of pain greater than rumors could generate.

Guilt washed over Lika at her quickness to judge. Some boy had done something bad to Amber, something really bad, and no one else had a clue.

"Did you call the police?" Lika said.

"Are you kidding?" Horror bloomed on Amber's features, then she clamped her mouth shut for several long moments, scrutinizing her untouched lunch. "I can't put myself through that. Colton's the wide receiver on a championship football team. I'm the new girl in school. You do that math."

"Does your mom know?"

"I can't put her through that again…"

"Again?" Lika said.

"I used to go to West." Then Amber clammed up.

Deductions clicked in Lika mind. Amber had left West because her school had become too toxic for her, probably because of a boy. A boy who had gone too far.

Amber tried to force some brightness into her voice, but didn't quite get there. "If Mom knew, she'd hunt Colton down and slice his Achilles tendons, and then she'd go to jail and I'd be stuck in foster care. A whole tragic story."

"I think that would be a great start, the Achilles tendons," Lika said, looking across the lunchroom toward the convocation of athletes, where Colton was eating with his buddies. "You need to tell someone about this."

Amber shook her head, then shrugged. "I guess I just told you." Then she laughed bitterly, but there was deep, deep hurt in her eyes.

Lika reached across the table and squeezed Amber's hand. "Oh, girl."

"Thanks. Thanks for being my friend." Amber smiled back.

Her hand was warm in Lika's, and Lika sighed at what Amber had already gone through in her life. "Anytime." Lika's judgmental undercurrents drained away. All she saw now was a poor kid in more pain than she knew how to deal with.

Amber sniffed again, then said, half-jokingly, "Looks like it's going to be you and me, Sister. I've sworn off males for the foreseeable future." She made a shuddering sound, then laughed.

Her laugh drew Lika into a sympathetic chuckle. She could certainly see how Mike was so smitten with this girl. She had charisma to burn.

Then Lika's phone rang. It was a number she didn't know, which normally she would have let go to voicemail, but a flash of intuition spurred her to answer. "Hello?"

"Hello! Is this Lika Walker, Mikey's friend?" It was a woman's voice with a Spanish accent.

"Yes! Is something wrong?"

"This is Imelda, his neighbor."

"Oh, hi!" Lika had encountered Imelda numerous times. She was a little eccentric, but a sweet lady. "Is Mike okay?"

"His whole life is trouble, *si?* But no more than normal today."

Lika relaxed a little. "So what's up?"

"I have an idea for how to help him."

CHAPTER FORTY
REHAB

Otter thanked Odin and Thor that he didn't have to go to work today, however much he needed the money. The rain came down with a vengeance like a biblical flood. Thor's hammer smote thunderclaps across the sky.

Poring through Zeke's book on Norse myths, Otter finally reached the chapter on Ragnarok, the Twilight of the Gods, the end of the world. They were just cool stories. How could Lika be right about the Nazis using them as a rallying cry for racial purity?

He spent much of the afternoon calling all the guitar stores but found no success. Whoever had stolen his bass either still had it or had sold it to someone who wasn't talking. Big Jimmy's Fender Jazz was still the only one within reach. Several dealers offered to order him a cheap beginner model, but none of them would arrive in time.

His plan for the day had been to go to the library to see if there were any guitars to be found used on the internet, and maybe do a little digging into Odin's Warriors, but Mrs. Pritt had thwarted that plan.

The more hours that passed with her sitting outside in her car, the more he hated her.

When he finally put the mythology book down, he checked the window. With dusk drawing on, Mrs. Pritt's beige sedan had finally disappeared. His annoyance simmered. He'd been forced to sit in dim half-shadow all day long, not daring to turn on the lights and reveal his presence inside. He hated feeling like a rodent hiding in its burrow.

The ship in the bottle rested now in the middle of the kitchen table, a classy ornament, he thought, lending a nautical flair to the 1970s wood-panel decor.

He thought back about his "trip" to Nagasaki, the strange mix of horror and wonder of it, past and present like a Chinese yin-yang symbol, black and white, dark and light, Grandpa's joy at being there infused with suspicion that radiation might have given him the cancer that killed him.

"What do you got for me today, Grandpa?" he said as he reached into the cardboard box.

A red plastic keyring in the shape of a loader that read Kowalski Konstruction.

So strange to be thinking about Uncle Sal so much lately, when he'd been gone for so long. The memory of him with the baseball bat on the front seat, ready to throw down hard on somebody threatening family, was a side of him Otter had never suspected.

As he rubbed the keychain, Otter caught snatches of recollection, flashes, almost like photographs, of Misty lavishing affection on Salvatore and Sal grudgingly accepting it with a dark-eyed wink. Bursts of an ecstatic father doting over three towheaded toddlers. A happy family. Then six-year-old girls crying when he held them and told them daddy wouldn't be coming home anymore, while Misty heaved great, ragged sobs in the bathroom.

With snotty noses, pink cheeks, and streaming tears, the girls cried, they asked questions, they cried some more, all trying to feel their way to the truth of it, the finality of it. Then the sudden, horrid funeral, with Donovan supporting Misty to and from the car and Maggie trailing Misty's little blonde ducklings, hand in hand.

The memories here were more disjointed than usual, less focused, like a mirror reassembled from shattered pieces.

Otter had his own memories of Uncle Sal, a guy with a ready laugh and a good-natured chuck on the arm for the only little boy in the family.

These memories melded with his own until he lost track of whose was whose.

Only Maggie and Donovan were left to support Misty as she fell apart. Her mother was gone. Her big brother was gone. She had three kids to support. Fortunately Sal's life insurance paid off the house and the business, leaving Misty with something to live on. Without Sal to manage it, though, Kowalski Konstruction soon started to founder. Donovan had talked Misty into selling the business before it disintegrated completely.

"Dad, I need your help at Misty's," Maggie had said over the phone, sounding frustrated, frightened.

"What's going on?" he said, rolling out of bed. "It's one in the morning."

"Misty was babysitting Mikey for me, but I got here and she's…not."

"Not what?"

"Not *here!* All the kids are upstairs sleeping, but she's not here. Her car is gone."

"I'll be there in fifteen minutes."

He pulled up outside Misty's house behind Maggie's car. Misty's car was in the driveway, two wheels in the unkempt flower bed. The front door stood ajar. Harsh voices echoed through the foyer from the kitchen.

"You're such a needy whore. You've been sponging money from Dad for years for you and your illegitimate brat."

"I haven't 'sponged' a thing. I've never asked Dad for money! I work my ass off!"

"Yeah, in a *bar.* You like all those college guys hitting on you. Good Lord, you got more cleavage than I don't know what. Mom would be horrified." Misty's words slurred together, barely intelligible.

Donovan glanced around for the kids. They should all be long asleep by now. Fortunately the top of the stairs was dark and empty. He hurried into the kitchen.

"And if I'd have known I was leaving my kid with a drunk I'd have taken him to the bar with me!"

As he stood frozen for a moment at the mouth of the hallway, terrible words blasted between the two sisters, the kind that leave scars and can never be taken back.

"Hold it right there, you two," he said. His voice silenced them, drawing them apart. "What the hell is going on?"

Misty's eyes were red-rimmed, tears glossing her cheeks. A bottle of bourbon sat empty on the countertop. Another bottle of something, wrapped in a paper bag, stood next to it.

Barely controlled rage flared in Maggie's eyes, and her fists clenched at her sides. She wore a revealing black dress and high heels, her face tired, her hair a little frazzled from a long work shift.

"First of all," he said, "you should both be ashamed of yourselves for the things I just heard. You're sisters, and there are kids in the house."

"Oh, you don't know the half of it," Maggie snarled. "I come to pick up Mikey and…"

"And what?" he said.

"She'd gone to the liquor store! Already, drunk as a skunk!" She turned on Misty. "It's lucky you didn't kill somebody!"

Misty's eyes were bleary, her voice defensive. "I needed something to help me sleep."

"You *need* professional help!" Maggie said, then turned to her father. "The only reason I caught her was because they sent me home early." She yelled at Misty again. "How many times have you done this?"

Misty burst into sobbing tears. "I'm such a mess! I'm useless..."

If someone didn't prop her up right now, she was going to fall. Donovan crossed the room and wrapped her in his arms. She collapsed into him, wailing.

"I'm nothing without him!" she sobbed over and over. "Nothing, nothing..."

He murmured soothing words to her and stroked her greasy, unkempt hair.

Across the room Maggie simmered. "She needs to pull herself together. I'm not bringing Mikey back until she does. And Dad, you might want to think about having the girls come to live with you for a while."

Misty tore herself away. "You wouldn't dare!"

"I sure as hell would!" Maggie said. "You could have killed someone tonight! You could have orphaned three sleeping babies upstairs! You can't even walk a straight line! If you can't take care of yourself, how are you going to take care of your kids? Take a shower this week! Do your dishes!"

Maggie was right about the shower. And the dishes. Dirty dishes were piled high around the sink.

"Oh, listen to you talk!" Misty sneered. "You look like a hooker!"

Donovan caught Maggie's glance, and she crossed her arms. "I get better tips this way."

"Oh my god I'm gonna be sick!" Misty cupped a hand over her mouth and ran for the bathroom. The kitchen sink was too full of dishes.

Moments later, the sound of vomiting into a toilet came from nearby.

Donovan and his younger daughter shared worried glances.

"You should find a different babysitter for a while," he said.

"I can't afford to pay a babysitter until I start getting the weekend shifts when the tips are better. And we have to do something. She is *not* well."

A tremulous voice came from the bathroom. "Don't talk about me like I'm not—" Another puking heave drowned the last of her sentence.

"You deal with her," Maggie said. "I'm done being called a slut and a whore."

With that, she stalked out of the kitchen. Her footsteps thumped up the foyer stairs to the second-floor bedroom where the children slept.

He caught her coming back downstairs. "I'll babysit for a couple of weeks."

She had a sleeping seven-year-old draped half over her shoulder. Her eyes softened. "Are you sure? He's a handful."

"I'm sure. You need to make up with your sister, though."

"When she's sober, maybe I'll think about it."

"You used to be so close."

"Until I got pregnant. Ever since, she's been a holier-than-thou, judgmental bitch."

"She needs you."

"She needs something, but it isn't me."

"You're stronger than she is, and she knows it. She doesn't know what to do without Sal to support her."

Maggie snorted. "Maybe she's not as dumb as she acts." She came the last few steps down. "'Night, Dad."

He leaned over and kissed her, then kissed the sleeping Mikey on his forehead. They disappeared into the night, leaving him to pick up the pieces of his shattered daughter.

It was a long night of sobbing, flip-flopping with anger at Sal for abandoning her and the girls, at herself for being thirty-five years old with a fourteen-year-old college diploma and no real work experience. He talked her through endless spirals of despair and self-recrimination until she finally faded into sleep on the couch. He covered her with a quilt Rebecca had made and then took a spot in the easy chair. The triplets would need someone to make breakfast for them in a couple of hours.

The threads of family were fraying as quickly as he could mend them. Mike was gone. Rebecca was gone. And now Sal. Maggie had always been independent enough to stand on her own, but not Misty. The road ahead of her would be long and rocky. As the sun came up, he was still thinking about what to do.

Otter sat in the darkness of his trailer. Curtains of rain slashed across the countryside.

He remembered that night from a smaller perspective, the last night he had played with the triplets at their house. He had broken something and Aunt Misty had screamed at him. He didn't understand it at the time, but he remembered the whiskey bottle on the kitchen counter before she had yelled at all four kids to get their butts into bed. He had curled up in a sleeping bag at the foot of the bunk bed. He didn't remember Mom coming to get him.

And Grandpa had never babysat him after that.

What had happened to that plan?

CHAPTER FORTY-ONE
DIRTY DEEDS DONE DIRT CHEAP

When Toby called Otter before school on Tuesday morning to tell him about rehearsal that night, Otter knew it was a backhanded way of asking if he had found his guitar or acquired another one. The disappointment apparent in Toby's voice was more than he could stand. "Don't worry, Toby. I'll take care of it. I can't make rehearsal tonight, but you can count on me for the show. I'm working on it."

Toby said, "Okay," but he didn't sound okay.

In fact, Otter was preparing a trip to the public library, where he could get on the internet and do some searching for anyone in town who might have a bass guitar for sale.

He spent much of the afternoon at the library. The librarians gave him some side-eye, perhaps thinking he should have been in school, but they were kind enough to answer his questions about websites to look for such things. He already knew about various auction sites, but he didn't have the time to have a guitar shipped to him, even if he could come up with the prices the sellers were asking.

While it felt good to be trying, the hopelessness still overwhelmed him to the point where he often caught himself staring at the screen in despair. So then he would go outside, sit on the curb, and sigh, letting the warmth of the autumn sun suffuse him and drive back the chill of the breeze.

He found a couple of listings for super-cheap beginner guitars, but when he called them, those guitars had already been sold. All the others were as out of reach as the one in Big Jimmy's Pawn.

No one he knew had a car who could help him pawn his stuff. He didn't feel right bumming rides from anyone, and Lika wasn't old enough to drive. Mia might help him, but Misty wouldn't come all the way across town for this. Besides, after he delivered the choice words he was itching to lay upon her, she wouldn't be inclined to help him. That family certainly had money, but he'd be damned if he'd ask Misty for any.

It was his guitar. It was his stupidity that had lost it. It was his problem to fix.

The trouble was, he had no good solutions for coming up with that kind of cash in three days.

He once typed "Odin's Warriors" into a Search window, but then closed it. The things Lika told him about Odin's Warriors made him squirm, but he was going to give them one more chance. Zeke was his friend. Maybe she was wrong. Maybe Duke's group was on the up-and-up. Maybe it was just a name mix-up. Besides, they were supposed to show him some cool fighting moves, and he'd given Zeke his word.

The hour neared for Duke to pick him up, so he rode back home eat some waxy, chocolate-covered snack cakes.

A subsonic rumble outside alerted him to Big Red's approach. The massive diesel pickup ground through the gravel of his short driveway, sounding like a semi had just come to nest.

He waved as he stepped out, then locked his door. Zeke jumped out and allowed Otter to climb up into the middle.

"A sucky thing about your guitar, little bro," Zeke said, "That's why you need us around." Zeke looked a little more awake and alive, more jovial, than the last time Otter had seen him.

"Yeah, that sucks," Duke said, maneuvering the Red Beast out of the driveway.

"Well, I've been keeping my eyes open. Doing some looking around," Otter said. "Something has got to come through for me by Friday. After all, I still got my lucky guitar pick." He pulled it out of his pocket and performed magical ritual movements with it, humming in gibberish.

Duke grunted, "What's lucky about it?"

"'Johnny Cash,' see there?" Otter pointed at the silver script.

"Lucky is right!" Duke said with a whistle. He seized Otter's wrist in an iron grip. "You got any idea what that's worth?"

"No, why?" Otter said.

"That's a collector's item right there. The companies that make those do it for the artist. They don't do it for fans. They made a run of a few hundred guitar picks *for Johnny Cash his own self.* Where'd *you* get it?"

"It was in this box of stuff my Grandpa left me in his will. My mom got it from the hand of the Man at a concert." Otter's thoughts immediately flashed to what he might get for it and would it be enough to buy himself a guitar. But would anyone seriously trade him a single pick, awesome as it was, for a whole guitar?

"Is that so?" Zeke peered closely at it. "Might be you got other valuable stuff in that box."

Otter held up the pick proudly, basking in this fresh perspective on its awesomeness.

"Say, Duke," Zeke said, "how'd you know all that?"

"Worked in a pawn shop when I was a kid about Otter's age. I got all kinds of strange collector facts rattling around in here." Duke tapped his temple.

Both Zeke and Duke chain-smoked as Big Red rolled through the streets of town, looming over every vehicle they passed.

"Say, Duke," Zeke said, "our little bro here is getting himself some action."

"What?" Duke said. "Hot damn."

"That's news to me," Otter said, bewildered.

"Yeah, I saw his band do a little show at Ziggy's a few nights ago. Totally kicked ass. And boy, that little drummer…"

"What?" Otter said. "What are you talking about? We're just friends!"

"Just friends, my ass." Zeke leaned forward and said to Duke, "This little chocolate honey looked like she wanted to throw him down and go all jungle on him."

A sudden heat washed up Otter's face. "We're just friends."

"It's okay to admit it. We're all dudes here. You're getting in her pants, right?"

"No! We're just friends!" Sudden flashes of unbidden imagination, with Lika in them, just felt…weird, and he didn't appreciate the lascivious look on Zeke's face when he talked about her that way.

Duke's flinty gaze raked over him. "Just be careful with them colored chicks, kid. It's okay to dip your wick. Just remember who your people are."

With those words, the last of Otter's illusions shattered like mirrors, shards raining everywhere. Lika had been right about everything. His stomach turned sour and queasy, and awareness struck him that both of these men were much larger than him, and he was a long way from home. He crossed his arms and slouched into his seat.

Zeke said, "I do believe we have offended our little bro here, Duke."

"Offended, how?"

"I do believe he thinks we're being politically incorrect." Zeke sneered the last two words.

"Is that true, Otter? Are we being politically incorrect?"

Otter's mouth turned dry as old sandpaper. "I—"

Duke's voice was dark and threatening. "'Cause 'politically incorrect' is just faggot talk for the truth. You're not calling us faggots are you?"

"Uh, no—"

"That's good. 'Cause, you know, I saw plenty of those in the joint. Knew some niggers too, a few good ones but mostly bad ones. Let's just say we ain't meant to live together."

Thoughts of defending Lika's honor disappeared in a wave of fear for his personal safety. Sweat trickled down one cheek. His armpits were sodden. If he survived this and made it home unscathed, the first thing he was going to do was call Lika and tell her she was right and he was sorry for not believing her.

For several blocks, he kept catching Duke's gaze on him, a gaze filled with scrutiny and calculation. The silence hung like an accusation in the cab of the pickup.

How had everything suddenly turned so vile? Otter pulled his arms in and tried to avoid touching either of them, but he couldn't help it. Contact with them made his skin crawl.

Conversation between the two men turned to sports, then women. Duke said some lewd things about Baby that Otter would have to Brillo Pad out of his imagination.

An hour passed. The two men talked and smoked, and Duke cruised around town like a knight surveying his territory. They offered Otter a beer from a twelve-pack on the floor, but he declined.

"What's up with you anyway?" Zeke said. "Got your panties in a twist?"

Otter wanted to go home, but the looming brute to his left did not appear ready to agree to that wish. He wrapped his arms around his queasy stomach. "I'm not feeling good. My stomach."

They resumed talking past him, this time with Duke lapsing into a story about a run-in he'd had with some Mexican bikers a few days before. It was then Otter noticed the livid scabs and swelling on Duke's knuckles.

"Surely we're not gonna get skunked again tonight," Zeke said. "Let's have some action."

Otter tried to shrink even smaller, but even as he did so, his blood chilled. Something Zeke had said rattled itself loose so he could examine it. Zeke had said Lika was looking at him as girl-boy like, not friend-friend like. Could Zeke be wrong? Was he lying? Exaggerating? Regardless, Otter should have stood up for her. He shouldn't have let them say such awful things about her. She was his best friend. And he was a coward for letting it happen.

It was getting late, and the streets outside turned into those of Toby's neighborhood. He immediately wished he had gone to rehearsal tonight, even if all he could do was hang out with them.

The dark, grainy anger of betrayal settled behind his breastbone. He'd been wrong about Zeke. All this time, Zeke had been leading him down a dangerous path. A little danger had titillated him at first, but—

"Hey, look!" Zeke pointed to a man walking on the sidewalk, away from them. A man in a turban.

Otter's mouth went dry, and his hands started to tremble.

"What the hell is a rag-head doing in this neighborhood?" Duke snarled. He gunned the engine to catch up to the pedestrian, then whipped the truck up onto the curb in front of the man. The bounce of the tire jumping the curb lurched Otter half out of his seat.

The man in the turban jumped back.

Zeke and Duke flung open the doors and bailed out.

Otter tried to call out, but it came out as a hoarse whisper. "No."

"What the hell are you doing here?"

"Go back where you came from!"

"Don't lie to us!"

"You a terrorist?"

"Can't understand a word you're saying!"

"You speak English?"

The man held up his hands, eyes wide, babbling.

They fell upon him like dogs, snapping at him, shoving him.

Otter sat frozen on the front seat, arm outstretched. The man was Mr. Mukherjee. Otter had known from the first moment, but he couldn't believe this was happening. He was talking about his daughter, pleading for his life for her sake. Could he see Otter in the truck?

Then Duke buried his massive fist in Mr. Mukherjee's belly.

It was all happening so fast, like a horrible dream.

The Indian man's slight frame toppled like a snapped sapling.

"Don't!" Otter said, "I know him." But his voice was like the whisper of dead leaves.

They rained blows and kicks, spewing curses and combinations of words and F-bombs Otter had never heard before. "Go back to the desert, towel-head!"

Mr. Mukherjee curled up like a roly poly bug, covering his head with his hands.

There was blood on the sidewalk.

"Stop!" Otter called, but his voice was dry leaves in a hurricane.

Mr. Mukherjee's arms sagged from their defense.

Zeke laid a hard kick to the side of his head. The turban went flying, and the sight of his head snapping back and forth as if on a spring brought Otter's gorge into this throat, like a finger snapping in his grip. Mr. Mukherjee flopped onto his back, eyes closed, blood streaming from his face.

A distant scream, a woman's or a girl's, echoed in the night.

Duke spat on Mr. Mukherjee, then said, "Let's go." He and Zeke piled back into the pickup and he threw it into reverse, squealed off the curb, then slammed into a forward gear and roared up the street, leaving a cloud of black smoke in their wake.

CHAPTER FORTY-TWO
SOUND OF SILENCE

"Did you get the license plate?" Lika's father said, notepad and pen in hand.

"No, I'm sorry. It was too far away," Lika said. Her cheeks were wet with tears, stomach tight with nausea.

The lights of the ambulance and her father's police cruiser turned the dark street into a blinding frenzy of red and blue. Neighborhood residents watched from their porches and sidewalks. Her father's partner stood up the street interviewing a group of them. The way they shook their heads told her that nobody had seen or heard a thing.

"With a vehicle of that description, though," he said, "we should be able to find it without a plate number."

Lika wanted to throw up. She had never seen anything so brutal. She would never forget the sight of him curled up on the sidewalk, soaked in his own blood.

The paramedics slid Mr. Mukherjee's gurney into the back of the ambulance. His face looked like raw hamburger, and a brace circled his neck. She had never seen so much blood, soaking his clothes, spattered all over the sidewalk.

"Is he gonna be okay?" she said. "Is he gonna be okay, Daddy?"

"Oh, baby. I hope so." He wrapped her in his thick arms and held her close. The hardness of his badge, the weapons on his belt, the stiffness of his Kevlar vest all formed a wall between them, but she cried against him anyway.

When she could speak again, she stepped back. "Why do something like that? Why?"

"My first instinct is, this is a hate crime. Do you think you could identify the two men?" The war between duty and fatherhood raged on his face.

"I don't know. Maybe? It was so dark, and I was half a block away."

"And they drove off after you screamed?"

She nodded.

He took her face in both hands and lifted it to look into his eyes. "That was a brave thing, baby girl. I'm proud of you. And I'm glad you're safe. You might have saved this poor guy's life."

How did her father deal with violence like this every day? She would never be able to wipe the memory of what she had seen. She would never forget the feeling of the sickness, the helplessness, the way those two men had fallen upon Mr. Mukherjee like wolves for no other crime than walking home from work.

"Is there anything else you remember?" he said.

She hesitated, then shook her head.

He hugged her again. "Momma's gonna be here to get you soon. She'll take you home. I'm going to get right on this."

She nodded against him, his implacable, unassailable strength surrounding her.

But she had lied to her father. She had seen something else, somebody else sitting in the front seat of huge, red pickup truck, bathed in the dome light from the open doors. A familiar silhouette. A familiar baseball cap. And the memory of it made her so sick she could barely think. She wanted to punch Mike for being so stupid, for not listening to her.

Or worse, maybe he had known all along.

After the beating, Duke and Zeke clinked beer bottles and congratulated each other on a job well done, so keyed up that both of them talked at hyper-speed about what had gone down.

Meanwhile, Otter felt like puking on the dashboard. There was nothing he could do. Duke was an ex-convict, a man steeped in violence. Zeke would follow Duke's lead anywhere. Otter couldn't physically stop them. He could only watch the blows fall, hear the thud of fist against flesh, the meaty crack of bone, feel the bruise-black darkness close in about him, a suffocating weight upon his chest, a cold wet trickle of sweat down his neck.

"Cops wouldn't appreciate it, but we showed that Muslim scumbag he don't belong here," Duke said.

"He wasn't Muslim," Otter said. He was using past tense. He didn't even know if Mr. Mukherjee was alive.

"What'd you say?" Duke said, his voice dark and threatening.

"I said he's not a Muslim. He's a Sikh."

"What the hell is a seek?"

"It's a religion from India. I don't know much about it, but that's why he wore the turban."

"Screw it," Duke said. "A rag-head is a rag-head."

Zeke said to Otter, "How do you know this?"

"He told me," Otter said.

"You know him?" Zeke said, his voice now filled with threat as well.

"I tried to tell you," Otter said, his voice thick, his vision blurring with tears. "He owns that convenience store there."

Duke swore. "Did he see you?"

"I don't know."

Duke's gaze speared Otter to Yggdrasil, the World Tree. "You keep this to yourself, you hear me?"

Otter didn't know what to do except nod and say. "Take me home. Please."

They dropped him off at the mouth of the driveway into Starlite Trailer Court. Otter stood on the gravel and Zeke climbed back in the pickup.

"You know," Otter said, "you guys are assholes. You shouldn't have done that." He glanced at the dark bushes leading into the woods, gauging his chances if they wanted to chase him.

Duke leaned forward and stabbed a meaty finger toward him. "Like I said, you keep your mouth shut. Anybody talks to the cops, we'll know it was you."

"Fine," Otter said. "Just leave me alone."

Duke put the truck in gear.

Zeke said to Duke, "Hold up a sec, bro." He got out of the truck and faced Otter, arms and ankles crossed. "Is it because of that little nigger girl you hang out with? She's a cutie. I get it. I get it."

"Don't talk about her that way," Otter said, his throat tight, his voice trembling.

But Zeke seemed not to hear him. "People are complicated, little bro. I dig Asian chicks. You hanker for a little chocolate action. You go find her and cuddle up. Just remember who your people are."

Otter turned away and gave them the finger.

"Remember who your people are!" Zeke called as he got back in the truck. The engine revved, and the pickup roared away.

The gravel of the drive turned every trudging step into a grinding indictment.

He wiped his eyes. "The Coward Cometh," he said.

His legs were Jell-O. A sob hovered at the edge of every breath. His mouth tasted like bile.

He should have stopped them. He should have done something. Even at the cost of himself.

The sound of the blows reverberated in his skull. He thought he'd seen Mr. Mukherjee breathing when they backed away from him, and his hopes clung to that image.

Should he call the police and confess that he was there? At best, that would land him squarely in the hands of Louisa Pritt. Could he leave an anonymous tip? If he called from his own telephone, the number would be traced instantly to his address.

But the thought of talking to anyone, of saying what happened, speaking the words, filled him with such dread his limbs felt made of lead.

Inside the warm glow of Imelda's house, he heard the sounds of some game show in Spanish.

Geri and Freki glared at him from inside their fence, eyes glowing the streetlight.

The nights were still warm enough for crickets, and their songs filled him with loneliness and desolation. Terror at the trouble he could be in. He was done for. He was in trouble for simply being in the car. If he turned himself in to the police, Zeke and Duke might go to jail, but he'd likely end up in juvie. This would be all Pritt needed to chuck him into foster care, which would be just as bad, as far as he was concerned.

Inside his house, he collapsed into the sofa, clutching both hands to his chest as if trying to protect his heart, sniffling back tears.

Why was he worried so much about himself?

Was Mr. Mukherjee even alive?

He needed to do the right thing.

But doing the right thing meant he would lose everything he'd worked for, everything he wanted.

Everything.

Goodbye, Black Line show.

Goodbye, Lika. And Amber.

Goodbye, independence.

Goodbye, home.

He felt the overpowering urge to call Lika, to tell her she'd been right all along, but he couldn't bear the thought of how *wrong* he had been.

A nerveless fugue settled over him like a black, smothering blanket.

The ringing phone jerked him back out of it.

How the clock came to say 1:30 a.m. he could not fathom.

The caller ID read Lika's number. If she was calling at this hour, it had to be important.

The phone kept ringing.

And yet he yearned to tell somebody, to shed the massive weight of terror and remorse that cinched his chest so tight he could barely breathe, and there was nobody but her to tell.

He answered the phone.

Tears thickened Lika's voice. "I can't sleep."

"Why?"

"Because I saw something terrible tonight."

An unspoken meaning in her voice gave him pause. "What happened?"

She flashed into barely controlled anger and accusation. "You were there!"

His mouth ceasing functioning.

"You got about two seconds to talk or I'm gonna hang up and never speak to you again."

"Wait! Lika. Wait. I feel awful, too. I've been thinking about calling you. I need to talk to somebody."

"Why do you feel awful?"

"Because nothing like that was supposed to happen. And…"

"And what?"

And I didn't stop it. But he couldn't say that, could barely accept the thought. What kind of warrior was he? He was supposed to protect the downtrodden, not become the downtrodd*er*.

Otter said, "And…is he okay? Do you know?"

"They took him in the ambulance. That's all I know."

"What hospital?"

"I'll ask Dad when he gets home. What did you expect was gonna happen? They're white supremacists! I told you!"

"I know you did. And I'm sorry."

"So why did you ignore me? Why didn't you listen?"

Coming from her, the accusation slashed across his face like a blade, even though he already knew it to be true. "Because Zeke was my friend. He helped me a lot."

"How?"

"He lives across the street. I could go play video games and eat pizza and get drunk and not think about how much I miss Mom." His voice cracked, then hardened again. "But not anymore."

"You have to go to the police."

"They said they'll come after me if I do. The leader, Duke, he's been in prison. At least one of the other guys, too. God, I don't know if I'll ever sleep again."

"Yeah, you got it rough, all right," she sneered. "You're not in the hospital." His legs gave out and he sank into the couch with a tortured groan.

"I saw the whole thing," she said, "walking to the bus stop after rehearsal. I've seen a couple fights at school, but nothing like this. All because he has dark skin."

"Mainly because he had a turban. They thought he was Muslim."

"Hate don't pay attention to details. It just tears shit up, and when there's nothing left to tear up, it feeds on itself. I thought you were my friend, Mike. I thought you cared about me, about my family."

"I am! I do!"

"Then you gotta help get those guys off the street before they do it again. Mike, maybe there's something hasn't registered in your brain. I was thirty seconds away, on the *same street*. That could have been me." Her voice crumbled.

The truth of it punched him in the stomach. What might they have done to a pretty black girl walking alone at night? A little "chocolate action." The thought made him want to throw up.

He swallowed the taste of bile in his mouth. "You were right. About everything," he said, but he didn't think she heard him because she was talking and her words were a jagged, sluicing tumble.

"You don't know what it's like to walk on eggshells your whole life for fear of ticking off some white person. You wanna know the kinds of talks black kids have with their parents that white kids don't? Talks about how to behave with white cops to avoid getting arrested or shot for nothing. Talks about how to act around white people."

"Do you…act different around me?"

She sniffled, then blew her nose. "I don't know. Maybe? Do you act different around me?"

"I don't think so. But maybe? I just know you're you, and I know you. I mean, I know you're black and your life is different than mine because of it. It's one of the things I like about you. You're such a cool person, I've always been proud you're my friend. I know you got my back. I just—" His voice shattered, and he couldn't finish.

"What is it?" she said.

He stammered until he rammed it forth, blubbering be damned. "I don't know, after tonight, if you can trust me to have your back. I couldn't stop them. I wanted to. But I was afraid. I was so scared."

"So what are you going to do? Are you going to call the police?" Her voice was sharp with challenge.

He leaned over his knees, clutching his forehead. "I don't know."

Her voice caught as if she had just been struck. "Then we're done."

She hung up.

CHAPTER FORTY-THREE
BOULEVARD OF BROKEN DREAMS

Otter tried calling Lika back right away. The first try rang and rang. The second went straight to voicemail. After five more tries, he gave up. The cinch around his heart tightened. He despaired ever getting a good night's sleep again. He paced. He slouched. He pondered. He pulled his hair. He marinated in blackness and guilt.

Hours passed. He sensed dawn approaching, even though the night outside was still pitch black.

The cardboard box sat quietly there, a calm presence, like it was Grandpa himself there watching him, offering nothing, but waiting to see what he would do.

"What do I do, Grandpa? What do I do? What do I do?"

You have a greater destiny than this.

What did that mean? Would this trouble take care of itself? Could he find a way through it?

A true warrior protects the weak and the downtrodden.

"But I'm the downtrodden."

No, you're the warrior.

The items he'd found in the box thus far, the memories he'd absorbed, had formed a patchwork of new experiences, new knowledge, new ways of thinking that somehow made him feel older than fifteen, wiser than he had been even two weeks ago. But there was still so much to learn. Would he ever know *enough*?

What wisdom could Grandpa impart to help him through this awful mess?

Become the warrior.

But to protect the downtrodden, he had to give up everything.

It is the duty and fate of some warriors to die for the greater good.

No one liked to think about that. In battle, someone had to lose.

Sometimes even the winner loses. Sometimes there is no return.

He crouched above the box and peeled back the flaps. "Tell me what to do, Grandpa."

His eye caught a little plastic figurine of King Kong beating his chest atop a screw-top Coke cap.

Recollection snapped into focus. Otter remembered this little King Kong. Grandpa had given it to him to play with once. Grandpa and Mom had been angry at each other and told him to run off and play in the back yard. He'd taken the King Kong and some Star Wars figures into the sandbox and played until Mom had come and told him it was time to go. But he'd been having so much fun building sand forts and knocking them down he didn't want to go. Mom had yelled at him, half-crying.

But now he heard a child's voice that sounded so familiar. "Can I play with this, Grandpa?"

"Of course you can," Grandpa said, smiling.

"Go play for a while," Mom said. "Me and Grandpa have to have a talk."

The words resonated with his memories in strange mental stereo. He saw Grandpa's kitchen from two different perspectives at once, kicking his brain into vertigo.

Little Mikey bounced away with his eight-year-old fists full of Star Wars figures and King Kong.

As soon as the patio door to the back yard closed and little Mikey bounded off toward the sandbox, Maggie turned on him. "I can't believe you sold all of Mom's jewelry."

"I had to do something. I'm not made of money." Nevertheless, Donovan couldn't look her in the eye. The words came thick. He hugged his elbows.

"Mom promised those to me. Misty wanted the furniture. I was supposed to get the jewelry. I'd have taken them a long time ago, but I thought they'd be safer here."

"There were extenuating circumstances."

"With Misty, there always are. Here's the thing, Dad." Anger turned her voice thick and brittle. "You know what Mom told me to do with them? Sell them and use the money to go to the best damn acting school I could find. I've been dreaming of that for *years*. You know I have."

"I'll send you to school." He was hardly destitute. He could find some way to help her with tuition to a local college.

"That's not the point! They weren't yours to sell!"

His thoughts scrambled to shore up defenses against her rising anger. His heart pounded. "They were *my* wife's!"

"But *she* promised them to *me*! You blew *my* inheritance on an addict! I suppose I'd be less furious if the rehab had stuck. How did you pay for this third go-round?"

"Your grandfather's antique furniture," he said, shame tightening his throat and stomach.

She cupped an ear. "What's that? Don't mumble."

"Your grandfather's antique furniture."

"The stuff he brought from France after the war."

"I had to. She's my daughter—"

"So am I! What makes you think the rehab will stick this time?"

"I have to believe. She needs help. So do the triplets."

"This was *my* shot, Dad! I had the paperwork all lined up! They loved my audition. They *never* take new students my age. But they took *me*."

"I'll pay for your school, like I said."

"How? You're selling *furniture*."

"Give me a year and—"

"And what? You'll have Misty straightened out? I've been waiting *eight years*, Dad. Mikey is getting big enough that I can finally—finally!—go to school. There was enough in that jewelry to pay for Juilliard."

"You got into Juilliard?"

"Yes! The audition video cost me a week's pay. And there's no way you can afford Juilliard if you're selling furniture to pay for Misty's rehab."

"You were going to move to New York?"

"That was the plan, yeah."

His own anger, a bit of manufactured outrage, rose up to deflect hers. "And you weren't going to tell me."

"I wanted to surprise you. And don't you *dare* turn this around on me." Tears streamed down her cheeks. He had never seen such hurt on her face, such betrayal.

The guilt in his belly turned into a choking black cauldron. He had always pitied her for the life her ferocious independence had demanded when Mikey was born. Donovan loved that boy deeply, but she had given up everything she was to raise him. And just when she was once again taking steps to pursue her own dreams, her own father yanked the rug from under her. "I'm so sorry," he whispered.

There was nothing he could do. Rebecca's jewelry was long gone. Otto's furniture, too. Misty's addiction to alcohol and sleeping pills clung to her like a tumor, and three little girls needed her desperately. But Maggie was right. There was no way he could afford to send her to Juilliard. Living expenses and daycare in New York would be through the roof.

"I could help you out, but it would have to be at a local school. State College maybe?"

"Dad, if I start now, I'll be almost thirty when I graduate. Actresses don't start their careers at thirty. They start them when they're barely in their twenties, because by forty, there are no roles left for them. It was *Juilliard,* Dad!" Tears of fury sparkled in her eyes. Behind them, her dreams were burning.

He slumped onto the edge of a stool.

In that moment, she was so much like Rebecca. After the anguish of Michael's death, Donovan discovered that his beautiful, educated, rational wife could hold a grudge like no one he had ever met. He could almost smell the bridge burning now. How could he have sacrificed one of his children's life for the other? How could he have betrayed her trust like that? "I'm sorry, sweetheart. I'm so sorry." He grabbed a tissue from a nearby box and blew his nose.

"Sometimes sorry doesn't cut it," she said. Then she walked outside, took Mikey by the hand, and dragged him to her twenty-year-old car.

He wanted to follow her, but shame held him frozen in place, a fist of guilt squeezing his heart, and then she drove away, his angel.

He never saw her again.

He tried to call her, but she never answered the phone. He prepared paperwork to mortgage the house to pay for her way to Juilliard, but he never reached her, so he never went through with it.

King Kong turned up in the lawn clippings a week later. Donovan kept it on his desk.

Some things you couldn't take back. Some bridges were destroyed so completely, you had to build a whole new one on different foundations. And you didn't even know that until the smoke cleared. He waited for seven years for bridge construction to begin, but it never did. They talked on the phone a couple of times. He invited her over for holidays, but she always had an excuse, even when it was clear that Misty's last stint in rehab had been successful, that she was staying sober. He always thought maybe someday Maggie would come around, always hoped for it, and yet hesitated because seeing her again would force him to consider his own act of betrayal. He had, of course, known about Rebecca's promise to Maggie. But it hadn't mattered enough to stop him. Would he do it again if he knew the cost was going to be losing Maggie forever?

That was a question he didn't enjoy considering.

Otter found himself sitting cross-legged on the floor, holding King Kong, feeling a profound regret for having done something awful that he couldn't take back. He didn't know what Juilliard was for sure, but it sounded like a capital-B Big Deal.

The first question was: whose regret was it, his or Grandpa's?

The next was: could he stop the bridges from burning?

He vaguely remembered a long, dark period where his mom barely spoke to anyone, including him. She slept a lot. Dinners were sometimes a peanut-butter-sandwich afterthought. Little Mike hadn't known that day would be the last he ever saw his grandfather. He remembered asking many times about going over to Grandpa's house or going to play with the triplets, but Mom always had a reason they couldn't. Eventually he stopped asking.

Yellow-orange morning painted bright stripes on the walls. Imelda was singing "Pink Cadillac" in the shower.

His eyes felt full of sand. His entire body ached. The dead mouse had crawled back in his mouth. But there was something he had to do now, and it was more important than a guitar.

CHAPTER FORTY-FOUR
RIDERS ON THE STORM

The bus ride to St. Francis Hospital took an hour and a half. The only flowers available in the hospital gift shop were equivalent to half a week's pay, but he bought them anyway, a dazzling array of colors and flower varieties he could not name.

The flowers buoyed his leaden spirit only slightly. He even wore his best shirt, a nicely pressed button-up his mom bought him a few months before the funeral, but he'd grown so much the cuffs only reached two inches above his wrists. He still felt like a man going to face the gallows. The nurses seemed to look at him with undisguised accusation. They couldn't possibly know anything, but it didn't stop the shame from flushing his ears with warmth.

Mr. Mukherjee shared a room with someone hidden behind a curtain. As Otter stepped into the doorway, a woman and a little girl stood up to greet him, Mr. Mukherjee's wife and daughter. Surprise painted their faces. Mrs. Mukherjee had a brilliant red dot between her eyebrows. The girl, perhaps eleven, with enormous dark eyes that sparkled with intelligence, smiled at him. In a few years, she would be a stunner.

"Oh, hello," Mrs. Mukherjee said awkwardly, expectantly.

Mr. Mukherjee's eyes fluttered open, and it took several moments before recognition displaced the bewilderment, during which time Otter could only stand there. Even so, seeing the man with his eyes open and alive sent such a rush of relief through Otter that his legs almost crumpled.

Finally he offered the flowers and said, "These are for you."

Mrs. Mukherjee stepped forward and accepted them with both hands, her eyes widening. "Oh, they're so beautiful! Aren't they just gorgeous, Rana?"

Mrs. Mukherjee placed the flowers on the stand near the bed and said something in another language to her husband.

"Hello, young man." Mr. Mukherjee's thick voice was difficult to understand, his cheeks puffy, his face covered in stitches and bandages. "Thank you for this gift." A cast covered one hand like a great, pale mitten. He lay back in the partially raised bed. The blood vessels of one eye had burst and turned the white red.

Tears welled at the sight of him. "I'm sorry for what happened to you," Otter said. "Um, how are you?"

The woman said, "It hurts him to talk. He has three broken ribs and two broken teeth. We will talk to the oral surgeon later today. And his nose is broken, and a bone in his forearm. He has a concussion, but thank God, his skull is intact."

"It is thick!" Mr. Mukherjee said, grinning feebly.

"I'm really sorry," Otter said again. Nothing else seemed to want to come out. "Do you remember what happened?" The presence of the open door behind him made him want to make a quick exit.

"Just two big men in a big, red truck. That I will never forget."

"The police are investigating," Mrs. Mukherjee said. "Animals!" She fussed with the blankets around her husband's feet.

"I'm sure the police will catch them," Otter said. "I should let you rest."

"May I ask," said Mrs. Mukherjee, "how do you know my husband?"

"I go to his store sometimes."

"How did you hear about what happened?" she said.

"Uh…it's all over the neighborhood. Then I called all the hospitals until I found the one he's in. How long are they saying you'll be here?"

"A couple of days," Mrs. Mukherjee said. "Until the swelling in his brain goes down."

"Who's running your store?"

"There is no one. It is closed," Mr. Mukherjee said.

"We lose money every day," his wife said.

"I could help you," Otter said. "You don't even have to pay me. I could work there for you until you're back on your feet."

"That is very kind of you," Mrs. Mukherjee said, "but you are too young to sell beer and cigarettes."

"Could I clean up around there or something? You don't have to pay me. I just want to help."

The two adults exchanged glances. Mr. Mukherjee's gaze, hemmed by swelling and bruises, fixed upon him strangely, piercing. "I have some things to do there. You come tomorrow at 8:00 a.m. My wife will show you."

In the lobby of the hospital, Otter found a pay phone, took a deep breath, then took another and called 911.

The operator came on immediately, "9-1-1, what is your emergency?"

"I have an anonymous tip for you. Last night, there was an Indian man, Mr. Mukherjee, got beat up along Pine Street by two guys in a big, red pickup. The guys who did it, their names are Zeke Halvorsen and Duke Cochran. Zeke's address is Starlite Trailer Court, number 27. He drives a Harley with green lightning on the gas tank. Duke's address is on Cedar Ridge. Duke has the big, red pickup. I saw it happen."

"What is your name and address?"

He hung up.

Otter made it to the car wash just in time for his shift. Bussing around town added hours to anything. Having not slept, he felt like a zombie, going through rote motions without vigor or attention. Jeff yelled at him to get his poop in a group. Otter grumbled but tried to work harder, especially when the new guy Dashawn paused to joke around with Jeff. Jeff and Dashawn laughed uproariously at some joke. Their camaraderie made Otter think he might as well quit now to save Jeff the trouble of firing him.

But he needed this job now more than ever. Everything was crumbling in on him. Lika wasn't speaking to him. If he couldn't come up with a guitar by Friday night, none of them would ever speak to him again. The cops would hopefully arrest Duke and Zeke soon, but chances were, they would get out on bail. They would come after him.

All of this was a thick, black stew in his mind, so inescapable he hardly noticed when his shift was over and Jeff was locking the doors. Otter slumped in the locker room, weary to the core, and stared at the wall until Dashawn came in.

"You all right?" Dashawn said.

Otter blinked and sighed. "My life is a black pit of disaster. Thanks for asking."

"That bad, huh?"

"Yeah, one of my friends turned out to be a neo-Nazi douchebag who beat up somebody I know and somebody stole my guitar last weekend so now I can't play the gig my band has lined up for Friday night and I just blew most of the money I had in the world on flowers for the guy who got beat up and the government wants to put me in foster care but I'll be lucky if I don't end up in juvie after what happened and my best friend won't talk to me because I seriously, ginormously screwed up."

Dashawn raised both hands and backed slowly away.

"Wow, saying it all out loud makes it sound even worse," Otter said. There was nothing to do, though, but keep moving forward, even if the road ahead was a black abyss and he had no headlights because, if he stopped, all of this mess would overtake him.

So he shucked his coveralls and headed home. He ditched his bicycle in the bushes at the entrance to the trailer court and crept through the trees to his trailer. Running into Zeke would be bad.

Peering through the bushes between his and Imelda's trailers toward Zeke's place, he saw no sign of Zeke's Harley. Geri and Freki were standing at the gate watching him, preternaturally still and attentive, as if he were a rabbit they had known was there all along, soon to be ripped to bloody pieces. He shuddered at the sight of those dogs now, knowing what he knew about Zeke.

The next thing he noticed was his front door hanging ajar.

The key was in his pocket. He remembered locking it when he left.

He burst out of the bushes and ran for the door. The wood around the door latch was splintered, torn out. The metal door frame showed the teeth marks of a crowbar.

His heart fell into his shoes, and the hair on his neck rose like a hedgehog's spines.

He cocked an ear, but only dead silence lay within.

He'd been away for almost twelve hours. Whoever did this had to be long gone by now, didn't they?

Why would anyone want to break into a trailer? Nobody around here was rich or had anything particularly valuable. Imelda's front door was intact. Why *his* place?

He swung the door wide and steeled himself for action, either fight or flight. His nerves pulsed with his heartbeat. Right now, he would hear a mouse fart.

Stepping inside, his gaze immediately registered formerly occupied spaces. The TV was gone. The stereo. The CD rack.

"Bastards!" he yelled at the ceiling. He pulled out his phone, saw that it was shut down. When he turned it back on again, a brief message popped up saying that he needed to buy more talk minutes for his phone.

Maybe he could use Imelda's phone. He knocked on her door, but she wasn't home, and her door was locked. Until her place was vandalized, she left her door unlocked.

He rubbed his face, his eyes, and went to inventory what might have been taken.

The electronics, as old as they were, were the only easily hockable items. There was nothing else remotely valuable here, a fact he'd been beating his head against since Saturday night. A quick survey of the rest of the house told him nothing else had been stolen.

Then he noticed the living room floor was strangely empty. He cast about for a moment until his fatigued mind registered what had been there.

Grandpa's box.

Gone.

His legs collapsed and he sank into a cross-legged slump in the middle of the living room, a manic laugh bursting forth. The thing that was at once the most useless and valuable thing in his life was gone.

Whatever junkie tried to sell that stuff was in for a rude awakening.

Why his place? Why not Zeke's? Zeke at least had a few guns lying around, a big screen TV and a nice video game console.

But then a sick realization washed into Otter's brain like an incoming tide full of oil slick and toxic waste.

Had it been Zeke who broke into his house?

Zeke had known about the box, and the valuable guitar pick. Maybe he thought to find more valuable stuff in there, so he took Otter's electronics, too.

Then another wave slammed him against the rocks.

Had Zeke stolen Otter's guitar that night at Ziggy's? He'd been alone in the back of the room, in reach of the instruments. Otter hadn't seen him leave.

Otter's teeth clenched for a moment at the thought of all those nights hanging with Zeke. What had been going on in that guy's mind? He had never been Otter's friend.

Had it been Zeke who vandalized Imelda's house?

How could Otter have been so stupid? He clenched his fists.

Geri and Freki burst out barking. Someone was coming.

It wasn't long before he caught the sound of footsteps in the gravel.

Imelda's voice called in, "Are you here, *mijo*?"

"Yeah, I'm here."

"What happen to your door?"

He heaved himself upright and went out to speak to her. "Somebody broke in and stole everything I own. Well, not everything. But everything they can sell."

And the box. That stupid, damned, precious box.

Imelda threw her arms around him. "Oh, *mijo*, you having such a terrible week!"

Surprised, he returned her hug awkwardly. The embrace broke something loose in him, a glacier of rage and despair calving into the sea, but he'd be damned if he cried on her. He clamped down hard on the sobs, but he let the spark of rage bob to the surface.

"If I ever find out who did this…" he growled.

"You call *policia*?"

He shook his head. The thought of cops coming to his house, asking question he didn't want to answer, made him queasy. Worse, he had no expectation they would do anything. Just another unsolved burglary they didn't have the resources to pursue. And worser still, they could use it as a chance to nab him for Mrs. Pritt.

He had nothing left now except a roof and the clothes on his back.

"You stay with me tonight," Imelda said. "Sleep on my couch like when I babysit."

"Nah, thanks, you go to too much trouble for me. I'll stay here. I can tie the door shut with some rope around the doorknob and use the back door."

"No, you stay with me. I make enchiladas. You eat today?"

"Not yet." The thought of going inside to heat up some ramen noodles filled him with dread, for a reason he couldn't quite pin down. This wasn't just the theft of his stuff. He felt violated in ways he couldn't name.

And the box was gone. Just as he began to feel reconnection with his family, with the grandpa he had never really known, all of that was wrested away, too. All he had now were memories. Grandpa's strange "presence" in his life for the last couple of weeks had made him feel less lonely. Now, he was truly alone again.

As he stood outside with Imelda, looking into the void inside the house, darkened by the descending sun, the trailer felt less like home now. Someone had robbed him of that, too.

He had no idea how to fix the door. All he could do was secure it against animals. Everyone in the trailer court talked of raccoons in their garbage bins. What would raccoons do inside his house?

"I need to fix my door," he told Imelda, not knowing what else to say.

"You fix your door and I make us enchiladas. Do not argue."

By ten p.m., exhaustion had crashed over him in a twenty-foot wave, and he lay snuggled under a brightly woven wool blanket on Imelda's couch, drifting off to the sound of a Mexican soap opera. The wildly buxom women in skin-tight dresses on those shows held his attention for a while, but the rapid-fire Spanish fatigued his brain, and soon his exhaustion was such that even dazzlingly beautiful women couldn't keep him awake. On a bookshelf across from him was a little shrine to the Virgin Mary, complete with scented candle and incense. The couch and scratchy blanket smelled like spices, clove cigarettes, and vanilla incense. It was all so familiar, even though Imelda hadn't babysat him for several years.

An hour ago, he had finished tying his front door shut from the inside with a rope around the door knob, using the back door to come and go. He had no idea what it would cost or how to fix the front door.

As he was fading into oblivion, strange flashes, bright enough to see behind closed eyelids, prompted him to open them. Red and blue strobes flashed across the ceiling and walls.

Hair netted up and in curlers, Imelda sat up straight in her easy chair and gave him a cautionary glance.

A bolt of alarm at the flashing lights rolled him off the couch. Still groggy, he scuttled on all fours into the dark recesses of her house, to the bathroom. He shut the bathroom door and sat in the dark on the edge of the bathtub.

The lights of the police cruiser spattered the curtains in their blinding pattern. Through the open window came the sounds of a car door, feet on the gravel, crickets on the night air, and pounding on a door, his front door.

A male voice called, "Michael MacIntyre, open up! This is the police."

Imelda opened her door and went out onto the porch. "He is not home."

"Do you know where he is?"

"Somebody broke into his house today. Broke his door. Stole everything. Why you looking for him?"

"We need to question him."

Other footsteps moved through the gravel and the grass to circle to the far side of his house.

"He in trouble?" Imelda said.

"We need to talk to him. Do you know where he is?"

"I told you, I don't know. He was very upset. Left on his bicycle."

"We found a bicycle in the bushes."

"I don't know about that. Maybe he don't feel safe in his house after today. Where were you then, huh?"

"We have no reports of any break-ins here today. How long has he been gone?"

"Maybe eight o'clock."

"How well do you know him?"

"I know him since he was lee-ttle. This high. He's a good boy."

"If he comes back, tell him to call this number. He's not in trouble, but we need to talk to him."

"Why?"

The second set of footsteps came back toward the police cruiser. "No sign of him here."

"Just have him call us, okay?"

"Okay. You guys find who rob him, huh?"

"He needs to report it. Then we'll send someone over to investigate the break-in. Good night, ma'am."

Footsteps going back to the car. Imelda's door closing. Otter didn't move until the police car was gone.

In the living room, Imelda handed him a business card from the officer at the door.

"I heard everything," Otter said.

Imelda's eyes were wide with concern. "What's this about?"

"Something bad happened last night," he said. "I was there, and I should have tried to stop them, but I didn't. Today, I fingered the guys who did it, and they probably fingered me. But I didn't do anything."

"How bad?"

"An innocent guy got beat up pretty bad. He's in the hospital. Zeke was one of the guys who did it."

"I knew it! That guy *es pendejo*! *Cerote*! Maybe they arrest him."

"I hope so. But I was there, and that means I'm in trouble, too. It all happened so fast."

"Oh, *mijo!*"

"I should go. I don't want to get you in trouble, too."

"No! You put little white butt on my couch and rest. Try life again tomorrow."

"But—"

Her eyes flashed. "Do it!" She smiled warmly, and her eyes bore a look that also suggested a secret she was not ready to divulge.

Leaving the candle burning for the Virgin Mary, she turned off the lights, then turned off the television and went back to prepare herself for bed.

In the warm light of the candle, he pulled the scratchy blanket up to his chin, head couched on his arm, and stared at the ceiling, reflecting.

He was in more trouble than ever, with catastrophe looming on every side, but when he finally fell asleep, it was the sound, untroubled sleep of the just.

CHAPTER FORTY-FIVE
HURT

Otter arrived at the Kwik Trip promptly at 8:00 a.m. on Thursday morning, his stomach flipping flapjacks, and found the place open. He hadn't seen much of 8:00 a.m. in the last few months. Mr. Mukherjee's wife recognized him through the window as he approached the front door. Meeting her gaze was difficult, but he gave her a sheepish smile.

Had Mr. Mukherjee seen him in the pickup that night? Would they guess his gesture was one of making amends rather than simple altruism? What would they do if they knew? Turn him in to the police? He didn't know what to do. Every option filled him with dread.

He took a deep breath and went inside.

"Good morning," he said.

"Good morning," she said, her expression guarded.

He shoved his hands into his pockets halfway to his elbows. "So, um, what would you like me to do?"

"We were not sure you would come," she said. "People say many things, you know. People are all talk sometimes."

He nodded, scuffing his shoe across the floor tiles. "How's he doing?"

"Why do you care what happened to my husband?"

The edge in her voice turned Otter's hands into fists. "Me and my mom used to come here a lot. He was always very nice to us."

"Are you certain that's all?" She looked at him askance, and his ears flushed hot. Her gaze was a mirror he couldn't look into.

"Um, what else could it be?"

"You don't want to steal something?" The anger in her voice slashed sharper.

"No! Honest!"

"Then why else do you wish to work for free?" she snapped.

"Because I was there, okay?"

The words blurted out before he knew they were there, and then hung between him and her like a visible cloud, long moments passing. Her hands were fists, fingers wringing themselves.

"I didn't do it! But I was in the pickup, and I couldn't stop them. After I came to the hospital yesterday, I called the police and told them who did it. I don't know if they've been arrested yet. And…and…" His throat squeezed off the words.

Her jaw was a block of stone, her lips a thin, dark line, hands clasped tightly before her.

"I'm here because I want to make it right, and this is the only way I can think of, besides turning in the douchebag son-of-a-bitches who did it. I'm sorry I didn't stop it. I could have done *something*, I *should* have done *something!*" The tumble of words rattled to a halt, and still she did not speak, just looked at him with that piercing dark gaze, simmering with anger. "If you don't want me here, I understand. I'll just go. But I really just want to help."

More long moments passed, and finally he started to turn away. "I'll just go. I'm sorry."

"My husband gets to come home tomorrow," she said.

"And he's going to be okay?"

"When the bones heal, yes."

Otter's sigh of relief weighed a thousand pounds. "That's good."

"Perhaps it is God's will that brought you here," she said. "Perhaps your presence here has much to teach both of us." Her own sigh was heavy and trembling with emotion. "Follow me."

She led him into the back and put him to work at his first task, which was thoroughly mopping the entire store, then sweeping the parking lot and pump stations, then washing the storefront windows, then scrubbing the restrooms, then tidying up the storage room, then stacking great piles of recyclables behind the store in preparation for pickup.

The hours passed quickly. The work was hard, a bit tedious, but each completed task felt *right*. He would leave it up to Mrs. Mukherjee to inform him when he was finished for the day, at least until three o'clock when he had to make his shift at the car wash. It was too much to finish in one day, but he would come back. At lunchtime, she gave him his pick of sandwiches and soft drinks, and he thanked her sincerely. The hard set of her jaw had softened somewhat.

The work also gave him an excuse not to think about the missing guitar, or about the way his heart ached over Amber, or about how he had let Lika down, or about how his house had just been burglarized, or about how his only link to his grandfather had been stolen, all of which wasted no opportunity to creep back into the cracks between other thoughts.

He had no hope.

There was simply no way he could acquire a guitar by tomorrow night, short of stealing one.

Amber would never speak to him again.

He would never be able to win back Lika's friendship.

When the time came for him to leave, Mrs. Mukherjee told him, "You may come back tomorrow, if you wish. We are most grateful for your assistance. You have done well today."

She wouldn't meet his eye, but the tone of her voice removed a couple of boulders of guilt from the avalanche that had buried him.

Otter took off his Mudskippers hat and unpinned the Superman emblem. "Would you please give this to your husband?" He offered her the pin. "It's got magical powers. It might help him recover faster." His hand trembled as he gave it to her, his most powerful talisman, the symbol of his destiny.

She smiled indulgently. "Magical powers, you say. I will accept your gift and give it to my husband."

Giving away the pin had been sheer impulse, instinct, and the second it left his touch, panic rose in him. He had just given away his greatest talisman. All he had left was the Johnny Cash guitar pick in his pocket. He had nothing left. From somewhere within him, he sensed approval.

Superman is Superman, regardless of whether he wears the suit.

Otter was puffing with exertion. A coal train crossing had held him up, and he'd had to pound the pedals for a mile or risk being late for work.

He hurried into Jeff's office two minutes before his shift was to begin.

Jeff was sitting behind his desk with a steadfastly neutral expression. "Mike, you're here."

"I'm on time, right?"

"Just in time to pack up your stuff and clear out," Jeff said brightly. "You're fired."

"*What?*"

"I am not known to stutter."

"But why?"

"The police were here earlier looking for you."

"Oh god," Otter groaned. "Look, Jeff, I'm sorry. It's about this thing that—"

"I don't care what it was about. There's too much government breathing down your neck. Makes me antsy. I warned you. Here's your last check." Jeff slid a white envelope across the desk. "Now, go pack up your stuff."

The utter lack of regret in Jeff's voice, the resolve, told Otter that pleading would be pointless. He snatched up the envelope.

In the locker room, he tore open the envelope, hope flashing that it might be enough to bring home a guitar today, any guitar. His shoulders slumped. The check represented a mere down payment on the Fender Jazz at Big Jimmy's.

As he gathered up the handful of things from his locker—a comb, some baseball cards, a burrito wrapper, an empty potato chip bag—he spotted something that had fallen into the back corner. A photograph.

A photograph of him, Mom, and Lika standing around a birthday cake with twelve candles. Back then, Lika wore her hair in a wild array of gnarly pigtails. In the photo, a raucous laugh plastered her face, and her fingers were covered with icing. Rainbow icing smeared his face like a mustache. Mom smirked knowingly. It had escalated from there. When the debacle ended, both he and Lika had had icing in their hair, and his mom had slunk off to gloat over her incitement to birthday cake riot. He recalled being somewhat of a pain that day about what he wanted to wear to the party, more of a pain than Mom cared to tolerate, and she had enlisted Lika to take him down a notch, a charge Lika had gleefully undertaken. In the end, only a couple of pieces of the red-velvet cake had been mortally wounded.

He tucked the photo in his pocket, missing Lika terribly.

Plank by plank, the floor continued to fall out from under his world.

Having nowhere else to go, he wobbled his bike to the library to pore over online classified ads for bass guitars. He didn't dare stop moving or the darkness would overtake him like it almost did the week before. He could feel it behind him, the darkness, sniffing along his trail. The depth of that blackness, the ease with which he might still succumb to its seduction, frightened him.

After two hours, his guitar search efforts came up dry, by which point it was the library's closing time.

In the last minutes before sunset, he wobbled his bike to Blue Spruce Park and sat on one of the swings near the picnic table where Amber had broken his heart, watching a couple of skaters work the half-pipe.

He couldn't blame Amber for not being into him. He was a piece of work, wasn't he?

No!

Like a thunderclap, the echo of that negation exploded in his brain. He would not immerse himself in that poisoned pool. That way lay the darkness.

He'd had minor crushes before, since he'd first become aware of his feelings for girls in the sixth grade, but none of those girls had mattered like this one. None of them had set him so completely on fire with fascination and fervor.

But just because he loved her didn't mean she owed him anything, no matter how much he wanted it to.

He'd laid his heart at her feet, and she had stomped on it.

Or had she?

Was there still hope? Had he given up too easily? Amber's mom had heard about him. Had Amber been talking about him at home? How many shreds of hope could he cling to?

Could he still win her heart somehow? But why would he want to, after the pain she'd deliberately caused him?

Darkness fell around him, and these thoughts immersed him in waves.

The skaters left. A woman walked her dog. A police cruiser passing on the street fifty yards away made him turn his face away. A homeless man camped under a towering blue spruce tree. The night carried the nip of coming autumn and he hadn't worn his jacket, but he let the chill seep into his bare arms.

He thought about the day he had watched two kids swinging, both of them a little younger than him, the day of the funeral, and he thought about how he had convinced himself he had no more time for swinging, that a man didn't swing. He'd certainly made one catastrophe after another out of that idea, hadn't he?

With nothing left to lose, he might as well swing. So he kicked himself a little higher, then a little higher, then higher still, until at the apex of his rise, he swung so high the chains went slack and his body felt weightless. The chains creaked and rattled. And he wanted to keep swinging higher until he didn't have to come back down ever again.

But that was not possible.

He stopped pumping his legs and let himself settle back to the bottom until he was still.

For the first time in he didn't know how long, his mind was still.

He moved to lie atop the picnic table and stared up at the stars, arms behind his head, contemplating the vast gulfs between worlds, appreciating how his concerns dwindled to pettiness in the face of entire civilizations out there being helplessly eaten up by supernovae and black holes. He was just an ant on a tiny, blue marble spinning through space.

He wasn't dying of cancer.

He dreamed of getting out of here in the first colonial space ship, putting together the first rock band amid the red sands of Mars, with new friends, new loves, people that wouldn't remember his failures or the fact that he was an orphan.

At some point he drifted off between the stars, imagining greater destinies than ending up homeless or in juvenile detention. He let the cosmic void draw him up, up, up into sparkling darkness, where the dreams awaited him.

He awoke a couple of hours later, shivering, his breath forming clouds above his face.

Sitting up, he rubbed his arms fiercely until the shivering abated.

With a harsh laugh, he said, "Well, let's call this practice for being homeless."

Only a dresser full of warm clothing gave home marginally more appeal than sleeping outside. After the burglary, the trailer still felt like a broken empty shell of the sanctuary it had once been. But his bed was there, and his clothes, and a couple slices of bread to quell the roaring beast in his stomach.

At least he still had a bed.

Even though he had no guitar, no friends, no family.

And oh yeah, no job.

He looked at the dark, shapeless mass of the homeless man sleeping under the tree.

Tomorrow was going to come, no matter what.

The sun would rise. And he had less than twenty-four hours to find a guitar.

CHAPTER FORTY-SIX
HOLDING OUT FOR A HERO

Friday afternoon, Lika sat cross-legged on her bed, vibrating with excitement, sick with fear, praying that somehow, today, everything would work out. Today at school had been a relentless agony of jitters and worry, peppered with questions as people came to ask her about the show from the posters she'd made. She'd counted down the minutes until the final bell, consumed by the truckload of momentous *ifs* floating around her in dizzying orbits.

Now, in her bedroom, still counting down the minutes, Maya and the Angelas gazed down at her.

You are *a strong woman,* Angela Davis said to her.

Your heart is great and kind, as expansive as the sea, Maya Angelou said.

You are tough, and I know talent when I see it, Angela Bassett said.

The sheer exuberance, the transcendence, of the night at Ziggy's had become a specter that haunted her sleep, made her yearn to experience it again, while simultaneously striking terror that she never would. That Zone. That Perfection. That Land of Wonders.

But what if it eluded her for the rest of her life? What if it had been a fluke?

What if the chance never came again?

And still the Wrong Decades had no bass guitarist.

They had a bass guitar, but no guitarist.

When Imelda had called Lika a few days ago, she let Lika in on her plan to surprise Mike with a new guitar. She was collecting money to buy him one, asking coworkers and other neighbors to chip in. When Lika heard this, she leaped with joy. "Absolutely we'll chip in!" So she, Amber, and Toby had collected all the money they possessed, and Imelda came by to pick it up. How many hours on the bus Imelda must have spent just to do this amazing thing, Lika could not guess. Each of their parents had chipped in as well.

Imelda had called her again yesterday. "I have *guitarra*! It's so pretty! Where is Mike? Have you seen him?"

A spike of emotions shot through Lika, too complex to easily tease apart, closing her throat for a moment. Had something happened to him? Then again, she shouldn't care, because if he was hanging out with neo-Nazis, protecting them, he should go take a walk on a busy freeway. When she was able to speak again, she said, "Sorry, Imelda, I haven't seen him for days."

"Hmm, he is not home. Somebody break into his house. Don't know where he is. If he call you, tell him call me right away. *Si?*"

"*Si, señora.*"

She heard Imelda smile at the Spanish.

"Bye-bye, *mija.*"

At rehearsal last night, Toby and Amber had been so relieved they practically collapsed. The three of them discussed performing whether or not Otter showed up—but without a bassist, they would suck. They would sound shallow and incomplete without the depth of a bass line.

No one had been able to reach Otter all week long. It was like he had fallen off the earth. Toby had tried to call him a dozen times and gone to voice mail a dozen times. All of which made Lika think something was seriously wrong. Which made her question the hard line of her last conversation with him—until she remembered the brutality of what she had witnessed and Otter silhouetted in the dome light of that monstrous truck.

This week at school, she had looked up a half-remembered quote: *The only thing necessary for the triumph of evil is for good men to do nothing.* The man who said it was some ancient British politician whose name she'd already forgotten, but the words resonated. She was going to slap Otter in the face with that one at the first opportunity.

Fortunately, the scales of justice were already being balanced. Her dad told her that an anonymous tip had named the perpetrators of the assault on Mr. Mukherjee. One of the perps had been arrested, Duke Cochran, the ringleader of this little branch of Odin's Warriors. The other was still at large, although his house was under surveillance. Her dad thought Zeke Halvorsen might have skipped town until the heat died down. Dad's regular reports on this case helped assuage her fears. The thought that such men were walking around free, that there was a local network of people who thought and felt like they did, when she was a witness to what they had done, had kept her awake for most of two nights. What frightened her even more was that they were part of a *larger national organization* of such people. The online research she had done on them had been like sticking her face into a cesspit of hate, like the bottom of a campground toilet, and the stench still clung to her thoughts.

The alarm she had set on her phone chimed.

She jumped off the bed like she'd been sitting in a nest of spiders.

She checked herself in the mirror for the thirty-sixth time. A fledgling rock star had to look the part.

Knee-high, suede boots.

Sparkly, black leggings.

A loose, crimson, sleeveless T-shirt, knotted tight at one hip, showing an upraised fist silhouetted against the sun—a shirt with something to say, but which also gave her freedom of movement.

Bright red lipstick.

And the new hairdo.

After school yesterday, Momma had taken her for a new 'do, and Lika *loved* the way it looked now, a glossy ebony mane of tight, spiky ringlets with a few subtle touches of light-brown highlights. She looked *grown up*, a woman, stylish, sophisticated, and utterly badass.

But inside, still terrified nonetheless.

She was still turning and posturing, scrutinizing from every angle, when Momma's voice filtered through the closed bedroom door. "Baby, I got your dinner ready."

Lika opened the door. "How can you expect me to eat at a time like this, Momma?" Her stomach was in full, gymnastic frenzy.

Momma's eyes bulged at the sight of her. "Oh my word, where did my baby go?"

Lika rolled her eyes, but the compliment warmed her.

Tears burst into her mother's eyes and she covered her mouth and nose with one hand. "Oh my word." Momma's arms extended and enfolded her. "Oh, my beautiful, beautiful baby. I just don't have the words."

"Oh, Momma," Lika said, burying her face in the comfort of her mother's neck, getting all teary-eyed herself.

Momma held her at arms' length, then hugged her, thrust her out to arms' length again. "Oh my word."

"Momma!"

"Okay, okay, give your poor mother a chance to get her mind around this…change. This morning I was changing your diapers."

"Can we just go? I want to get there early. Maybe the jitters will go away." Her stomach was like a washing machine full of underwear.

"Jitters like last time?"

"What if I blow it?" Lika said. "What if I blow it in front of a thousand people? If not for Mike, I don't think I'd have been able to make it last time."

Her mother sat on the bed and patted it beside her. Lika sat.

"You ever read Aretha's book?" her mother said.

Lika shook her head.

"You want to know something? Aretha used to get stage fright."

"Really?"

"So bad she could barely manage to go on stage. She was terrified, everyone looking at her, is her hair right, checking her out from head to toe."

"How did she get over it?"

Momma squeezed Lika's knee. "She didn't."

"What? Oh god…"

"Her whole life, even after she was the Queen of Soul, she had stage fright something awful."

"But what did she *do*?"

"She went out there and sang anyway. Every time. *Every* time. She felt the fear and she did it anyway. You hear me, baby?"

Lika looked into her mother's eyes, tearing up. Then she nodded. "Feel the fear and then do it anyway." She leaned in and her mother squeezed her close.

After a time, her mother said, "All right then. I'll get my coat."

Lika wiped the warm tears from her cheeks and nodded.

"Did Mikey find himself a guitar?"

"We got one for him, but we haven't been able to reach him."

"We could swing out by his house."

"No time for that. Either he'll be there or he won't."

"Something wrong between you two?"

"He's just an idiot, that's all."

Her mother's gaze held on her for several long, uncomfortable moments. Finally she said, "Just make sure you give him a chance to make it right. Don't hold no grudges."

"That's up to him."

PART V

BACK IN BLACK

CHAPTER FORTY-SEVEN
THANK U

Otter spent the first part of the day working at the Kwik Trip. He felt more than a little grungy after sleeping outside without a shower, but the sun woke him up at the first crack of daylight, so he had time to go home and shower. At least no one had stolen that.

As he stood under the hot water, it struck him how tired he was of killing himself over the guitar. He was just going to disown everyone and move to Argentina or California or something, start over. He was sure to find a band in L.A. After tonight, after alienating everyone he knew, there would be nothing keeping him here.

Mrs. Mukherjee looked genuinely pleased to see him that morning. She told him that her husband was at home and doing reasonably well, with suitable painkillers to keep him comfortable.

Otter had done so much work the day before that he had less to do today, so she sent him away at noon with a bag full of food, for which he was incredibly grateful.

He ate the food out front of the library, after which he launched himself into one last vain online search for a guitar he could afford. It seemed the entire universe was against him. As the hour approached library closing time and he was still unsuccessful, he was forced to ask the hard question.

"Do I go to the show or not?"

What need was there for a musician without an instrument? If he didn't have an instrument, would they want him there? Maybe he could borrow a bass guitar from another band, just for one set. That idea gave him a little hope. Surely not everyone in the world could be as awful as Duke and Zeke.

You have a greater destiny than this.

It was like he could hear Grandpa's voice—still so, so corny—but was it Grandpa's or his own? Were they his own thoughts, or some strange Grandpa overlay? The places he'd seen, the women he'd loved, the regrets he'd borne to his grave. Being in Grandpa's head had broadened Otter's world in ways he was only beginning to fathom.

Maybe he could at least go and cheer his bandmates on. If nothing else, he felt like he should be there to apologize, to heighten the focus on his failures, to sear the lessons into his brain so that he'd never do anything stupid ever again. He needed to face them.

When he returned home, Geri and Freki watched him glumly from the shadows under Zeke's deck, whining pitifully.

To Otter's knowledge, Zeke hadn't been home since Tuesday, before the incident. That meant the dogs had had no food or water for three days.

He immediately went inside and fixed them two peanut butter sandwiches each, ran some water into a big mixing bowl and carried it all across the road. As he neared Zeke's yard, the stench of sun-warmed dog poop wafted over him. The meager grass inside the fence had been flattened to bare earth by the dogs' incessant pacing. He tossed the sandwiches over to them, then reached over the gate and set down the water bowl while the dogs were busy gobbling.

He stepped away from the gate before they were finished, but instead of charging at him and snarling, they came and buried their muzzles in the water, slurping and slobbering desperately. Then they looked at him with big grins, tails wagging their thanks. He slowly reached over the gate, let them sniff his hand, then set about scratching their bristly ears.

"Maybe if you guys had a decent master, you wouldn't be such jerks," he said. When Imelda came home, he would use her phone to call an animal rescue shelter.

Zeke's sharp voice made him jump. "What the hell are you doing with my dogs?" Zeke stood on his front porch holding his duffel bag.

Otter's stomach and all his internal organs fell out and hit the ground between his feet. The instinct to run surged up in him, but a greater surge of anger nailed his feet to the ground. His voice quavered. "They don't deserve to starve to death just because you're on the lam."

In two strides Zeke leaped over the low, chain-link fence. "Was it you turned us into the cops, you little shit?"

Otter clenched his fists.

Two more strides and Zeke loomed over him. His breath smelled like a beer-soaked dead fish left in the sun, and there was more red in his eyes than white. "It was, wasn't it!"

"You guys are assholes! The things you said about Lika! What you did to Mr. Mukherjee! You suck!" He was shaking so badly he could hardly get the words out.

Zeke seized him by the shirt and flung him six feet away to splat against the gravel. "I treated you like my little brother!"

Otter's arms and hands burned with road rash.

Geri and Freki threw their faces against the fence like crazed, rapid beasts, barking and snarling, lips flecked with foam.

Otter raged back, "You beat him up, too, shit stain?"

Zeke's fists clenched and he reached for Otter, but Otter scrambled backward like a crab out of reach. "I thought you were my friend!" Tears of rage filled his eyes, and his heart pounded so loud he could hear little else. "How much did you get for my guitar, you son of a bitch?"

Zeke stopped and flinched as if struck. His hands flexed at his sides, his teeth grinding. But he couldn't look Otter in the eyes.

The sound of more footsteps in the gravel, running nearer.

"*Pendejo,* you leave him alone!" Imelda shouted, her breath huffing as she approached. "Or I call *policia* right now!"

Zeke gave her the finger. "Go back where you came from, you beaner bitch!"

Imelda snatched up a stone the size of a small egg from the edge of the road and hurled it at him. Her aim was true. It glanced off the side of his head. He howled in pain and clutched his skull, eliciting more barking from the pit bulls.

Otter leaped to his feet and prized a stone the size of his fist from the roadside. He hefted it and cocked his arm.

Zeke held up a hand. "Stay away from Duke or he'll kill you." Then he leaped back over the fence, snatched up his duffel bag, and ran around his trailer.

Imelda stopped beside Otter and gave him a worried look. "You okay, *mijo?*"

Otter nodded.

The rumble of Zeke's motorcycle rose from behind his trailer, engine revving toward thunder. Then it burst into view, skidded, and spun onto the road. Zeke's hand cranked the throttle, and the machine fishtailed as it accelerated toward them.

Otter pushed Imelda out of the way. The motorcycle flashed past with a cloud of dust and exhaust. Then he spun and flung the rock after Zeke. His aim was not as good as Imelda's. Zeke had to dodge something lying in the street from the spot where Imelda had thrown the stone.

A guitar case.

Otter's heart leaped but he had just spent too much of his courage facing down Zeke to ask.

Imelda turned to him. "*Madre de Dios, Miguel, te encontré!* I look for you since yesterday!"

He pointed down the road. "What are you doing with a guitar case?"

She gave him a secretive grin. "Come!" She took him by the arm and led him toward it.

His heart thumped even harder.

She picked up the guitar case and presented it to him. "Open."

He took the hard-side case, laid it gingerly on the ground, and unsnapped the clasps, half-expecting something she might have dragged out of a dumpster. Then he opened the lid and revealed one of the most beautiful objects he had ever seen.

The guitar's body was ivory-colored, with a pickguard of iridescent crimson shell and a dark, rosewood fretboard. Four fresh strings gleamed in the sun. The head said *Fender*.

"This okay?" Imelda said.

"Okay! Imelda, are you kidding me? It's…*amazing!* Where did you get it?"

"Man at *tienda de guitarra* says this one just came in. Is used but—"

"Oh, my god, it's *gorgeous!*" He lifted it from the case as if it were pure gold. Then he put it back. "But I can't take it."

"What?"

His ears grew hot and his chest tightened. "I can't take it. It's too much. I can't accept it."

"Nonsense, *mijo!* You take this guitar. Is for you!"

"Please just take it back." He couldn't bear owing anyone a debt this huge.

"No!" Her voice hit him like a physical blow.

"But, Imelda—"

She stuck a stubby finger in his face, dark eyes flaring. "*Silencio! Escucha!* You will take this *guitarra* or *Madre de Dios* I will spank you! You ask me for help! So I help!"

He drew back. "But, I can't pay you back for this for a long time. I just lost my job and—"

Imelda raised a hand. "I talk to people, uh, what is English words…? I pass the hat."

"You collected money for this? From who?"

"Your friends. They worried about you." Then she waved around at the trailers of the Starlite Trailer Court. "Also, everybody." Her vehemence disappeared into a beaming grin. "Well, almost everybody. I tell them all the bad things happen to you. I tell them you want to be a musician. They all give me a few dollars to help. At work, too. Señor Beck in number twelve is a cheap bastard. But Señor Simpson gave me fifty dollars. He's cheap bastard, too, so I was very surprised."

Otter's mouth fell open. Imelda had talked to Lika, Amber, Toby, plus everyone in the trailer court, everyone at her job, and asked for their help. For him. And they had helped. Even Old Man Cheapson. Fifty dollars was what he had owed Otter for that summer of lawnmowing.

But he had asked Imelda to help. The word could not contain the enormity of what she had done. He was just an orphan from a trailer park.

Then he remembered how Grandpa had accepted the Superman pin at the moment he needed it most. Marvin had talked with him about being man enough to accept help when he needed it. Otter had even given the pin to Mr. Mukherjee.

"I…I don't know what to say," he said.

"You say thank you," she said with big *duh!* in her voice.

He hugged her. "*Muchas gracias!*"

"*De nada, mijo,*" she chuckled, hugging him back.

He backed away and admired the bass's exquisite contours, familiar and yet new at the same time. "I don't know how I'll ever repay you."

She raised her thick, coal-black eyebrow and gave him a smirk. "How about a ticket? We call it square."

"Done!"

He reverently closed the case, unwilling to let the instrument leave his sight, but if he didn't leave now, he might not make it in time. He couldn't carry this beauty on his bicycle. It was the bus this time, and he didn't dare miss it.

He ran back toward his house.

Imelda called after him, "I beauty up! Let's go together!"

CHAPTER FORTY-EIGHT
I BELIEVE IN MIRACLES

Lika didn't know what to expect from the Black Line. She'd never been there. Thanks to the seedy, post-industrial neighborhood, it was the kind of place nobody went by accident. An old carpet factory reconditioned to be a dance club, the Black Line was a three-story brick behemoth with small-paned windows filmed by the grime of age and industry. The refurbishment of the old factory district was part of the city's attempt to reclaim places the times had long since left behind.

Around the neighborhood, graffiti spattered the walls of all the buildings, boarded-up windows, and doorways. Tufts of grass elbowed through crevices in street and sidewalk. The sidewalks were so old and cracked the concrete looked more like old flagstones.

But the neon sign and the marquee were shiny and new, and a thrill rippled through her when she saw *The Wrong Decades* on the marquee below two other bands, *Della and the Rhythm Kings* and *Guitarmageddon*.

She checked her watch. Two hours until showtime. No word from Mike.

Momma parked the car across the street in a vacant lot the venue conscripted to serve as a parking lot.

At school this week, people had been all over her about the show. She, Amber, and Toby had made some fliers and passed them out to *everybody* at lunch today. No less than thirty people had told Lika they were coming to the show, and every affirmation filled her with a sick combination of jubilation and dread. She heard several comments like: "You're playing with Guitarmageddon? My brother/sister/cousin saw them at [insert venue here] and they burned the place down!"

But one thought overrode all others. Where the hell was Mike?

The alley by the stage door smelled like old vomit. A bouncer the size of a grizzly bear crossed his arms and looked down at her. He was the closest she'd ever seen an uncostumed human resemble Chewbacca.

"We're with a band," Lika said.

The bouncer made a wookiee-like huff of skepticism until she opened the tailgate of her mom's minivan to reveal the drum set. Then he said something that sounded like, "You're a little young, aintcha?"

Momma got out of the car. "I can assure you, sir, my little girl is going to bring the house down."

Lika gave her mother a grin, and they set about hauling the drum set inside. Since The Wrong Decades were the first act, she took the drums straight to the stage.

The interior of the Black Line was cavernous, empty, and looked like a gutted factory of poorly patched brick, complete with old industrial fixtures and incomprehensible machines, which were sequestered from the public by acres of Plexiglas windows. The smell of the place was a veneer of cleaning chemicals over an undercurrent of stale beer and decades-old dust. The floor was a wide-open swath of tiled concrete that was so old and stained by gum, booze, and cigarette burns it was impossible to tell what color it might have once been, stretching from the stage to the street-facing side of the building. The stage stood five feet above the dance floor. A long, hardwood bar stretched along the side wall. Interspersed between the ancient machines along the opposite wall were great canvas posters explaining them in faux techno-gibberish, calling them things like "The Bi-Selectric Transmogrifier," designed to echo the poster of Rosie the Riveter and others of the World War II era.

A balcony circled the dance floor about twenty feet up, above the masses of strange machinery. An area of the balcony at the corner of stage left had been roped off for special guests, such as the parents of The Wrong Decades.

The stage was smaller than she expected, maybe fifteen by twenty feet, with a backdrop of deep crimson velvet upholstery, making the back of the stage look like a luxurious, antique, overstuffed seat cushion.

Still no Mike.

She didn't see Amber or Toby either.

The sound guy was fiddling with the sound board. Bartenders were stocking the bar. None of them paid her any attention.

She found her breath growing short.

It was real.

It was going to happen.

And without Mike, they were going to bomb so hard, she'd never find her way out of the crater.

Amber walked in with the handles of her keyboard case clutched in both fists.

Lika couldn't help her double take at the sight of their lead singer.

Amber wore black denim short-shorts over black fishnets, a black fishnet body stocking over a black bra, scarlet suspenders that matched her lipstick, black platform boots, and a black derby with a scarlet feather in the hat band. Her scarlet forelock curtained one side of her face. Lika's eyes bulged that Amber's mother had let her leave the house looking that sexy.

This week, Lika had come to understand how Mike had fallen so completely in love with Amber—and how his heart had gotten shattered. Amber was one in fifty thousand. Talent, beauty, and a vibrant, rainbow-colored heart all rolled up in one incredible package—with a love of attention as powerful as her disdain for those who paid it.

Amber gave Lika a grin filled with the same apprehension that Lika felt. "I can't believe this," Amber said, putting down her keyboard. Then she started vibrating in place, emitting a high-pitched squee that built until she launched herself at Lika and they splatted into a hug.

When they separated, Amber's face was serious. "Otter?"

"I don't know," Lika said.

"Do you think he'll show?"

"I don't know." There was a time when Lika had trusted him implicitly. That trust had been shaken to the foundations.

The simple act of coming to the Black Line was an act of faith on all their parts, an act of hoping for a miracle. Imelda had found a guitar, but no one had found Mike. He had apparently been swallowed by the earth or eaten by wolves.

Amber took a deep breath and let it out, a sickened expression on her face. "The show must go on, right?"

Toby showed up two minutes later, stopped at the foot of the stage, guitar case in hand, gazed around the hall, and whistled. "I'd be more excited if I didn't think we were going to die." He cut a splendid figure in a dark gray suit, white shirt, thin, black tie, and sunglasses. That boy was going to have girls swarming the foot of the stage.

Faith and hope clung to the pillars of Lika's heart. "He'll be here."

Toby's mouth twitched. "I guess we'll see."

Lika checked her phone. An hour and a half until show time. Across the room, the double front doors were still closed, but she could see people gathering outside.

A voice blasted over the speakers. "You guys ready for sound check?" The sound man was looking at them expectantly from his raised booth along one side of the room.

Toby called back, "Almost."

"Aren't there supposed to be four of you?" the sound man said.

"Yeah, but we'll sound check with three," Toby said. The way he paced almost aimlessly revealed his uneasiness.

Lika's mother withdrew to the balcony. Lika finished setting up her drum set, while Toby tuned and plugged in and Amber set up her keyboard stand.

When they were all set up, they proceeded with sound check, and still no sign of Mike. The dread in Lika's belly became a dark, writhing snake that filled her entire torso and squeezed her lungs.

They were going to bomb.

The industrial clock above the bar gave her one hour left to live.

This was going to be the worst night of her life.

For sound check, they played the first half of "Under Pressure," or tried to. Without Mike's bass riff, the sound was empty, hollow.

They couldn't do it without him.

Lika's drumsticks felt like floppy lumps of dough in her trembling fingers. The rhythms wouldn't hold. She fiddled with the placement of the high-hat, the cymbals, the snare drum, over and over and over, her throat tightening and tightening.

The sound check guy finally said, "I think we're good. When is your fourth supposed to show?"

"He'll be here soon," Toby said.

With the sound check complete, they left their instruments on stage and retreated to the dressing room, a drab, overgrown closet with mirrors and makeup lights, rough plywood walls painted flat black.

Toby slumped into a ratty old couch. "I don't think I can do it. This was a mistake. We should have pulled the plug."

Amber folded herself over the top of a stood and spoke to the floor. "We're going to bomb."

Lika eased onto a rickety stool, clutching her hands together like a prayer. "He'll be here."

The minutes passed. The clock hand crawled its circle. A general hubbub began to grow outside the dressing room.

"Doors are open," Toby said, like a man walking toward the electric chair.

The stage doors opened and another group of musicians filtered in, dragging their equipment. A pretty woman with latte-colored skin in her early twenties sauntered in wearing a gold lamé halter minidress, leopard-print vest, and clear acrylic platform shoes. Three men followed, their arms full of equipment.

"Hi, I'm Della," the woman said, her mouth full of chewing gum.

"I'm going to throw up," Toby said. Seeing Della's strange expression, he added, "Not about you. You're gorgeous."

Della smiled.

Toby turned back to Lika and Amber. "We can just clear out. We can cancel. We'll say we're all sick—"

"He'll *be here!*" Lika shouted.

Della said, "You guys got a problem?"

"Yeah, our bass player," Toby said. "He's MIA."

"That sucks," Della said, her tone sympathetic but it was clear she was glad it wasn't her problem. "Show business, right?"

Simultaneously, they all said, "Right." And sighed.

"I can't handle it," Toby got up. "I'm going to go find the manager and apologize my butt off. And then maybe throw up."

Lika wanted to collapse into a pile and bawl, but it would destroy her makeup.

The sound guy's voice came over the dressing room speaker. "Fifteen minutes to go-time."

"Oh god, oh god, oh god…" Toby said as he left the room.

"He'll show, he'll show, he'll show," Lika whispered.

Amber sat beside her, put her arm around her, and they hugged silently as the minutes ticked toward their destruction.

"I'm going to have to transfer schools," Lika said. "I'll never be able to live it down."

"I'm moving to Antarctica," Amber said. "I hear penguins like to dance."

"I saw that in a movie once."

A sudden scuffle outside the alley stage door caught Lika's attention. "I'm in the band!" came Mike's voice. "Get out of my way, you walking carpet!"

Lika jumped to her feet.

Otter burst into the dressing room, gasping for breath, sheened with sweat, eyes wide.

There was a guitar case in his hand.

Lika threw herself onto him, driving him back two steps, flung her arms around him, and kissed him on the mouth.

CHAPTER FORTY-NINE
A KISS TO BUILD A DREAM ON

A kiss from Lika was the second-to-last thing Otter expected when he threw himself through the dressing room door. The last would have been a kiss from Amber.

She pulled her lips from his, eyes wide with shock at her actions. Then her eyes flared with anger and she punched him square in the chest, hard. His breath exploded out of him and the fire of impact tore across his breast. He staggered backward, clutching what had to be a crater. That was more in line with what he had expected.

Lika's outfit launched her into contention for the Jaw-Dropping Award. He had never seen her look so beautiful, so vibrant.

"Hi," he wheezed.

"We're on in ten minutes!" Lika cried.

"I made it," he said.

"You got the guitar!"

He released a long breath and straightened himself, rubbing his chest. "Barely. I need to tune. Love the hair."

Amber jumped in. "We didn't think you were going to make it!" A vision in fishnets and scarlet, her beauty drove him back another step, and his mouth went dry as an old bone. She looked like a rock star, ready to break loose and fly.

He swallowed hard and managed to say, "I didn't either until about an hour and a half ago."

Lika's fists punched her hips. "Where have you been?" With the taste of her raspberry lip gloss still on his lips, her beauty and presence shared the room equally with Amber's, and it was this metamorphosis that held his gaze. The new hair, the makeup, the long, lithe legs swathed in black tights and boots.

"My phone is dead," he said. "No minutes. I haven't been able to use it for days. And Zeke broke into my house and stole everything. We don't have time for the story of my week right now, do we?"

Otter peeked around the stage backdrop, and his stomach flopped onto his sneakers.

There had to be two hundred people out there, with room for five or six hundred more.

Toby appeared at his elbow. "Dude, thank god you're here!"

Otter turned, and Toby threw his arms around him.

"I don't have to kill you now," Toby wept, with a level of joking Otter had a hard time pinning down.

The sight of Toby in a suit made Otter conscious of his own slovenly appearance. An ancient Queen T-shirt, once red but faded to weird, pinkish-salmon color, worn so thin it was practically gauze; blue jeans, complete with frayed holes; old sneakers, stained and grimy; Mudskippers hat; fresh road rash on his arms and hands. His standard look. Attire-wise, he was all set for a Grunge revival, but his bandmates all looked like a million bucks.

But no matter. He was so happy to be there, so incredibly fortunate to be there. Imelda was a pure miracle, and now she waited in the balcony upstairs with all their parents, a look of pride and expectation on her face. He waved to her. She waved back, grinning and bouncing.

After tonight he would have some cash in his pocket that he might use to scour the graffiti off of her house, pay off the rest of his bills, fix his bicycle...
"So what's our cut for this? That crowd outside is going to fill this place."

"Cut?" Toby said.

"Yeah, how much are we getting paid?"

Toby looked away.

Otter frowned, processing Toby's reaction to the question. Then the floor dropped out from under him.

His voice rose. "Are you telling me we're playing *this crowd* for *free?*"

Toby still wouldn't look at him.

"You said you were working that!"

"The manager said it would be good exposure," Toby said sheepishly.

"Exposure for what? This is the Black Line, not Carnegie Hall!"

"It's the only way I could get the gig."

"You got screwed, man, got us *all* screwed."

"Hey, it's our first show, all right? What do you expect? We gotta pay our dues."

"*I* got dues to pay and 'exposure' doesn't do it! I've been counting on the money from this to *live!*"

"Maybe you ought to find a different way to live. This isn't real life."

"Really?" Otter said. "Who's been telling you that? You think this is a hobby? This *is life*, Toby! This is all of it! The long haul!"

A vision came to Otter of Toby in ten years, working as a dentist, his guitar and amp safely, innocuously stowed away in the closet, hidden from his kids and the world, a relic of the "glory days." How many more shows would he play before succumbing to "being sensible?"

Otter poked Toby in the chest. "This is more real than anything any of us have ever done." Then he snorted. "I'm going to go get tuned up."

Not having played this new guitar, he would be getting acquainted with it onstage. But there was no time for anything else. Fuming, he stalked out onto the stage with his new axe to a smattering of whistles and applause. In spite of the roiling disappointment in his belly, a grin emerged on his face, one he could hardly wipe off. In the crowd, he spotted a few familiar faces from school.

Even as he slung the bass around his shoulders, the beauty of it struck him, all gleaming ivory and deep-red iridescence. If it played half as well as it looked, Imelda had done incredibly well. As he tuned, the inevitable differences between this guitar and his old one started to emerge. Tiny variations in the action, the feel of the neck, the width in the fretboard. Guitars all looked much the same from a distance, but every one had its own personality, its own quirks.

"Be good to me, baby," he murmured as he adjusted each string.

Something else struck him then, the memory of his mother's last vibrant performance onstage. This would *not* be his last performance. There would be many, many more, no matter what else happened.

It struck him then how much the guitar in his hands resembled a key.

With tuning complete, he stood the guitar in a stand and looked up toward the balcony. Imelda sat beaming beside Loretta. He gave them the thumbs-up and turned to rejoin his bandmates backstage.

That was when he spotted Louisa Pritt and a uniformed sheriff's deputy, a thick-set woman with a stubby blonde ponytail and mirrored sunglasses, watching him from near one of the bars.

Mrs. Pritt's face bore a smirk that said, *I've got you.*

CHAPTER FIFTY
WE WILL ROCK YOU

Otter trudged back to the dressing room, unable to erase the memory of Pritt's smug expression. He wasn't getting out of there a free man. He might as well go down with a bang.

In the dressing room, Amber noticed that something was wrong. "What happened? Did somebody just shoot you or something?"

He swallowed hard, his mouth dry, and gave her a wan smile. "Just jitters is all."

Toby called them into a huddle. "Everybody remember the set list?" he said, his voice fluttering slightly. "Otter, we made a couple changes. Just follow my lead."

"Got it," Otter said. His guts were vibrating like a stand-up bass.

"Just like we talked about," Amber said, looking pointedly at Toby.

Toby said to Amber, "You sure it's ready?"

Amber nodded, glancing at Otter. Her gaze transfixed him, but like always he could read nothing about what this look meant, and there wasn't time to ask.

A deep stentorian voice echoed through the building. "Welcome to the Black Line!"

Applause rose from the crowd, whistles, hoots.

Toby gathered them closer and put his hand in the center. They covered his hand with theirs. Amber's hand was warm and soft under Otter's, as was Lika's on top of his.

The emcee continued, "Thank you all for coming, and for supporting our local music scene. There's absolutely nothing in this world that beats live music from musicians with heart, and this first band is about to bring you that, in spades. They're young, but they'll put a smile on your face! Please welcome The Wrong Decades!"

Toby raised their hands high. "Go!" they chorused.

They ran out onto stage where the emcee, a short, pudgy man in an ill-fitting suit, stepped aside from the microphone and waved them on with a flourish. "Knock 'em dead, kids."

Polite applause rose from the audience as the house lights dimmed.

They took their places, geared up, plugged in, strummed a few notes and chords, thumped the bass drum a couple of times, rattled the high-hat.

Otter studiously avoided looking in the direction he had last seen Louisa Pritt. Surely she wouldn't have the deputy yank him off stage and destroy the whole show…Would she? After everything he'd been through?

Instead, his eyes went to the three beautiful blonde girls standing at the foot of the stage. The M&Ms waved at him with enormous grins. Maya and Mara waved at Toby. Mia clasped her hands under her chin, gazing up at Otter, eyes gleaming with anticipation.

He flashed Mia a smile, but it was time to get his head in the game.

Thumping a few notes from the first bass riff, he tested the feel and voice of this new creature in his hands, this wondrous thing of wood and wire that laid the foundation for everything. Without a bass, be it stand-up or guitar, it was not rock-n-roll. The strings rumbled with fresh power, strong and clear.

It was time.

Toby counted down quietly to initiate Lika's high-hat, and Otter jumped into the bass riff of "Under Pressure."

Bumm-bumm-bumm-bumm-bumm-bump.

Bumm-bumm-bumm-bumm-bumm-bump.

No, the rhythm was wrong. His fingers stumbled over the strings, tripping over the eighth-note syncopation. His shoulders snapped taut. His breath quickened, his throat cinching closed.

Keep playing, keep playing. Get it together. Find the groove. Settle in. Breathe. He'd played these bars a hundred times.

Nevertheless, his flubs filled the hall with flubby flubberness.

Amber's bright piano chords quickly covered them, however, and Toby jumped in with the lead guitar. Within moments, the audience was shuffling their feet and dancing along. Somewhere in the diminished halls of conscious thought that weren't taken up by music, Otter wondered how many of the kids from school had even heard of the music they were about to experience, Queen included. Or did they just assume that teenagers should only care about the current music on Top 40 radio? Amber launched into her resurrection of Freddie Mercury, Toby again singing the David Bowie part. Waves of applause and cheers washed through the hall. The two voices danced around each other, resonating, harmonizing, flashing apart to belt out their own lines, Toby slashing through epic guitar chords.

By the final, upbeat piano chord, the audience's surprise was palpable. But they wanted more.

Toby launched Lika directly into "Back in Black." The AC/DC classic ripped through the audience like a turbo-charged muscle car. Otter's heart swelled at the sight of so much recognition and pleasure sweeping the crowd, and the moment he stopped thinking about his flubs from handling his new baby, his fingers fell into the rhythm and thrum of the music. By the first chorus, half of the crowd was singing along, arms pumping the air. Toby hit the guitar solo like he was on fire, and a grin of sheer exuberance plastered Otter's face.

They were doing it. This was real.

As "Back in Black" faded, the audience roared.

The four bandmates looked at each other in burgeoning joy. They were *killing* it.

Toby paused a moment to let them all bask in the applause, then stepped up to the microphone. "Thank you! As you might have guessed by now, we were all born in the wrong decade. We hope you don't mind."

More cheers.

Toby introduced all four of them to the crowd, himself last, then said, "You ready for more?"

"*Yeah!*"

He cocked an ear. "Are you ready for more?"

"*YEAH!*"

The sounds of an acoustic guitar emerged from Amber's keyboard, and just like at Ziggy's, flowed into "What's up?" This time, Amber managed to make it sound even more mournful, more insistent, more force to change the world. The way she could make her keyboard sound like a rhythm acoustic guitar by pushing a few buttons, even including strum patterns and arpeggios, made the band sound like it had at least two more guitarists. Toby laid into the electric guitar counterpoint, bending into the melody with feeling and eloquence. Guilt flashed through Otter at how Toby's riffs had improved over three weeks ago, even since the open mic night. Meanwhile, Otter was back to tripping over notes and turnarounds, maybe because he was playing an unfamiliar instrument, maybe because he was living a train wreck. Toby had poured everything into this show, and it showed. Otter was doing his best at times just to keep up.

Amber had the audience eating out of her hand. Otter couldn't take his eyes off her. The fishnet leggings and body stocking set his imagination on fire. At one point, he blinked and realized he'd missed two whole bars, his mind engulfed in this vision of her. Fortunately, the crowd seemed not to notice.

She led the band into a huge finish, and as the final chord reverberated in the roof trusses three stories above, the audience, which had doubled in size since their set began, gave it back with roars of approbation.

Next came Lika's turn as lead singer. Amy Winehouse was one of her favorites, and she'd chosen "You Know I'm No Good." She loved the hip-hop beat and the bluesy, heartful minor riffs. Otter loved the super-groovy bass line and Toby's reverberating surf guitar. After the way Amber had been owning the stage, Lika sounded tenuous at first, tight, afraid to cut loose.

The lighting guy brought the house lights into a dark, smoky dimness to match the song's mood, bringing a spotlight onto Lika.

Somewhere along the way, Otter had stopped tripping over notes. He found the groove, and his new guitar sang like an operatic baritone, clean and clear and heavy, strings vibrating into amplifiers, amplifiers vibrating into speakers, speakers vibrating into sound, sound vibrating harmonic kisses through his clothes into his very flesh.

When the second chorus rolled around, Lika had found her voice, warmed up to it, delved into the sexy undercurrents mixed with struggles against impulses and betrayals, a song about love that shoots itself in the foot. In the balcony, Loretta's eyebrows rose at some of the lyrics.

Otter saw, but Lika didn't. She was swimming in the music. She drummed and sang, lifting her voice to the microphone and opening her heart, and the audience took it in and embraced it.

Memory of her lips on his leaped back into his mind.

He hadn't kissed a girl since the eighth-grade dance, and that had been more awkward than exciting, a dare.

But Lika's kiss had been real. Followed up by a punch, nonetheless, but every sliver of it warm and real.

He looked out over the crowd, and every eye in the place was on Lika.

The M&Ms were dancing and swaying with the rest of the crowd at the foot of the stage, ten feet from him, immersed in the beat and the mood.

When the song ended and the audience roared and whistled, Lika beamed. She had pulled it off. Otter tried to catch her eye and congratulate her on a great job, but she would not look at him.

Toby stepped up to the mic. "You all having fun?"

"Yeah!"

"We're sure having fun! Are *you* having fun?"

"*Yeah!*"

It was time for Alanis Morrisette. Again the audience's faces lit with recognition as Toby, Lika, and Otter jumped in together, leading into the biting melody of "Hand in My Pocket." He loved the bass riffs in this one, too. Solid and subtle behind Toby's strumming, at times almost taking over the melody. With this one, one of Amber's choices, Otter marveled at the way a song could exemplify a person's character. Every lyric could have come from Amber herself. Trying to figure out a world of inhumanity, youthful, hopeful, an array of emotional contradictions, a song of piano and peace signs.

Halfway through, Otter caught sight of Louisa Pritt near the bar, deputy at her elbow, head bobbing to the song with a look of rapture, singing along.

When they came to the end, fading into a keyboard "harmonica" solo, Mrs. Pritt clapped with fervor.

Maybe she was human after all.

Next up was "Kashmir." Toby was a nut for Led Zeppelin, and rightfully so. They had debated long about "Kashmir" versus "Black Dog" versus "Immigrant Song." Toby had doubly assured them he was *not* ready to try the fiery riff of "Black Dog" in public yet, and "Immigrant Song" was a little short to fill out their set. "Kashmir" would bring the crowd back to rocking so their set could build to a crashing crescendo through Aretha's "Respect," ending with AC/DC's "You Shook Me All Night Long" at the summit.

Otter took a drink of water from the nearby bottle to wet his desert-dry mouth, gearing himself for John Paul Jones' driving bass thunder.

But Amber leaned into her mic. "We're going to play an original song now."

Otter did a double take. They hadn't developed any original songs, and the few days he'd been incommunicado were not enough time.

The stage lights dimmed and the spotlight fell on Amber. Her face glowed, her smile radiant, but did he detect a hint of nervousness there?

"This song was written by our super-stupendous bassist, Otter, A.K.A. Mike MacIntyre," she said.

"Oh god," he whispered.

Lika had not seen the song Otter had written for Amber, but she'd long been curious. Would it have the effect on Amber that he desired?

Did Lika want it to? If he got his wish, would she be happy for him?

She couldn't believe she had kissed him. She hadn't planned it, hadn't seen it coming. But the sight of him there at the back stage door, smashing all her anxieties and fears into a million glittering shards, had overwhelmed her. The flood of emotion filled her again until it overflowed and her eyes leaked. Otter—Mike—had turned into a handsome young man, tall and lithe, with an adorable grin and disarming blue eyes, but his life was an utter mess. It didn't matter to her that he'd been walking with one foot in the gutter since his mom got sick. She knew lots of poor kids. What did matter is that he often succumbed to a kind of shiftlessness that frustrated her, which included his reluctance to turn in the racist scumbags he'd been hanging with and also his refusal to go back to school. That path would most certainly drive both his feet into the gutter, the way it so often happened in the black community. Kids who dropped out of school eventually went to jail or ended up dead. That was the rule. Too many of them once "good kids." She had no intention of watching her best friend dash himself to pieces against the jagged rocks of the modern world.

But then again, she had just kissed her "best friend." What did that mean?

Maybe she had a few things of her own to figure out.

Amber had said at one of this week's Otter-less rehearsals that she was working with Otter's lyrics and chords, adding a few bars of melody, a couple of touches in the minor key to give it an edge of uncertainty, and pronounced the song "as ready as it'll ever be."

Amber said to the audience, "You are the first audience ever to hear this. It's called 'Everywhere You Go.' We hope you like it."

Otter's eyes looked like a flaming meteor was streaking straight toward him.

Amber eased into the first chords of the intro, her keyboard sounding half-harmonica, half-guitar. Without Otter, the three of them had discussed doing this song, and Amber told them she had it well in hand. She just needed some simple backup chords and a little rhythm. Lika improvised an easy, bass-and-high-hat thump and counterpoint, Toby following with some rhythm strumming.

Amber leaned into the microphone.

> *From across the great divide*
> *Shines the one who makes me sigh*

A few bars in, Otter appeared to recover his senses and sidled in with some easy bass heartthrob along with the chord progressions. It was his song, after all.

> *A meteor flashing bright*
> *She can be my world delight*

Amber's embellishment of a shift to a minor chord caught Otter off guard, but he corrected quickly.

> *Or my darkness*
> *Or my darkness*
>
> *But you're my queen*
> *In a world of drones*
> *So I'm caught between*
> *The gold and bones*

At the chorus, Otter stepped up to his mic and sang harmony, his eyes fixed on Amber.

> *Everywhere you go*
> *You leave a trail of honey*
> *For me to follow*
>
> *Everywhere you go*
> *You leave a trail of honey*
> *For me to follow*

Amber led her keyboard into a heartful solo, exuberant in the hope of love, but tinged with fear that it wouldn't be returned, that the world was too complicated for true, pure love. She signaled with her head for Toby to take the solo, and he stepped to the front of the stage, his guitar singing a bluesy lament of yearning and hope.

Otter's three gorgeous cousins stood at Toby's feet, staring up, enraptured, practically melting into the floor.

> *I'll give my heart to you*
> *Terrified of what you'll do*
> *Pick it up and hold it tight*
> *Bring my love into your light*
>
> *Or your darkness*
> *Or your darkness*

Above the heads of the crowd, pinpoints of light appeared, cigarette lighters and "cigarette lighter" phone apps, candle flames held aloft for love.

> *Everywhere you go*
> *You leave a trail of honey*
> *For me to follow*
>
> *Everywhere you go*
> *You leave a trail of honey*
> *For me to follow*
> *For me to follow*
> *For me to follow*
> *For me to follow*
> *For me to follow*

The final chord was a minor one, offering the sense that being inexorably trapped, unable to turn away from that trail of honey, was dangerous for both the pursuer and the pursued.

Lika rested her drumsticks. Her heart could not help but be moved. What would she have done if he had written that song for her? How would she have felt about that? She was not exactly lacking in interested males. A fair share of awkward or ham-handed love letters had come her way since middle school, but they were merely a titillating curiosity. None of them had set her heart aflame. Her dad forbade her from dating until she was sixteen anyway.

The stage lights went dark, and hoots and whistles exploded.

Ten feet away from Lika, Otter stood like a wooden statue. The spotlights flooded over Amber, then him.

"For god's sake, take a bow!" Toby said to Otter.

Otter stepped forward sheepishly and bowed his head a few times, waving to the audience, humbly accepting the applause.

Amber came and stood beside him, took his hand, and made him offer a proper bow along with her. Then she chunked him on the shoulder and they exchanged some words Lika couldn't hear.

Then something happened she could never have imagined.

Otter yanked Amber close, cupped her cheek in his hand, looked into her eyes, and kissed her.

Amber's eyes bulged with surprise, but then she kissed him back.

The crowd went berserk.

Lika's heart burst and deflated, collapsing upon itself like a rotten melon left in the sun. And that was how she knew.

CHAPTER FIFTY-ONE
JUST LIKE HONEY

Otter held Amber's hand and took a bow before the crowd. A grin spread across his face, his heart pounded in his chest like a rocking bass line. He looked at the beautiful girl beside him, her perfect skin gleaming in the spotlight, her eyes sparkling, her lips full. Her eyes met his.

"Why did you do it?" he said.

"It's a good song," she said. Bewilderment showed on her face.

"You made it better."

Something tugged them together like a golden thread. Here she was, right here in his arms, her body warm and soft against his. A hundred things fell together at once, like the sweet spot on a baseball bat that effortlessly sends the ball over the fence, like the perfectly timed photograph that catches a lightning strike, like the perfect song at the perfect moment where the melding of melody and lyrics smashes your heart wide open. He found himself in such a moment, and he did the only thing that moment would allow.

His eyes closed, because that's what you were supposed to do, right? He kissed her.

Right there in front of hundreds of people. An endless moment of surprise. Then she kissed him back.

His heart roared. The wonder of that moment, that exquisite point of soft contact, echoed through his life, ripples from a pebble dropped into a still pond, ripples in a Zen sand garden.

She tasted of cherries, warm and soft against his lips. Scents of jasmine, vanilla, and a touch of sweat tickled his nose. It could have lasted only for a couple of seconds but it stretched into infinity. With his lips against hers, she shed the divine raiments his heart had imagined for her, her goddess aspect, and became just a fifteen-year-old girl, soft and alive, with her own secret hopes and secret dreams.

As their lips parted, her eyes met his, sparkling, and he saw into her hopes and dreams—and found himself in none of them. That moment lasted long enough to see deep into the soft, vulnerable core that she kept carefully shielded with walls so high and thick she herself couldn't escape them. Then the portcullis slammed shut.

But it was enough.

He became aware of the tumult of the crowd, washing over them, the looks of shock from Toby and Lika.

Lika.

Amber squeezed his arms with both hands, then looked up into his eyes. "We *all* made it better."

He nodded.

"We're both a little broken, aren't we," she said. Then she pulled away resolutely and resumed her place behind the keyboard.

He stood for a moment alone in the spotlight, his consciousness spinning. Then he bounded back to his place, energized by what he'd just had the guts to do, feeling every thread of his clothing, the smooth shell of this ivory and crimson creature slung around his shoulders, the energy of the crowd pumping into him, filling him until he must burst before he could hold any more. He had just kissed the girl of his dreams, and she'd responded. In this moment, he needed no more than that.

He gave Toby the nod to continue.

"Kashmir" erupted from their instruments like lava, plowing across the hall, through the crowd, making heads start bouncing, fists start pumping, bodies start jumping, arms raised like branches in a hurricane. If Amber's vocal cords could handle Freddie Mercury, they could emulate Robert Plant as well. Suddenly they were in Shangri-La. Goosebumps blasted up and down Otter's arms and legs. The song's deceptively plodding tempo charged the air itself, major and minor chords dancing, intertwining, rising until the song receded in the distance.

The applause swelled to the roof. The crowd jostled forward, squeezing Mia and her sisters against the stage, but they didn't seem to care.

The next song put Lika in the spotlight again with "Respect," and in the moments Toby counted down to the start, her eyes were fixed on Otter.

CHAPTER FIFTY-TWO
R-E-S-P-E-C-T

The sight of Otter kissing Amber left diminishing reverberations in Lika's heart, settling in her belly like wet cement, but the moment Aretha Franklin's lyrics started coming out of her mouth, she knew she had never sung "Respect" like she was about to sing it.

Laying a kiss on him when he finally showed up had been an accident, a rush of emotion.

Amber was the girl he wanted, Amber who would break his heart and grind up the pieces. She was like trying to trap mercury or harness a rainbow. But he had to go there on his own. There was no way around it, only through.

Lika had to do the same.

She powered through the rhythms and raised her voice to the rafters, singing her demand for respect as an affirmation to herself. No one, not even her best friend, would *ever* walk all over her. R-E-S-P-E-C-T? *You're damn right.*

A grin emerged and her eyes closed, immersing herself in a waterfall, emotions dashing over her, through her, and she let it pour out of her with all the soul of a gospel choir lost in rapture.

As the final chorus neared, she caught Otter looking at her, his eyes flashing with appreciation and admiration. His gaze said, *We'll talk.*

With a little nod, her gaze replied, *Oh, yes, we will.*

Just a little bit, just a little bit.

This unspoken understanding settled into her that no matter what happened, they would always talk.

Toby stepped up to her drum set and signaled the final slowdown and chord with his guitar neck, evoking another intoxicating wave of applause.

The spotlight fell upon her, and she stood and waved to the crowd, her heart galloping, her blood surging, her skin tingling.

"Wow," she whispered, and only she could hear. She would never be Whitney Houston or Aretha Franklin or Clyde Stubblefield. She would be Lika Walker.

As the wave of applause broke over the stage, Otter glanced down at Mia. She winked at him and grinned. In the balcony, the parents were on their feet. Loretta's hands covered her mouth, tears of joy and pride streaming down her face, blowing kisses at Lika. Toby's parents were jumping up and down with their fists in the air. Imelda's face beamed with pride. Where was Chrissie, Amber's mother?

The Wrong Decades stood there for several timeless instants, basking in the energy of the crowd, dripping with sweat. Elation filled Otter like nectar sweeter than he had ever imagined.

A sudden strange vision of Christmas lights came to his mind, stars strung together, gleaming on a night dark enough the wires connecting them disappeared, stars like moments in time, moments of people's lives, moments that shone in memory forever, strings being fashioned one lustrous point at a time. Periods of darkness interspersed with brightness and warmth. Always yearning for the next pinpoint of luminous wonder.

How many points of light will your life be, Michael?

Otter didn't know.

Here's a secret that people forget: we all create our own points of light in the string, but you have the power to do it with purpose. You can build a string of lights so dense it can light the path for other people.

Some of these lights could find a sort of home in items, trinkets, otherwise useless objects becoming symbols of those moments, associations of those moments, depositories of those moments.

Thunderstruck, he contemplated this. These trinkets, these useless things, represented the bright spots, the shining pinpricks of a connect-the-dots picture, moments that when taken all together formed the shape of a person's life. A life filled with pain, love, regret, joy. His grandfather had not been any sort of superhero, but his life had touched people, had touched the world in a way that sent ripples through the lives of many.

This is your destiny.

Otter's throat choked closed for a moment, and he wiped his nose.

Now is not the time for me to bawl like a baby, Grandpa...

...Because Toby had just struck Angus Young's intro riff to "You Shook Me All Night Long."

Instant recognition swept the crowd, and the deafening cheer kicked Otter's heart once again into hard-driving rhythm.

Lika kicked her thumping bass into gear. Amber charged into the first verse. Immediately the crowd sang along, a crashing tumult of exuberant sound. Her keyboard brought Malcolm Young's background rhythm guitar to life. Otter waited for his moment to come in, a couple of bars before the chorus when the song really took off, and when his moment came, he played it with everything he had. With the sudden added depth of the bass, the audience roared.

Toby threw himself into the guitar solo like he had something to prove, like this would be the last show he ever played. Passion flooded his face, the buoyant energy of the crowd chasing electricity through his fingers. He went on for several bars too long, but he was on fire, so they let him.

Otter's earlier vision of Toby as a dentist sneaked back into his mind, and the certainty settled over him that, while The Wrong Decades might play a few more shows, Toby would someday take the "sensible" path.

Amber would move on and do fabulous things.

Lika would move on.

Someday, Otter would be in a band that toured the world like AC/DC, a world that was phantasmagorically bigger than a fifteen-year-old's first love. And he would have a cooler nickname, like Cougar or something. And he would still be rocking in his sixties and seventies, like AC/DC, and the Stones, and McCartney, and Chuck Berry, and Johnny Cash. This love, this want for Amber that had so consumed him these past months, still felt the size of the world. Maybe together they would grow it even bigger, make it more real, but more likely he would move past it, and that kiss would become a pinpoint in the string, a thing he would look back on with a mixture of warmth and regret, like walks on forested mountainsides or brief brushes of passion in intense times.

He stood before a forest of pumping arms and surging faces, his fingers forming the driving rhythm of deep sound.

He wanted to stay here forever, but he knew he couldn't. Songs always had to end.

Then, as quickly as it began, the song neared the final crescendo, so unbelievably brief, a flare. It could do nothing except end with Lika's crashing cymbal flourish.

The applause gushed over them, drenching them like a fire hose.

The emcee stood just offstage with an expression of awe.

The crowd cheered and cheered.

Finally Toby stood up to the microphone. "Thank you! Good night!"

He and Otter unplugged and unslung their guitars and led the two girls offstage, waving as they went.

The emcee's mouth was open, and he gave them a slow clap as they passed.

In the narrow hallway to the dressing room, all four of them flung their arms around each other, hugging and jumping, laughing and crying.

"We did it!"

"Oh my god can you believe it!"

"That was beyond beyond!"

"You're amazing!"

"And you!"

"And that solo!"

"Listen to them!"

Sound rushed over them, into their elation. The audience was still cheering, and something new emerged.

"En-CORE! En-CORE! En-CORE!"

Their mouths fell open. Seconds passed as they stood stunned.

The emcee came down into the hallway. "So are you going to oblige them or what?"

"Holycrapwhatarewegonnaplay?" Lika said.

They hadn't even considered the possibility they could play an encore. They hadn't rehearsed anything else.

Then, just like the kiss with Amber, Otter's mind blossomed with an idea. "Folsom."

The genius of it worked through Toby's face. It was an easy twelve-bar blues. They had played it a number of times just for fun. Toby said, "Great idea. But you have to sing it."

"Me?" Otter said. "Uh…"

"Yeah, you. You know the words better than any of us."

"En-CORE! En-CORE! En-CORE!"

"Okay," Otter said.

The emcee beckoned. "Then let's go!"

They ran back out onto the stage, and the audience cheered again.

Otter had never sung lead before. He could sing well enough, but being in the spotlight made him uncomfortable. Like most bass players, he liked to hug the shadows and let the attention fall on the lead guitarists and singers.

But he was going to do this.

He stepped up to the microphone. "So you want one more, huh?"

"*Yes!*"

"We've had so much fun playing for you all, I think we could do this all night."

"*Yes!*"

At the side of the stage, the emcee was holding up one finger, as if to say, *You get one more.*

Otter shoved his hand into his pocket and squeezed the Johnny Cash guitar pick between finger and thumb. Someday, maybe he would have a pick with his own name on it.

He looked over his shoulder at Toby and nodded the signal.

Toby picked the iconic opening riff to "Folsom Prison Blues."

More expressions of surprised pleasure bloomed across the surface of the crowd, but Otter only had a moment to notice before he jumped into Johnny Cash's immortal lyrics. He did indeed hear a train a-comin' and he was going to roll it straight through this audience.

A year ago, he would have sounded like a squirrel trying to sing Johnny Cash, but his voice had dropped far enough into adult male range that he could approximate Cash's hearty baritone. It was a song he had known by heart almost since he'd first picked up that old, battered six-string. He sang about yearning for freedom from prison, from regrets, from a life gone awry.

As the audience sang along, excitement reached such a peak in his chest that he forgot his place and sang the second verse twice. But they didn't seem to care as Toby and Amber traded solos.

As the most tremendous rush of his life crashed through him, as he rode the crest of this wave, he thought about his mom. How proud would she be of him right now? For a moment, he might have caught a glimpse of her in the balcony, jumping and cheering and dancing.

He gave each of his bandmates a long look, trying to burn into his memory this moment, this brightest pinpoint of his life thus far, the way they looked, the way they played. When each of them finished their solo, he introduced them to the audience again to more cheers and applause. He caught Lika's eye and shot her a meaningful expression.

He leaned into the mic again. "And on the drums, the beautiful, the stupendous, the Princess of Rhythm, Lika Walker!"

With a serious nod, Lika poured herself into a sizzling drum solo, crashing and thumping and skittering and jumping, raising a riot of sound. Her drumsticks flew and twirled. Her cymbals exploded. Her bass drum was a cannonade.

The crowd cheered, driving her to a greater frenzy.

Sweat sheened her beautiful skin. Her eyes slid closed as she lost herself in the rhythm.

And then she gave Otter the signal.

The other three picked up again, the last time through the chorus, and cheers and whistles and howls for Lika echoed out of the crowd.

Then Toby stepped forward using his guitar neck to signal the slowing of tempo to the final chord. They all hit it together, resonating, cascading, dying out like an exuberant, primeval cry.

Just like that, their set was over, and the four of them stood at the front of the stage, rock stars, bowing again and again.

CHAPTER FIFTY-THREE
WISH YOU WERE HERE

They rode the wave of exuberance back into the dressing room, laughing and grinning. Otter didn't know if his heartbeat would ever go back to normal.

Della and the Rhythm Kings were lounging back there, waiting for their turn. Della stood and smoothed her gold lamé dress, grinning. "You all expect us to follow *that*?"

"Thanks," Otter said.

Della turned to Lika and hugged her. "Girl, you got you some pipes. Aretha would be proud." Then she hugged Amber. "And you, too! Lord a'mighty, girls. You need to take yourself on the road."

"Maybe when school's out," Lika said with a wink.

Della laughed. "You boys be good to these ladies. They'll make you stars."

Otter and Lika shared a grin.

One of the Rhythm Kings stood up, a tall, lanky man with a shaved head and a pointed goatee. "Let's go, fellas. Time to set up." They picked up instruments and carried them out.

A stage hand brought two pieces of Lika's drum set into the hallway outside the dressing room and went back for more.

Then a massive, uniformed figure filled the dressing room door, polished badge glinting.

"Daddy!" Lika cried, charging Marvin. She jumped into his arms, flinging her arms and legs around him. "You came!"

Marvin laughed and squeezed her tight. "You think I'd miss this? I'm on 'patrol,'" he said with a wink. Loretta was right behind him, her face overcome with pride. Lika released him and threw her arms around her mother.

"We're so proud of you, baby!" Loretta said, squeezing Lika again. She turned to Otter. "And you, too, Michael." She crossed the room and hugged him. "That was one wonderful show. All of you."

"Thank you, Mrs. Walker," Amber said.

"Yeah, thanks!" Toby said.

Marvin pulled Lika aside. "Here's some extra good news. State troopers caught the second perp, Zeke Halvorsen, hiding out in a cheap motel. Thought you might like to know."

Otter's legs went wobbly, and his muscles sprang loose like a twisted coil spring. He saw the relief flood Lika's face as she sagged against her father.

"Thanks, Daddy," Lika said.

Marvin looked straight at Otter. "Someone called in an anonymous tip. Then the victim IDed the perps. We found a bunch of stuff in Halvorsen's house that was probably stolen, plus some drug paraphernalia. Looks like he was trying to support a crystal meth habit."

Otter's mouth wouldn't work. The wave of relief couldn't quite drown the knowledge of how wrong he'd been about a great many things.

Marvin looked hard at him. "You got something to say, Mike?"

Otter tried to gather enough spit to talk. "I was the one who called in the tip."

Marvin said, "I recognized your voice from the 9-1-1 tape."

Lika spun on her father. "Really? And you didn't tell *me* this?"

"Figured you knew."

"No, I didn't know! I've been furious with him all week for nothing!" Lika gave Otter an apologetic look.

Marvin said, "Mike, we're going to need you to give a statement, but we're not looking to file any charges against you."

Another set of coil springs in Otter's shoulders broke loose, and he almost collapsed, letting out a long sigh. "Thanks. I can do that."

"If they don't plea it out and it goes to trial, you'll probably have to testify, but Cochran and Halvorsen will not be getting out anytime soon. Bail on Duke Cochran was denied and probably Zeke's will be, too, since he's a proven flight risk."

"What about the stuff Zeke stole?" Otter said. "He might have some stuff of mine."

"That's all taken as evidence. Sorry."

"My guitar?"

"Sorry, Mike, they didn't find a guitar."

"What about cardboard box full of random junk?"

"That I don't know. Like I said, they're still cataloging evidence."

So if Zeke hadn't thrown Grandpa's box into a dumpster, the police had locked it up in the black hole of the evidence locker. He would miss Grandpa's presence in his life, the wisdom he had somehow found a way to share.

At least they got Zeke. Otter would sleep easier.

"There he is, Deputy!" a voice shrilled.

There were two cops in the room now, complete with different colored uniforms, and Louisa Pritt standing in the dressing room doorway like a hockey goalie.

Marvin turned to her. "Really? You're going to do this now?"

Louisa Pritt crowed, "This little rapscallion has eluded me long enough!"

"You don't need to treat him like a criminal," Marvin said.

Her face twisted. "Then he shouldn't have acted like one!"

"What's going on?" Lika said.

"What are you doing?" Amber said.

"Taking him into state custody," Pritt said.

"No way!" Amber said.

"Not a chance!" Lika said.

Both girls jumped in front Otter. Toby looked confused for a moment, then shrugged and stood in front of the girls, facing Mrs. Pritt. He crossed his arms and said, "You're gonna have to go through us."

Marvin began, "Lika, honey—"

"No, Dad!" Lika said. "Can't you do something?"

"Children!" Pritt shrilled. "You will not stand in the way of the law. Unless you wish to be arrested yourselves."

The three of them planted their feet in defiance.

"Deputy," Pritt said, "arrest them if you must."

The deputy's gaze went from Marvin, to Pritt, to the kids. She edged forward, but her eyes said her heart was not in it.

Now it was Marvin's turn to round on Pritt. "Now, lady, you need to cool your jets."

Pritt glared at all three hundred pounds of him.

The deputy said, "Michael, why don't you come quietly? Spare your friends the scene."

Warmth filled him at the way they all defended him.

But there was nowhere to run. He was cornered. No exits. The deputy's hand rested on her night stick. He didn't relish the idea of being dragged out in handcuffs.

"Thanks, guys," Otter said. "It's okay. I'll go." But the bitterness was thick in his voice. In this moment, he was going to lose every single thing he had ever fought for. But Pritt would never stop harassing him. Never. And he was so tired of running.

"Mike, no!" Lika said.

"A wise choice," Pritt said smugly.

"But not without my guitar." He held it up and said, "Thank you all for this. You're amazing." Then he laid it lovingly into its case's velvet bosom and snapped it closed. He had been so, so stupid for so long. His friends had done this for him, and he hadn't even asked. That's what people who cared about each other did. As Marvin told him once, it took a strong man to accept help. His eyes teared up and snot trickled inside his nose. He sniffled, then swallowed hard, suddenly filled with warmth. "All right, let's go."

"No!" Lika said again. "Please, Daddy!"

Pritt said, "We are taking him into temporary custody until the court can decide his disposition."

"Mike," Lika said, "come and live with us!"

Marvin said, "The offer is still open, son…"

Otter looked back and forth between them. He had already put Lika through so much, he felt fortunate she still wanted to be his friend. "It's kind of you to ask, but…"

"Please?" Lika said.

He met her gaze for a long moment. This whole crazy mess was his responsibility, his consequences. "I should have listened to you about Zeke. I'm sorry about that." For that matter, he should have listened to his *mom*. "You tried to give me good advice, tried to protect me, but I didn't listen. That was really stupid."

Lika's big brown eyes brimmed with emotion.

How could he have been so blind to the red flags waving in his face? He had some things to think about, some things to make up for. And there was one other thing. He had just kissed more girls in one night than in his whole life up to this point. One of them was the girl of his dreams, and one of them was Lika. He needed a little time to think about that. Living down the hall from Lika would complicate that significantly, and Marvin might well rescind the offer if he knew.

Otter took a deep breath. "I can't. I have to do this." Then he threw his arms around both girls. He kissed each of them on the cheek. "We came and went with a bang, didn't we?"

Amber whispered in his ear, "You know we did." Her breath warmed him all the way to his heels and back up his spine. God, he wanted to kiss her again, but this was not that moment. She drew back and poked him in the chest. "I'll be seeing you." And how he wished he could see through the walls behind her eyes to know what she meant by that.

Toby clapped him on the shoulder and hugged him. "We sure did. We're gonna be legends. And about what you said. I might have to rethink some things. And I'm sorry about not talking to you guys about the money."

Otter smiled at him. "Good. Because you got the chops, buddy."

Amber crossed her arms and gave Toby a suspicious look. "What about the money?"

Otter picked up his guitar case and said to the deputy, "Let's go."

Louisa Pritt's car was parked behind the deputy's cruiser out front of the Black Line. The line of people still waiting to get into the building stretched halfway down the block, no doubt waiting to get in to see Guitarmageddon.

A musician being escorted out by the deputy caught the attention of many of the idle curious, but Otter walked with his head high.

Louisa Pritt led the way. "I was so surprised at how good you all were! You really do have talent and potential."

"Yeah," he said, "we're so great you have to destroy the band. Because that's what you're doing." He could have piled on more sarcasm and bitterness, but it would have taken a dump truck.

She was impervious to it apparently and kept rattling on about the high points of the performance.

As they neared the deputy's cruiser, a voice called, "Hey, wait! Stop with that kid! Mike! Hey, Mike!" Mia and her sisters shouldered through the crowd at the front door and came running toward them.

"Mike!" Mia said, skidding to a stop. "What's going on?"

He shrugged and pointed to Mrs. Pritt. "Ask her."

Louisa Pritt's voice was clipped but polite. "We are taking him to a proper home. His emancipation is going to be revoked, and he will become a ward of the state."

The three girls burst into a torrent of speech.

"You can't!"

"No!"

"Leave him alone!"

"Let's not drag this out, shall we?" Mrs. Pritt said. "Come on."

A woman's voice said, "Forget that. He's coming to live with me."

Aunt Misty emerged from behind her daughters.

Anger surged up in Otter at the sight of her. She had said so many awful things to his mom. But behind the anger were surprise and pleasure that she cared enough to come. He crossed his arms and glowered at her. "Uh, no."

Misty flinched at his refusal.

"And who are you?" Mrs. Pritt said with a sharp challenge.

"I'm his aunt. His mother's sister."

"He says he does not wish to go with you," Pritt said.

He turned on Mrs. Pritt. "Oh, shut up! Don't pretend you actually give a damn what I want. You still going to frame me for something? Hit me with your car again?"

Pritt's cheeks reddened and she opened her mouth, but nothing came out.

Aunt Misty straightened herself, smoothed her stylish wool jacket. Even after a concert, she looked like a catalog model. "Can he and I have a minute to talk? We have some things to work out."

"Well, I—" Mrs. Pritt began.

"You just got a free concert," Misty snapped. "You can give us five minutes."

Mrs. Pritt glanced at the deputy to indicate she should keep a sharp eye and then nodded her approval.

Otter let Aunt Misty guide him away from Pritt and the deputy, around the corner of the next building. The deputy moved to keep them in sight, but otherwise kept her distance.

Then Aunt Misty's look of hardened determination melted to one of concern. "First things first." She stepped up to Otter and hugged him.

He couldn't bring himself to hug her back. Misty's voice yelling *whore! slut! hooker!* boiled out of his grandfather's memories.

"I'm not going with you," he said.

She released him and clasped her hands. "I came here because I wanted to see you. I wanted to talk to you. Can you give me a few minutes?"

He crossed his arms.

Misty said, "I know you don't know what to do with me. You haven't seen us in so long."

"It's more than that," he said.

"Oh, how so?"

"You said some terrible, awful things to my mom. You called her a slut and a hooker—"

"She told you that?" Her eyes bulged with mortification. "Oh god…" She clapped a hand over her mouth. "How could you know that?"

"Grandpa told me. Sort of. You're not going to deny it?"

Her voice was thick, and her eyes glistened with tears. "No. I did say those things. And probably worse. It was the darkest time of my life—"

His voice rose. "And that's supposed to be an excuse?"

"No, not an excuse." She wrung her hands and swiveled her body as if pacing in place. "I was so awful then. And I'm so ashamed of it. If not for the girls, I wouldn't have lived through it. Some things, though, you can't take back, no matter how much you want to."

"You couldn't ever say 'sorry'?"

"I *am* sorry. I came here tonight to see you and tell you I'm sorry. The truth is, your mom could be…a little stubborn. That was one of the things I both loved and hated about her."

After the last couple of weeks, he knew the cost of being stubborn.

Misty continued, "The truth is, I always envied her, and I have a lot to make up for. I hope you can forgive me."

"She was stronger than you."

She flinched at the hardened edge of his words, then nodded. "She had the talent." She gestured to herself. "Looks will only take you so far. She had enough to go all the way, the talent, the drive. I didn't."

"And she gave it all up to have me." Remorse for something he hadn't done crept into his voice. "And *then* Grandpa spent her inheritance on rehab for *you*."

Her face crumpled again and she wiped away more tears. "I never asked him to do that, but I wouldn't be alive today if he hadn't." She took several deep, shuddering breaths, gathering words. "Sometimes lives fall apart and we spend years trying to rebuild them. I was a drunk. I was awful to my kids. I was awful to my dad. I was awful to my sister. I was probably awful to you. But not anymore. I have been sober for six years. I have a wonderful husband, and I try to prove myself worthy of him every day."

"You don't miss Uncle Sal." The moment it came out of his mouth, he felt awful. Missing Sal had almost killed her. He said it because he had wanted to hurt her the way she had hurt his mom, and that realization made him feel like the worst person ever.

Her face held its composure this time. "Of course I do. That man was my first love, and he gave me three amazing little girls. Well, not so little anymore. Losing him almost killed me, too."

"I'm sorry," he said. "I shouldn't have said that."

They both sighed heavily.

She said, "I want to help you, Mike. Truly. We're all the family you have. You're all I have left of my sister."

"Why didn't you all help when she got sick?"

"She didn't tell us. We didn't speak for years. We could both be stubborn—and a little spiteful. And then she wouldn't even let us have a funeral. Your Grandpa was already sick by then. Hearing that his baby girl had just died of cancer almost put him in the ground the same day. That was a mean thing she did, refusing to let us mourn for her. The ultimate middle finger to get back at me."

She was on a roll and he wanted to hear what she had to say, so he didn't stop her to say that they couldn't afford a funeral; but Misty's surety made him wonder if his mom had had more complicated motivations.

Misty went on, "But all that is in the past, and this is not about me. Wrecking things is easy. Rebuilding is hard. I want you to come home with me, right now, tonight. I'll introduce you to Scott. He's almost nothing like your Uncle Sal, but…If you decide to live with us, you will have your own room. You'll have to go to the same school as the girls, of course, but they can help you get your feet on the ground there. We can go over to your house tomorrow and pick up your things—"

"When we talked on the phone, you didn't sound very enthusiastic about having me." Was it still skepticism about her, or was he holding his breath?

"My dad had just died. Without Maggie in his life, with Mom gone, your grandfather had come to lean on just me. He'd been leaning on me for years, even though he'd swear it was the other way around. I had a few things of my own to sort out." She took him by the hand, warm and gentle. "The important thing is that they are now sorted. Please, come and live with us."

Tears threatened to come at the earnestness of her voice, but he clenched his teeth against them. "What about the band?"

"What about it?" she said with puzzlement.

"Would you let me stay in the band, keep coming to rehearsals?"

"Mike, you're really talented, just like your mom. I wouldn't dream of depriving you of that."

Something warm rose up inside him, something that hadn't been there for a very long time. "Even if rehearsal is several times a week?"

"Even then."

"And bringing me to gigs?"

"I can't wait to hear you all play again."

"What about my house?"

"It's your house. You can keep it until we figure things out."

Something bloomed inside his chest. A chunk of emotion broke loose from it and fell free, diffusing through him.

"And a Mudskippers game once in a while?" Otter had had meant it half as a joke. He and Mom hadn't had the money to go to a Mudskippers game since summer the previous year, before her diagnosis, and it just now occurred to him how much he missed it.

"Oh, sure. Scott loves baseball," she said with a smile.

How could he say no to the Walkers and yes to Aunt Misty? The Walkers had been better to him over the years than Aunt Misty ever had. And yet, somehow, it felt important in this moment to rebuild bridges. Plus, cousins felt more like sisters than he wanted Lika to be. That kiss lingered in his mind. The thought of kissing Mia or her sisters made him cringe. Plus, baseball.

He put his hands in his pockets to tamp down the bloom of hope that would make him look like a total goofball. "Okay."

"Really?" Her voice rose with hope, eyes gleaming.

He nodded.

She threw her arms around him, and he hugged her back.

Under the veneer of expensive perfume and makeup, she smelled much like Mom, felt much like Mom. A single sob shuddered out of him. "I miss her. I miss Mom."

"Me too, kiddo."

For several long moments, they held each other and sniffled.

Then she walked him back to the cruiser, one arm around his shoulders.

Mrs. Pritt watched them come, her brow a dark, wrinkled shoreline, her mouth a thin line. "This boy has led me on quite a chase, I'll have you know. Are you sure you would not prefer that I deal with him?"

Aunt Misty squeezed him tighter. "I'm sure."

"Then I shall stop by on Monday with the necessary paperwork. May I have your identification please?"

As Misty retrieved her driver's license from her Dolce & Gabbana clutch, Mrs. Pritt thrust a finger into Otter's face. "We *will* be checking in on you, young man."

He couldn't tell if Mrs. Pritt was happy or disappointed that her arrest was thwarted. She was as stiff and tightly wrapped as barbwire around a baseball bat.

Mia and her sisters sidled up around him, anxious, expectant grins on their faces. Mia bit her lip. "Mike, you guys were amazing!"

"Incredible!"

"The greatest show I have ever seen!"

Otter gave them a lopsided grin, "Thanks!"

He traded awkward looks with the three girls. Maybe having pseudo-siblings wouldn't be awful.

CHAPTER FIFTY-FOUR

IT'S THE END OF THE WORLD AS WE KNOW IT (AND I FEEL FINE)

TWO MONTHS LATER...

"Off to take the world by storm?" Aunt Misty said as Otter passed through the kitchen. She was meticulously constructing some sort of pastry, her hands and blouse powdered with either flour or confectioner's sugar. Saturday sunlight spilled through the French doors to the back yard, gleaming on countertops and stainless steel.

He grinned at her and gripped his guitar case in one hand. "One city at a time. Lika is coming to pick me up for rehearsal. We're working on some new stuff. Original stuff," Otter said.

In a suggestive, ribbing tone, she said, "Are you dating?"

"That's a good question. We've been friends for so long..."

He was looking forward to simply seeing her. They lived on opposite sides of town now, and they hadn't seen each other since the Black Line concert. Even though they talked via phone and text almost every day, he still missed her, lately in ways that he hadn't considered before.

Misty asked, "But didn't you kiss the other girl on stage?"

"I had to. No choice." He had not kissed Amber since that night, nor Lika for that matter. His life since that night had been a cloud of confetti only now starting to settle to the ground. He and Amber had talked on the phone a few times, but something was not properly clicking between them. Perhaps it was her vehement avoidance of the slightest whiff of boyfriend/girlfriend status that kept her a little standoffish, but he could tell she truly cared about him. Of that, he had no doubt. She still naturally generated a male entourage, but she was slowly, by infinitely small degrees, drawing him into the inner circle. So, as much as he couldn't take his eyes off her, as much as he still thought about her, that was enough.

"Well, be careful," Misty said, "Don't be careless with anybody's heart, okay?"

He stopped and thought about that for a moment. Was Misty referring to Amber or Lika? Both? Regardless, it was a good policy. "Okay. I'll be home around dinnertime."

"Oh, and Scott told me to ask you if you're still up for fishing tomorrow."

Otter smiled. "Sure." Scott was antsy to get out there before everything froze over.

Misty's husband—Otter wasn't quite ready to call him "Uncle Scott" yet—had quickly warmed to the idea of a second male inhabitant to help dilute a house full of estrogen. Scott seemed like a decent sort, even though the schedule of an anesthesiologist took him away at all sorts of crazy hours and they seldom saw each other. One thing was clear: Scott was desperate for a fishing partner. The females all adamantly refused to go fishing with him. Otter was still learning how to do it, but he liked the quiet solitude.

Everybody here seemed happy.

Including him.

He still missed the feeling of independence, of being in charge of his own life. He missed Imelda and her enchiladas. He missed the familiarity of his neighbors. He missed the house he had grown up in, rickety shack that it was. He missed the sound of crickets outside his bedroom window. Aunt Misty's house was too big and well-insulated for the sound of crickets.

Since moving in here, little by little he'd come to realize something. All along, he'd had people who wanted to help him, resources he could have gone to for help. Lika and her parents. Imelda. All he had to do was ask. He'd been so stubborn, so blinded by the belief he had to do it all alone, that he couldn't see what was right in front of his nose.

One night on the back patio, listening to the crickets, he sat with Mia, looked out over the city, and confided this all to her. This subdivision had been built on a hillside, and this house had a spectacular view of the sparkling tapestry of streetlights.

She had listened intently, and when he finished, she elbowed him.

"Dude. Go easy on yourself. You're a teenager. No one expects us to see every angle. But you're right. Take it from an old, wise woman like myself, knowing everything we know now, you were blind as a bat and twice as dumb."

"Bats aren't blind. Read that in science class."

"Okay, a mole then."

"Neither are moles. Well, mostly."

She sighed dramatically. "Fine. A freakin' jellyfish then."

"You suppose jellyfish get lost in their own little hells?"

"I'm sure of it," Mia said.

He nodded, and she gave him a little smile. He got along well with the other two triplets, but it was Mia he had bonded with. She was starting to feel like a real sister, and he liked that a lot.

She said, "But we're learning, right? We have our whole lives ahead of us, right?"

"Damn straight." Lots of things would never happen to him again.

But he was excited to play some music today. He'd printed out the songs he wanted to try, having found them on the internet in a late-night exploration binge. It was nice having high-speed internet at his fingertips.

He went outside to wait, sitting down on the step. Autumn had stripped the trees, turned the grass brown, and put a bite in the air. He zipped up his jacket. The denim jacket he'd worn since he was twelve had gotten tight, the sleeves short, but he wasn't quite ready to give it up.

He recognized the car coming up the street and…his mouth fell open.

Lika pulled up to the curb with a beaming white smile—driving her mom's old minivan.

She flung open the door and bounded out of the driver's seat like a crazed bunny.

"You're *driving!*" he said.

She bounced up to him and threw her arms around him, continuing to bounce. "Ohmygoditssostressfulandsoawesomeatthesametime!"

Her sixteenth birthday had been two weeks ago. "Congrats on getting your license."

"Got it on the second try. They tricked me the first time, but hey, I'm here!" She flung her arms wide. "Dad said he's going to sign me up for the police pursuit driving course." She laughed, then imitated his voice. "'Get through that, and you can be a stunt driver in the movies and I'll never have to worry about you.'"

Lika being old enough to drive felt like an alien idea. It would take some getting used to, much like the way it felt to hug her was different now. He was starting to wonder if there would ever be a time when he could properly kiss her again. The more he thought about it, the nicer the memory.

She held him at arm's length. "You seem older now somehow." Her eyes narrowed. "Have you grown?"

He laughed. "Maybe."

But there was something about him that felt older now, he agreed. He knew things that most fifteen-year-olds did not know. He had seen things, been places, and he had Grandpa to thank for it. It was difficult now for him to tell the difference between Grandpa's memories and his own, except to step back from them and consciously think, *Okay, being in love with your own grandmother is just icky and I could not possibly have been to Japan. At least not yet.*

A delivery truck rumbled up the street at the forefront of a cloud of exhaust. The truck pulled up behind Lika's car. The driver climbed out of the back carrying a large box wrapped in cloudy plastic and approached them. "Either of you live here?"

Otter raised his hand.

"Got something for Mia Kowalski," the driver said, holding forth an electronic sign pad and a stylus. "Have to sign for it."

"Okay," Otter said, taking the pad and stylus. Mia and her sisters were at volleyball practice. Their high school was aiming for the state volleyball finals this year and their coach called for special practice sessions on Saturdays. The girls were built like perfect volleyball players, tall and lithe, and the coach was delighted to have them in triplicate.

Otter was still trying to make up a month of missed school, but the teachers were being really patient with him. Mia and her sisters had helped ease his social transition. They were popular, and hanging with them gave him enough of a social toehold that he was starting to make his own friends. The kids on this side of town weren't much different than his old school, where Lika, Amber, and Toby still went. It also didn't hurt his social status that The Wrong Decades had become legends. A band of kids no one had ever heard of brought down the house, and the stories of it spread through every high school and middle school in town.

He signed his name on the pad and handed it back.

The driver handed over the package and departed.

Through the cloudy plastic he could see a large sticker that read

"EVIDENCE." On one flap, written in marker, were the words, "FOR MIA KOWALSKI," the words that he had written there.

Lika's dad had told him that the police department returned evidence when trials were over or when it was no longer useful. This box had had a name on it.

Heat washed through him, his heart going *ka-thump* like Lika's bass drum.

Sudden excitement coursed through him to share the box with the girls. Would Grandpa's junk be magical for them, too? He ran the box inside to Aunt Misty.

"What's this?" she said.

"Grandpa's stuff. From the will. The stuff Zeke stole from my house."

She covered her mouth to hold back tears. "Really?"

Maybe there was something in there for Aunt Misty, too.

Since he had moved in, he and Misty had talked a lot about Grandpa, about Grandma, about sisters and memories and regrets. She had been surprised at all the things Otter knew. He had been vague about how. He enjoyed talking about Mom with someone who knew her almost as well as he did. Misty's recollections of her glowed with love, admiration, and remorse.

He ran around the counter and kissed her on the cheek. "Gotta go!" Then he pelted back outside where Lika waited.

"Okay, let's go," he said.

They jumped in the minivan. Lika started it up, going through some sort of mental checklist as she belted in and checked mirrors. She bounced in her seat with a look of terrified glee as she put the car in Drive. Otter clutched the armrest but gave her a grin. And so they were off.

As they drove out of the neighborhood, Otter spotted a park ahead. "Hey, stop over there."

"Why?"

"Just do it."

"We'll be late."

"Maybe we'll be five minutes late. And we have all afternoon."

She acquiesced and pulled into the park near the playground. He bailed out and headed toward the playground.

"Hey, where are you going?" she called.

"Come on!"

He heard her growl in exasperation, then shut off the car and follow him. He didn't know exactly what he was doing, only that he had to.

The swing set stood before him, swings creaking lazily in the breeze. The gooseflesh up his back and arms might have been from the biting autumn breeze, or maybe from something else. He jumped into the swing and started pumping himself higher. The taste of Orange Crush filled his mouth, and the smells of hot dogs and popcorn wafted into his nose. Somewhere, children snickered and squealed with joy.

Lika giggled at him.

"Come on, Stick-in-the-Mud!" he called.

She jumped into the swing beside him.

And they swung as high as they could, pushing each other to ever greater heights.

"Come on, higher!" she cried.

They laughed with delight and swung for the sky.

AFTERWORD

Music shapes us.

In many ways, it is a kind of cultural glue. We grow up with the songs of our generation, and if we're open minded enough, we acquire the music of our parents' or grandparents' generation. It's not uncommon to hear Billy Idol, the Beatles, the Rolling Stones, and Journey at high school dances right now. And if we're really open minded, we'll pay attention to our children's music, and their children's.

Writing this book was in many ways a musical journey, discovering new and rediscovering what has stuck with me. I hope the reader will close this book with the desire to look up music with which they're unfamiliar, because with the lingering sunset of broadcast radio's importance, there's so much amazing stuff out there we've never heard of. Artists of today stand on the shoulders of giants. It has always been so.

Musicians need to be told they're good enough. Writers need to be told they're good enough. Most creative people go through their lives believing that the Quality Police are going to kick down the door at any moment, yelling, "You suck! You don't belong with the *real* writers/musicians/artists." It's a delicate balance, having enough ego to put one's art in front of people, and having the humility to always be learning, striving to improve, honing one's craft. The moment you think you know everything, you're sunk.

Sometimes all it takes is one person to tell you that your dreams are worth pursuing, that the world needs your unique, creative energy. It does. The world needs music, poetry, words, beauty, now more than ever. So you, yes *you*, go forth now and do your thing. Maybe someday you'll become the giant that inspires someone else.

T. James Logan
January 2020

ABOUT THE AUTHOR

T. James Logan writes a lot of different kinds of things, from science fiction, fantasy, and horror to working on roleplaying games and screenplays. In this persona, he loves to recapture bits of childhood, those dreams of becoming a comic book artist, a musician, a writer, those times when crushes were crushing, and those moments of youthful exuberance when the world was all possibilities. He lives in Denver, Colorado with his family, plus a dog and a cat, neither of which are particularly good musicians.